Dancing Between the Beats

In ballroom dance, movements blend over the beats.
This merging of movement
means that one dances "between the beats" rather than on each
beat of music.
In this respect, dance is like life.
We live, as we dance, between the beats.

To Isabel
The best part of
writing this book is
making a new,
writer friend.
So pleased to meet you

Lynn Nicholas

a novel by
Lynn Nicholas

Dancing Between the Beats

Published by Wheatmark®
2030 East Speedway Boulevard, Suite 106
Tucson, Arizona 85719 USA
www.wheatmark.com

ISBN: 978-1-627878-755-8
LCCN: 2019914137

Bulk ordering discounts are available through Wheatmark, Inc. For more information, email orders@wheatmark.com or call 1-888-934-0888.

Author's Note

The events that unfold in this work of fiction could have taken place anywhere, in many different locations and venues. But dropping my characters into the world of studio-based ballroom dance offered a unique environment in which to ground them. During my own foray into ballroom dancing, I've met more remarkable dance professionals and amateurs than there is space to mention. Entrance into this world triggered my imagination with all the what-ifs and exaggerations that keep writers up at night. I hope I stayed true in my descriptions of dance to give an air of authenticity to the fictitious ballroom studio in this book. I also hope I delved deeply enough into the world of make-believe to have created unique, imaginary characters.

The real-world ballroom community overflows with students and professionals steeped in integrity and good will. Any flaws that my characters possess are purely the result of my overactive imagination.

ONE

Enter Stage Right

Katherine Carrington
8:05 a.m., Tuesday, 13 October, 2015

Key ring dangling from a gloved hand, Katherine hesitated. She snuggled into her soft cashmere wrap and took a deep breath of the crisp, apple-cider air. On a picture-postcard morning like this, it was tempting to ditch the recirculated stuffiness of the dance studio for a play day outside, but…Katherine chewed on her lower lip. Playing hooky wasn't within the realm of her reality.

With a martyred sigh, she inserted the heavy key into the lock. No response. She raised her artfully plucked eyebrows and tried the key again, with more force this time. No welcoming click rewarded her efforts, only a stubborn refusal to budge. Katherine jerked on the door handle.

"Damn it to hell." A sudden gust of wind tugged at her coiled chignon, snapping strands of blonde-streaked, brunette hair across her eyes. She pushed the errant tresses out of her face and, swearing softly under her breath, delivered three rapid-fire kicks to the heavy door's metal baseplate. Katherine leaned her forehead against the coolness of the thick glass. She was plagued by the temperament of her instructors all damn day; she didn't need attitude from an inanimate object. Holding her hair back with one hand, she forcibly jiggled the key and pulled hard on the door handle. With a reluctant click, the tumbler gave way and slid into place.

"About bloody time," Katherine announced, enunciating each syllable through gritted teeth as she pushed open the door. As much as her British mother's sayings grated on her nerves, there simply weren't any satisfying substitutes for British swear words in exasperating situations.

Katherine punched the passcode into an alarm keypad. She flipped on the overhead lights, narrowing her cornflower-blue eyes at her reflection in the lobby mirror. She pulled the ever-present vial of Visine out of her pocket and blinked back the drops. She could wipe the effects of stress off her face with a high-quality face cream and facial, but the strain in her eyes couldn't be camouflaged as easily. She was letting the pressure from balancing the books get to her, and she had to stop. Really, the money game wasn't much different from playing with a child's toy top—one strong pump to the handle was all it would take to stop the wobble and restore balance. She had no doubt she could alleviate the studio's monetary imbalances before anyone was the wiser.

"Enough," she said. Negative thinking too quickly leads to self-pity.

Crossing the lobby in three long-legged strides, Katherine tossed her cashmere cardigan over the reception counter. It landed with one-shot perfection over the back of her receptionist's tall barstool. Jill would moan and bitch to anyone within earshot about Katherine's "casual attitude about expensive things" and claim she "shouldn't be expected to pick up after the owner like a slave," but Katherine dismissed Jill with a characteristic shrug. Annoyed or not, the girl would hang the cardigan with care, and that was the point. Besides, she was the boss, a fact everyone had to deal with.

A frown tried to form on Katherine's brow, but it was Botoxed into submission. Her lips formed a tight line. It was too bad it was necessary to reinforce an understanding of everyone's place in the hierarchy of the studio. Because of her generous nature, which no one seemed to either appreciate or acknowledge, people took advantage, but she always managed to stay ahead of the curve. Katherine's taut face relaxed into a satisfied smile. With a lilt in her stride, she swept down the hall to the main ballroom.

The heavily draped ballroom was cave dark. Katherine felt for the line of switch plates and ran her hand along the rows. One by one the banks of fluorescent lights brought the ballroom to life. Wood floorboards gleamed their greeting, announcing the official start of the day. She scanned the room with the possessiveness of a mongrel dog with a bone. This studio was her heart and soul, and, disregarding a few minor technicalities, it was essentially hers alone.

Thank God for small favors like automatic timers, Katherine thought, as the scent of freshly brewed coffee pulled her down the hall like the business end of a bungee cord. The lobby featured a dual-burner Krups, designed to grind fresh coffee beans before brewing. Beside the Krups was a box of assorted organic tea bags. A tray of cheap, colorful ceramic mugs, displayed on a tiled Mexican table, completed the small vignette. The scenario imparted a homey feel to the studio's reception area for clients. There was also a ubiquitous Mr. Coffee and plenty of generic ground coffee in the employees' break-room. Caffeine was a cheap, legal drug, essential to keeping the staff's energy levels high.

Katherine retrieved her personal coffee mug from under the high top of the reception counter. It was a Vestal Alcobaca mug from Portugal, hand-painted in shades of lavender and pale green. She washed this mug herself. No one else dared touch it. She poured her first cup of the day, carefully sipping the hot brew as she strolled behind the reception desk to scan the appointment book. From the edge of her peripheral vision, the blinking red light on the office phone signaled a silent alert.

"When in the hell did a call come in?" Katherine muttered. "Must have been when I was in the ballroom." Katherine hit the button for voice mail and put the phone on speaker.

"You have two messages," the machine's nasal voice intoned. "To hear your messages, hit Play." She hit the button and waited.

"Hi there, it's Jill. Whoever gets this message, please tell Katherine I won't make it in today. I'm pretty sure I'll be in tomorrow. I'll explain later. Thanks." Jill's words faded into a girlish giggle.

The machine's digital voice added, "Eight thirty-five a.m.," before it played the second message.

"This message is for Katherine Carrington. Katherine, this is Felicia from New Haven Adult Care. I do apologize for calling you on your office phone, but I've already left two unreturned messages on your cell. It's imperative we speak at your first opportunity. There seems to be an issue with your mother's last check. I'm sure you can clear this up quickly, but I do need you to call me back as soon as you can."

"Eight forty-two a.m.," the machine stated.

Katherine's eyes flattened like a cat poised to pounce. Her fingertip hovered above the number seven on the keypad for a brief moment before she pushed down.

"Message erased," the machine confirmed.

Katherine leaned against the edge of the reception counter. She stared out the glass front door, her eyes focused on nothing. She pursed her lips.

"Cripes." Katherine opened the appointment book and traced the hourly schedule with one long, perfectly manicured red nail. Everyone was booked for at least four lesson hours. Katherine nodded in satisfaction. Running her nail tip down the roster, she noted a full schedule for her bread-and-butter teacher, Joey. He might be background noise, the chorus line to the rising stars, but without him the show couldn't go on. She wished she had three more Joeys. The charm he oozed captivated and kept clients, and his clients kept the dance heats filled for studio showcases. And then there was Paige. Time to turn the new kid on the block into a moneymaker. The hours Marcos put into Paige's training were bordering on excessive.

Katherine tat-tatted her bright acrylic nails on the equally high-gloss reception desk. She stared into space. The working man's bible emphasized the tenet that effort pays off. She shook her head. That was a myth force-fed to the peons to keep them plugging away. What pays off is being shrewd and fearless. Katherine was both, but she also knew her success was rooted in being observant and recognizing an opportunity when one presented itself.

She sipped her coffee, her thoughts wandering. The formats and procedures she instigated at Desert DanceSport might be recycled concepts—and the word was *recycled*, not stolen, as her ex-boss mistakenly tried to contend—but it was her personal spin that made the difference. Katherine shrugged. "Stolen" had such a negative connotation. One simply takes inspiration wherever one finds it. Clothing designers did it all the time. Such a fuss over nothing.

"The crew ought to be straggling in at any moment." There was an odd satisfaction to filling the well of silence with the sound of her voice.

Coffee mug in hand, she slipped along the north hall, past the practice rooms and her private office, unlocked the back entrance, and stepped outside. The wind was much stronger, flipping the eucalyptus tree's silver-dollar leaves, exposing their whitish undersides like Victorian ladies showing their petticoats. A whisper of mesquite-scented smoke spiraled under her nose, tickling and teasing, demanding to be noticed. "Why would anyone build a fire this early in the season?" Katherine muttered. She pressed her tongue hard against the roof of her mouth to avert a sneeze.

She laid her head against the wooden doorframe, lost for a moment in memories. It had been a crisp, windy October day like this when, forty-three and newly divorced, she had opened the doors to Desert DanceSport. How could twelve years have passed so fast? Back then it was just she and Marcos running the whole show. Marcos was in his playboy prime back then, just thirty-seven. What an opening day! She and Marcos drank too much champagne and ended up...well, perhaps that was best forgotten. Katherine smothered a Cheshire Cat smile. She remembered raising an empty champagne bottle and declaring her emancipation to the world. She promised herself and anyone within earshot that she'd never, ever be under a man's thumb again. No one would get the best of Katherine Carrington, especially not in the queendom of her own dance studio. And Marcos, to his credit, had never infringed on her reign.

Katherine took a deep breath and released it slowly. There was no time to linger and luxuriate in reminiscing. Fall heralded the start of snow-bird season. Winter visitors would soon be signing contracts for lessons. Maybe, for a change, her young instructors would buckle down and upsell contracts like the pros they were supposed to be. Katherine shook her head. Everything fell on her shoulders. Nothing got done if she didn't keep an eagle eye on the kids.

She took one last deep breath and willed an aura of authority to permeate her being. Game face on, she blocked out the tantalizing scents of fall and turned back to the more familiar scents of the studio—coffee, waxed wood floors, and the light undernote of locker-room sweat fused with a layer of citrus air freshener.

~

Marcos Stephanos
9:00 a.m., Tuesday, 13 October

"Where in the hell are those damn gloves? Why aren't they where they're supposed to be?" Marcos's voice rose in direct proportion to his impatience. He detested being late. Twenty minutes ago, he'd backed his roadster convertible out of the garage, but the unexpected snap to the air had sent him back indoors for his treasured driving gloves. They were lambskin, made by Fratelli Orsini, in the classic open-back European style, and they were not in the top-right drawer of the mahogany chest of drawers.

"So much for getting to the studio early," he grumbled as he rummaged through the dresser drawer. To catch Katherine for an uninterrupted chat, his best bet was to get there before her day spiraled out of control. He needed her on board with his continued training time for Paige. If he could finagle a few hours a week for the next couple of weeks, he could test Paige out of the Bronze teaching level and into Silver. Thanks to the girl's dance background, she'd caught on to the basics of ballroom very quickly. At least Katherine agreed that Paige was making great strides and the mentoring process was a success. With a little more time, he could polish Paige to a shine, and besides, he genuinely enjoyed the one-on-one time with her.

Marcos rubbed his temples. He found a missing silver cufflink and a twenty-dollar bill, but no gloves. He worked his way through the lower drawers, eyes focused but mind wandering.

Lately it was difficult to gauge Katherine's mood. It was like she was on an emotional teeter-totter—one minute too preoccupied to engage, the next in-your-face intense. The woman could be intractable as hell, but he'd never seen her quite this volatile before. He was concerned but…if he asked her what was wrong, she might tell him, and then he'd have to get all involved in her stuff, and that could get complicated. Women had a tendency to make life messy really fast if you let them, and Marcos was happy to keep his life uncomplicated and unencumbered.

"Ah, there they are." The gloves were hidden in a protective tissue-paper nest in the bottom drawer of the dresser. Marcos slowly pulled them on, luxuriating in the softness of the leather against his skin. It amazed him that something as simple as the feel of these gloves could completely change his mood.

He glanced at the Baume & Mercier wristwatch he bought on his last birthday. Now he really was running late, and he'd have to rush. Marcos hated to rush. He dashed downstairs, reset the alarm code by the garage door, clicked open the silvery-gray roadster, and slid into a cocoon of leather. The freshly detailed car exuded a new-car scent, even more enticing than the French-press coffee he treated himself to every morning. Marcos was unapologetic about his love of luxury. Life was too damn short.

He hit the power button to raise the lowered hardtop and glanced into the rearview mirror. The fits of wind had undone his carefully coiffed do. His one vanity—well, maybe not his *one* vanity as much as his *main* vanity—was his full head of thick, silver-threaded, black hair. At forty-nine he had as much hair, if not more, than he had as a twentysomething young stud. This drove his balding buddies crazy. Marcos grinned. His hair insinuated virility and vitality; their lack thereof screamed Viagra. He reached for the emergency supply of personal care items in the armrest console. A quick touchup with the comb and a spritz of unscented hairspray—to not compete with his signature fragrance, Gucci's Guilty pour Homme—and he was back in perfect form. With one hand on the steering wheel, Marcos backed the car out of the driveway.

Marcos nosed the car onto the narrow, desert-lined road. He pursed his lips. He'd never forget the Latin dancer, a picture of sleek-haired perfection, who'd loaned him his non-aerosol, Clinique hairspray in a rare moment of warm-spirited camaraderie. It was at the Emerald Ball in Los Angeles. Marcos arrived in the dressing room with bedhead hair and no hairspray. A quick combing and a lung-choking amount of his competitor's hairspray saved him from the judges' wrath. Appearing on the dance floor with messy undressed hair would have won disapproving looks from the judges and cost him points. It was crazy to think that hairspray could make or break a guy's career, but with all factors equal, a professional couple's final placement can come down to costuming and grooming, a direct reflection of their respect for the sport.

Marcos's car zipped along the saguaro-lined roads winding from the foothills to Sunrise Road. The Mazda MX-5 Miata handled well, and it was neither pretentious nor ostentatious. It was just snazzy enough to bolster what Marcos hoped was an image of urban élan and sophistication. As Katherine once told him, ballroom is a superficial business. It's all about appearances, and no one gives a rat's ass about intellectual expertise.

The wind gained strength, and a dust devil tossed a brittle tumbleweed into his path. Marcos swerved with the skill of a racecar driver to avoid catching this bit of desert debris in the Miata's undercarriage. The potential for rain was looking more like a promise than a threat. Marcos shook his head. This time of year in the desert, the weather changed as swiftly as a woman changed her mind.

~

Paige Russell
9:45 a.m., Tuesday, 13 October

Paige cupped her hand protectively around the lit match. The feeble flame arm-wrestled with the wind, fighting for its few seconds of life. Cigarette clamped between her teeth, Paige increased the shield, tightening the curve of her hand and bending her head until her nose twitched from the pungent scent of phosphorous. She by God needed this cigarette, and right now. Damn this wind anyway and the neighborhood idiot who was stinking everything up with mesquite-wood fumes. If she wanted smoke in her lungs, she would smoke.

Paige leaned against the old eucalyptus tree in the corner of the studio's back parking lot. The wide trunk made a great wind break. Her pale cheeks hollowed as she dragged hard to light her cigarette, pushing the tip deep into the base of the flame. The delicious scent of tobacco filled her nostrils and a gentle stream of smoke swirled through her fingers. She'd started smoking only two years ago, but the habit was so embedded, it was as though she was born with a cigarette clutched in her tiny baby fist. Without her smokes, she was a bundle of hot-wired nerves. She hated herself for her weakness, even as she closed her eyes in pleasure. Smoking brought her back from the brink of insanity but landed her on the ledge of despair.

"I'm such a mess," Paige muttered, shaking her head. There were still too many mornings when her mother's face was the first image that popped into her head. Sometimes she would wake up thinking she heard her voice. Grief didn't march through five neat stages. That was complete bullshit. Grief spirals and turns back on itself. It hides, and then springs out at you like a lunatic ghost in a not-so-fun Halloween corn maze.

How can I miss my mom so much and still be so damn confused and mad at her all at the same time? Paige felt angry tears damming behind her eyes. She blinked rapidly to stop them from spilling over. She wound another loop of her knit scarf around her throat and pulled her wide Mexican poncho closer. It felt colder than when she left her midtown apartment forty-five minutes ago—more like Flagstaff than Tucson. The quickly moving clouds obscured the blue desert sky she'd come to love. Dirt-filled dust devils ripped hidden bits of litter from under the bushes, creating a careless collage of rubbish, only to dump the discards helter-skelter. The exposed litter brought back an old saying of her mother's—something about not airing your dirty laundry in public.

Paige's shoulders slumped, and a familiar hollow bubble formed in the pit of her stomach. She had to stop thinking about herself as someone's dirty secret. Paige ached to confront her, and cry, and scream, "Why, Mom? What was so bad you couldn't tell me?" But you can't ask a dead person questions.

She rubbed the back of her neck and lifted the strap on her shoulder to reduce some of the weight of her heavy, hand-tooled leather bag. She'd only kept the bag because it was her mother's favorite, but it was cumbersome. Paige sighed. Mad or not, she just plain missed her mom. Twenty-two was too young to find yourself alone in the world. Her mom had kept her grounded, and now, at twenty-four she still felt untethered—a Mylar balloon, adrift and buffeted on the breeze. Paige took a deep drag of her cigarette, willing herself to relax.

A blasting shotgun sound broke through the quiet. Paige jerked around in time to see an overloaded old pickup truck, backfiring its way down the street. The truck bed was piled with who-knows-what kind of junk, concealed under a dirty beige tarp. She bit her lip. Keeping big secrets was like that bulging pile of crap, restrained under the tightly stretched tarp. If the tarp's bindings came loose, and all the junk underneath it sprang free, it would be impossible to ever get it all under control again.

The wind tugged at her hair, which she'd tidily restrained in a knotted bun. The thick blackish mane flew free, dancing a street salsa with the wily westerly wind. Clamping her cigarette between her teeth, she scooped her hair back, twisted it into another knot, and secured it as best she could with a long hairpin. Here she was, trying to cultivate a professional demeanor, and instead she looked like a disheveled gypsy. Her hair would need some serious pinning and spraying before Katherine caught sight of her.

Paige shifted her position against the tree, hoping her new dance pants weren't covered with grit from the bark. She wasn't ready to go inside just yet, even knowing time with Marcos was on the schedule. Being able to work so closely with him was more than she'd hoped for when she signed on with Desert DanceSport. Every day she learned a little more about him.

Paige extinguished her cigarette, ready to head inside, but there was Marcos, waving as he walked across the parking lot, cigarettes and lighter in hand. With the rueful laugh of someone caught with his hand in the cookie jar by someone who already has a cookie stuffed in her mouth, he joined an ally in addiction.

"Ever wonder why so many dancers smoke?" Marcos said, shooting Paige a companionable sidelong glance. "The dance community is composed of smokers, with the exception of Katherine. I'm sure you've heard her warnings about smoking creating wrinkles around your mouth." Marcos paused to inhale.

Paige nodded. That phrase was one of Katherine's mantras.

"I actually quit smoking once," Marcos continued, exhaling a grayish stream. "It's odd, but I never got over the feeling that a part of me was missing. It's like having your right arm in a sling. You don't realize how much you need that arm until you suddenly can't use it. Know what I mean?" Marcos tilted his head.

Paige didn't have a clue what he meant but nodded anyway.

"After I quit smoking, I'd find myself not knowing what to do with my hands. When I was out with my smoking friends, I'd lean in to get a whiff of tobacco. I so missed the smell, the taste, the way I stood with a cigarette between my fingers. Smoking was part of my demeanor."

Marcos's black, raised eyebrows made him look like a romance-novel pirate. Paige camouflaged a giggle with a throat-clearing cough.

"I'd been clean for about two years," Marcos continued his monologue. "I was at a dance competition when my partner came out of a spiral on the outside edge of her foot and snapped a tendon. It was horrible. She actually hit the floor. I took her to the ER right away, of course. I was so distraught; the fall cost us a shot at a championship. Dancer's priorities, right?" Marcos laughed as he gave Paige's shoulder a little nudge. "I hit the first cigarette machine I could find, and that was that. I've been smoking ever since."

Paige hung on Marcos's every word like he was a revered East Indian guru. He seemed to enjoy having an audience. She noticed he pulled himself up a tad taller under her gaze.

"Yeah, I get it," Paige said, finally finding her voice. It was the most erudite response she could muster. She hated feeling so flustered. Marcos spent time with her, teaching and coaching, but not simply chatting. Paige's mind rapidly shuffled memories to share to keep this going.

"I never smoked in my life until my mother got sick," she said. "Wanna hear the story? It's good one." Paige lit another cigarette.

"Sure. All of us addicts have our justifications. I will gladly play the priest and hear your confession." Marcos bowed, hands palm-to-palm, in a namaste pose.

"It was about two years ago. I'd just learned my mother's cancer had metastasized." Paige cleared her throat, took a long drag, fixed her eyes on some unknown spot on the horizon, and continued. "Mom had finished her second round of chemo and radiation, but a PET scan showed hot spots. The cancer was alive and well. I went outside to be alone. Mom was at St. Joseph's hospital in Phoenix. They have a meditation garden. I was crying, trying to find a private corner, when I honest to God literally stumbled over a young ICU nurse. She was hiding out on a small bench behind a hibiscus bush."

Paige stopped for a minute to take another thoughtful, slow drag. She didn't look at Marcos. She'd retreated into the past.

"I didn't even see this nurse. I crashed right into her. Joan—her name was Joan—was also crying. She was about my age. I apologized all over myself, but she grabbed my hand, pulled me beside her, and apologized herself. She was embarrassed at being caught looking so unprofessional. She told me that nursing school never prepared her to deal with the patient's grieving families. Trying to maintain emotional detachment was too draining, and she'd finally hit a wall. I told her my mother was on the cancer ward. This nurse was smoking like crazy the whole time she was talking to me. She offered me hugs and my first cigarette, 'to calm my jitters,' was what she said. I gulped in the calmness and never looked back."

Paige dropped the half-finished butt, crushed it with the toe of her boot, and retrieved it to put in the trash later. Marcos was looking at her with raised eyebrows.

"So, your mother? You've never said much about your mother before."

"She didn't make it."

Marcos shifted, but Paige ducked out of his reach before he could place a comforting hand on her shoulder. She knew she would split wide open at the slightest touch.

"My mom had esophageal cancer," Paige said. "The survival rate is very low. By the time you're diagnosed, it's usually too late. It's a bitch. She died a few months after the PET scan. She was sixty-three." Paige felt tears welling and ran her index fingers roughly under her lower lids. "If you don't mind, I'd rather not talk about this anymore, and I need to get inside anyway." Paige gathered the softness of the multicolored poncho around her, slipped the strap of her bag over her head, and walked briskly toward the building.

Behind her she heard Marcos mutter, "When will I ever learn to keep my mouth shut?"

TWO

BALLROOM 101

Paige Russell
10:15 a.m., Tuesday, 13 October

"Good morning, Paige."

Katherine's voice was cheery and friendly. It sent quivers of uneasiness down Paige's spine. Katherine was behind the high, curved counter of the reception desk with the appointment book open. She'd pushed the tall barstool out of her way.

"Good morning back," Paige said. She kept her voice friendly, but neutral. Fresh from a quick tidying, Paige tucked the last few stray strands into her dancer's bun. She discreetly chewed some minty gum to mask the aftermath of smoking to avoid incurring Katherine's wrath.

"I'll need your help at the front desk today, Paige. Jill won't be in. Between you and Brianna, though, we can keep the desk covered," Katherine said. "The first lesson on the books isn't until eleven, which gives you plenty of time to put the sign-in book out, clean the break-room from yesterday, and give the restrooms a quick check."

"Okay, Katherine. No problem." Paige swallowed a sigh. Why

couldn't this studio afford a regular cleaning service? Check the damn bathrooms, and hop to it? What the hell? Paige glanced at Katherine's lowered head, stifling the urge to stick out her tongue. Geez, like when the owner drives a classic Camaro and wears cashmere, the studio can't afford to take the housekeeping burden off the instructors—the female ones anyway. Paige smothered a giggle at the mere thought of the top male instructors running a disinfectant cloth over the pissers in the men's room. Never gonna happen. Not in this lifetime. She was none too anxious to get moving on this task, either. Paige grabbed an *American Dancer* magazine and flipped through the pages.

"Paige, I just saw Sylvie's car. She's early. Maybe she can share some of the front desk duties today as well. And there's a clipboard on the corner table for Halloween party sign-ups. Make sure it's seen by students as they arrive. Paige? Paige, did you hear anything I said?"

The magazine tumbled out of Paige's hands. Katherine was pointing toward the corner of the room with her pen. Before Paige could untie her tongue to respond, a rush of cool air and a swirl of leaf debris announced Sylvie's arrival.

The fresh fall air added a flush to Sylvie's cheeks and a sparkle to her azure eyes. Paige tried not to gawk at the studio's top female instructor. She exuded an intimidating confidence. As usual, Sylvie's blond curls were restrained by a wide white headband, emphasizing an attractive widow's peak. She had the perfect dancer's body: slim-hipped and tiny-waisted with rounded, high breasts. Her flared dance skirt showed off strong, perfectly shaped legs. Sylvie was petite, but her athletic frame translated into pure power on the dance floor. Paige always felt clumsy next to this tiny dynamo.

"Has anyone heard from Tony? I didn't see his car in either the front or back lots," Sylvie said, glancing from Katherine to Paige.

"Not me," Paige responded, walking behind the counter to stand beside Katherine. Katherine responded with a shrug.

"Darn," Sylvie said. "I texted Tony last night to come in early, so we could squeeze in some practice time. He should have been here by now. Our routines need serious polishing before the Orange County Open."

Paige discreetly watched Sylvie turn her head from side to side and pout at her reflection. Only Sylvie could wear a pout so well.

"Do you know what Tony said to me last week, Katherine?" Sylvie spun around to face the reception counter. "He had the nerve to say I need to remember he's the center of our partnership and I revolve around him. Can you believe it?"

Paige knew better than to toss in her two cents. This was all Katherine's.

"Can you name even one male champion Latin dancer who doesn't have a huge ego, Sylvie?" Katherine said, jiggling a pencil between two fingers. "I'm not excusing Tony, but for perspective, Tony's been there, done that. He made a name for himself long before I asked him to partner you and jump back into the competitive circuit. Tony's earned his attitude."

"Yeah, I sort of know that, but it gets worse. Tony said I make everything about me, and my need to win is on overdrive." Sylvie's hands were on her slim hips. "He said he feels like a prop in a play, like his only purpose is to showcase me. And get this, he said he feels disrespected—like a husband."

Paige put her hand over her mouth to stifle a laugh, but it burst through her fingers as a muffled squawk. Even Katherine let loose with a low snicker.

"Moving on now, Sylvie. Have the new costumes arrived?" Katherine asked.

"Not yet, but any day now. I need to move in this new Latin dress to get a feel for its weight and movement. It has to be a showstopper," Sylvie said. She turned back to the lobby mirror to pat her curls and straighten her dance skirt.

Paige bit her lip. She felt too awkward around Sylvie to initiate a conversation, but she was dying for details about the competition—

who would be there, who was judging, what division Sylvie and Tony were dancing in. Better to be the fly on the wall for now.

Sylvie pulled her gaze away from the mirror, plonked both her dance bag and her forearms on the counter and, on tippy-toes, leaned over the top. "Did you know Tony and I will be competing against the snarky couple who placed second at Nationals last year?"

"I heard through the grapevine they're in Vegas this week, being coached by one of the visiting Romanian coaches," Katherine said.

"Yeah," Sylvie replied. "I heard the same." Sylvie's voice lost its confident edge, and her words came out mumbled. "I don't know how they afford it. The cost of competing this past year has maxed me out. Tony and I need this win so we can get invited to teach workshops at next year's competitions. Then we can begin to break even."

Paige felt embarrassed for Sylvie, who looked close to tears. Sylvie's shoulders dropped simultaneously with the rise of Katherine's perfectly plucked eyebrows.

"Sylvie," Katherine said, drumming her nails on the counter. "You have to compete smarter. You should know to cover your costs by encouraging top amateurs to enter the Pro-Am heats. It's a money ripple effect. Students need additional lesson hours to prepare for comps."

Sylvie straightened and smoothed her skirt. She cocked her head to one side and nodded slowly at Katherine.

"You're right," Sylvie said. "I need to broaden my focus to include the Pro-Am sections of the comps. This could make a huge difference to our cash situation."

"Exactly, Sylvie. And, if you take more than one student and they enter enough heats, who knows, you might place for Top Teacher. That's real cash money in your pocket. Cash money! Some comps pay out at four levels," Katherine said. "And Paige, since you are standing here listening rather than taking out the trash, I hope you are taking notes. It will be your turn soon enough."

"I…uh…yes, ma'am," Paige mumbled. Geez, it's not like she was eavesdropping. She was standing right there, for God's sake. What was she supposed to do? Pretend to be deaf? Paige stifled a yelp as Sylvie sharp-elbowed her out of the way. Sylvie dragged the barstool around Paige and wedged it next to Katherine.

"You have me feeling more positive, Katherine," Sylvie said.

"Keep one more thing in mind." Katherine paused. Her left hand rested on a jutted hip; a nail tip tapped rapid-fire on the countertop. "Your ambition alone isn't enough. Tony must be one hundred percent on board with everything from taking your practice times more seriously to encouraging students to compete Pro-Am. I don't see the same drive to win coming from him that I do coming from you."

Paige could see Sylvie's bright balloon of happiness burst, showering her blond curls with bits of drooping colored plastic. She came close to feeling sorry for her. This seemed like good timing to get moving on the tasks Katherine assigned her a half hour ago.

The back door handle jerked out of Paige's grip. She stumbled onto the stoop and the tightly knotted garbage bag flew out of her hand, landing with a soft *mmumph* on the asphalt. At least the strings on the bag held.

"Hey there, mamasita. Slow down. You could have knocked me over." With one hand still gripping the outside door handle, Tony Moreno grabbed Paige's arm to steady her and prevent both of them from landing in a tumble on the concrete stoop. Paige felt a rush of heat rise from her neck to her cheeks.

"What were you doing, barreling through the door like a running back? You could hurt someone."

How dare Tony scold her like it was her fault? What the hell?

"Me?" Paige exploded without thinking, "It was me who was pulled *out* the door. You jerked me right off my feet." Paige tried to release herself from his grasp, but Tony's hold was firm. He pulled her toward him.

"We've never been this up close and personal before." A flirtatious smile played across Tony's face. "You're always in the corner, so quiet. You should get angry more often, little one. Anger puts fire in those gorgeous gray-green eyes, and they sparkle like gemstones."

Never loosening his grip, Tony rubbed his thumb across Paige's well-toned bicep. She felt the heat in her face increase and tried to twist free.

"Take it easy, spitfire, or both of us are going to land on our back-sides."

Paige saw the teasing look in his eyes, but this wasn't funny. This was embarrassing. Tony Moreno was like her dance god. He was sexy and sultry and moved like quicksilver on the dance floor. He might be an ass, but he was the best Latin dancer she'd ever seen. This was not how she'd pictured her first real encounter with Tony. Now he would think she was an idiot—the stupid new girl on trash duty. She felt Tony pull her a little closer until her nose was inches from the deep vee of his partially buttoned shirt. Paige couldn't help herself. She leaned in, intoxicated by the scent of his crisp, spicy cologne. What was she doing?

With a flustered-sounding yelp, Paige jerked her arm out of Tony's grasp and pulled herself into a balanced stance. She only reached the top of his shoulder, and she had to stretch her head back to look Tony in the eye. She imagined herself a female tiger.

Tony chuckled and smiled his familiar self-assured, artificially whitened smile. He tipped an imaginary hat, bowed graciously, and stepped aside.

Paige moved quickly past him, retrieved the trash bag, and strode across the gravel to the dumpster with her head high. Damn Tony, anyway.

Paige huddled behind the reception desk, cradling her third cup of coffee, still trying to piece together the shattered remnants of her composure. Tony had really rattled her cage, and not just hers. She'd overheard Sylvie bitching about him strutting into the ballroom like a visiting celebrity, awaiting paparazzi. What did Sylvie expect? That he'd grovel like some timecard–punching peon? Nope, not Tony. He was The Tony Moreno, and he made sure everyone around him knew it.

"Paige? Earth to Paige." The irritation in Sylvie's voice startled Paige out of her magazine.

"S-sorry." Paige felt her face warm at being caught off guard. She crimped her page and put the magazine down. Sylvie was looking at her with an expression somewhere between amusement and exasperation.

"I asked you about Jill," Sylvie said. "When exactly is she coming in? I'm not a receptionist, and this gig is getting old fast."

"All I know is that Jill called Katherine to say she wouldn't be in today at all. Katherine didn't say why. I'll try to stay at the desk as much as I can."

"You have that wedding couple coming soon, though, right?" Sylvie said.

"Yeah. Pretty soon actually. After my lesson with them, Marcos is going to work with me. He's been amazing. He thinks I'm ready to test out of Bronze and move into Silver. I didn't expect to advance this quickly, but Marcos has been very generous with his talent and time."

"Yeah, I'll bet he has," Sylvie said. "When exactly is your next *special* coaching with Marcos? Wait, don't answer. I'll have a look." Sylvie leaned over Paige to check the appointment book. She ran her finger across the top of the columns. "So, Marcos has two hours later this afternoon with Barbara Bradshaw, then you can snarf him for a quickie in the rehearsal hall." Sylvie snorted.

Paige felt her cheeks get even hotter. She studied her shoes and sucked in a lungful of air. Before Sylvie could have any more fun at her expense, the front office glass window slid open, accompanied by a loud rapping.

"Paige, let me know as soon as Edward Dombrosky arrives," Katherine called through the partially open window. "I need to get Ed's deposit today and signature on the contract for the Vegas Holiday Dance Classic in 2016, late January. Got that?"

"You bet, Katherine," Sylvie called back before Paige could answer.

Paige caught Katherine's glance. Damn. Now Katherine thinks Sylvie stepped in for her 'cause she can't handle the front desk. Sylvie always had to butt in and be the star of the show.

"I sure wish I could find myself an Ed Dombrosky," Sylvie whispered to Paige.

"Edward? Katherine's student? Seriously?" Paige whispered back, curious but confused. First, Sylvie was actually talking to her in a sort of friendly way. Second, she would have never thought Sylvie preferred older men. Much older men. Ed had to be in his sixties.

"Ed's a dream student," Sylvie said.

"Oh. A student like Edward. I get it," Paige said. She felt more than a bit stupid.

"What the hell did you think I meant?" Sylvie frowned. "Whatever. I don't even want to know where your mind goes. Just listen and learn. The man is a retired IBM engineer. Think megabucks. He's a widower, no children. Not only does he spend a ton of money here, but he keeps our computer system running. He's a love. Last summer he tweaked the sound system when it tried to die on us. And last spring he spent a whole Saturday installing mirrors in the rehearsal room."

"And he gets along well with Katherine?" The words were out before Paige could edit herself. She put her hand over her mouth and turned toward the front office window. Katherine, looking irritated, was on the phone, not even glancing their way.

"Ohhhh, our Katherine is all smiles and honey with Ed," Sylvie said. She leaned closer to Paige and gave her a naughty nudge. "Personally, I think she's hoping to work her way into his will, if not his heart. Maybe there's a spot for her somewhere between the Humane Society and the Elephant Sanctuary."

Paige felt her face shift into what her mother used to call her frowny face.

"You are still such a baby about this business, Paige. Didn't they teach you anything at that Astaire studio in Flagstaff?" Sylvie narrowed her eyes.

"I was only part-time," Paige said. "I taught beginning group classes, answered phones, and filled in where needed. I wasn't trained to sell contracts."

"Well, that explains a lot. So pay attention." Sylvie turned to Paige and folded her arms. "Many of our retired students spend hours here every week. The studio becomes their second home, and we become like family. Some of them can be very generous toward us."

"Isn't that, well, sort of taking advantage and a little against the rules?" Paige ventured.

Sylvie tossed her curls and gave Paige a steady, schoolteacher stare.

"It's no big deal, Paige. Pay attention to the jewelry these women wear and listen to what they talk about: gigantic homes, vacation cruises, stockbrokers, housekeepers, and personal trainers. So what if it makes them happy to spend some of their money on us? The closest we'll get to their lifestyle is to marry into it or get written into some-one's will." Sylvie raised her chin. "Ed's expenses to go to the Las Vegas competition with Katherine are more than you'll make in six months."

"I never thought about it like that." Paige revolved from side to side on the leather bar stool. She held on to the counter with one hand. Hearing all this nitty-gritty stuff sort of killed the fun of thinking this gig was all about the glamor.

"Speaking of money, answer me this." Sylvie grabbed the barstool, abruptly stopping her swinging motion. "You don't have enough students yet to be making any kind of money, but you don't wait tables for the breakfast rush or have a part-time job. You don't live at home? What is it, then? Rich parents, or are you a trust-fund baby?"

Paige took a deep breath. Sylvie sure wasn't one to beat around the proverbial bush or let things go. Her money situation really wasn't anyone's business. Sylvie moved in nose-to-nose. Why couldn't the phone ring now? Paige cleared her throat, mentally editing.

"So," Paige said, "you know my mother died not too long ago, right?"

"Yeah. I heard, but I guess I forgot. You don't talk about it." Sylvie stepped back, out of Paige's face, and folded her arms. "So your dad foots your bills, then?"

"Um, no. My mom was a single mom. I've never met my dad."

"Oh. That sort of sucks. Then what? Your mom left you a lot of money?"

"Well, there was some money from the sale of the house and the life insurance. It's enough for living expenses until I get on my feet. When I came to Tucson for this job, I paid my first three months' rent up-front."

Sylvie stared, unblinking, and didn't ask any more questions.

"Ladies!" Katherine's voice cut off any thought of further conversation or questions.

They both jumped into action. Sylvie fumbled with a pen, and Paige dusted the counter with a tissue.

"It's nice to see you both so busy."

Paige glanced at Sylvie. Katherine's sarcastic tone wasn't lost on either of them.

"I have to make a private call. I don't want to be disturbed."

"Yes, ma'am." Sylvie's tone was formal and courteous. Katherine disappeared back into the front office.

"Crap," she whispered to Paige. "Good thing she didn't hear us talking about Ed. Okay, I'm gone. I'm heading to the ballroom. You're on your own for a while."

Sylvie's words were still hanging in the air when their coworker Brianna gave a yelp from the front door. She was trying to push the heavy door open with one hip and was stuck.

"Get this door for me, okay?" Brianna yelled. The signature aroma of Ricardo's Mexican Food drifted out of the white paper bag she clutched in one hand. The other hand held a half-eaten burrito, partially wrapped in yellow waxed paper.

"How do you stay so cheerleader slim?" Paige ran over and held the door open. "You're always stuffing your face."

"Good metabolism." Brianna shot Paige a good-natured smile. "I'm booked today until nine so I'll be working it off." She paused mid-step to take a bite out of the burrito. "Yum."

"I guess I'll just stay here and play doorman," Paige said. She held the door open. Joey Bustamente was running across the parking lot, hot on Brianna's heels. At least Joey wasn't *in* Brianna's heels. Paige felt her face redden at her visual of Joey prancing through the front door in four-inch stilettos; she covered her mouth to hide a giggle as he brushed past. The Italian dance instructor's expansive gestures were so effeminate, Paige always assumed he was happily and blatantly gay. But under the layers of gold chains, tight-fitting dance pants, and see-through shirts, it turned out Joey was a married man. As if to confirm his heterosexuality, he patted Brianna's spandexed backside before she could dart out of his reach.

"Hello, lovely." Joey directed his attention to Paige. He winked and circled to give her a playful hug. "Oh, I caught that blush," Joey stage-whispered. In full singsong voice, he crooned, "I think Paigey has a crush."

"Give it a rest, Joey," Paige said, moving back behind the counter. She turned to hide her smile. Joey's peacock train would deflate pretty darn fast if he knew his dashing demeanor came across more Elton John than Justin Timberlake. And absolutely no one took him seriously.

"Pretty Paige, you go take a break. I need to use the computer to check the webpage for updates to the group class schedule and stuff."

Paige changed places with Joey, who started clicking onto the studio's webpage before she could get out of his way. A loud expletive accompanied by a hand slap to the counter made her jump. Paige was astonished. Joey had his quirks, but he very rarely swore.

"God damn it," Joey repeated. "This fucking class schedule is two weeks old. Katherine promised to promote an advanced rumba class if I would teach it. What the hell! I'll update the damn webpage myself."

Paige glanced at the front office. Joey's voice projected. Yup. Time for that break. There was no way she wanted to get caught in the crossfire if Katherine heard his comments.

THREE

Bedlam or Ballroom?

Paige Russell
1:30 p.m., Wednesday, 14 October

Paige walked her wedding-dance couple to the door and sighed with relief. She watched them argue all the way to their car. This was her second lesson with Nikki and Brandon, and so far, choreographing their wedding routine was not the fun time it should be. Today, Nikki never stopped taunting her fiancé about his inability to be the man and lead. That girl needed to be bitch-slapped. You can't lead someone who refuses to follow. Nikki was just plain mean.

"What's with those two?" Sylvie asked, peeking out from behind the reception desk's computer monitor.

"I wish I knew," Paige answered. "Honestly, as much as Katherine wants me to push them to buy a contract, I think their money would be better spent on premarital counseling."

Paige walked around the counter and pulled out a bright pink marker to highlight the appointment book. Katherine wanted her to mark open spots for the week, but before she had a chance to get even one pink streak onto the page, Joey's biggest client, Linda Wilson, burst through the front door. Paige cocked her head. She'd seen Linda on the floor but hadn't actually met her. From her cropped red hair and sunset-coral lipstick to her bedazzled shoes, Linda was a substantial woman. Her jewelry was big, her voice big, her personality bigger.

"You know I simply can't relax in a messy house." Talking in full voice, Linda sloughed off her wool jacket and tasteful silk scarf. "Visual disorder equals mental disorder. The mess was shifting my axis off center. I thought about canceling my lesson but decided the discipline of dancing would calm my mind. So, I recruited my neighbor's cleaning ladies to do my house, and I dropped the Mercedes off to be detailed. The dealer will pick me up here. I'll drive home in a freshly washed and waxed car and enter the calming environment of a clean house." Linda took a breath, palms outstretched in the universal gesture of "Am I not the brightest bloom in the field?"

Paige felt like she should applaud.

Right on cue, Joey Bustamente slipped into the reception area and greeted his best client with a big hug.

"Sounds like your day is off to a great start," Joey said, taking Linda's hand. "Let's make it even better. While you change into your dance shoes, I'll get some music queued up for us. How about we warm up with our foxtrot routine?" Joey's voice drifted away from the reception area as he maneuvered his student to the ballroom.

"Wow," Paige said. "It feels like all the air has been sucked out of this room."

Four long and boring hours later, Paige settled into the sofa closest to the entrance of the ballroom. As a visual learner, observation was her best tool—a better teacher than any syllabus or dance methods book.

A circus of sound and movement swirled through the ballroom. All the instructors, except Brianna and Joey, were on the floor with clients: Jackson, who had about a year of experience over Paige; Carrie, a part-timer who had yet to share two words with Paige; Marcos, of course; Tony; and Sylvie. Paige smiled a contented smile. A nice cross section of Tucson's multicultural community was represented in this one room. Desert DanceSport's clients were as diverse in ethnicity as they were in their ability to dance.

To the uninitiated onlooker, the scene was more bedlam than ballroom. Teachers shouted counts and instructions over each other and over the sound system. Everyone observed one informal rule: each instructor waited their turn for their choice of music. It was everyday normal to shout out the count of the *one-two-three-hold* of a salsa for a student while the *slow, slow, quick-quick, slow* of an American tango blared overhead. Focus was the word of the day.

Across the ballroom, Jackson created an invisible wall around his Preliminary Bronze couple to narrow their focus and train them to block out distractions. A few feet from them, a lithe Hispanic woman, wearing earbuds and a short dance skirt, ran her Latin cha-cha choreography. Paige was more than a little envious of this woman's professional-level technique. She was Tony's most advanced student. Having her on the floor was a selling point for walk-ins. On the far side of the rectangular ballroom, Carrie maneuvered a very rotund but energetic red-haired guy through some country-western basics. Katherine made sure Paige knew Carrie sold a full lesson package to this new student. There was no mistaking the underlying message of Katherine's tone. Carrie's sales pitch focused on how dance skills would improve his dating life, and by the looks of things he was super motivated.

A middle-aged East Indian couple tried to stay out of everyone's way while practicing their West Coast swing moves. Paige could hear their *one-two, three and four, five and six*. Paige rubbed two fingers under her bottom lip. She taught the same dance but counted the steps as *one-two, triple-step, triple-step*. It all danced the same way, but what worked for one person didn't work for another. Flexibility—another teaching gem to tuck away.

It was Tony's turn at the sound system. Arm-in-arm, he led his most elderly student—an eighty-four-year-old dynamo—to the middle of the floor. In seconds they were bounding through an old-fashioned Peabody, a 1950s ballroom dance few people knew how to do. Everyone in the studio loved this student for her wicked sense of humor and enjoyment of performing. Paige once heard her announce, with a full-throated chortle, she was happily spending every dime of her ungrateful children's inheritance on ballroom.

A few tables away, Marcos and his favorite student, Barbara Bradshaw, were hydrating after a two-hour lesson. Paige hoped she'd still be dancing when she hit Barbara's age. She gave Barbara a discreet once over. The woman must be in her midfifties. She was attractive, with stylishly layered and streaked chestnut hair. The little lines around her eyes softened her face, making her look more mischievous than old. She was super friendly, too, always asking Paige how she was "getting on." Barbara was at home enough in the studio to answer the phone when everyone was busy, water lobby plants, and even wipe smudges off the ballroom's mirrors. The more Paige got to know Barbara, the more she saw why Marcos spoke so highly of her.

Paige curled her feet under her just as, a few feet away, Sylvie pulled her couple, Eric and Amy Fromme, into a less crowded space on the floor. Eric was a tall African American, and Amy was an equally tall pale-blond Scandinavian type. They complemented each other well. Sylvie's music queued up—Michael Bublé's "The More I See You"—an easy foxtrot in a four-four rhythm. Paige compressed her lips to hide her amusement. Eric was loose-limbed, a bit uncoordinated, and completely unselfconscious. His approach to ballroom dance was entirely his own. No matter what technique Sylvie employed to get Eric to glide and slide and brush his feet along the floor, up went those knees and off he went, prancing like an overgrown colt around the ballroom. His lack of talent was more than balanced by sheer determination and enthusiasm. His idea of leading was to muscle his partner in the direction he wanted her to go. Sylvie looked like she was ready to break into a nervous sweat. Eric's wife, Amy, calmly followed with a patient smile on her face. She was the polar opposite of her husband, as gentle and quiet as he was strong and outspoken, and actually quite a lovely dancer when she got the chance.

"Heel lead, Eric," Sylvie called out. "Push from your standing leg, let your traveling toe caress the floor, then flip to a heel lead as your back heel raises off the floor. Smooth as silk, Eric. Brush the floor and lilt on the three-four."

Sylvie caught Paige's eye and winked as she tried another approach with Eric.

Paige held her breath. Sylvie didn't act annoyed with her for watching, and that wink made her feel like an insider. This was a moment.

"Eric, instead of counting the *one, two, three-four,* try *slow, slow, quick-quick,* and you'll get a nice little lilt on the *three-four.* Remember, foxtrot is jazzy." Sylvie clapped to the count for emphasis.

Amy glided. Eric pranced, humming and counting out loud as he marched his way across the floor. Sylvie sweated and called out encouraging comments. Eric jerked Amy into the turns and danced like a machine gun in short, rapid bursts of energy. Paige wondered if Sylvie ever thought of switching him to something more staccato, like the Latin paso doble.

"Ouch." Sylvie rubbed one elbow. Eric had spun Amy hard so hard she flew right into Sylvie, who quickly reached for Amy to steady her. Smiling and oblivious, Eric bowed.

"Okay, kids. That's it for today," Sylvie said. She turned to Paige and rolled her eyes. "What do you think about Tony Moreno joining us for the first hour of your next lesson, Amy? Tony can take you through all your new patterns, while I work with Eric on his lead."

"Sounds great," Eric said, and gathered Sylvie into a big bear hug before heading off the floor to change into his street shoes. Amy beamed.

"The man really thinks he's as debonair as his idol, Fred Astaire," Sylvie whispered to Paige after she ushered her clients off the floor. Sylvie leaned against the arm of Paige's sofa.

"You suggested an exchange lesson with Tony?" Paige asked. "What's your thinking?"

"I don't want Amy to burn out," Sylvie replied, rubbing her elbow. "You learn to be sensitive to undercurrents. Amy won't complain, but I know she needs time dancing with an expert leader, and Eric needs some serious one-on-one. I hope to channel some of Eric's energy into technique. He'll never compete, but he might make a decent social dancer in time. Maybe."

The Frommes turned to wave as they headed out to the hall.

"Bless his heart," Sylvie said, waving back. "Eric really is a sweet man, but he's like an overgrown Great Dane puppy. Okay if I sit here for a few? I'm so done."

Paige nodded and made room on the sofa. Maybe things were looking up between her and Sylvie? This was someone she could really learn from if Sylvie would let her.

"Sylvie, about earlier today. Is Linda Wilson always that wired?"

"You saw Linda on a slow day." Sylvie laughed. "Want the scoop on her?"

"Sure," Paige said, going into sponge mode.

"So," Sylvie started, her voice taking on a superior tone, "next to Katherine's Edward Dombrosky, Linda Wilson is the studio's prized bread-and-butter client—lots of money and happy to spend it. She's a top real estate agent but still finds several hours a week for lessons. She enters two or three major competitions a year with Joey. Her loyalty to him is unwavering. Joey totally understands the gold mine he has in Linda."

Paige bit her lip, and Sylvie responded with a wagging finger.

"Don't misunderstand. Joey genuinely likes Linda, but he has no qualms about continually selling to her. She has the money. And, before you go all judgmental, look at it this way. Joey is doing Linda a great service. Dancing keeps her agile in middle age, and dancing is more social than a solitary workout at a gym. Linda gets to fulfill a childhood fantasy of being Anna, twirling around the ballroom in *The King and I*. Joey gets both a fat paycheck and the status of being the studio's top moneymaker. It's a relationship made in heaven."

Paige absentmindedly chewed on the edge of her finger as she sorted out her thoughts. She got what Sylvie was saying, but did most students understand that all the attention lavished on them wasn't personal? It wasn't fake exactly, but it was contrived to create a bond that made it hard to refuse to buy into everything their instructors tried to sell them. Paige was about to ask Sylvie if big-spending students ever overstepped their bounds and assumed this friend-ship bond entitled them to an instructor's time on a personal level, but...Marcos was heading their way. Coaching time with Marcos! He raised his hand and gestured toward her. Like a happy puppy, Paige obediently ran to her master. Sylvie and her question were forgotten.

9:30 p.m., Wednesday, 14 October

Paige stepped onto the small apartment balcony. With the tip of her thumb and index finger, she picked up one chic leather boot and held it to her nose. Not too bad. At least the smell didn't make her nauseous anymore. Two nights on the balcony, and the stink was fading. The boots were a mega deal, but the jury was still out on whether they were the deal of a lifetime or her biggest error in shopping judgment. The tag on the boots read *Made in China from natural materials*. Like what? Old rubber tires? Other possibilities were too disconcerting to think about.

Paige grabbed the balcony railing and leaned out. She could see to the far end of the heated pool where a light vapor rose in the cool evening air. The fronds of the surrounding palm trees, illuminated by spotlights, shimmered against the blue-black sky. The pool area sure looked more appealing at night than it did under the unforgiving light of day. Paige rubbed her arms and shivered. Time to go back inside. She shut the sliding glass doors behind her and pulled the faded blue folder out of a drawer. She tucked herself into a corner of the loveseat sofa and propped her bare feet on the upholstered wood crate that served as a coffee table.

With her big toe, she nudged aside the book *Midlife Orphan* by Jane Brooks—the book that started it all. The word *orphan* put a label on exactly how she was feeling. Until she stumbled across this book, she had no words to explain her pit of emotions when well-meaning friends asked how she was doing. The word *orphan* was an identifier. At twenty-four, she was alone—mother gone, no father in the picture, no family to visit at Thanksgiving, no home to go home to, no one to be a grandparent to her unborn children. Her aunt was still someone she barely knew, and besides, she'd gone home to Florida. The plain fact was, she was an orphan and didn't belong anywhere or to anyone anymore.

Paige ran her hands over the blue folder's ragged faux leather. She still couldn't wrap her head around finding this folder hidden away in a box of junk files. It darn near hit the trash can. The folder was beaten-up, and the worn flap was held closed by elastic, which had long lost its stretchiness. It didn't look important, but the papers inside—some stapled, some in plastic sleeves, some loose—completely changed her world. Why hadn't her mom kept something this major with the tax files, or the important receipts, or the insurance papers, or even with Paige's birth certificate? Instead it was stuck in a shoebox with child-hood vaccination records and Paige's old report cards. She chewed on her thumb. All those hours sitting by her mother's hospice bedside were now missed opportunities when her mom could have told her to look for this folder. So many questions could have been answered. The whole thing just made her want to bawl.

The doorbell's shrill ring, followed by abrupt banging on the door, cut through her thoughts. "Hey, Paige. Open up. It's me, Kristi."

"Okay, hold on. Be right there." Paige slid the blue folder under a chair, out of the way. She sighed. Her spontaneous invite for Kristi to drop by sounded like a good idea at the time, but now.... Who knows, Kristi might just be exactly what she needed. She was one of those people you feel like you've known forever right after you meet them. That didn't happen very often, at least not in Paige's world.

Paige held the door open and slim, broad-shouldered Kristi swept into the apartment. Her dark hair, heavily streaked with blond, was shampoo-commercial perfect. The chin-length cut flowed and rippled when she moved, falling right back into place, emphasizing her high cheekbones. Her almond-shaped brown eyes were bright and full of mischief.

"Sorry I'm late, and thanks for the invite. I'm so glad we ran into each other doing laundry. Chatting definitely took laundry from boring to bonding." Kristi brandished a brown bag and held a colorful Mexican bowl in the other hand. Tucked under her arm was a bottle of red wine.

"I brought salsa and tortilla chips and, of course, wine. Where?" she said, glancing around. "Okay to put this stuff on the wood tray on…what is that exactly, an upholstered crate?"

"Yup. That's exactly what it is. A thrift-shop find. Works as both a coffee table and an ottoman," Paige replied. She pointed toward the small slice of kitchen counter, where she'd placed two wine glasses next to the corkscrew.

"Grab this bottle before it slips out from under." Kristi raised her elbow after Paige wrapped her hands around the enticing bottle of Ménage à Trois red.

"You've done a great job with this place, Paige," Kristi said. She put the snacks on the crate table and looked around. "Those old-fashioned fabric lampshades soften the light, and I adore the vintage telephone table. I can't believe you actually have a landline and an old rotary-dial phone that actually works."

Paige let Kristi deal with uncorking the wine while she busied herself ripping open the bag of tortilla chips. She dipped a large chip into the salsa and cupped her hand underneath the drips. Munching on the chip, Paige glanced around the room, seeing her living space for the first time through someone else's eyes.

The glow of lamplight hid the worn carpeting and softened the generic motel-room feel of an apartment where too many occupants had come and gone. Woven Mexican blankets from nearby Nogales added the right touch of color. She'd hung one red-and-cream blanket on the longest wall and draped a brightly colored fringed blanket across the back of the loveseat. A few furnishings from the house in Flagstaff made the small living room comfortable: the loveseat and a vintage floor lamp were from her mother's bedroom, and the padded rocking chair was from the den. Books of all sizes fought for space in the oak bookshelf beside large pinecones, odd-shaped rocks, and beach shells from a trip to California with her mother. She ran her thumb along her lower lip, giving in to a contented smile.

"So, were you able to connect with your Aunt Teresa?" Kristi settled into the rocking chair beside the sofa and placed the wine bottle within easy reach.

Paige bit her upper lip and sighed. "We talked last night. She's not very happy with me right now. She and my mom might not have had much in common, but they were on the same page about there being no future, no money, and no security in dancing. Me bailing on school was not part of the plan. She wants me back at NAU."

"Hmmm," Kristi murmured. "You never really did say why you left NAU and how you came to be teaching at Desert DanceSport."

"Well." Paige shifted her position and savored her first sip of wine. "In a nutshell, when I applied for a job at Desert DanceSport, I already had a part-time job at the Fred Astaire studio in Flagstaff. Katherine, the owner at Desert DanceSport, hired me based on a recommendation from the Astaire studio and a short interview on Skype."

"Well, that sounds easy enough. But why Tucson?"

Paige shifted in her seat and sipped more of the delicious wine before looking over at Kristi. "I dunno," she mumbled. "I was still pretty raw from my mother's death and was floating emotionally. I needed to find my tribe, so to speak. I saw some dancers from Desert DanceSport at an expo in Flagstaff, and something clicked. It was like a magnetic pull. I Googled the studio and applied."

"So, who did you see? How many dancers from this Tucson studio were at the expo?"

"Well, only one, actually. A pro dancing with a student." Paige loaded another chip, dribbling salsa on her shirt. "His name is Marcos. I couldn't get him of my head."

"Isn't Marcos the instructor who's mentoring you?"

"Yeah, that's the one. He's the Dance Master at the studio."

Kristi cocked her head, one finger tracing a line under her lower lip. Paige waited for Kristi to speak, but she just nodded.

"And it's working out," Paige said in a rush. "I'm learning so much."

"Well, that's great, then. How about your friends from NAU? Don't you miss them?" Kristi asked.

"Well, I do, and I don't. I guess I have issues with friendships. A few months after my mother died, my friends all started telling me how I needed to get over it and move on." Paige reached for the bottle to refill her glass and then settled back, one leg curled underneath her. "And I suppose I started to withdraw, avoiding phone calls and not returning texts. I was worn out with the effort of smiling and having to say I was okay when I wasn't."

"That sounds tough, Paige," Kristi said. Her eyes were filled with sympathy.

"Sorry, I didn't mean to play the death card," Paige said. She forced a tight smile and continued. "Being here is good. Part of me needs to start over with new people." She spoke without meeting Kristi's eyes. "But the other part of me is afraid to dive into friendships. So many people turn out to be piranhas. They'll eat you alive if you let them," Paige blurted. She felt a warmth creep all the way from her neck to her cheeks. Damn, wine had a habit of loosening her up too much.

"Strong statement," Kristi said, leaning forward. "Women especially need friends. We couldn't survive without other women to talk to. I'm hoping you and I can become friends."

Paige noticed two little frown lines forming between Kristi's eyes. Paige took a small sip, trying to compose her thoughts. She felt more comfortable with Kristi than she had with anyone in a very long time and didn't want to scare her away.

"My mother always said that, too, about how women need friends.

But between my friends not understanding where I was coming from and my mother's friendships seeming so lopsided, I just don't know anymore," Paige said.

"That's just sad. If it's not being too pushy, can you explain what you are talking about with your mother's friendships?" Kristi asked. She leaned back, twirling the stem of her glass between her hands.

"Here's the thing." Paige hesitated. If she totally spilled her guts, she could sink this friendship boat before it even left the dock. "My mom put a ton of energy into her friendships. She was the one who always offered help, listened without judgment, remembered birthdays, celebrated successes, but I didn't see her getting that back." Paige pulled at her bottom lip. "I know I sound bitter, and trust me, I don't like it much. Are you sure you want to hear this?"

Kristi topped off her wine, and nodded. "I do. It might be good for you to talk anyway."

"Okay, then. My mother was a nurse. She went off the rails after her stage-three cancer diagnosis, and who could blame her. She over-indulged and got ticketed with a DUI. She got off with a fine and probation. Nurses know a lot of cops. Anyway, her so-called friends, who didn't know about the cancer yet, were like a flock of chickens pecking an injured chicken to death. Even after they found out how sick she was, only one or two stepped off their self-righteous pedestals to apologize. It was like these women needed to believe that my mom's kindness was all a big phony act. They acted like this person, the one nailed with a DUI, was the real Patricia." Paige stopped to breathe.

Kristi shook her head and made a sympathetic sound. "She must have been very hurt and disillusioned. I can see how this affected your thinking."

"It did. My mother taught me to live by the Golden Rule, and I get it. That's the way to be. But when you try to be thoughtful and kind all the time, people take advantage." Paige gave Kristi a sheepish shrug. "I'm sorry to be such a downer." She placed her empty wineglass on the table and folded her hands in her lap.

"Paige." Kristi sat straighter and made eye contact. "I'm not trying to invalidate your feelings. Your mother's treatment after the DUI was callous. People are judgmental for sure, and there are too many bullies on the playground. But, what you said about her friendships being lopsided, well…." Kristi tucked her streaked hair behind her ears. She reached across to the sofa to touch Paige's hand before continuing.

"Maybe your mother bonded people to her by being there for them and put more energy out than anyone expected or even wanted. Maybe she needed to feel needed, and that gave her the warm fuzzies. Were her friends really truly friends or just acquaintances? Most of us can have only one or two real friends, and you can't buy real friendship." Kristi paused to dip a tortilla chip in the salsa and eyed Paige.

Paige cocked her head, twisted her lips to one side, and slowly nodded.

"Let me pass along something my grandmother told me," Kristi said. "She was generous with people to a fault until the day someone pushed the envelope too far. It finally hit Nana that too many people were taking advantage of her good nature. She told me there's a difference between helping people and people helping themselves. In Nana's words, 'There are too many fat people with their hands stuck in the cookie jar.'" Kristi raised one eyebrow and smiled. "Maybe my nana wasn't very PC, but she was right."

"You are, for sure, more insightful than I would expect for someone who does nails for a living," Paige said. "Oh crap, Kristi. I'm so sorry. I shouldn't have blurted that out."

Kristi's laugh was soft, and her eyes brightened with warmth. She wasn't the howling-with-laughter type but seemed to appreciate unedited honesty.

"As I've gotten older," Kristi said, "and I'm hitting the big Three-O this year, I don't get offended so easily." Her smile lit her face. "Truth is, working as a nail technician pays my college tuition, mainly online. I'm working toward a degree in psychology and counseling."

Paige looked at Kristi with renewed interest. A small smile curled around the edges of her mouth. She really liked this girl. "I think you are going to make a super-great counselor."

"Thank you." Kristi smiled and yawned. "I'd love to talk more, but I'm booked for a set of acrylics at seven in the morning, and I have to get some sleep. Let me do your nails one day. They're strong and well-shaped. A shame to neglect them. No offense."

"None taken." Paige stretched out her fingers. Her cuticles really did look pretty ratty.

Paige hugged Kristi at the door, carefully locking the deadbolt behind her. She kneeled and reached under the chair for THE FOLDER—the words not just capitalized in her head but flashing in electric blue. Paige rubbed her palms together and pulled out a well-worn page, every word memorized. She bit her lip and slapped the paper back into the folder. Why did her mother keep this stuff such a huge honking secret, leaving her to draw her own conclusions? But, between the stuff in the folder and her own gut instincts, she had enough to go on to bring her to Tucson. Holy crap, if she told Aunt Teresa why she was really in Tucson, she would be on the next plane from Florida to drag Paige back to Flagstaff by the short hairs. She'd probably take her to a shrink while she was at it.

FOUR

DANCING TO YOUR OWN BEAT

Paige Russell
10:30 a.m., Thursday, 15 October

Jill's high-pitched shrieks and giggles became more annoying the closer Paige got to the reception area. Jill bounced from person to person, her blond ponytail flipping back and forth. Her outfit was classic Jill—a hot-pink, boat-necked, rhinestone top stretched over a very short black skirt. The pink bedazzled cowboy boots took it over the top.

"Look, Paige, look," Jill squealed. She thrust out her left hand, wrist down, pink-tipped fingers splayed. A flash of diamonds and gold glittered under the fluorescent lights.

"I got married Monday night!" The words tumbled out with the tremulous rush of a teenager's giggle. Jill's flush matched her pink shirt.

Before Paige could lean forward to have a better look, Jill bobbed away, dancing around the room to show everyone the ring again.

"And check this out." She slipped down a corner of her blouse, exposing a two-inch tattoo: a banner, outlined in red, with small American flags on either side. A bright-blue *Steve* was carved into the middle. "Red, white, and blue—my skin being the white," Jill said. "Steve has one that matches, only with my name instead of his." Jill's eyes were wide and luminous with the brilliant flame that can only be lit by reckless passion.

Paige closed her eyes and shook her head. Jill was at least ten years her senior.

Stunned silence filled the reception area, broken finally by Marcos's gentlemanly, cultured voice. "And for how long, my dear, have you known this Steve, um, your husband?"

Jill's little chin jutted out, and she folded her arms in a defensive posture.

"Not long, but when it's right, it's right. And anyway, Steve is an American hero. He was deployed overseas with the reserves. Now he's joining the Border Patrol and is going to New Mexico for nineteen weeks' training."

"So where did you meet this American hero, Jill?" Paige asked. Marcos winked at her.

"We met at The Boondocks. He picked me out of the crowd, and we danced all night. Our very last dance was to a George Strait song where the last line is 'And now that I've found you, I'm never gonna let you go.'" Jill closed her eyes in romantic ecstasy.

"Hmmm. Nothing like a country western song for life-changing philosophies," Marcos said in an unenthusiastic monotone. Paige caught Katherine elbowing him before he could expound any further.

"Jill, I'm sure everyone wishes you well," Katherine said. "But we need to focus on our day." She shooed everyone away from the reception area with a back-to-work gesture.

Jill didn't look too happy at having her audience dismissed so abruptly. Paige signaled Brianna to follow her into the instructors' breakroom.

"So how much do you know? You talk to Jill more than I do," Paige asked. She grabbed a super-caffeinated Monster Energy drink out of the fridge.

"Jill mentioned this Steve guy to me a few weeks ago." Brianna's words were muffled by a mouthful of sesame bagel and cream cheese. She stood in front of the mirror, sucking in her midriff as she munched. "This is what I know. Steve walked over, tilted his cowboy hat back with his thumb, and swooped her off her feet. And I mean physically picked her up. After the bar closed, Jill followed Steve to his place—a double-wide on six acres out near Picture Rock—and they talked until sunrise. Then he made her homemade waffles with strawberries and whipped cream, and, in Jill's words, 'the sweetness of it all won my heart.' This is her dream guy—an honest-to-God working cowboy with a roping horse in the corral and a country drawl."

Paige couldn't suppress a snarky little giggle. "Hasn't Jill been married once?"

"Twice," Brianna answered. She rinsed out her coffee mug, set it on the drainer, and turned around to face Paige. She leaned against the breakroom counter. "Here's the thing. The Boondocks is Jill's regular Saturday night hangout. I've watched her in action. She wears tight jeans and unbuttons the top of her shirt to maximize her advertising dollars. Then she strolls across the dance floor as the band warms up. Drinks start arriving at the table within minutes."

Paige didn't know whether to be amused by or embarrassed for Jill.

"Hey, changing the subject. I want to ask you something real quick," Brianna said. Her voice lowered to a whisper. "Did Katherine ask you to hold off on cashing your paycheck?"

"No. Geez. Holy crap. Did she actually ask you that?" Paige said.

"Yeah. It's never happened to me before, but I've heard rumors Jeremy quit over paycheck issues. This check has my bonus money on it from the competition, and the bonus is late coming to me as it is."

"That stinks, Brianna. Did Katherine at least give you a reason?" Paige asked.

"She said there was a minor mix-up with the bank, which would be straightened out in a day or two. I also overheard Joey on the phone talking about delaying mailing a couple of checks. I'll bet it's just me and Joey because of competition bonus money." Brianna made an apologetic face. "I probably shouldn't have said anything."

"Don't worry. I don't gossip," Paige said, pulling open the break-room door. "Guess we should both get back to making money we might never see."

~

Katherine Carrington
1:30 p.m., Thursday, 15 October

From the front office window, Katherine kept an eye on Jill's antics as she waved her wedding-ringed hand at every client who came in the door. The stupid girl, believing she'd found the Holy Grail of love, couldn't keep her attention focused on her job for more than the flick of a cat's tail. Katherine pursed her lips. Enough was enough. Brianna and Jackson were at the desk trying to check the appointment book, and now Jill had them corralled.

"Brianna, Jackson. Could you both step in here for a moment?" Katherine cracked open the office window as she spoke and tapped on the glass to emphasis her words.

The pair of fledgling instructors stood in front of momma bird's desk, looking like they were about to get booted out of the nest before they could fly.

"What's up, Katherine?" Jackson was the first to speak.

"What's up, Jackson, is that I haven't seen any paperwork cross my desk for either the Student Specialty Showcase or the December Midwinter Ball. We have to get the heats filled, especially for the ball, so I can reserve the hotel ballroom. What about your new student? The one who recently tested out of Preliminary Bronze? She should enter fifteen heats minimum: three waltzes, foxtrots, and tangos, and then two heats for each of her basic American Rhythm dances. What's the holdup?" Katherine leaned back, arms folded.

"I don't think she can afford to enter," Jackson said. He gripped the back of one of the chairs facing Katherine's desk. "She has kids in school still and—"

"Can't afford? That's an unacceptable excuse. People find the money for the things they really want to do. It's not your job to be this woman's financial advisor or worry about what she can and can't afford. Do you know her husband's an endocrinologist?"

"Um, well…she might have mentioned it to me once—"

"Stop fidgeting, Jackson, and pay attention," Katherine said. The sharp edge to her voice was honed to cut through perceived bullshit. "It's your job to make your student understand how entering events provides an opportunity to take her dancing to a new level. Talk to her about the value of the adjudicator's comments and how you'll use them to shape her future lesson plan. Are we clear?"

"Yes, ma'am." Jackson's knuckles were turning a whitish pink.

"And Brianna." Katherine leaned forward, tapping a pen on her desktop. She paused long enough to catch each rabbit in her coyote-like field of vision. "What about that youngish cop? The one who hangs around and talks to you after his lessons. What in the hell are you talking about if not dancing? He's on the books for later this afternoon, so check back with me at the end of the day." Katherine laid her hands flat on the desk in her *I'm done* gesture. "I think we're all clear on what's expected. Back to work, both of you."

Katherine shook her head. As pleasant a diversion as that was, she had to get back to the business at hand. Two spreadsheets were open on her screen. The more colorful spreadsheet resided on a bright-red thumb drive she kept either locked in a desk drawer or safely tucked into her purse. Fingers steepled and one eyebrow raised, Katherine rocked back and forth. Her eyes were beginning to glaze over, and her neck had started to ache thirty minutes ago. Feeling like she had ADHD, she swiveled her chair and glanced into the reception area. Jill was on the phone, deep in conversation. A section of her ponytail was tightly wrapped around one finger. Katherine quietly cracked open the window.

"Yes, I called the order in a couple of hours ago. Uh-huh. Billed to our account for delivery tomorrow. What? Are you sure?" Jill turned her back on the two students signing in for their lessons and cupped her hand around the mouthpiece. "Yes, I understand. I'm sure it's a mistake. I'll call you back as soon as I can. No. Hold the order until I get back to you."

"Jill, I need to speak with you," Katherine called out. She kept her eye on Jill as she rounded the counter and dragged her feet to the door.

"Sit." Katherine pointed to an office chair. "What was that all about?"

"Ummm...that was Abbott Office Supply on the phone. I called in an order this morning. They called back and said our account is way overdue, and anything we buy has to be on a cash-and-carry basis until we pay the balance." Jill's voice trailed off, and she wouldn't look Katherine in the eye.

"Who did you speak with, Jill?"

"A man called Jerry Burke. He said we need to pay the past due amount right away. He sounded pretty angry, Katherine." Jill finally raised her eyes to meet Katherine's. "I told him it had to be a mistake. Right?"

"It's fine, Jill. I'm sure it's a mistake and this Jerry is just having a bad day. You go back out to the front desk. I'll call him and get things straightened out." Katherine gave Jill her most reassuring smile and ushered her out.

Katherine rubbed her temples. Was Jill going to become a problem? Last week she'd had the impudence to question Katherine about not returning calls. Katherine's knee jiggled. As if Katherine's word wasn't good enough, the persistent sales manager from the Hilton kept calling to harangue her about a deposit for the Midwinter Ball. She pressed her fingertips against her lips, head bowed. Jill saw the incoming mail before anyone else, screened phone calls, and could place minor orders. Maybe Jill was under the mistaken impression she was an office manager rather than a receptionist?

Katherine folded her arms and stood by her desk, watching Jill. The girl might not be the brightest berry on the bush, but even she could add two and two and get four. The last thing she needed was ditzy Jill drawing her own misguided conclusions about the studio's business. Jill needed to stop asking questions above her pay grade.

She was tempted to pass along some insights, but...Katherine shrugged. If Jill thought life was the personification of a poignant country western song, who was she to waste her breath trying to change her mind? In reality, this new marriage of Jill's was doomed to be closer to a Greek tragedy than a romantic Keith Urban love song. Whatever. She had more important things to do than try to run Jill's personal life. The stupid girl would get lost going in a straight line.

One thing her own disastrous marriage taught her was the importance of detaching long enough to take a cold, hard look at the other person before you ever say "I do." The fog of love obscures the simple fact that people don't really change, and character traits exaggerate with age. You have to put your lover's worst traits under a microscope to decide which behaviors you can shrug off and which ones you can live with. The beast you see today is the beast you will be living with until the day you die, file for divorce, or commit murder.

"Not my circus, not my monkeys," Katherine muttered. She sat back down at the front office desk and turned to the numbers dancing across the Excel spreadsheets.

∼

8:45 p.m., Thursday, 15 October

Tucked away from the noise and distraction of the main part of the studio, Katherine's private office was a woman's version of the coveted man cave. Soft green walls served as a neutral backdrop for her collection of colorful acrylics. Each painting featured a traditionally clothed Hispanic female caught in a private moment: joyfully dancing, lost in thought in a bougainvillea-draped courtyard, or eating a mango, the juice dripping down the woman's coffee-with-cream forearms.

The walnut shelf held several pairs of dance shoes. A selection of hand-painted silk scarves hung from pegs attached to the shelf's underside. There was an antique walnut-framed mirror that graced the wall behind her sleek desk, and a few select pieces of her barware of choice—Godinger crystal from Dublin—sat on a tray on top of the demi-fridge. The anomaly was the five-foot-tall cat tree tucked into a corner of the office—a perch for the frequent cat guests Katherine kept in the studio. A litter box disguised as an attractive wooden table was situated beside the carpet-covered cat tree.

To temper life's little stresses, Katherine kept her girl cave well-stocked with a few small luxuries. Tonight she needed every luxury in her arsenal after her mother, in one of her more lucid spells, persuaded a nursing assistant to dial the phone for her. Lucidity for Joan Carrington meant amusing herself by berating her youngest daughter. The list of Katherine's failings was endless. In her most shrill, upper-class British accent, she rebuked Katherine for her lack of grandchildren, for not playing her cards right and missing opportunities to remarry, for "handing your own mother over to a nursing home after all I've done for you," and for not being her dead sister. Every time Joan Carrington mentioned Katherine's sister, it was a knife to her heart—a reminder of how different Katherine's life could have been. Finally someone with at least the sense of a chicken heard the tirade and took the phone away from the ranting woman. On top of all the verbal abuse, it looked like the damn woman was going to live long enough to use all her bloody money.

Katherine's fingers drifted over the lock on her file cabinet. She needed, she deserved, a nightcap. The tip of her tongue lingered on her upper lip. She could taste the Ketel One Vodka nestled in the bottom drawer, but Marcos was still in the building. He was a major pain in the ass when it came to drinking in the studio. Katherine compressed her lips. She'd have to wait.

She stood, riffled behind her Latin practice shoes, and pulled out a black-and-gold box. For now she'd placate herself with chocolate truffles from Fran's in Seattle. Katherine settled into her chair and stared blankly at the computer screen. She popped one truffle after another into her mouth.

Edward Dombrosky kept flitting through her mind. They spent a very pleasant hour chatting yesterday after his lesson. Ed was about twelve years her senior but still quite athletic-looking. He was tall but not ungainly, had an intelligent face and quick smile, and was very easygoing. He loved animals and was behind Katherine's fostering of rescue cats, which turned out to be a great idea. Cats calmed her nerves. If a very annoying student hadn't made such a fuss about his allergies, she'd still have a permanent studio cat.

Edward was one of the very few students Katherine chose to take on these days. Limiting her teaching hours was a major benefit of being salaried and the boss. The days of being financially dependent on the number of lesson hours taught per week were long behind her. And the number of students Katherine chose to teach was her business and hers alone, as an ex-employee found out the hard way.

The very thought of that traitor Jeremy Fines had her fingers itching for that vodka bottle again. Damn him anyway. His refusal to wait a few days to cash his paycheck showed how selfish he was and how lacking in dedication to the studio. He must have been seriously mismanaging his money not to have a cushion. She wrinkled her nose in distaste. Jeremy had a smarmy edge about him anyway, like an over solicitous, money-hungry funeral director. He played into the hearts of more than one attention-starved female client. The hopeful looks in their eyes were matched by Jeremy's rapacious hunger to build a nest egg before his boyish charm hardened to cold cunning. She should have fired him way before the day he stormed into her office, smacked his hand on her desk, and accused her of not carrying her share of the load by not putting in her share of lesson time on the floor.

A loud meow erupted from the corner of the office as Katherine's latest rescue stretched awake from its nap. She opened the cat carrier's metal door. New Cat stretched, exited the carrier, and raised her tail in I-own-the-place cat speak, and jumped right into the cat tree. Katherine held the cat's chin in her hand and snuggled New Cat's face.

Why couldn't she banish thoughts of that cursed Jeremy! In the face of his outburst, she'd stayed in control. She calmly thanked him for sharing, and then told him that since he obviously wasn't happy with how she ran her studio, he could clean out his locker and vacate the premises. And then, after the bastard left, he convinced his highest-spending students to break their contracts and follow him, hurting the studio big-time. As far as Katherine was concerned, stealing students was an unforgivable breach of professional ethics. She bit her lip. It had been months ago, but she really should sue him anyway.

Katherine sank into her comfortable office chair, folded her arms, and closed her eyes. People in general annoyed the hell out of her these days. If it wasn't an employee thinking they knew more about running her business than she did, it was a student butting their nose into studio business under the guise of being helpful. Everyone thought they knew more than she did about how to run the studio. Opinions were like assholes: everybody has one, and no one needs to share theirs, especially with her.

"Bloody hell," Katherine muttered. She walked over and plucked New Cat out of the cat tree and cradled her. She was rewarded with a deep rumbling purr.

Katherine plopped into her leather chair with the cat curled on her lap. She wrapped one hand behind her head and tugged at her hair. The studio had lost revenue, and juggling her mother's meager savings and social security income for adultcare expenses wasn't helping her stress level. Her mother's house needed to sell for enough money to allow Katherine to get out from under a few unfortunate loans.

"Ouch!" Katherine pried the contented cat's claws out of the silky fabric of her dance skirt, which was forming ratty-looking runs. "First thing on the agenda for you when I get you home is a claw trim." Katherine held the cat nose-to-nose as she spoke. She snuggled into New Cat's fur. "Why don't people like cats?" she murmured to the purring creature. "Cats are so much more honest than people. You always know where you stand with a cat." She leaned over and popped New Cat back into the carrier.

She tried to settle back in, but, as tired as she was, her cushy office chair didn't feel comfortable this evening. Katherine tapped the desktop with a long fingernail, unconsciously keeping time with one jiggling knee. Her thoughts wandered back to Edward. The man was comfortably retired, not wealthy exactly, but in a position to never have to worry about money. He'd told her he'd retired when companies still offered defined-benefits pension plans, and he also had money coming in from a patent. He'd retired at sixty-two, after his wife passed away, which meant he must be...sixty-seven or sixty-eight? She rested her chin on her hand. Underneath Ed's contented demeanor, might he actually be lonely? He spent an awful lot of time in the studio. Ed was, as they used to say, a darn good catch, and the man liked cats—a real plus.

"Katherine, I'm heading out." Marcos poked his head in Katherine's door, car keys dangling from his fingertips. "Everyone's gone. Are you okay locking up alone?"

"I'm fine, but thanks for asking. By the way, we really do need to discuss the Jill situation. Between her being out without prior permission and her nosy attitude, I'm ready to wring her neck."

"Jill is Jill," Marcos said. He had one arm raised, palm against the doorframe. "We've cut her too much slack in the past and probably set a bad precedent. We should talk to her, but I'm not optimistic that she'll change."

"That damn girl needs to up her game." Katherine folded her arms across her chest. "Or she might find herself marching out the door faster than she walked in."

"No argument from me. Hey, I've been meaning to ask: how is it going with the sale of your mother's house? Any offers pending?"

"Not yet," Katherine said. She pulled her arms even tighter across her chest and shrugged. "I know the housing market is sluggish, but this is a great house. Thankfully I got my mother's POA signed before her mind slipped any further. Old age isn't mellowing her in the slightest, and now she's accusing me of robbing her and taking her money. It's the adult-care home that consumes her social security and savings, not me."

"Sorry to hear that. Must be hell."

"And how would you know, Mr. Trust Fund?" Fatigue made her reckless. She couldn't stop the words or temper the biting tone in her voice. "Daddy may not be talking to you much, but the soft landing is always available. Didn't his law firm recently win some high-profile case in Phoenix?" Katherine knew not to push any further.

"I'm not going there with you, Katherine. You know I don't discuss my father." Marcos's voice was controlled but held a warning. "So, how late do you plan to stay?" His jangling car keys signaled his impatience.

"I need a few more minutes here before I head home. Lock the door after you leave, and please make sure the outside light is on. Don't worry. I'm fine." Katherine flashed Marcos her classic disarming smile. This was not a good time to start a squabble with him. She could do charming. It was all a matter of choice and benefit.

"Okay, then. I'm taking you at your word. I'm beat and ready for a scotch." Marcos flipped his keys into his palm and waved goodbye. The back door clicked shut behind him.

Katherine pulled out her beloved bottle of vodka and poured a double shot. The warmth cascading down her throat was familiar and soothing. Katherine relaxed into the welcoming leather of the chair. She rubbed her knuckles along her jawline. Men really force women into being manipulative, she thought. They don't give us a choice. When a woman is young and attractive, she can't get a man to hear what she's saying because they're either focused on her boobs or wondering how she sounds when she comes. And once a woman hits fifty, men don't listen to her because they don't even see her anymore. And they wonder why we resort to shouting or tears to get them to pay attention to our words.

"Bloody hell." Katherine took a ladylike swig from her glass. She swept a strand of hair out of her eyes and shrugged. The beginning of a headache crept out from her temples and tap-danced on her forehead. With a sigh, she turned her attention back to the rows of numbers on her computer screen. She'd always managed to keep the ship afloat; this time was no different. There'd be no calling for a lifeboat. It was simply a matter of borrowing from Peter to pay Paul.

FIVE

Everyone's the Star of Their Own Show

Katherine Carrington
8:30 a.m., Friday, 16 October

Katherine stifled a deep yawn. Last night was one of those miserable toss-and-turn nights. This morning she was stiff, achy, and tired enough to wish she could lock her office door and take a rejuvenating little doze. She leaned into the leather office chair, inhaled deeply, and stretched her arms high above her head, fingers laced and palms facing toward the ceiling. She exhaled. Her best bet might be to dance out her stiffness before the heedless herd stampeded through the front door and upended her day. With a resigned sigh, she pushed herself out of the enticing comfort of the soft leather.

Katherine opened the demi-fridge and poured some organic orange juice into a crystal highball glass. Hesitating long enough for a polite pass at propriety, she unlocked the bottom drawer of her desk. The silver label from the Ketel One Vodka glinted a greeting. Maybe just this once, a little boost to her morning juice—she applauded herself for her clever little ditty—to kick-start her day. She doused the juice with a generous splash of vodka and, careful to hold the overfilled glass steady, drifted down the hall to the ballroom.

Edging in on fifty-five, Katherine was proud she still moved with the grace of the ballet dancer she'd once been. Toes pointed outward, she kept her tail bone tucked, abs in, shoulders back, and chest high and open. Her salon-enhanced brunette hair was swept into a dancer's bun. Katherine glanced at the gold watch encircling her narrow wrist. It was a Patek Philippe, one of the few gifts from her ex-husband she'd kept. Paul might have been a cheating, self-centered ass, but the man really had exquisite taste. He wasn't a keeper, but this watch certainly was.

Just thinking about her ex dredged up memories of the naïve, easily manipulated young woman she'd once been. Between kissing prima donna ass in the corps de ballet and later being shoved aside by the more seasoned, cutthroat ballroom instructors, she'd toughened up. And just when she was beginning to develop some cajones, Paul the Prince entered the picture, sweeping her onto his mighty white steed with promises to make her his queen in happily-ever-after land. Right. The minute she lost her youthful glow, the bastard tossed her in the mud for a younger princess. Lesson learned. Any future using or tossing would be done by Katherine.

She took a deep swallow of her juiced-up juice and placed the tumbler on one of the café tables skirting the ballroom. Katherine's suede-bottom shoes shushed across the floating wood floor. The lights were at half bank, and the flattering softness reflected a younger Katherine—the only version of herself she would accept.

Facing the mirrors, she rolled her shoulders back and down, and pushed her elbows together to stretch the upper-back lats. The release of tension felt as good as her juice tasted. She eased into a few deep knee bends. Toes turned out, she executed a perfect *grand plié*—knees spread and over toes and heels raised—stretching the inner-thigh adductor muscles. Katherine smiled a small, self-satisfied smile. It might take longer to warm up this cold engine, but once revved, she could hit the cruising speed of any thirty-year-old. She rose gracefully out of the last of eight pliés and critically appraised herself in the mirror.

Ballet exercises and Pilates kept her slim hipped and nicely muscled. There was nothing graceful about aging in the ballroom dance world, which is all about strength, stamina, and sexiness, or maintaining the illusion thereof. She leaned in closer, hand to jaw, to examine the effects of her favorite cosmetic surgeon's work: a bit of Botox, regular chemical peels, a simple demi-lift around the jawline, and a few Restylane injections to remove lines around her lips. Dr. James was worth his weight in gold, which she'd paid him at least twice over. Maintaining a youthful image was bloody expensive, but one did what one had to do to survive in this business. Katherine's stubborn chin tilted, and her eyes narrowed. After all, she was the face of the studio, so cosmetic procedures weren't selfish indulgences but legitimate business expenses, advertising dollars well spent.

Katherine cupped her breasts and turned sideways to the mirrors. The breast augmentation was enough to keep the girls perky and make her an ex-customer of the padded bra section of Victoria's Secret. She'd had the procedure on a Friday and was in the studio the following Tuesday. She gently probed the area around her eyes. Those sagging upper eyelids and under-eye bags had to go. Recovery time would be longer. She'd say she needed a few weeks at a luxury spa. God knows, the way she worked, everyone knew she deserved it.

Pushing away from the mirrors, she glided across the floor, humming a melodic waltz. Katherine moved with strength and elegance to the rise and fall of the one-two-three, four-five-six count. Her arms rose gracefully, and she ended the pattern with artfully extended fingers. She spun to face the mirrors. Graying roots were pushing their way into her dark hair. Time to refresh the blond streaks. Streaking hides the incoming gray. *Incoming.* It sounded like a battle cry. "Well," Katherine said to her mirror image, "fighting age these days is a battle, and one I am going to win, cost be damned."

~

Paige Russell
10:30 a.m., Friday, 16 October

"Crap! That was stupid." All she needed was a ticket for running a red light. She whipped into the Ben's Best Bagels's parking lot, and spotted Kristi getting out of her car. She wasn't the only one running late. Kristi raised a hand and waited for Paige to lock her car and walk over.

"Hi. Sorry. Hit the snooze button too many times this morning," Paige said.

"I don't even have an excuse," Kristi replied. A gracious white-haired gentleman held the café door open for them. They slipped inside as Kristi smiled and thanked him.

Brianna, already seated in a red leatherette booth, nursed a coffee. The table held a carafe and two extra cups.

"Brianna…Kristi." Paige swept an open palm from Brianna to Kristi. The two girls were chalk and cheese: Kristi edgy and stylish with her big earrings and heavily highlighted hair and Brianna with her all-American, cheerleader wholesomeness. "Kristi lives in my apartment complex. She's a nail technician at M'Lady Salon. Kristi, Brianna is the dance instructor I've told you about.

"Hi." Both girls spoke at once, friendly smiles lighting their faces.

Paige glanced around the brightly lit café. Country-style shelves were crowded with an assortment of vintage coffee pots, ceramic mugs, and, of all things, ceramic pigs in varying colors. Posters ranging from coffee plantation scenes to old ads for coffee products hung on the walls.

"It was super nice of Marcos to tell us it was okay to come in later today because of the workshop tomorrow and the Halloween thing around the corner," Paige said.

"What's going on for Halloween?" Kristi asked.

"I guess Katherine goes all out," Paige said. "Everyone wears costumes. The studio offers group classes, raffle drawings, and special pricing. Everyone brings treats, and in the evening there's a potluck dinner and open dancing. I've never worked an event like this before. Is getting ready always this crazy, Brianna?"

"Yup." Brianna's brown eyes danced. "Chaos is what happens when a bunch of dancers try to get organized. But somehow it will all come together at the last minute."

Paige glanced toward the bakery cases. "Do we order at the counter, or will the server come to the table? My stomach is growling."

"I ordered a bagel basket for us: six different bagels and two kinds of cream cheese. I hope that's okay," Brianna said. "Our server was waiting for you guys to arrive." She signaled to a ponytailed young man behind the counter. Within two minutes the warm bagels and generous tubs of cream cheese were sitting in the middle of the table.

"You find the best places," Paige said between bites. "These bagels are killer."

"Carbs are my drug of choice," Brianna said from behind her hand, mumbling through a mouthful. "I'm not a bar girl. I find a specialty bakery and drown my sorrows."

"Here's to carbing ourselves into a happy daze." Paige raised her coffee cup.

"To happy days," Kristi said with a wink, clinking her cup on Paige's.

"I've been wanting to ask you, Paige, about the NAU thing. Are you going to stay at Desert DanceSport or go back to Flagstaff next semester?" Brianna pushed her long, golden-brown hair behind her ears.

"Well, after Mom died, I took this ballroom gig to give me time to figure things out—you know, school and all—but thanks to you, I want to get good enough to dance competitively. And the studio is starting to feel like home." Paige paused to tear open two sugar packets and stir them into her coffee. She took a deep swallow, sighing in satisfaction. "I enrolled at NAU in the first place because my mother kept harping on the fact that most dancers are broke and the career lifespan of a dancer is short. She said only trust-fund babies don't have to plan ahead for a steady job and income, and I wasn't a trust-fund baby."

"Sounds like something my mother would say," Brianna added.

"Yeah, the whole financial-security thing," Paige said. "My mother steered me into Early Childhood Education—a steady teaching job with benefits and lots of vacation time." Paige picked up a second bagel half and generously slathered it with strawberry cream cheese.

"And Brianna, how did you get into ballroom dancing?" Kristi asked.

Brianna put down her bagel and dabbed at her lips with the napkin. "A friend invited me to a local dance competition where she was styling hair. She was pushing me to quit waitressing and go to beauty school. Her hairstyles were works of art, but for me it was all about the dancing and the glamor. Desert DanceSport advertised at the competition for dance instructor trainees, and I signed on." Brianna shrugged and smiled. "There's nothing like the energy and glamor of being at a competition, even dancing Pro-Am."

"Kristi," Paige said, "speaking of glamor, I watched Brianna morph into a pure glamor queen a few weeks ago. Sylvie—the one who competes all the time—helped Brianna get glammed for a local competition hosted by Southwest Dance Divas. Brianna wore these huge blue-tinged false eyelashes." Paige wiggled her fingers in front of her eyes. "Sylvie netted Brianna's hair into a fancy twisted 'do and extended her eyeliner with tiny rhinestones."

"That sounds pretty wild," Kristi said.

"And Brianna's gown…" Paige sighed and clasped her hands. "It was turquoise with sheer long sleeves. The bodice was all studded with crystals. Gorgeous, huh, Brianna?" Paige felt her face get hot. Even to herself she sounded like Cinderella on the kitchen stoop, watching the wicked stepsisters head off to the ball. What must Kristi think?

Brianna raised her eyebrows and smiled. "You'll get there, girl-friend."

"As long as I continue coaching with Marcos, I think I might have a chance. I'm so lucky he's mentoring me. The man is an amazing dancer, and he knows how to teach. He's also fun to be around."

Paige caught Kristi and Brianna eying each other over their coffees.

"Really, guys, he's not the playboy type everyone seems to think he is. Actually, I'm surprised Marcos is single. He'd make a great dad." Paige rested her case.

"What?! Geez, Paige." Brianna choked and then sneezed. "Now I have coffee up my nose. Damn." She wiped her face with a napkin. "I know Marcos oozes charm, but you haven't known him very long. Marcos would not, definitely not, make a great dad."

"Why would you say that?" Paige said, embarrassed to find herself close to tears.

"So, here's the scoop. About a year ago, this elegant woman stopped in to buy lessons. I was in the lobby. The woman stopped cold when she saw Katherine. She turned around and walked out. Sylvie and Katherine were buzzing like busybody bees after she left." Brianna paused. "Sure you want to hear this? Might disillusion you."

Paige flattened her back against the booth and nodded.

"The story was that Marcos was married to this woman several years ago. They met at some art gallery opening. She had a young son and made it clear the boy came first. She wanted permanence and wouldn't settle for living with someone. Marcos, who Katherine said never wanted to be either married or a parent, convinced himself and her that he could be the perfect husband and stepdad."

Paige lowered her eyes to avoid Brianna's penetrating stare.

Brianna took a sip of coffee. "From what I heard Katherine tell Sylvie, the marriage barely lasted two years. In Katherine's exact words, 'He was an abysmal father and a self-centered husband.' Since the divorce, which he never talks about, he's been a confirmed bachelor. Any young woman who thinks she's found the solid, older man, someone who has sown his wild oats and is ready to settle down, better look elsewhere. Marcos is Peter Pan."

Paige just grimaced. She wasn't sure what to say. Brianna didn't see Marcos the way she did. Maybe the woman he married was too demanding. Maybe the child was a brat. Who knows?

"Oh, I forgot." Kristi's voice broke the silence. She put her cup down so fast coffee sloshed onto the table. "I have a new client at the salon. She's a longtime student at your studio. Barbara Bradshaw? About five foot five or so, average weight, short dark hair with long bangs. You guys know her?"

"Barbara is Marcos's best student. She's super nice, and she and Marcos are pretty tight. Right, Brianna?" Paige said, looking at Brianna, who nodded.

"I really liked her," Kristi said. "Barbara didn't talk much about the studio, and we covered more in-depth topics than I usually discuss with my clients. I enjoyed her."

"Do you usually keep it sort of light with clients?" Brianna asked.

"I have to. Some of my clients don't know the difference between being passionate and being evangelistic about their political and religious views. I listen but keep my opinions to myself. Even if I offered a differing opinion, hitting someone over the head rarely changes their perspective; it just gives them a headache."

"That's something I'm going to have to remember before I open my mouth without filtering first," Paige said, reaching over to nudge Brianna, who laughed in agreement.

"So, right on topic about opinions and attitudes, let me tell you what was running through my head last night before I closed my book and turned out the lights," Kristi said.

Paige leaned forward, elbows on the table.

"One of the characters made a crack about men and penis size. You know, the size-doesn't-matter line, even if it takes a pair of tweezers and a magnifying glass to find it."

Paige sucked in her breath, then let out a laugh that wrapped around a breathy, "Oh my God, you are too funny."

"It got me thinking," Kristi continued. "Women spend half their lives reassuring men they are perfect just the way they are and then spend the other half making themselves over into men's image of the perfect woman. How many women, even teenagers, get breast implants? If men's balls were as exposed as breasts and if men were judged on the size of their testicles, would they buy padded ball-holders?" Kristi created ball-holders with her hands. Her catlike eyes widened with fake innocence.

Paige snorted into her coffee cup. Brianna had stopped in mid-motion—bagel poised ready to bite. Paige wiped coffee off her face and waved at Kristi to continue.

Kristi's voice rose as she warmed to her topic. "And what if penis size became the number-one marketing tool to sell everything from new cars to chocolate bars? What if women would only date men with a big one! Would a man ever put his penis under the surgeon's knife to meet the unrealistic expectations of a girlfriend or wife? Not a chance. What women do to meet Barbie-doll expectations is completely ludicrous, and we all need to turn the ship around."

Brianna giggled. "I'm so glad Paige invited you to come today. I needed this."

"I knew you two would hit it off," Paige said, with a smile that started from deep inside. "But, I need a ciggie really badly and, Brianna, now we're running late." She tucked a nice tip under her coffee cup. They'd occupied this table far longer than they should have. She might actually be on her way to making her first real friends in Tucson, next to Marcos, of course. But then, Marcos couldn't exactly be classified as a friend, under the circumstances.

~

Marcos Stephanos
12:30 p.m., Friday, 16 October

"What the hell is this?" Marcos shook his head. Hanging outside Katherine's office, next to a display of tasteful commemorative plaques from dance competitions, was an ostentatious, gold-leaf plaque. It stood out like a Harlem Globetrotter at a convention of little people. The plaque was inscribed in cursive script: "It's a kind of spiritual snobbery that makes people think they can be happy without money. —Albert Camus." Marcos rubbed the back of his neck and sighed. Katherine's choice of inspirational quotes was…well, uniquely Katherine.

Marcos's dance-shoe bag swung as he strode toward the lobby. He was as close to Katherine as anyone could be, and he would always have a soft spot for her, but the woman was definitely not someone to cross. She possessed both cunning and wits and used them to her advantage. Katherine was as theatrically gifted as anyone he knew, able to melt from aloof to disarmingly congenial in a heartbeat. Only those with a keen eye and perceptive nature ever noticed the hard edge to Katherine's mouth and the predatory glint in her eyes.

He glanced at the framed photograph of him and Katherine taken in their heyday at the Chicago Crystal Ball. Her silver dress swirled around her ankles, and the arch of her back was perfection. They placed first, but Marcos always wondered if they outdanced everyone or if Katherine unnerved their strongest competitors before they walked onto the floor. With a captivating smile, like a cobra hypnotizing its prey, Katherine darted in for the kill. Her unwitting victims were verbally sliced, diced, and tossed into the trash before their naïve smiles faded from their faces. Marcos watched their rivals exchange dazed, confused glances as they tried to reconcile the biting remarks with the gracious Katherine they knew. She was a master.

Marcos perched on one of the lobby chairs and slipped off his street shoes, his thoughts still on Katherine. Yesterday, after running a quick check on the accounts, she nearly bit his head off when he questioned why, when everything looked solid, she was waffling on having some basic repairs done to the building. She took his question as a personal assault on her ability to manage the business. Maybe it was hormones? She was at, if not past, that age. He'd have to tread lightly, but tread he would.

Dance shoes tied, he had time for a cup of coffee, and he wanted the good stuff Katherine usually reserved for clients. The lobby was quiet. No one paid him the slightest attention. Jill was busy organizing party materials; Tony and Sylvie were side by side at the reception desk, checking the afternoon schedule. Tony's white silky shirt was open halfway to his waist, disco style, revealing his spray-tanned six-pack abs and an array of gold neck chains. The boy looked like a refugee from the set of *Saturday Night Fever*.

"G'day, all," Paige chirped. She trotted in the front door, full of energy and glowing.

"Looks like your late morning did you some good," Marcos said, smiling at his protégé. Paige's dark, cocoa-colored hair was loose and softly curled, her eyes were bright, and she looked more relaxed than she had in days. Her energy was contagious. At least until Tony Moreno strutted her way, winking and posturing and making the poor girl blush.

"Hey, baby girl. Lookin' good this morning. Come give papa Tony a hug." Tony flashed his center-stage smile at Paige.

Marcos didn't miss the narrowing of Sylvie's eyes.

Rising color stained Paige's cheeks and flushed her neck. She ducked to one side to avoid Tony's outstretched arms and reinforced her stance with a couple of backsteps.

Marcos felt his state of mind shift from sunny-and-clear to thunder-and-lightning.

"Time to get our A-game on, everyone." Katherine's voice came out of nowhere. She emerged, weary-eyed, from the darkened front office, sounding more apathetic than motivating. Her energy was so low, no one even responded.

Marcos nodded a curt hello to Katherine. He was already halfway to Paige's side. What game was Tony playing? Was her fresh-faced innocence a joke to him? Could he actually have a thing for her or was he just making a fool of her? Either way, Tony was trouble Paige was not equipped to handle. Neither was the studio.

"Oh, Paigey girl. You are breaking my heart," Tony wailed with both hands over his heart. His smile flashed like a neon sign outside a cheap motel.

Marcos shot Tony a warning glance. "Come with me." Marcos

grasped Paige under one elbow and guided her out of the reception area. Glancing backward, he glowered at Tony again. Tony's body language said, "I surrender," but his expression signaled, "Up yours."

Marcos had grabbed a stack of papers off the desk. "I want you to start folding some of these pages. They're promotional flyers for the Halloween party. We'll begin handing them out to everyone today. Note the specials on lesson packages, okay?"

Consumed by his own thoughts, he led Paige toward the ballroom like a prize show dog he was parading around the breed ring. Maybe it was time for him to let it be known he was staking his claim. This young woman needed his protection. Sure, Paige was twenty-plus years his junior, but one couldn't let minor obstacles clutter the playing field. Age was only a number, and there was many a young dancer more than willing to put her shoes under Dance Master Marcos's bed any day of the week—many an older dancer, for that matter.

Marcos appraised Paige with the eye of a seasoned art critic. She was a knockout in a natural, subdued sort of way: thick dark hair usually worn simply in a bun or a ponytail, lovely large eyes, great breasts set off by her dancer's slim hips and muscular thighs. Paige was sexy, but her sexiness was girl-next-door. What was it about this young woman that pulled at his impregnable fortress of a heart? It was more than physical attraction. Paige moved with a natural grace that reminded him, oddly, of his own mother—a very successful Broadway stage dancer before she married his father. What was that old saying about men marrying their mothers? Marrying?! MARRY! He choked on his thoughts. What was he thinking? What was wrong with him? His aversion to the very thought of the M word sent a shudder down his spine, tingling all the way to the fingertips he'd so skillfully placed on Paige's elbow to guide her along.

SIX

REVELATIONS

Paige Russell
9:00 a.m., Saturday, 17 October

Still in her red-and-white Hello Kitty pajamas, Paige settled onto the sofa, coffee mug in hand. She slumped back. What was wrong with her? She wanted to scream her frustration at her mother—her dead mother, no less. How cold and useless was that?

She was angry on so many levels. Her mother had been a nurse. Why hadn't she recognized the symptoms of esophageal cancer? Or had she and chose to ignore them? Maybe if her mother had acted sooner, Paige wouldn't be a stinking orphan at twenty-four? And worse, once her mother knew she was terminal, why didn't she come clean about the secret she'd hidden from her only daughter for her whole life? "Why, why, why?" Even to her own ears, her voice sounded whiney.

The infamous blue folder lay where she'd tossed it last night. With the tip of her big toe, Paige nudged it away from its precarious spot at the edge of the table, reached over, and retrieved it. The folder's frayed elastic closure unraveled in her hands. Well, no surprise there.

It was pretty shot. She grabbed her cigarettes, tucked the folder under her arm, and headed out to the balcony to contemplate. She lit up, clearing the fog from her head with a happy lungful of nicotine, but "why" always drifted back in. As many times as she'd riffled through this folder, how could she have missed the stuck-together pages? This info clinched the deal on why she'd come to Tucson. It was a game changer.

Paige flicked an ash skeleton off her cigarette. She pulled out the tattered handwritten page that had started her search. The writing was in faded pencil. The edges were ripping. She'd add Scotch tape to her shopping list. Until last night, it never made sense for this page to be in a folder with her mom's medical history, blood tests, and a reference to some therapist or counselor. Until now she figured the therapist thing was her mother working out the crap she'd told her about getting knocked up after an uninhibited night with a stranger at a medical conference. Paige took a very long drag of her cigarette. Her mother was never, at least not to her knowledge, the one-night-stand, party-girl type. Why would she want her daughter to believe something like that rather than the truth?

She smoothed out the handwritten page. She could make out a man's name, an age, the city was Phoenix, a date about eighteen months after Paige was born. Some scribbled comments followed: attractive, personable, intelligent, and the last notation was *dancer*. Until last night, Paige figured her mom must have tracked down her birth father, and her worst-case scenario was the guy was a male stripper in a bar in Phoenix.

Paige dropped her cigarette butt into a clay pot of sand, and tucked the note back inside the plastic sleeve. She ran her fingers over the pages she'd unstuck last night. She still couldn't wrap her head around the sperm-donor clinic stuff. Keeping this kind of a secret implied shame. Was that what she was: a shameful little secret? Did her mother think the truth would make her feel like a laboratory experiment, like something grown in a petri dish? Or was she protecting her from embarrassment? The only thing Paige knew for sure was if you wanted a secret to die with you, don't leave a paper trail. The shredder is your friend.

She knew she shouldn't, but she lit another cigarette anyway. A child had the right to know the truth about themselves, their medical background, their ancestry and biology. A father is half of who they are. How could her mother not believe that kind of information was a gift?

Paige hooked her toes on the cold balcony railing and took slow, soothing drags of the dwindling cigarette. She wanted so badly to see herself reflected back in a father, a grandmother, or maybe even a half-sibling. It wasn't as though she hadn't loved her mother to pieces, but she didn't look like her at all. Her mother was mousy-haired with brown eyes; Paige's hair was dark brunette, almost black, and her eyes were greenish gray. Besides wanting to confirm where half her DNA came from, she needed to know if her dad was the kind of man who might wonder if he'd conceived a child. Surely he would want to know?

Yawning, Paige extinguished the butt and laid it to rest in the clay-pot cigarette graveyard. Tucking the folder under her arm, she slid the glass doors open. "Holy crap!" The clock on the electric stove said 9:40 a.m. "I'm going to be late. The workshop!" She had an hour to shower, dress, and get to the studio in time to practice with Marcos.

~

Marcos Stephanos
12:30 p.m., Saturday, 17 October

"Paige," Marcos said. With his hand on the small of her back, he guided her behind the tall reception counter. "I need you to work the desk for the next hour or so. Check in everyone arriving for the afternoon session. Hand out flyers so they know what will be covered in the afternoon class. And if you get any walk-ins wanting information on the studio, tell them about our introductory special, and then call someone to conduct a studio tour."

"Happy to do it," Paige said, already reaching under the counter for a stack of flyers.

"I'll come and get you before my class starts. Okay?" Marcos said.

"No problema. I've got it covered," Paige answered.

Marcos had started to edge past Paige to get back around the counter when Katherine burst through the front door—hair flying, no hello.

"Katherine! What are you doing here?" Marcos couldn't hide the surprise in his voice. "Wasn't the plan for Joey and me to run the workshop so you could have a day to yourself?"

Wordless, Katherine strode straight to the coffee pot and poured herself a black coffee.

"Good morning—"

Marcos halted Paige's greeting with a warning finger on his lips. He moved in front of her, shielding her from Katherine's view.

"I was at New Haven this morning," Katherine said, turning to look at Marcos. "I had to speak to Felicia in person, and so I popped in to see my mother. The studio's on my way home. It's easier to grab a coffee here than stand in line with the unwashed masses at Starbucks." Katherine pulled off her sunglasses, revealing reddened, angry eyes. She took a sip of her coffee. She held the cup between her hands. "Mother actually beckoned me to sit on her bed, reached for my hand, and started talking, and then..." Katherine paused, looked away, and took a breath. "She called me Kimberly—her *darling* Kimberly."

"I'm so sorry, Katherine," Marcos said. He kept his voice low and consoling.

"When I tried to correct her, she became so agitated I had to call a nursing assistant to calm her. The NA suggested it might be best if I left, so I did." Katherine stopped. "Paige? I don't remember putting you on the schedule."

Marcos nodded at Paige, who looked like she wanted to blend in with the walls.

"Um...yes. I'm going to demonstrate the lady's part in Marcos's waltz class."

"It's good exposure for her, Katherine," Marcos said, before Katherine could criticize the idea. "And, since we finished our practice early, Paige can check in the afternoon stragglers and call students who haven't volunteered as yet for Halloween party refreshments. Time well spent. So, you're not staying, then?"

"No." Katherine brushed past Marcos as she spoke, ignoring Paige. "I'll be out of here as soon as I retrieve my box of chocolates from my office and finish my coffee in peace."

Marcos could feel Paige looking at him. He sighed and turned his head. "What...what?"

"Marcos," Paige whispered, moving closer. "What do you mean, what? Who's Kimberly? What was that all about? Katherine seriously looked like she'd been crying."

"Follow me." Marcos spun around on one foot. He ushered Paige into the breakroom, shut the door, and leaned against it. "Okay. This is not something I would ordinarily tell you, or anyone else for that matter, but you were right there, and you heard what you heard. But first, I have to know you'll keep what I am going to tell you to yourself. Can you promise?"

"Yes. Yes, I promise," Paige said and sat on one of the hard metal chairs.

"All right," Marcos said. He clasped his hands under his chin and momentarily closed his eyes. He took a deep breath. "Understand this, though, if I hear you've gossiped, you will be fired immediately, and by me personally. Are we clear?"

Paige nodded, her beautiful eyes as big as quarters.

"Kimberly was Katherine's older sister—four years older. She died when Katherine was eight." Marcos paused, pulled out a chair across the table from Paige, and sat. "Kimberly was the apple of her parents' eyes. She was their precious baby daughter. Eventually they tried for another child, expecting a son. They got Katherine," Marcos said. "Are you getting the picture?"

Paige nodded. She sat very still.

"Anyway, when Kimberly was nine-years old, she was diagnosed with leukemia. Katherine was five. The next three years were filled with hospitals and cancer treatments. Katherine was shunted between aunts, family friends, and babysitters. And then, against all odds, three years later Kimberly went into remission, right after her twelfth birthday." Marcos leaned both elbows on the table and rubbed his forehead with one hand.

"B-but—" Paige stammered.

"Be quiet and listen," Marcos interrupted. "Everyone was overjoyed. But Joan, Katherine and Kimberly's mother, never stopped waiting for the other shoe to drop. She became extremely overprotective of Kimberly."

Marcos stopped to look at Paige. He folded his arms. "Now, here's the rest of the story. The year Kimberly went into remission, both girls begged their mother to let them go trick-or-treating. Kimberly wanted the fun of taking her little sister out, if only to a few houses on their block. Their first and last Halloween together was before the leukemia, when Kimberly was eight and Katherine was four. Their parents finally gave in, even buying the girls matching black cat costumes. They let them go out alone." Marcos paused to clear his throat.

"The girls were headed home after trick-or-treating on their block. Katherine told me they were with a group of kids, laughing and trading candy. The next thing she remembers was the sound of screeching tires, metal ripping against metal, and a huge bang. It was the sound of a tire blowing out as it hit the curb. Kids were screaming. Kimberly pushed Katherine out of the way, and Katherine fell, face down, onto someone's lawn. Later she learned that a drunk driver hit another car, spun out of control, and careened onto the sidewalk. Two children were seriously injured. Kimberly was killed." Marcos let Paige absorb what he'd told her.

"Oh my God, Marcos." Paige's hands flew to her mouth. "That's so horrible, so awful, but it doesn't explain why Katherine was so upset about her mother getting confused and calling her Kimberly."

"This part might be hard for you to understand, Paige, but try. Joan,

71

Katherine's mother, has never stopped grieving for her dead daughter. She also blames Katherine for Kimberly being out on the street. After Kimberly died, it was like Katherine didn't exist. Her parents divorced, and then Katherine's father died. Katherine's mother poured all her energy and money into charitable work for a foundation for childhood leukemia and into Mothers Against Drunk Driving. Katherine felt cheated and abandoned. She was robbed of her childhood, her sister, and basically lost both her parents. Katherine was never allowed to celebrate Halloween again. So, partly to commemorate her sister's wish 'to celebrate Halloween like a normal kid' and partly to get back at her mother, Katherine now makes a huge deal out of Halloween."

"So, that explains all the craziness about the studio Halloween party," Paige said.

"Right," Marcos said. "Knowing her backstory might put some of Katherine's quirks into perspective. But remember, this is not a woman who wants sympathy. She wants her privacy, so let's make sure we give her that, understood?"

Marcos was already on his feet. He opened the door and motioned Paige back to the front desk. He turned toward the ballroom. He badly needed to switch mental gears, and focusing on today's workshop was the ticket. The sign-ups for this first-ever Saturday workshop were much higher than expected. Marcos smiled a small smile. This idea could become an excellent moneymaker for the studio.

Joey's class must have just finished. Marcos had to weave through the crowd to get to the ballroom. From what he could see, everyone got their money's worth. Sweaty students were busy refilling bottles at the water fountain or crowding around the refreshment table. A few stragglers were in the ballroom, feet propped on the café tables. Barbara was among them, watching him from across the room. She raised her well-shaped eyebrows and waved. Her dance shoes and crumpled knee-high stockings lay on the carpet beside her.

"How's my favorite glamor queen doing today?" Marcos asked, pulling out a chair.

"Not feeling so glamorous if you really want to know." Barbara scrunched and flexed her bare toes. Her water bottle was just about empty.

"Joey killed us this morning. I don't think he quite grasps the reality of being in one's fifties. His cha-cha lesson sabotaged my youthful mental image." Barbara massaged one foot, all the while looking at Marcos. "I was trying so hard to keep my chest forward, it felt like I was standing on the edge of a cliff. You know how he describes the correct posture for cha-cha?" Barbara said, leaning back in her chair, smiling.

"Don't tell me he's still saying TOT, tits over toes?" Marcos said.

"How'd you guess?" Barbara replied with a soft chuckle.

"That boy is going to get us sued." Marcos folded his arms but tempered his body language with a head tilt and an upturn to his lips.

"I think I'm going to stick to American Smooth from now on," Barbara said, shaking her head. "All that Rhythm business about never having two knees bent at the same time and keeping one's toes pointed outward, and the whole Cuban motion thing. My hips are not made to move in a figure eight. Joey makes Cuban motion look so easy, but it's darn tough."

"It takes time to perfect the movement, but you're a great dancer. In fact, you're my best student, Ms. Barbara." Marcos couldn't remember ever seeing Barbara blush, but there it was, a gentle flush of color warming her cheeks. He reached over and patted her hand. "Now that I know how to challenge you, we'll add some Rhythm dances to your lesson plan. It will keep you young, I promise," Marcos said, with a wink.

From the corner of his eye, Marcos watched Edward Dombrosky tip his cap to a young female student he passed as he entered the ballroom. Ed was quite the gentleman, something even Marcos found refreshing, and he knew the ladies loved Ed's courtly, old-fashioned gestures. Marcos waved him over.

"Ed. Join us. You two know each other?" He glanced from Ed to Barbara, who exchanged friendly smiles.

Edward spoke first. "Marcos, this lovely lady is in the studio every time I'm here, and I spend half my life in this darn place, which means she must as well."

"Sad but true," Barbara responded. "This studio has become my second home."

"You and me both. I need the socialization as much as the dance lessons," Edward said. "I've been a widower for nine years. I've come to realize it's the female side of the marriage partnership that brings the humanity into the home. And I mean that literally. My wife planned parties and invited people over for dinner. Why, I hardly even cook. My golf buddies are acquaintances more than friends, and I know my neighbors on a hi-and-wave basis, but that's it. Being a widower is a different life."

"I get it," Barbara said. "I knew everyone at my husband's firm but lost touch with all of them after he passed." Barbara took a sip from her water bottle.

Marcos had no life experience here to offer, so he sat back to listen.

Edward leaned one forearm on the table. "After Betty passed away, the people who'd swept across my doorstep like rising river water were absorbed back into the sponges of their own lives." Ed laughed and shook his head. "Sorry, didn't mean to wax so dramatic." He turned toward Barbara. "I need this place as much as you do, and I think there are several of us in the same boat." Edward winked at Marcos. "And it's up to you and Katherine to keep this particular boat afloat for all of us strays."

"And I've told Marcos many times, dancing is a better use of my money than therapy, which I came pretty close to needing before I started ballroom lessons." Barbara twisted her lips into a self-deprecating smile.

"Therapy? I feel a story there," Ed said, with an encouraging "go on" wave of his hand.

"My story is nothing unique for someone who's lost a long-time spouse. My natural optimism—my ability to see the silver lining—evaporated. But, then I walked through the door of Desert DanceSport.

74

I was mesmerized watching one couple float across the floor. I wanted their happy glow. I signed up for lessons on the spot."

"So, now I have to ask, what brought you in the door in the first place?" Edward said.

"We've touched on this before," Marcos added, nodding at Barbara. "But I'm not sure I've ever heard the full-blown version."

Barbara's sigh was audible. "Colin's death knocked the wind out of me. He was only fifty-seven and wasn't even ill. One morning he collapsed lifting weights at the gym. He died of an undetected aneurysm." Barbara glanced from Marcos to Edward as she spoke. "I felt like life was over, and I was barely fifty-one."

Marcos held back from giving Barbara a consoling touch. Tears flirted around the corners of her eyes. He felt guilty not ever asking about the exact circumstances of her husband's death.

"Michael, my son, finally had enough of my widow's weeds and wallowing. He decided I needed to try something new, and he suggested ballroom lessons. Michael is a stage dancer, Edward, but his roots are in ballroom." Barbara shrugged in a way Marcos interpreted as "What the hell did I have to lose?" This was the *insouciant* Barbara he knew.

"I was afraid I'd look the fool," she continued, "but women older than me were dancing and having a wonderful time. Everyone acted so alive, and their sense of camaraderie was enviable. So, I dove in headfirst. Michael says ballroom dancing gave him his mother back."

"You're the poster child for middle-aged rejuvenation." Marcos ducked his head and glanced sideways at Barbara.

"Middle-aged poster child, huh?" Her heart-shaped face entertained a gentle, affectionate smile. "Let me tell you, losing the love of your life can age you before your time. But life goes on, and if you want to go on with it, a good place to start is stepping out of your comfort zone to become a novice at something. Getting out on the dance floor, in front of all those mirrors, pushed me way, way out of my comfort zone."

"I like your positive, can-do energy, Barbara. Your enthusiasm is contagious," Edward said.

"I second that," Marcos chimed in. He quite enjoyed watching these two interact. He could be wrong, but he thought he detected a new twinkle in Ed's eye.

"Thank you, gentlemen," Barbara said. "The change from negative to positive was like stretching out a new pair of leather pumps. At first they feel constrictive and make you a bit self-conscious with their shiny newness, but then one day you realize your toes don't feel pinched anymore. The new shoes not only fit but give your walk a new, lively lilt. How's that for an analogy men probably can't relate to?" Barbara said. She stretched her fingers in an outward gesture, displaying artfully manicured, but not overly long, nails.

Marcos leaned forward, forearms on the table. Barbara's eyebrows were raised, as if she were surprised at her own outburst. Barbara shared amusing stories but rarely divulged this kind of personal information. Marcos watched her watching Ed. If he could risk a guess, Barbara was looking at Edward with a tad more interest than wariness.

"Let me share something with you now," Ed offered, gently touching Barbara's hand. "There's one piece of philosophy that's pulled me through many difficult times in my life: "Desiderata" by Max Ehrmann. Are you familiar with it?"

Barbara nodded. "Yes. It's one of my all-time favorite pieces of writing and a lifetime source of inspiration."

Ed compressed his lips and nodded. "I still want to believe 'the universe is unfolding as it should.' And some days, I admit, I struggle with that one." Edward stood. "Now I'm going to leave you both for a few minutes before Marcos's workshop begins."

Marcos glanced at his watch. He had to get Paige before he started the class.

"Remember this one thing. Life is like dancing between the beats. One never stops moving as long as the music is playing." Ed took Barbara's right hand, raised it to his lips, and placed an old-world kiss on the back of her hand. Barbara colored like a schoolgirl.

Marcos leaned back, hands on the edge of the table. An unfamiliar feeling of shame washed over him. These two people, not much older than him, were shaped by all the highs and lows, the loves and losses, the challenges of life he'd so studiously avoided for most of his adult life. He had a new vision of the studio as well. To them, Desert DanceSport was more than a place to take dance lessons. It was the beating heart of belonging for them. Running this place didn't feel like such a game anymore. Ed and Barbara possessed a depth you could see in their eyes. Uncomfortable, Marcos excused himself. He wondered what his eyes revealed to others. Probably not depth.

~

10:30 p.m., Saturday, 17 October

Marcos slid into the steaming heat of the Jacuzzi. The embrace of the hot water on his body, juxtaposed against the coolness of the night air on his face, fed his senses. Not even cold weather stopped him from using his Jacuzzi. Last winter he soaked in its heat during one of Tucson's rare snowfalls, watching fluffy snowflakes drift around him and dissolve on the water.

Marcos's tumbler of Scotch whiskey was within easy reach. The liquor went down smooth and warm, spreading its relaxing heat throughout his chest. With a contented sigh, he leaned his head back and watched the world around him slowly shift to silver under the soft light of the full moon. The topmost fronds of palm trees shimmered under the moonlight; an owl hooted from the neighbor's mesquite tree. Maybe the same owl that nabbed his neighbor's cat two nights ago?

Marcos shifted, positioning the base of his spine against the pulsing jets. The workshop had been a success, but his back felt the weight of every beginning student who couldn't hold her dance frame. He felt all of his forty-nine years and then some.

Hard as he tried to focus on his scotch and the soothing hot water, he couldn't shake a nagging feeling of unease about Katherine.

Lately she was more like a discordant piece of jazz than a smooth and flowing saxophone piece. The changes were subtle, and to anyone else they might not be so obvious, but few knew her as well as he did. Their long-ago affair might have been a brief one, but it had been a great one. It might be all business now, but he could still sense when the pistons weren't all firing.

Marcos stretched to reach the bottle of Glenlivet and, slippery fingers and all, slid it over to refresh his glass. Lately Katherine avoided anything but the lightest of exchanges. She brushed off his attempts to get up to speed on the financials and refused to discuss even something as mundane as hiring another advanced male instructor. His questions or suggestions were met with defensiveness. Maybe handling the financials alone for too long made her possessive of them? Marcos sipped his drink. If he was honest with himself, he was guilty of sticking to the fun side of the business, teaching and coaching. The money end was all work and no play.

The first phrase of "Strangers in the Night" mingled with the vibrating hum of the phone's motion on the cool decking around the hot tub.

"Marcos here."

"Marcos. Hi. It's Michael Bradshaw, Barbara's son. I hope I'm not disturbing you by calling so late."

"Michael, hello. No, you're not disturbing me at all. Barbara mentioned you might call. Hold on for a second, please." Marcos pulled himself out of the water and wrapped himself in a thick terry robe. He grabbed the phone and his tumbler of scotch and settled into a cushioned chaise lounge under the patio roof. "Thanks. I needed a minute to get situated. Okay, right down to business. Can you fill me in on your ballroom dancing background? You'll be required to take some certification tests."

"Of course," Michael said. "When I was at the University of Arizona—fine arts major with a business minor—I was president of the ballroom dance club. I always placed in the top three in competitions, dancing at the Open Gold Level. In Seattle I taught ballroom dance for a semester at a junior college and, believe it or not, as a volunteer at a senior center."

"Ah, a ballroom instructor with a college education. A rare breed," Marcos said, pausing to sip his third—or was it his fourth?—scotch. "You might want to keep that to yourself. People expect their ballroom instructors to be debonair, dashing, and maybe a little dumb." Marcos laughed, pleased to hear Michael join right in. There was a vivacity in Michael's voice that reminded him of himself at Michael's age but, at the same time, made him much too conscious of bordering on fifty.

"So, Michael, talk to me about where you are in terms of your career, and fill me in on your stage-work history."

Marcos lit a cigarette and stretched out on the chaise. It was a lovely, starry night, and between the Jacuzzi and the scotch, he was finally relaxed. Michael was an enthusiastic talker, and Marcos was in the mood to sit back and listen. Fifteen minutes later, Marcos jumped back in.

"Michael, there's only so much we can cover over the phone. Here's an idea. Come and spend a day or two at the studio. Teach a couple of classes, meet the staff. I think we'll both know soon enough if you joining us on a permanent basis is a fit. That's the best I can give you right now. But first I have to ask…your mother mentioned you have a commitment with *Kinky Boots* until the end of the show's run in late December, or is it early 2016?" Marcos said.

"Late December, but as far as my commitment goes, I'm okay. Because I've been exploring career options, I've worked to bring one of the junior dancers up to speed. I can exit gracefully without leaving the show in a bind. The young man I'm training is biting his nails at the chance to step into my part for the final few weeks of the show. I can make plans for a short trip to Tucson if that will work for you."

I'll tell you what," Marcos said. "Why don't we have a little fun with this? Our next big studio event is a Halloween costume party dance on Friday, October 30…"

SEVEN

PLAYING WITH MATCHES

Katherine Carrington
9:30 a.m., Monday, 19 October

Katherine wrapped the Scottish cable-knit sweater across her chest, folding her arms to hold in the warmth of the wool. With one hip, she pushed the back door closed and, head down against the wind, walked across the parking lot. She needed uninterrupted time to think, to breathe. Like a chameleon, she blended into the mottled shade of the eucalyptus and leaned her back against the wide trunk. Katherine unknotted the wide belt of the cardigan and thrust her hands deep into its pockets. It was days like this she came close to flirting with the idea of smoking. The repetitive motion of hand to mouth seemed to relax those who indulged. But she simply couldn't bear the thought of smelling like a dirty ashtray.

Katherine unclenched her teeth. Her jaw ached. She stretched her lower jaw from side to side to force relaxation. What was her dentist thinking? Inserting one of those nasty mouth appliances every night to prevent grinding her teeth was misery. Two nights and she'd had enough. Also, the damn device made her drool, an unthinkable indignity.

Katherine carefully nibbled on the inside edge of her finger to avoid ruining her manicure. She scanned the length of the building—the biggest ballroom studio in southern Arizona. A short five years ago, she rented only part of this building. Luckily, the yoga studio at the end went belly-up, motivating old Harry Weinstein to sell the building and retire to Florida. He was a stocky, tough-talking New Yorker with a soft spot for Katherine, and he gave her first right of refusal to purchase the building. It was tricky, but, with the addition of some investment capital, she qualified for the mortgage. It was a sweet deal that would have been sweeter if the mortgage were in her name only. Still, the contract was written with an *or*, not an *and*, so Katherine could still do whatever she wanted without a lot of unnecessary discussion.

The wind dropped the air temperature, and Katherine snuggled deeper into the soft warmth of her sweater. Low, murky-looking clouds tumbled over the granite ridges of the Santa Catalina Mountains, streaking the deep canyons a misty gray and obscuring the ubiquitous silhouettes of the saguaro cacti. She could feel the temperature drop as the storm approached. The warning tinges of a barometric-pressure migraine tugged at her temples. Katherine closed her eyes. They burned all the time lately. She pulled the Visine out of her pocket and blinked back the drops. Her thoughts drifted and tumbled with the approaching clouds.

The squeal of tires wrenched Katherine's focus away from her thoughts. A Dodge Ram pickup truck whipped into the loosely graveled lot. Dust rose in its wake. Jill jumped down from the high cab before the driver brought the truck to a full stop. With a metallic thud, the passenger door slammed shut. Jill raised her sunglasses to her forehead and directed a death glare at the driver—the husband, maybe—followed by the slam-bang of her fist on the hood as she cleared the front of the vehicle. Katherine narrowed her eyes. Jill's husband responded to her fist on the hood with more screeching tires as he gunned the truck backward. Small gravel stones flew everywhere. Katherine shook her head at the stream of profanities Jill directed at the retreating truck. And then Jill's eyes made contact with Katherine's. She froze in her tracks, bit her upper lip, gave a half-hearted apologetic shrug, and ran for the back door.

"Well, I sure as hell hope this unfortunate display of temper isn't going to set the tone for the rest of the day," Katherine said, pushing herself away from the comfort of the tree trunk's embrace. She sighed and followed Jill into the studio.

～

Katherine settled herself into the front office. She left the door ajar and slid open one side of the window. Jill's purse was still hanging from her hand; her back was toward Katherine. She then threw the purse under the counter and stood facing the front door, the heels of her hands pushing against edge of the counter.

"Okay, I have to focus." Jill's words were muffled by a tremulous sigh.

Katherine chose to remain quiet. Jill obviously had no idea she was being observed and her every word could be heard. She rocked slowly forward and back. She pushed away from the counter. Her deep intake of breath was visible.

"I have to check the appointment book for the week, tidy the coffee area, check today's schedule… I can do this." Jill's voice quavered. She opened the vinyl-bound appointment book and, with a hot-pink marker, checked empty time slots under each instructor's name. She dropped the marker and furiously fanned her eyes with her fingertips. "Damn, damn, damn," Jill said, as she pulled several tissues out of the box.

Katherine couldn't take it anymore. God forbid clients should start arriving, expecting a cheery good morning, only to be greeted by this unfolding melodrama.

"Jill."

Jill dabbed her eyes and turned around.

"Jill," Katherine repeated. "I can't have you out here greeting our clientele in such an emotional state. What on earth is going on? And what was that scene in the parking lot?"

"I'm sorry, Katherine." Jill hesitated, but once the dam broke, her words tumbled like rapids over rocks.

"Steve and I have been fighting, and last night was the worst. We argued until past two in the morning." Jill hugged herself and paced in the confined area behind the desk. "Some stupid TV program got us talking about church and believing in God. Turns out Steve and his parents are devout Southern Baptists. Then Steve started asking about how I vote, and I had to tell him I'm not even a registered voter. That was really bad." Jill punctuated her speech with a grimace and eye contact with Katherine. "Several beers later, Steve opened the argument door on homeschooling and how children should be raised, which circled us right back to religious beliefs and patriotism. I don't understand how being Republican and Baptist equals being a true American." Tears crept out of the corners of Jill's eyes. She reached for another wad of tissues.

Katherine folded her arms and pressed her lips together.

"His voice keeps bouncing around in my brain," Jill wailed. "Then he started in about how a wife has to follow her husband's way of thinking, and he'd made that mistake once and would never go there again. I asked what he meant, and it turns out he has an ex-wife he's never before mentioned."

"All right, Jill," Katherine said firmly. "You need to take a breath or two and calm yourself." Katherine walked over to the shaking girl and placed both hands on her shoulders. "It sounds to me like you're getting to know your husband after the wedding instead of before, and it's not the romance and roses you expected. I am sorry for the reality check, but, as difficult as it might be, you have to leave your personal life at the door when you come to work."

Jill rubbed the back of her hand across compressed lips.

"So," Katherine said, "I want you to take a few minutes to compose yourself. Pour some coffee, and then see if getting some work done might distract you from your problems. There's a stack of mail to sort. You can also reconcile the instructors' hours against the students' sign-in sheet. There's plenty to do to keep your mind occupied."

Jill nodded and reached for another tissue, but, before she could dab her eyes, the phone rang. She grabbed it on the second ring.

"Desert DanceSport. How may I help you?" Jill said, her voice waxing professional. "I'm sorry, could you repeat that? Did you say Felicia from New Haven?"

Katherine stood stock-still. She signaled a "no" and whispered, "I'm not here."

"I'm sorry, ma'am," Jill said, nodding at Katherine, "but Ms. Carrington isn't in the studio today. May I take a message?" Jill's face reddened, and she turned away from Katherine.

"Hmmm. Yes. I'll let her know, but I'm not sure you can reach her at home today, either. I believe she said she was driving to Phoenix to interview a dance coach." Jill looked back at Katherine, who could hear the caller's voice rise a decibel or two.

"Okay. Yes, of course I understand the urgency, and I will be sure she gets a message to call you as soon as she checks in. Thank you. Goodbye."

Jill took a deep breath. She exhaled audibly and slowly. She shifted from foot to foot and pulled at a strand of hair. She looked like she would rather be at home fighting with her husband than in the office right now.

Katherine raised her hand before Jill could say a word.

"Consider me duly told that Felicia called," Katherine said, turning her back.

"But...but, I think maybe you should—"

"You think I should maybe what, Jill?" Katherine placed one hand on her hip.

"This Felicia called from New Haven last week as well. She called twice, actually. I gave you her messages. Remember?" Jill's voice trembled as it rose in pitch and her brow furrowed. "She sounded very mad this time, Katherine. She said she thought you were going to stop by this morning, so she came in early, and then you didn't show. She expected a ch—"

"You've said enough, Jill. This is really none of your concern. Your job is to answer the phone and pass along messages, and that's where your responsibility ends." Katherine folded her arms. She took a deep breath and then exhaled a small explosion of air. "You know, Jill, I think you should take the rest of the day off. Paige and Sylvie should be here soon. The girls can cover the front desk. You can make up the hours during the week."

"But…but Katherine, I don't even have a car today. Steve dropped me off," Jill said. Tears pooled in her eyes again. She hugged herself, stroking her upper arms.

"Tell your Steve to come and get you then, Jill. He'd probably rather have you home today anyway so you can talk," Katherine said, already halfway through the door to the office. "I have work to do, so…"

"Yes, ma'am," Jill mumbled.

～

Barbara Bradshaw
10:45 a.m., Monday, 19 October

Barbara pulled into the back parking lot and waved at Marcos. He was about to extinguish one of his cherished Gauloises cigarettes. Why did the man smoke? He should know better.

"You are such a gentleman," Barbara said, as Marcos opened her car door. She handed him the tray holding their venti lattes and reached across the seat for her dance-shoe bag. "Looks like I caught you hiding out and smoking again." Barbara gently chided her instructor. She couldn't help herself. She was the mothering type down to her toes.

"Guilty as charged," Marcos said with a good-natured smile. "I'd raise my hands in surrender but I'd drop our coffees, which, by the way, I appreciate your bringing."

"So, what's on our flight plan for today?" Barbara asked as they entered the studio.

"Well, my thinking is to focus on your tango and then maybe work in time to begin practicing the new choreography for your rumba. You're entering the next Student Specialty Showcase, right?" Marcos asked as they made their way through the hall past the restrooms.

"Well, I...oh—"

A tearful Jill nearly knocked Barbara into the wall as she rushed past them. Marcos grabbed Barbara's arm just in time.

"Sorry. 'Scuse me. Sorry," Jill mumbled. She slammed open the bathroom door and ran inside.

"Oh my. What now? You go on ahead, Marcos," Barbara said, already turning toward the ladies' room. "I'll find you in the ballroom as soon as I can."

Loud sobs echoed off the walls and floor of the tiled ladies' room. Barbara tiptoed to the closed stall door and knocked softly.

"Jill? Jill, honey, can I do something to help? Why don't you come out and sit with me on one of these nice little chairs, and we'll have a chat?"

Murph, sniff, gulp, and the sound of a nose being blown was all Barbara got in reply.

"Come on out. Nothing is so bad that sharing doesn't ease the burden."

The crying quieted to a controlled gulping and sniffling, and the stall door slowly opened. Jill was a mess. Besides the outfit—a blouse stretched tightly across her chest, purple feather earrings, and a too-short purple skirt—Jill's mascara-smeared eyes were swollen and red.

"First, let's get you tidied. We can't have anyone seeing you like this, can we?" Barbara sat the girl down and wiped her face with wet paper towels. She then applied a thin layer of the only moisturizer on hand, the generic hand lotion by the sinks. Barbara pulled her own cosmetic bag out of her purse, and began to restore some order to Jill's ruined makeup. "Sit still, please, so I can do this, and then we'll talk."

Obedient and subdued, Jill let Barbara do her work.

"Now, tell me what has you so upset," Barbara said. She sat in the chair next to Jill. There was a Kleenex box on the narrow table between them.

"Everything has gone wrong. I tried to talk to Katherine, but she was so mean to me. And then she told me I should go home. I don't even have my car. Steve dropped me off. And he's so mad at me, he'll probably tell me to walk if I call him."

Barbara could see tears welling again in Jill's eyes. She pulled a paper cup from the dispenser, filled it with cold tap water, and handed it to Jill.

"Okay. Here goes," Jill said, sipping while she talked. The whole sad story emerged in an avalanche of words, blocked here and there by gulps and stifled sobs. "Steve really isn't a cool cowboy like Toby Keith at all. He's a right-wing redneck, all the way from the top of his hat to the tip of his pointy cowboy boots. A redneck!" Jill choked a bit. "His father is a preacher. Everything he told me about how he believed in marriage and how a woman was meant to be taken care of was really about his religion and his idea of a woman's place. A woman's place!" Jill wailed.

Barbara handed Jill more tissues. "It gets worse," Jill said. "Steve's parents expect us in church every Sunday and on Wednesday nights as well. And I'm ag...nos...TIC." She stared wild-eyed at Barbara. "And the man hunts everything that walks or flies, and I hate hunting. He owns reloaders, for God's sake. He eats like an Eskimo—all meat and hardly any salads or veggies. He wants me to make him a big huge breakfast every morning and then expects me to do all the dishes before I go to work. What happened to the man who made me strawberry waffles? And his father thinks we should get the marriage annulled because we are not 'equally yoked,' whatever that means."

Barbara sat back and folded her arms. She tried to stifle her natural tendency to go into overdrive and plow through a problem until a solution was found.

"I'm going to see if Marcos can reschedule my lesson," Barbara said. "You sit tight for a minute. No, I have a better idea." Barbara rummaged in her purse. "Take my car keys. Wait for me in my car. We'll go somewhere and have some tea. We can talk about expectations versus reality and then figure out how to get you back on track." Barbara's immediate thought was that Jill had never really been on track, but right now it was a moot point.

"But what about the no-fraternization rules?" Jill said. Her voice threatened tears again. "Won't both of us get into trouble with Katherine if I go somewhere with you?"

"Nonsense," Barbara replied, more sharply than she intended. "Those rules are meant to keep young and foolish instructors from making bad judgment calls with their students and jeopardizing the studio. There's a point where common sense and maturity, both of which I have, take precedence over rules meant for those with neither."

"Thank you, Barbara." Jill was already on her feet, car keys dangling from her hand.

~

Barbara glanced around, pleased the ambiance in her living room was cozy, in spite of it being a large room. A wrought-iron chandelier on a dimmer provided soft lighting, augmented by strategically placed table lamps. A granite fireplace with a polished-walnut mantel broke the pristine white of stucco walls, and hand-hewn, dark beams tempered the white ceiling. Soft leather armchairs formed a conversation circle around a square ottoman, encouraging guests to put their feet up. Right behind the generous-sized sofa, in which Jill was comfortably ensconced, was a floor-to-ceiling bookshelf. Handsome pieces of glazed pottery and bright floral paintings, purchased from local artisans, added color to the otherwise neutral room.

Jill's feet were tucked under a soft throw, a hot cup of tea was on the side table, and a plate of home-baked chocolate chip cookies were close at hand.

"I'm glad we decided to come to my house, Jill," Barbara said. "You can unwind in comfort, and we can talk in privacy."

"This is so nice of you, Barbara," Jill said. "I feel better already." Jill brushed cookie crumbs off the throw. "I tried to talk to a girlfriend before I left the house this morning, but it wasn't good. You know how when you are mad at a guy and you tell your girlfriends, and they get madder than you are? It's like they get to enjoy the drama without feeling any of the pain. This friend, Becka, was ready to get all up in Steve's face. Talking to you isn't like that at all."

"Well, I certainly hope not. I prefer to diffuse drama rather than escalate it," Barbara said. "The one point I hope to get across is marriage is not about the flash and dazzle of a princess wedding moment. It's about committing to compromise for the long term and about learning to listen, to be accepting and supportive."

Barbara waited until Jill made eye contact to prove she was listening. The girl had relaxed over the past hour and was beginning to see reason.

"Don't let someone tell you marriage is fifty-fifty, either." Barbara sat back in her chair and continued. "It's more like eighty-twenty, and the ratio shifts from one to the other all the time. The day-to-day reality of marriage is dealing with in-laws, laundering someone's underwear, sharing the remote, coping with messy finances, and arguing over how to squeeze the toothpaste tube."

"Sounds about right," Jill said. She croaked out a small laugh before putting her tea cup on the coffee table. She took a defensive posture, crossing her arms.

"What is it, Jill? Is there something more, something you haven't told me?"

"Yeah," Jill said. "There's something more, and it's big." Jill looked at Barbara, and her eyes held embarrassment. "Really big. I haven't told anyone, not even Steve," Jill said, lowering her head. Tears were threatening to fall again.

"Well, all right, then. We've made a lot of progress, so let's keep the ball rolling while the tea in the teapot is still hot," Barbara said, smiling and trying to sound encouraging.

"Okay," Jill said. She pulled herself out of her slouch to a normal sitting position. "Here goes. Steve and I were at a roping rodeo event about five weeks before we got married. Well, we drank way too much beer. Steve kept hugging me and singing sexy Kenny Chesney songs in my ear, and we were getting so hot for each other. There was also an RV show at the fairgrounds that day, so Steve and I sneaked into one of the RVs in the back of the lot, locked the door, and got it on. It was all passionate and spontaneous." Jill blew her nose. "And 'cause it was all so spontaneous, we didn't use any protection."

Barbara's back straightened. She mentally braced herself.

"Last night, before Steve and I got into the big fight, I took one of those pregnancy tests, the kind you can buy at Walgreens; it was positive." Jill hugged her stomach with folded arms and rocked back and forth. She looked at Barbara with pleading eyes. "Positive! If I tell Steve I'm pregnant, even though he's mad at me and after what his Dad said about an annulment, he'd want to stay married. So then what? He'd feel trapped. And if I don't tell him and we separate, what then? Even though I'm not religious, I would never have an abortion. I don't want to be a single mother." The tears started to streak her makeup again.

"Well, I think I'm going to put the kettle on and make us a fresh pot of tea," Barbara said. "You dry your eyes and have another cookie."

Barbara grabbed the teapot and headed through the Saltillo-tiled entryway to the spacious kitchen. Kettle on and fresh tea leaves in the pot, she leaned over the sink and stared out at the mountain view. Advice usually came easily to her, and she believed to her core that everyone makes mistakes and every problem has a solution. This time, she was at a loss for words. She chewed on her upper lip.

Barbara turned away from the window and looked across the entryway into the living room. Jill looked desolate. Poor girl. Jill's situation was not unique in itself, though. Half the human race was the product of an unplanned pregnancy. The same mistakes our great-grandparents made are repeated: people marry for the wrong reasons, husbands cheat, wives smolder with resentment, children disappoint their parents, and girlfriends and wives produce unplanned pregnancies. We spin around and around, a continual spiral of problem-to-solution and back again.

Fresh tea made and teapot in hand, Barbara walked back into the living room. The pattern of Jill's life was beginning to resemble a crazy quilt with uneven squares and too many loose threads. Pulling too hard on any one could unravel the whole piece. Even Barbara, a master weaver, wasn't exactly sure how to help Jill sort herself out. And, worse, she wasn't sure how deeply she wanted to get involved.

Jill had lain down, one arm thrown over her eyes.

"Jill, honey, let me pour you a nice hot cup of tea." Jill pushed herself to a sitting position and held out her teacup. "So," Barbara said as she poured, "do you think that maybe pregnancy hormones had something to do with last night exploding into a big fight?"

Jill looked at Barbara with a glimmer of hope in her eyes. "Maybe. Maybe that's exactly why I got so crazy I couldn't see straight."

"Let's go over the facts, then. You can't hide the pregnancy. Terminating the pregnancy is not an option. You also said Steve agreed you two love each other, but might have jumped into this marriage without enough forethought." Jill blanched and looked defensive. "But, you also said Steve's religious beliefs dictate that, once married, each partner *cleaves* to their spouse, not to the parents. 'Cleave' is the word he used, correct?" Jill nodded. "So, to me that means Steve will want to focus on what's best for your marriage rather than on what his father thinks."

Jill was quiet. She took a sip of her tea and looked over the flowered china cup at Barbara with big eyes. Barbara took this as a cue to continue.

"Jill, I was thinking. Why don't you call Steve, tell him I brought you over here and why, and he needs to come and get you. Once we get him here, you two can talk."

Jill nodded.

"Here's the plan." Barbara made sure she had eye contact with Jill. "So, without tears and dramatics, apologize for last night, tell him you love him and want to focus on all the things you have in common and all the things you love about him." Barbara sat back and softened her tone, trying not to sound like she was lecturing. "You said Steve is kindhearted and a hard worker. He has strong family values, which should translate to being a good father. Once you smooth things out and are both calmer, you can decide whether you want to tell him you think you're pregnant. Does this sound workable to you?"

Jill nodded again. She smiled, but her smile was as fragile as the china cup she was holding. "My cell is in my purse," Jill said. She dumped her purse upside down on the couch and rummaged through the untidy pile of contents.

"I'll give you both privacy, but I can mediate if things get ugly."

"But stay close by, okay?" Jill said.

"I will," Barbara said. "You and Steve need to try to figure everything out without his parents' input. Bringing a child into the world changes everything, Jill, regardless of the circumstances of conception. You are going to be a mother with or without this man, so it's time to play the cards you've been dealt. Okay? No one can fix this for you but you."

"Yes, ma'am," Jill said. She straightened her back and put away her tissues. The tears were gone. "I know he'll want to do what's right for us. My one condition will be what you said about Steve and me figuring this out alone. Could you make some coffee? Steve doesn't drink tea." Jill smiled an optimistic smile as she punched the numbers into her phone.

"I would be more than glad to. I'll refresh the plate of cookies while I'm at it."

"I feel really good about this," Jill called out to Barbara, who was already halfway to the kitchen. "I feel like I am finally in charge of my own life. I'm going to be a mother, and I'm not going to screw things up. Maybe I should celebrate with a new tattoo. What do you think about a tiny leaf with the tip sort of curling and turning over to signify my new, mature outlook on life? Isn't that a great idea, Barbara?"

EIGHT

Hits and Misses

Paige Russell
10:30 a.m., Tuesday, 20 October

"I just discovered a miracle of deliciousness," Sylvie proclaimed. Her words flew ahead of her as she sailed through the front door.

Paige put down the dance syllabus book and waited for the other shoe to drop. She was becoming desensitized to Sylvie's too-frequent, spontaneous outbursts, but today the gleam in Sylvie's blue eyes bordered on evangelical.

"This," Sylvie raised a very large, very empty, cardboard container from Angelo's Gelato, "is a wonder drug of velvety goodness." Sylvie cooed, "I'm totally, one-hundred-percent cured." She took off her sweater, tossed it on a chair, and turned her wide eyes back to Paige.

"What do you mean you're cured?" Paige stepped backward. Sylvie had the flushed, wild-eyed look of someone who's seen the image of Jesus on a dinner plate.

"This morning I was all achy and my throat was scratchy. I didn't have any orange juice and my stupid Mr. Coffee decided to die. The water heater in my third-world studio apartment is miniscule, so my shower was tepid, which made me feel worse." Sylvie shivered dramatically and looked at Paige, daring her to make light of her dilemma.

Paige took the hint. She kept her eyes glued on Sylvie, not sure whether to be amused, run, or call for the white coats. Sylvie was ready to spread the gospel according to Sylvie. The very thought made Paige uneasy.

"Anyway, on the way into work I pulled into a strip mall for a Starbucks but got totally distracted by this old-fashioned, flashing neon sign next door: True Italian Gelato. The pulsing lights pulled on my brain, and before I knew it I was ordering a honeycomb-flavored super-size." Sylvie paused, chin raised, eyes bright.

Paige held her hands out in a "So what does that mean?" gesture.

"So," Sylvie continued, "you know those people who knock on your front door, hand you a pamphlet, and ask if you want to hear The Truth?" Sylvie spread her arms heavenward, her voice only an octave behind. "*This* is the truth. When your head is splitting and your throat feels sore and cracked, bring on the big guns—gelato. Trust me on this. It's like a shot of B-12 right to the brain, an instant fix. Gelato has curative powers." Adrenaline rush spent, Sylvie plopped on top of the sweater she'd tossed on the chair.

Satisfied Sylvie's oration had reached its end, Paige ventured over and placed a hand on her forehead. Sylvie's bouncy blond curls were restrained with her signature wide headband.

"No fever, but definitely delirium," Paige declared with a smile. Sylvie could be off the wall, but today she bordered on crazed. "You're fine. Anyway, you can't get sick. With the comp less than two weeks away, I'll bet you're just stressed out."

"Maybe you're right," Sylvie said, crossing her muscled legs. "I think I have some classic signs of burnout, like yesterday I couldn't choose which shampoo to buy. There were so many choices, I was overwhelmed. So before my head exploded, I got the hell out of there." Sylvie looked at the lobby clock. "By the way, where's Jill? Shouldn't she be here by now?"

"She called in. She was running behind but said she'll stay late to put in the hours," Paige said. "Wait, there she is. That's her car heading toward the back lot."

"Good. I'm going to go stretch before my first student, Eric Fromme, arrives. Want to join me?"

Sylvie was out of the lobby before Paige could get off the stool. The amount of energy contained in Sylvie's tiny, athletic body was insane. Paige ran after her. "Hey, did you say Eric Fromme? What about his wife, Amy?"

"They're taking separate lessons now. Eric dances with me, and Amy with Tony. They practice together at the Friday parties." Sylvie situated herself on the floor, her legs stretched as wide as humanly possible. She dropped her torso flat onto the wood floorboards, arms outstretched to each side.

"I danced with Eric at the last party and noticed his lead had improved," Paige said.

"By the way, are you getting more comfortable asking the men to dance at the parties?" Sylvie's voice was muffled by her new position: legs stretched in front of her, hands grasping her upturned toes, and her face resting on her knees.

Paige bent over, her palms flat on the hardwood floor. "I'm getting better at coaxing them onto the floor. Marcos pointed out that a practice party could be the best part of someone's day, so I try not to correct their technique, but just make sure they have fun."

"Wise man, our Marcos," Sylvie said. "How's it going with the single male students? I noticed you have a couple of new ones." Sylvie let go of her toes and folded her legs into a lotus position.

"Good, I guess. My biggest issue is finding a balance between being friendly and keeping a professional distance," Paige said. She slid onto the wood floor, legs crossed, facing Sylvie, their knees inches apart. Paige twirled a section of hair from her ponytail around her finger and draped the tip under her nose, like a moustache.

"Yeah. That's a tough one, especially when you're in Smooth

dance frame and teaching body-to-body connection to a man you barely know. It's pretty easy for the intimacy to be misunderstood by someone who isn't used to ballroom dancing."

"Totally," Paige responded, stretching her arms in front of her. It was like Sylvie was taking her under her wing. Paige bit her lip. Maybe she should stop worrying about sounding stupid and naïve and be more open. People couldn't get in if you locked the door.

"And sooner or later," Sylvie said, "you end up tactfully telling someone that intimate contact in dance frame doesn't translate to intimate contact off the floor."

"Oh my God, that happened to me last week. I danced a few rumbas with one guy, and he got the wrong idea. He asked me out, and I had to say no. He accused me of leading him on. I apologized and explained about the flirtatious nature of the dance, that it's all playful acting. I told him I enjoyed dancing with him very much, but it's against the rules to date students. It wasn't personal. I'm still not sure he understood."

"It's a problem for all of us, the male teachers as well. Jackson had an issue with his new student, Mei Le," Sylvie said. "She couldn't understand why he wouldn't go out social dancing with her." Sylvie shook her head.

"It's hard to say no without someone taking it personally," Paige responded.

"When I started here, Katherine mentored me. She used to say young female instructors are the carrot dangling on a string to keep the male donkey moving forward."

"What…?" Paige said. "I'd laugh, but that's really not very funny."

"No, it's not," Sylvie responded. "And just wait until you're out of town at a competition with a student." Sylvie stretched her willowy arms over her head. "Yup, it's a delicate game of bait and switch, tease and halt. Sometimes selling lessons and your time is too much like selling yourself. The line is drawn very clearly in the sand, at least on my beach."

"Mine, too," Paige said.

Sylvie relaxed and crossed her legs. "I never thought I would say this, Paige, but you're turning into a good instructor. Being able to dance doesn't always translate into being able to teach, but you have the knack. And don't worry about the guys. You'll develop the right balance in time." In one smooth motion, Sylvie rose from sitting cross-legged to standing.

"Wow, thank you so much." Paige bit her lip. She suddenly felt self-conscious under the scrutiny of Sylvie's striking blue eyes.

"One piece of advice, then, one worth remembering. I learned this from a famous coach in a workshop years ago. He said, 'Practice, practice, practice, and then practice some more. Only in the dictionary does *success* come before *work*. In life it's the other way around.' Get it?"

Paige nodded, a little stunned. Maybe the ticket was to bring Sylvie some gelato once in a while.

~

Katherine Carrington
1:00 p.m., Tuesday, 20 October

Katherine clicked the Excel icon. She leaned forward, playing an index finger across her lips. Meeting this week's payroll could be challenging. Asking anyone to defer their paycheck for a few days would most likely get the same selfish response as always. Did none of her employees have savings accounts? So irresponsible. She folded her arms and studied the spreadsheet. One quick click of the mouse and she changed screens.

"This is more like it," Katherine murmured. Marcos's Saturday workshop had been a huge success. She scrolled through the numbers. He had a sixth sense about getting students fired up and signed up. Maybe he could sell the idea of monthly weekend workshops to the staff. Better him than her. If she had to deal with the inevitable whining about working one Saturday a month, she might just bitch-slap someone. What did these kids do with their time off anyway?

Drink and party? Play computer games? For all their complaining about not making enough money, they couldn't recognize a salary-boosting opportunity when it bit them in the butt.

Katherine straightened out of her slouch as her thoughts crystal-lized. Bottom line, this crew has to start bringing in more money. I've been too lax. It's about time all of them understood that hours on the floor equaled money in everyone's pockets.

Katherine drummed her desktop with one hand as she maneuvered the mouse with the other. What the studio needed was a few more Ed Dombroskys and Linda Wilsons. They never whined about not being able to afford to enter a student showcase or travel to a competition. She hated to hear someone who was well-heeled say they couldn't *afford* to enter a dance event. Of course they could afford it. They were just being cheap.

Edward understood loyalty. She'd talk to Ed. His enthusiasm motivated other students to participate in events. She rubbed her palms together, warming her icy fingertips. Edward! Katherine checked the time display on her monitor. His lesson was in less than half an hour. She jumped out of her chair and opened her small closet.

"What to wear?" Katherine mused, as she perused the selection of practice outfits. "The red and black." She held the outfit in front of the mirror. The top was designed to reveal a tempting taste of décolletage, and the dance skirt skimmed and flattered her slender hips. She pulled out her compact. Her eyeliner, light eyeshadow, and heavy coating of mascara—all applied with great skill—endowed her with a look of youthful, big-eyed innocence. She smiled coyly at her reflection.

Katherine sensed Edward standing behind her. She finished tacking the flyer on the announcements board.

"Hi, Kate," Ed said, resting a hand lightly on Katherine's upper arm. Edward was the only person besides her mother who called her Kate.

"Edward! You're early." Katherine tilted her head to show off the smile-induced dimple in her right cheek. Drawing from her well of performance skills, Katherine infused her eyes with a warmth designed to melt Mount Everest. Based on the one photograph she'd seen of Edward's deceased wife, Katherine knew she had the woman outclassed by a mile. Katherine put her arm through Ed's. He glanced at the wall clock and gently extricated himself from her hold.

"I see we have ten minutes before our hour starts. If you'll excuse me please, Katherine, I'm going to stop in at the men's room and then maybe make a quick phone call."

"Of course. I'll meet you in the ballroom. I'll get our music queued."

The ballroom was buzzing with activity. Katherine stifled a giggle, imagining dollar signs dancing above everyone's heads. She walked past café tables strewn with coffee cups, water bottles, shoe bags, sweaters, and student handbooks. As she chose music for Ed's lesson, her thoughts tumbled and her brow furrowed: scheming, reevaluating, and calculating options.

"I'm back, Kate," Ed called out.

On cue, Katherine's countenance transformed from Ms. Frownie to Ms. Congeniality.

"I'm totally yours for the next hour," Ed said, with outstretched arms.

Katherine smiled her sweetest smile. She was counting on exactly that and more. Edward Dombrosky was about to get the lesson of his life.

The hour flew. Katherine never stopped smiling. She presented her most gracious, charming self. She was a model of patience as Ed worked to learn the advanced elements and patterns of his new choreography. He was humming along to the "four-four" big-band sounds of the foxtrot. Katherine expertly back-led him thorough the jazzy, lilting movements as they maneuvered the crowded ballroom.

"Edward," Katherine whispered as they danced. "Great floorcraft. You are weaving and dodging like the young athlete you told me you were in your college basketball days."

"I was pretty darn good on the basketball courts, but my wife used to say I had two left feet on the dance floor," Ed said.

Wife—zero; Katherine—one. Katherine's smile widened. In perfect unison, their arms swept upward as they danced a series of side-by-side fallaways, free spins. Ed swept Katherine back into dance frame. She rolled off his right side into a perfect promenade position from a twinkle.

"You are quite the Fred Astaire today," Katherine cooed as the music stopped. "Great job, Edward. Your footwork was clean, and your lead for the sway-underarm-turn was spot on." Katherine directed her star student to their table. She handed him a bottle of water and took a deep breath. They had really danced.

"We'll work on the Viennese waltz next lesson. How many entries can I add for the Student Specialty Showcase?" Katherine asked. She paused to take a long drink from her water bottle. "Keep in mind this studio event will function as a trial run for the competition in Vegas in January, so take advantage of cheap floor time." Katherine maintained a light but possessive pressure on Ed's upper arm as she spoke.

Ed moved back in his chair. His arm slipped out from under Katherine's hand. He sipped his water, put the bottle on the table, and threaded his hands together as he leaned his elbows on the table. Katherine was encouraged by Edward's smile and relaxed demeanor.

"I think I'd like to stick to my usual number of entries, somewhere between thirty and thirty-five heats. I prefer to do mainly Smooths with only a few heats in the Rhythm section." Ed's eyes crinkled when he smiled. "I don't think I want to do any mambos or swing dances this time out. My knees aren't what they used to be."

"You, Mr. Edward Dombrosky," Katherine said with a wink, "are, as they used to say, a fine figure of a man." Katherine gauged Edward's receptiveness to her teasing. She sensed she should rein in the flirtatiousness but couldn't seem to help herself. She felt off her game, struggling to let Ed sense a shift in her attitude, without coming on too strong.

"Well, thank you for that. You're very kind," Ed replied. "However,

I'm feeling my limitations more these days." Ed gave Katherine a quick, closed-lipped smile and bent to unlace and kick off his dance shoes. He sighed as he flexed his toes. He leaned back, his posture relaxed, his socked feet casually crossed. His gaze was directed across the dance floor, as though captivated by the ongoing lessons.

Katherine leaned forward. She started a stream of chatter to reclaim Ed's focus, but even to her own ears it bordered on nervous. Before she could damn the creek, she confided about the studio experiencing a financial rough spot. Finally Katherine had Ed's full attention.

"Oh dear, I shouldn't have said anything. I'm sure I'm worrying unnecessarily. Carrying the burden of the business on my shoulders alone gets hard, and sometimes I wish I had someone to share it with." Katherine smiled demurely, looking at Ed from under lowered lashes.

Edward folded his arms behind his head. "You are one of the most capable women I know, Katherine. I have every confidence that you'll have the situation fully in hand in no time."

Katherine paused and ran the tip of her tongue over her upper lip. "A thought. I'm looking for a short-term influx of cash to the studio. Is there anyone, among your group of gentleman friends, who'd be interested in a quick-return investment? If you introduce me to the right person, I might even consider a relationship outside the realm of business." Katherine smiled to keep the statement light, punctuating it with a slow wink.

Ed tilted his head and smiled. "Your wry sense of humor sometimes catches me completely off guard, Katherine." Ed uncrossed his legs and rested his forearms on the small table. "I think I'm finally getting my wind back. We haven't danced our way through the hour like that in a long time." He leaned back in his chair before continuing. "I've also been thinking over your invitation of a few days ago. You offered to treat me to dinner in exchange for a few basic golf lessons at the club."

Katherine leaned forward in her chair, head cocked coquettishly.

"So, let me explain if I can. For me, golf is a palate cleanser of sorts.

It's a break from everything else in my life—from ballroom dancing and my volunteer activities." Ed's tone turned self-deprecating. "It's what the kids these days call *me time*—me, the greens, and the golf ball." Ed paused, as if lost in thought...or memories. "Even when my Betty was alive, she never joined me on the golf course. She accepted golf as my time and respected it as such." A tinge of sadness darkened Ed's eyes even as they crinkled with his ever-present smile.

Katherine bit her upper lip.

"However," Ed tapped the edge of the tabletop with the flat of his fingertips, as if to dispel any shadow of sadness and summon positive energy to the table, "if you are serious about learning to play golf, I can introduce you to the pro at the club. He's a great guy and an excellent teacher. I think you'd enjoy him and have a lot of fun."

Katherine slowly leaned into the backrest of the chair. She remained quiet, taking occasional sips from her water bottle. She kept her face a mask of pleasant attentiveness.

"Katherine," Ed said. He reached across the table and gently patted Katherine's hand. His expression was neutral, his body language benign and friendly. "I absolutely cherish our time on the dance floor. Our relationship works. It's comfortable because we both understand the rules. And," Ed paused for a beat, "as the example-setting older adults, we certainly can't break the 'No fraternization between students and teachers' rule, can we?" Edward winked, raising one eyebrow. "Oh, and by the way, since we are more or less on the subject of future dance events, what would you think about choreographing a couple of American Smooth numbers for Barbara Bradshaw to dance with me?" Ed asked. "Barbara and I are tossing the idea around of entering a few heats in the amateur couples section of the showcase."

Katherine realized that, with the skill of a diplomat, Edward had smoothly changed the conversational direction.

They continued a casual and friendly exchange. Ed's smile was open, his body language expansive and sincere; Katherine's relaxed and composed. Out of sight, under the table, Katherine's hands clenched and unclenched.

~

It was only four thirty, but Katherine felt wrung out. Needing coffee, she filled her favorite mug from the Krups in the lobby, and gazed mindlessly out the studio's glassed front door. She sipped and stared, willing the caffeine to jump-start her brain. Behind her, a conversational buzz emanated from the reception desk. Katherine tried to tune out the disturbance, but her peace had been broken. Annoyed, she glanced around. Jill was deep in conversation with a student of Tony's, who was gesturing like a traffic controller on steroids. Voices weren't raised, but Katherine could sense the intensity. Determined to stay out of it, she turned around and focused on the blur of traffic whizzing by. A sudden movement to her left caught her off guard, and she jerked, coming close to spilling coffee on her silk shirt. The front door pushed open, and Tony's student shoved past without even a glance. The door slammed behind her.

"Well, excuse me!" Katherine exclaimed. She turned to Jill. "What the hell was all that about?" She kept her voice low, but made sure there was no mistaking her tone. "That woman is one of Tony's best students, and she didn't look very happy. What you were two talking about?"

"Well, um, Mrs. Evans wanted to leave flyers here for a charity event her church is sponsoring to counsel pregnant teens. I told her we only post flyers about dance events. That's what you wanted me to say to people, right?"

"Yes. That's correct, Jill." Katherine paused. She wasn't in the mood for this. "However, your discussion seemed too lengthy and heated for a simple one-line response to a question."

Jill rubbed her palms on the hips of her too-tight denim jeans. "Mrs. Evans got sort of upset with me. She started talking about the Bible and stuff and said we should be proud to display her church's flyers about counseling pregnant teens. And then I guess I said...." Jill kept eye contact with Katherine, but her voice lowered. "I guess

I said something about sex-education classes and…and stuff." Jill's voice drifted into silence.

"Jill!" Katherine pinched the bridge of her nose and rubbed the inner corners of her eyes. Her exhale was audible. "Okay, I understand your point, and I'm actually more than surprised you can articulate a point of view, but…" Katherine sighed again. She was sure her words were going to drop like stones in a bottomless lake, but her choice at the moment was either to educate the girl or fire her. She had enough going on without adding "find a new receptionist" to her list. "Jill, I need your full attention right now. Are you listening?"

Jill nodded.

Katherine felt her features tighten as she folded her arms. She was in no mood to waste energy on pretense.

"What you choose to discuss with your friends on your own time is your business. But I'm telling you, not asking you, that in this studio, I expect you to fight your tendency to be outspoken if you disagree with one of our paying customers. Do you understand?"

"Yes, ma'am," Jill said. Her eyes were downcast, and she bit the corner of her lower lip.

"All right, I'll seek Mrs. Evans out as soon as I can and try to calm the waters," Katherine said. It seemed to be her day for audible sighs. "I have enough on my plate without your mouth adding to it. I need air. If anyone wants me, I'll be outside for a few minutes."

Katherine turned, coffee cup in hand, and headed for the back door. Once outside, she walked in ever-tighter circles, her thoughts spinning with her steps. There was too much to think about. Everything would be better once her damn mother's house sold. She stood still for a moment to take a swig of coffee. There was the home equity loan to be paid back, but taking out the loan couldn't be helped. Paying cash for her car was a smart financial move, and remodeling her condo increased its value significantly. She just had to keep all the balls in the air for a little while longer.

"Katherine. Hey, Katherine." Jill beckoned from the back door. "I just took a call from Felicia. She said she couldn't reach you on your cell. It's on the front office desk and was singing like crazy."

She tucked her windswept hair behind her ears and stepped inside the door Jill held open for her. Katherine moved quickly down the hall. "And what did you tell Felicia?" Katherine asked, keeping her voice neutral.

"I told Felicia I'd tell you to call her back as soon as I found you," Jill replied, trotting closely behind Katherine.

Katherine stopped abruptly. Jill slammed one hand into the middle of Katherine's back.

"Oh my God. I'm so sorry, Katherine."

"What the hell is wrong with you?" Katherine whirled around. She leaned into Jill, her voice low and hard. Katherine's lips formed a smile, but her eyes narrowed. She clipped each word as though speaking to an imbecile. "See if you can handle this simple request. I'm going into the front office. I'm shutting the door and pulling the blinds. No one is to knock, no phone calls are to be put through, no one is to bother me for any reason whatsoever, do you understand? And never again say to anyone that you are going to *tell* me to do something."

Jill nodded. A sheen of tears glinted in her eyes.

Katherine straightened and smiled at the students loitering by the front desk. She turned away, smile instantly gone, and shut her office door. Bracing herself against the door, she closed her eyes.

"Okay." Katherine dictated to herself as she jotted notes on a scratch pad. "First, Felicia at New Haven, the bank made a terrible mistake and moved monies into the wrong account. Then, the bank, ask for that nice Mr. Donovan. Hmmm, we have new accounting software and certain auto deposits did not get made. But before I call the bank..." Katherine strode into the lobby.

"Jill," she said, her voice a bit louder than necessary. Katherine reached underneath the reception desk for the petty cash box and the key. "From now on, I don't want you taking in any cash payments or using petty cash for studio purchases. Send anyone paying in cash directly to me. I'll be keeping the cash lockbox in my desk. Understand?"

Two students stopped their conversation to glance Jill's way. Their gaze lingered a little too long. Katherine smiled as a flush crept across Jill's cheeks. "Have a good lesson, ladies," Katherine said as she wiggled her fingers in greeting. She closed the office door with a sharp click.

NINE

THE BUSINESS OF BALLROOM

Barbara Bradshaw
9:15 a.m., Thursday, 22 October

"And so, it was a huge mess." The wind tumbled Barbara's long bangs. She pushed them to one side. "I really must make time for a haircut." She shifted on the bench, turning her back to the breeze, and glanced at Marcos. "Anyway, when Jill's husband, Steve, came over, he found her quite subdued. I think he grasped that they'd reached a crossroads. The boy isn't stupid, but for someone so young he's very set in his ways."

"Good luck to them, then. You and I both know Jill is quite the drama queen. Some people get addicted to the adrenaline rush." Marcos pressed his lips together and shrugged. "As one who avoids drama and conflict at all costs, I don't get it."

"I'm with you. I hope I gave Jill and her husband some needed detox time. I hung around as a referee until Jill could get all the words out and Steve could absorb them." Barbara paused long enough to take a quick sip of her coffee. "Then I discreetly disappeared into the kitchen, within shouting distance if needed. Jill and Steve stayed for well over an hour. Voices were never raised, and for that I was grateful.

When Steve came to tell me he was taking his wife home, he thanked me."

"That's good to hear," Marcos said. "Getting involved in a couple's issues is dicey."

"I could tell Steve was embarrassed to know I was privy to so much personal information, especially the RV incident." Barbara covered her mouth to stifle a giggle.

"I can't believe Jill actually shared that with you. The girl has no filter," Marcos said. He looked like he was ready to burst out laughing again. Barbara felt wicked, enjoying Marcos's struggle to keep a straight face. After all, this was one of his employees they were talking about. If she were telling this story to anyone else it would be pure gossip, but in this case she was only passing along information.

"Empathy is a better choice than apathy," Barbara said, "but everyone is on their own path with their own lessons to learn. I have no say in where these two go from here."

"I hope Jill appreciates what you're doing for her, but I think you're following in the footsteps of the patron saint of lost causes." Marcos gave Barbara a quick, one-armed hug.

"I guess I have to 'fess up. I also passed Jill a little cash in case she needed to get away for a few days. She thought a visit to her parents might clear her head." Barbara held up her hand in a "stop" gesture before Marcos could admonish her. "It wasn't much—a couple of hundred."

"I know you and Linda Wilson planned to meet before your lessons, so how are you doing for time?" Marcos tipped his head to one side. "I don't want to keep you too long, but there is something I'd like to share with you."

"I'm good. I'm a bit early for Linda, so feel free to share away."

"You might as well hear this story from me before it gets unrecognizably embellished," Marcos said. "But I need a cigarette. The ripples on the surface around here are turning into crashing waves, and I need my drug of choice to stay afloat. Can you indulge me?"

"Not one lecturing word," Barbara promised, hoping her smile conveyed understanding. She would never admit it to Marcos, but the truth was she didn't mind the smell of cigarette smoke. It reminded her of her father, a lifelong heavy smoker. A hint of cigarette smoke clinging to clothing was, to her, a very masculine scent. Something she would never say out loud.

Marcos pulled out his pack of Gauloises and a monogrammed silver lighter. He cupped his hand around the cigarette. Once lit, he took a deep drag and slowly exhaled a swirl of bluish smoke. "Yesterday, we had a near disaster in the studio." Marcos shook his head. He turned to face Barbara. "You know Joey's very elderly student, Irene?"

"Yes, of course. Everyone knows Irene. She's what…in her late eighties? She has the stamina of the Energizer Bunny." Barbara upended the cardboard cup and, with a sigh, watched the last drops of coffee dribble onto the gravel.

"Well, yesterday Irene got a little overconfident and tried to demonstrate some fancy one-footed spin she'd seen on TV. Before Joey could stop her, she lost her balance and hit the floor, hard." Marcos looked at Barbara and ducked his chin.

"How frightening, Marcos. Irene's eighty-something bones must be fragile. Was Joey totally panicked?"

The stress was evident on Marcos's face. His jaw twitched just slightly and deep folds furrowed his brow. His cigarette was fast disappearing.

"I wasn't in the studio. Paige was there and told me what happened. She heard a loud bang, like someone dropped a bowling ball, and, when she turned around, Irene was sprawled on the floor. The bang was Irene's head hitting the floorboards. Joey later told me Irene went down like a dead soldier. He's sure he saw her head bounce at least once." Marcos tapped the ash off his cigarette. "Irene pulled herself into a sitting position. She said she was all right, but after resting for fifteen minutes or so, she became dizzy and complained of a headache. Joey got her cell and called one of her friends, who came over and insisted on taking Irene to the ER."

"I'm sure that was the right decision," Barbara said. "How awful for her. How is she?"

"Fine now, I think. The ER doctor kept her a couple of hours for observation. When Irene's friend took her home, she was told to stay with her and to make sure she kept Irene awake for the next few hours. The doctor thought the concussion was slight."

"Concussion?" Barbara's back straightened and she lowered her chin.

"Yup." Marcos shook his head. "But, thankfully, not a serious one. She was lucky. Joey's traumatized. Nothing like this has ever happened before, either to him or to the studio. We're all grateful Irene didn't break a hip, or worse, her neck."

"Honestly, with all the aging dancers in the studio, I'm surprised you don't have an oxygen tank and a chiropractor standing by. But then, when I think about it, you aren't that much younger than either Linda or me." Barbara felt herself color as Marcos, thankfully, let out a choked bellow. "I don't know what's wrong with me this morning. I can't believe I said that. Maybe I should head inside before I embarrass myself anymore."

"You speak the truth, as much as I hate to admit it," Marcos said. He stood and offered Barbara his hand. "I came in early to make a few phone calls, and I need to get on with it. The first call will be to our insurance agent to review the studio's liability insurance. Do you think you can be flexible with our lesson time today?"

"Absolutely," Barbara said, smiling at Marcos as he held the back door open. "If you find yourself running late, let me know. I have a few errands I can run. Text me if you don't find me in the ballroom." She gave Marcos a quick hug before he disappeared into his small office.

Barbara wandered into an empty ballroom. It was 10:15, but pro dancers were usually not morning people. Just when she settled into a corner café table and pulled a bottle of water out of her bag, Linda's voice signaled her arrival.

"Hi there, lady," Linda Wilson boomed as she crossed the floor. She balanced a cardboard Starbucks tray in one hand, while the opposite wrist carried the full weight of her dance-shoe bag and an oversized handbag.

Barbara gestured to the chair next to her and gratefully accepted one of the two Starbucks cups. She fought the temptation to shade her eyes at the brilliance of Linda's outfit. An electric-blue tunic fell over a flared skirt in complementary mixed shades of blue, and a gold-toned Turkish head shawl was folded over one shoulder. But it was the turquoise cat's-eye glasses that sent the whole look sailing over the high jump. On anyone else this outfit would be ridiculous, but on Linda it somehow screamed fashion-forward.

"I've already showed an impressive property in Sin Vacas this morning," Linda announced. "And I have a later appointment on a property in the Tucson Mountains foothills. Tucson's hottest realtor will more than deserve her dirty martini by happy hour." Linda tugged off the expensive shawl like it was an outlet-mall reject and tossed it over a chair.

Barbara raised her Starbucks coffee in a toast. Even when Linda tried to lower it an octave, her vivacious nature vibrated through her voice. Linda carefully chose a spot to place her venti Starbucks. She was prone to talking with her hands and accidents definitely happened.

"Getting together before our lessons was a great idea, Barb," Linda said.

Without warning, big band music blared out of the speakers. Barbara twisted around to see Brianna leading an older gentleman onto the floor. "Any bets he's a retired doctor unable to break his early-morning habit?" Barbara said.

Linda nodded. "One thing I want to ask right off the bat is this," Linda said, edging closer to Barbara. "Has Katherine been in touch with you lately? Did she call you at home?"

"Me? No." Barbara raised her voice enough to be heard over the music without threatening confidentiality. "Katherine's never called me at home. We rarely speak unless I'm in her office signing a contract or exchanging a quick hello in the ladies' room."

"I remember when Katherine was more of a presence in the

studio," Linda said. "She wasn't so withdrawn. No, not withdrawn, *unavailable* is a better word. But even then, aside from the normal pleasantries, we never had a real conversation. And, as you know, conversation with me is hard to avoid." Linda let loose a rumbling burst of laughter.

"So, tell me. What did Katherine want?" The ballroom was still relatively empty, but even with lowered voices, discretion was tough when Linda was involved.

"I'm still trying to figure it all out." Linda shrugged. "Katherine called late in the evening, and, frankly, she was rambling. She started in on me being a successful businesswoman and so loyal to the studio. That led to a rant about the disloyal students who betrayed her and left to follow Jeremy when he quit. Then she hit me with what she called a businesswoman-to-businesswoman proposition." Linda leaned back and folded her arms.

Barbara raised her eyebrows. The folded arms were an uncharacteristically guarded pose for gregarious Linda.

"So?" Barbara's chin tilted downward, her lips pursed.

"So," Linda said. She placed her hands on her thighs, straightened her back, and took a deep breath. "Katherine wanted to *honor me* with the first invitation to become a patron of the studio. She's starting a sponsorship program called something like Studio Angels. Sponsors get a marked parking space, a locker with a key, a ten-percent discount on all events, and—get this—VIP sponsors will have their names inscribed on a Plaque of Gratitude in the lobby. The perks will be dependent on, as Katherine put it, the level of patronage.

"Level of patronage?" Barbara sat bolt upright, her eyes glued to Linda's.

"There will be three levels of patronage: Silver, Gold, and Platinum, ranging from fifteen hundred to 10K or higher. The monies would go to professional coaching for the instructors, their competition costumes, and improvements to the studio, like more mirrors and new carpeting and possibly paving for the parking lot. She's still working out details."

"You have to be joking?" Barbara pushed herself back in her chair. She snapped her mouth shut, realizing it was hanging agape. "You mean to say the money we pay for lessons and events isn't sponsorship enough? Is she equating studio sponsorship with being a patron of the arts, like donating to a nonprofit ballet company or the symphony? The key word here is *nonprofit*. What on earth did you say to her?"

"For once, I was at a loss for words. I think the best way to handle this is to pretend it never happened. And, unless Joey brings it up, I won't. The whole thing—asking for patrons—implies the studio is cash poor, and you know what happens when instructors think their paychecks might be in jeopardy: they jump overboard before the ship sinks."

"And students stop signing contracts," Barbara said. "I don't want to lose this place, so I hope we're wrong about possible financial issues. Marcos has said nothing, so I'll take a wait-and-see attitude. I wonder if Katherine called anyone else?" Barbara leaned back in her chair, popped open the water bottle, and rested her heels on the chair next to Linda's. She took a sip of her water, then leaned forward to nudge Linda's arm.

"Who's that woman? The one who just came in the door? She looks like an aging retired madame. I know I shouldn't say things like that, but...." Barbara gave a little shrug.

"The ancient redhead?" Linda arched one eyebrow. "She's tough, all right, but she's no madame. I heard she fought her way up the Manhattan nightclub ladder in the '50s as a jazz singer, married well, and divorced even better. She owns two hot restaurants in Scottsdale and fifty-one percent of a major nightclub in New York. She's retired. Bought a home near Pima Canyon. I wish I'd been her realtor."

"Oh my," Barbara said, rolling her eyes. "The only thing you can ever assume about anyone around here is they have money, whether they earned it, inherited it, or married it. Otherwise they'd be hanging around a bowling alley, not a ballroom-dancing studio."

"Someone's in a mood today." Linda shook Barbara's arm and rolled out her rollicking, life's-a-hoot laugh.

"I am. I admit it," Barbara said. "I'm achy tired. Thank you for the coffee, by the way. We get sold on the glamor of ballroom dancing, but I feel more grandmotherly than glamorous."

"Since we're on the subject of money, grandmothers, and aging, let me tell you what my buttinsky kids recently pulled on me," Linda said. She folded her arms on the table and looked at Barbara over the top of her cat's-eye glasses.

"I'm all ears," Barbara said, head cocked to one side. The decibel level of the music in the ballroom was ear-splitting, forcing Barbara put her feet back on the floor and scoot her chair closer. She assumed Linda didn't want whatever she had to say to become studio gossip.

"The two of them, Brad and Sydney, presented me with an estimate of what they think I've spent on ballroom over the past few years. They were *concerned*." Linda took a deep swallow of her coffee.

Barbara decided to never get on Linda's bad side. Linda's eyes had narrowed and darkened to a blue, rivaling the color of a stormy sea.

"I was infuriated. But I calmly informed them I'm financially secure and have not incurred a penny of debt from my ballroom dancing, and if I had, it was none of their damn business. Then Brad started in on how he thinks Joey's a con artist who flatters me into opening my checkbook." Linda ran her hands across the nape of her neck. "Well, that did it." She shook her head and folded her arms. "I set them straight and didn't mince my words."

The ballroom was beginning to vibrate with voices. Someone had turned the music down, and Barbara could actually hear Linda's voice without straining.

"I informed my kids I'm too intelligent to take Joey's flattery and tomfoolery seriously and too tough to be bullied into spending money I don't want to spend. My relationship with Joey is warm, but it's also all business." Linda dusted her hands together. "Discussion over. This old lady will keep dancing until I'm good and ready to stop."

"Good for you," Barbara said.

"Can't you see me twenty years from now: an oxygen tank strapped to my back, a cane in one hand, and Katherine steadying my other hand to sign contracts?" Linda's laugh bellowed.

Barbara joined her, pleased their conversation could end on a lighter note. Joey was walking toward them, ready to gather Linda in for one of his big hugs.

~

Marcos Stephanos
1:30 p.m., Thursday, 22 October

"Barbara, I'm going to demonstrate the last part of the triple twinkle in our waltz, from the promenade to feather finish." Marcos paused. With a dramatic lift of his head and perfect dancer's posture, he made eye contact. He wanted Barbra's complete attention. Then he assumed the woman's body position in promenade and danced through the pattern. "Your footwork, Barbara, for the feather finish is heel-toe, toe-heel, toe-heel. Now you do it on your own."

"All right, I'll give it a try," Barbara said. She ran through the footwork, calling out her toe-heel combinations as she moved.

Marcos stood with his arms folded. As friendly as their relationship was, Marcos knew Barbara was still intimidated by his expertise on the dance floor. This afternoon he was blatantly using this edge to keep their lesson on track. He enjoyed Barbara's company, but she was paying him far too much per hour to waste floor time chatting. To move her forward quickly with her Silver patterns, he needed to be all business.

"Let's dance through what we have so far. We'll work in our triple twinkle to feather, fallaways, and end with our chair-to-slip-pivot." Marcos signaled to Jackson, who was checking the music queue, and gave him a thumbs-up for the waltz music.

"Okay, I'm ready," Barbara said.

Marcos was pleased to see Barbara's head already in left poise as she walked toward him, connecting her right hand with his left to accept his invitation to dance. He led her into an open left box. They swooped across the long side of the dance floor in perfect harmony.

"Barbara, I'm really pleased," Marcos said as they finished their last waltz pattern. "I was keeping an eye on you in the mirrors. Your sternum was raised and your neck stretched. You're learning to elongate your movements with good arm styling. Today you kept everything large and round, and you continued the movement—shoulder, elbow, wrist—all the way to your fingertips." Marcos took Barbara's hand as they walked to the edge of the dance floor.

"Thank you," Barbara said. "See, I actually do pay attention when you say too many intermediate Smooth dancers rush the steps because they are trying to dance on the beat."

"Exactly," Marcos replied. Barbara was a quick study and a joy to teach. He wished he had more students like her. "Remember when you learned your first Bronze waltz box and you were taught to move your feet on the beat: one, two, three; step back, step to the side, and close? Silver is continual movement, counting *one-and-ee-ah-o-two*, constantly stretching, extending, reaching, or rising and lowering throughout the count. One movement flows into the next. It's all about dancing between the beats."

"I'm happy you're seeing some improvement." A smile brought out a dimple in Barbara's cheek. "But the more I learn, the more I realize how much I still have to learn."

"It's a never-ending process for all of us," Marcos said, letting go of Barbara's hand as they reached the carpeted edge of the ballroom. He hiked one foot onto a café chair and smiled at his favorite student. "Next hour we'll work on your rumba choreography. I think you're going to find several similarities between the Smooth and the Rhythm dances."

"I would love to get as comfortable with the rumba, and maybe even mambo, as I am now with the waltz and foxtrot," Barbara said.

"Marcos." Jill's voice rang out. "Can you take a call? He says it's urgent." Jill stood at the entry to the ballroom, waving a handful of papers to get Marcos's attention.

"Who is it, Jill?" Marcos asked. He tried not to let his irritation show. Jill knew not to interrupt a lesson, and, really, did the girl have to shout across the ballroom?

"He said his name is Mr. Donovan, and he's with the bank."

"I'm not expecting a call. Take a message. I'll call him back as soon as I can," Marcos said. He walked closer to Jill so he could speak at a normal level. He hated having to shout. "Jill, what on earth is on your leg? Is that a bruise?" Jill wasn't wearing the ubiquitous pink cowboy boots today, and there was something greenish with a burst of yellow on her calf.

"What? Oh, I forgot to show you my new tattoo." Jill turned her foot, angling her calf.

"Oh my," Barbara said, moving closer as Jill beckoned. "Are those... daffodils?"

"Yup, they are. The tattoo guy said daffodils mean rebirth and new beginnings, so I got this one instead of the curling leaf I talked to you about. It's perfect, right, Barbara?"

"Well...I..." Barbara stammered.

"Barbara can take a closer look later, Jill. We have a lesson to finish, and you should get back to the front desk," Marcos said. It took an effort to keep his tone light.

Jill gave Marcos a thumbs-up and bounced into the hall, as flushed and happy as a teenager with her first cell phone.

Marcos turned and whispered to Barbara, "So, the money you gave Jill to help her out...how much do you suppose a colored tattoo costs these days?"

～

Katherine Carrington
9:30 p.m., Thursday, 22 October

Katherine cupped the mouse with her right hand. Her left elbow rested on the desk, fingers folded and smooshed against her mouth. Her aquiline nose was accentuated in the blue-white light of the computer screen. Katherine's focus was absolute. Her eyes burned in protest, begging to be closed, but she wasn't ready to call it a night. She reached for the vodka and splashed a little more into her tumbler.

It was time to get the creative wheels cranking. Monies in the Midwinter Ball account weren't needed until she locked in the reservation for the hotel's ballroom. She could pull money out of the tax account and put it back before quarterly taxes were due. The credit card they kept for visiting coaches could be used for office expenses. And then, if she skimmed a bit off the top of cash payments…yes… that would weave a nice little safety net.

Katherine pushed away from the screen and leaned back in her chair. She took a long, rejuvenating sip from her half-drained glass. Her eyes drifted closed. She hoped they weren't as bloodshot as they felt. Katherine's nose crinkled in distaste at the memory of her father's bloodshot eyes and whisky-laden breath. She was young when her parents divorced, but some images burn into your brain. Her sister's death sent her father into alcoholic oblivion, but she wasn't her father. Her situation was entirely different, just temporary stress. Between Jill's instability, her mother's house not selling, and snippy creditors, the vodka calmed her. Calm was good. She could set this bottle aside any time she chose.

Katherine shrugged, reached for the Ketel One and poured herself another double shot. She sipped and sighed. It was too damn bad that a pervasive lack of appreciation of her efforts was palpable among her staff. They had nothing to complain about, not one of them. And then Marcos got some kind of wild hair and went all managerial on her today. What was wrong with everyone? Mercury must be in retrograde or some stupid star out of alignment.

Katherine put her feet on her desk, crossed at the ankles. First Marcos extended an impulsive invitation to Michael, Barbara's son, to teach a class at the Halloween party. Did he forget the studio had to pay guest instructors more than staff instructors? That was bad enough, but then he tells her—tells her, not asks her—that he's seriously considering offering Michael a full-time position. Katherine's lips compressed. Her fingernails thrummed a staccato beat on the varnished walnut desk, her knee jiggling in opposition to the beat. Michael's dance credentials could attract advanced students, and he could charge for coaching, but still.

Katherine tightened and released her upper back muscles. She pulled the pins out of her hair and shook it loose. What a nightmare of a day. She'd dodged the bullet on making a decision about Michael, but then Marcos went ballistic about the studio's liability insurance lapsing—what was the big deal anyway when all students have to sign liability waivers? What a fuss.

Marcos didn't butt into the business end of the studio very often, but once he got started on a money roll he kept picking up steam, and that train needed to be derailed. She'd keep him out of the books for a day or two and then show him a spreadsheet with better numbers. Katherine glanced at her wristwatch. Enough was enough. Tomorrow promised to be a quieter day with half the studio volunteering to participate in some charity flash-mob event. Katherine pushed away from the desk and then pulled herself back in. She'd forgotten to remove her special red thumb drive. She ejected it safely and dropped it into the depths of her purse.

"I'm surrounded by idiots. Don't need to become one myself," Katherine muttered, as she closed all the tabs and powered her computer off. She disliked feeling so tired and dragged out. Life was a bitch lately. On top of Marcos questioning her like she couldn't be trusted and dealing with ungrateful employees, the price of her favorite vodka kept rising. This sluggish economy was to blame for the uncomfortable position she was in. The one light spot in her life right now was the cats. Two new fosters arrived yesterday, and she could enjoy the hell out of them until they found forever homes. Cats she understood. People, not so much.

Tumbler in hand, Katherine strolled to the ballroom. It always fell to her to make sure the last one out remembered to turn off the lights. The lights were off but the ceiling fans were still on. "No one around here considers the electric bill," Katherine said, switching the fans off.

She raised the cut-crystal glass to the mirrors in a sardonic parody of a toast, watched herself finish her drink, and then placed the tumbler on a café table. A few stray chairs needed to be pushed under their respective tables before she could lock up for the night.

From a café table at the edge of the ballroom, the multifaceted crystal tumbler reflected light from the hall, and dozens of yellow sparks of fire danced across the mirrors. As Katherine turned the hall light out, the prisms dimmed and settled into darkness.

TEN

LET THE GAMES BEGIN

Marcos Stephanos
9:00 a.m., Friday, 23 October

Marcos manually flipped the switch on the Krups to override Katherine's autotimer. His headache was pounding nails into his brain, and he needed coffee now. Arms crossed, he willed the burbling coffeemaker to chew the beans and brew faster. One of his mother's favorite clichés crept in from nowhere: a watched pot never boils. "Screw it. Patience has never been my strong suit," Marcos muttered. He grabbed a mug to place directly under the flow, but the shrill ring of the office phone cut through the quiet of the empty lobby.

"Who the hell turned the ringer full on?" Marcos said. The still-empty coffee mug dangled from one finger.

Marcos cringed as the voice boomed, "This message is for Katherine Carrington. This is Mr. Donovan at Security National Bank. Before I can authorize a business loan, Ms. Carrington, I need to see two sources of repayment. Cash flow from the business as well as a secondary source, such as collateral—"

"Hello," Marcos said, grabbing the receiver, interrupting the message. "Mr. Donovan, this is Marcos. I'm so sorry. I apologize for not getting back to you yesterday. I'm afraid Katherine's running late this morning. Might I be able to help you?"

"Yes, of course, Mr. Stephanos. I've been dealing with Ms. Carrington on this loan request, but I'm not sure she understands the difference between equity financing and debt financing. There isn't enough equity in the building to qualify for the type of loan—"

"Pardon me for interrupting, but I've been preoccupied lately, and I'm out of the loop. Can you please bring me up to speed on when Katherine requested this loan?"

"Certainly. Ms....uh...Katherine spoke with me a couple of days ago. I tried to explain that when a company has a high proportion of debt to equity, I advise thinking about increasing ownership capital, or equity investment, for additional funds. Now, of course, we can review past financials to analyze cash flow, but—"

"Thank you, Mr. Donovan, but I think it would be best if I came by to review our accounts in person. Is it possible for you to squeeze me in today?" Marcos chewed his lip. "Yes. I can be there. Thank you." Marcos folded his right arm across his torso and rubbed the back of his left hand across his chin. The ceramic mug, still dangling from his right hand, clicked against his belt buckle.

"Hey there. I thought I smelled coffee," Paige said, bouncing into the lobby, "but I didn't see any cars out back. The door was unlocked, though, and the alarm wasn't set."

"Good morning, Paige." Marcos plastered a congenial smile on his face. "I parked out front and unlocked the back door. What brings you in before ten?" Paige absentmindedly separated long strands of hair from her ponytail and coiled them around her index finger.

"Well," Paige said, letting go of her hair, "with half the instructors and students out for one reason or another today, I thought I'd get in some practice time. And, since I found the breakroom a mess a few minutes ago, I'm volunteering myself to tidy it."

"Good girl. That's the team spirit I love to see." Marcos kept his voice chipper. "I came in early to clear off my desk, but my plans have changed. I have to head out in a few minutes. I'll be gone for a couple of hours but back in time to teach my afternoon lessons. Speaking of...don't you have a lesson on the books with your wedding couple later today?"

"I do, yes. Pretty sure they are scheduled for three this afternoon."

"Okay, then," Marcos said. He slapped his hand on the counter to emphasis it was time to get moving and turned back to the colorful Mexican-tiled table that held the Krups. "I need coffee pronto before I do anything." He filled his mug to the brim with the aromatic, strong coffee and took a careful sip of the steaming brew.

"Walk with me to the main ballroom." Marcos motioned toward the hall. He reached into his pocket and handed Paige a thumb drive. "There's a list of songs on this drive I'd like you to add into the main queue. Fit them in by dance category, please. I promise it won't take too long. You'll still have plenty of time to practice. Oh, by the way, you might want to use the rehearsal hall and leave the main ballroom available for Tony and Sylvie. They should be running through their routines later this morning."

"No problema," Paige said. She peered into the unlit ballroom. "Man, when the overhead lights are off and the curtains are drawn, this place is haunted-house creepy."

"Well, then, let's break the spell with some magic," Marcos said. He flipped on the switch for the lighted mirror ball. Silver and gold light fragmented across the ballroom.

"Marcos, what's that?" A glint of light twinkled from a nearby café table. Paige walked closer. "It's a fancy, cut-crystal tumbler." She reached for it and held it to her nose. "Yuck. Smells like stale booze, but who would be drinking in here?"

Marcos flipped on the main lights and was beside Paige in five huge strides. He took the tumbler away from her and held it to his nose.

"I'll take care of this, Paige. Please keep this to yourself, okay?" Marcos put down his coffee cup and placed his free hand over the top of the glass to stifle the stale alcohol smell. Without even a goodbye, he turned and left Paige standing alone. As he reached the hall, he heard Paige mutter, "What just happened?"

~

Paige Russell
10:30 a.m., Friday, 23 October

Paige hovered over the drinking fountain outside the main ballroom. As she gulped back the bubbling water, she tilted her head the slightest bit so she could follow Tony's every move reflected in the wall mirrors. The staccato beat of Tony's Cuban heels reverberated across the floorboards. Mr. Machismo was *on* this morning, his movements precise and powerful. His white shirt was open, and the elaborate gold cross he never took off was lustrous against his spray-tanned body. Paige could see the sheen of sweat on his chest. Tony oozed male Latin-dancer perfection. Yeah, Tony could be a total pain in the ass, but he was still sexy as hell. The trick was to make sure he didn't know that's what she thought.

She'd never seen a dancer embody the passion of the paso doble like Tony. Back arched, chin high, teeth bared in a matador's snarl, he swept a muscled arm backward and swirled an imaginary cape. He stopped mid-step to appraise his line in the mirror. The sudden silence caught Paige off guard, and she raised her head. With a wicked thrust of his pelvis, he winked at the reflection of Paige's wide-eyed stare. Tony grabbed his sweat towel and strode across the empty ballroom.

Flustered, Paige thrust her face back into the water fountain, gulping back water like a drought survivor. *Please, God, let him walk past me.*

"Paige?" Tony's voice was close to her ear. Her brain froze. She prayed to St. Jude—the patron saint of lost causes—for a sophisticated, witty quip. But her plea went unanswered.

Paige spun, water droplets flying off her chin, creating a perfect arc in the air. A delicate spray of water hit Tony and dribbled across his chest.

"Hey, sweetness, I took a shower already." Tony steadied Paige with a firm grip on her shoulder, and dabbed at her dripping chin with a corner of his towel. The scent of clean male sweat mingled with a delicious spicy aftershave muddled her senses.

"Paige," Tony said, lightly massaging her shoulder as he spoke. "I was about to say, before you drowned out my words, that I'm heading to the costume room."

Tony's melting-chocolate voice made Paige weak-kneed. She felt herself flush under his touch, his words not completely registering on her brain's receptors.

"Paige." He repeated her name, gently but firmly, like a parent waking a drowsy child.

Tony's lips twitched at the corners. He seemed to enjoy her discomfort. Was it that obvious? Paige raised her face to meet Tony's eyes.

"Our custom Latin costumes arrived late last night. Even Sylvie hasn't seen them yet, and she won't be in for quite a while," Tony said. He placed a practiced finger under Paige's delicate chin and tilted her head back.

Tony's eyes immobilized her. His pupils were dilated, and she felt like she could see into the depths of his soul. The frightened-rabbit feeling melted away. Trust replaced trepidation.

Tony smiled. He leaned forward and, in a conspirator's whisper, said, "Would you like to be the first to see them?"

Paige nodded. The nod was involuntary.

"Follow me." Tony was already walking down the hall to the staff dressing room.

"The new costumes!" Paige finally found her voice as she trotted obediently behind Tony. "Yes. I'd love to see them, Tony." She couldn't believe her luck. She was going to be the first one to see Tony and Sylvie's much-talked-about competitive outfits. Knowing Sylvie, hers for sure would be super gorgeous. She felt like a dazed groupie. Paige glanced at her reflection as they passed mirrored walls. The false eyelashes were a bear to put on, but between the eyelashes and the makeup Brianna was teaching her to apply, she was beginning to look like she belonged in the glamorous world of ballroom dance pros.

In the dressing room, one long table was strewn with makeup cases, magnifying mirrors on stands, hair ornaments, thread and needles to sew the ornaments into place, and an assortment of brushes and combs. Tony drew Paige behind a large, curtained-off changing area where the costumes were stored. He tossed his sweat-dampened towel onto a chair. Two racks of sequined, beaded dresses stood next to a shorter rack of men's stretchy dance pants, shirts, and vests. On the wall, large hooks held two opaque garment bags: magnets to Paige's steel. She shot Tony a questioning look. He nodded his permission.

Paige unzipped the bag closest to her. It held a man's costume. The nearly transparent silver-gray shirt had small ruffles in the front, defining the deep V-cut. Paige stroked the fabric, picturing Tony's ripped, tanned chest exposed by the neckline. She carefully zipped up the garment bag. She hesitated for a fraction of a second in front of the second garment bag, but once her finger touched the zipper, she couldn't unzip it fast enough.

"Ohhhhh," she sighed. The dress was the most exquisite thing she had ever seen. Her fingertip cautiously traced a line on the heavily beaded stretch fabric of Sylvie's Latin costume. The dress sparkled like a Christmas ornament in candlelight. Along with the beading, the dress was studded with hundreds of silvery Swarovski crystals. She felt her eyes dampen with tears of pure longing.

"Try it on, sweetness," Tony urged, pointing at the changing screen.

Paige hesitated, torn between temptation and uncertainty.

"You can trust me. Live a little, have some fun," Tony said. "Would I ever steer you wrong?" He placed open palms over his heart. "It's okay, Paigey girl. Sylvie won't care, and, if you're quick, she won't ever know. Go." Tony reached around Paige and released the delicate costume from the confines of the garment bag. He motioned her toward the changing screen.

Paige's reluctance evaporated as quickly as children's tears when they get their way. She snatched the hanger from Tony and disappeared behind the screen, the dress a white comet's tail trailing behind her. Her practice clothes fell to the floor, and she stepped into the confection of a costume, tugging hard to force a fit around her midriff and breasts. Paige was taller and at least one dress size bigger than Sylvie, and her breasts certainly didn't need padding.

She slipped out from behind the screen and stood in front of the mirror, open-mouthed and speechless at her transformation. She felt Tony's eyes graze her body. His possessive stare sent a tremor down her spine. The design of the dress bared one arm; the other was encased in a translucent, crystal-covered, silky sleeve. She felt her face warming and was tempted to cross her arms over her chest. The padded bra presented Paige's mounded breasts like an offering to the gods. She had never seen herself this way. Diamond-shaped cutouts revealed her taut tummy. She flicked her hips, sending the skirt's ten inches of fringe swinging.

"Come here." Tony's radio-announcer voice had gone husky. He pulled Paige into a close dance frame and began to lead her into a sensuous Latin rumba. He led Paige through a hip-snapping spiral turn and then out into a flirtatious Cuban walk. The beaded fringe flew around Paige's hips. She draped one arm over her head, running her hand down her side in an imitation of Sylvie's seductive arm styling. She felt sexy and powerful and more confident than she had ever felt in all the twenty-four years of her life.

The heavy drapes snapped open. Metallic curtain rings clanged against the steel curtain rod as Sylvie loomed in front of the startled dancers. The sensuous scene shuddered to a stop.

"What the fucking hell?" Sylvie's storm-cloud blue eyes radiated waves of palpable fury. Her tiny five-foot-three frame stretched tall, like a wildcat making itself larger to terrify its prey. "Paige. You scheming little bitch. And I was actually starting to like you." Sylvie's acrylic fingernails flashed in front of Paige's face—weapons designed to slash and maim.

"Oh my God, Sylvie," Paige whimpered, backing away. She

wrapped her arms protectively across her exposed breasts. "Please, please don't be mad. I'm so sorry. I didn't mean any harm. The dress was so beautiful, and Tony..." Paige turned pleading eyes to her Mr. Machismo dance hero.

"You son-of-a-bitch-in-heat," Sylvie shrieked at Tony. Her eyes narrowed to tigress slits, her face a mask of pure rage. "That's *my* 3,000-dollar costume you let this little nothing squeeze her fat ass into."

Sylvie lunged at Paige. Paige felt the tips of Sylvie's fingers slip through her ponytail.

"Sylvie, no, NO!" Tony yelled, springing in front of Paige. Sylvie cannonballed into his chest, and he staggered off balance. Her nails grazed his cheekbone.

Swifter than a striking scorpion, Sylvie drew back her hand and smacked Tony across the face. His head snapped to the left. Artfully tousled hair flew back off his forehead, revealing a purplish stain close to his hairline where black hair dye left its telltale mark. Tony raised a protective arm. Paige tried to dodge out of the way, but realized too late this gave Sylvie the opening she needed to dart around Tony. Sylvie's nails dug hard into Paige's bare arm. Paige yelped, and hot tears of shock trickled from the corners of her eyes.

"Get it off, you stupid bitch!" Sylvie screamed, shaking Paige by the arm and yanking at the clear plastic strap across the back of the delicate costume.

Paige wrenched free of Sylvie's grip and darted toward the changing screen to wriggle out of the clinging dress as quickly as she could. Sylvie dove after her, catching one long fingernail in the delicate beading of the costume's bodice. Paige's stomach dropped at the sickening sound of stitches ripping. Crystal beads clattered onto the hard wood floor, bouncing and scattering.

A dreadful, deafening silence filled the room, only broken by the gasping intake of Paige's breath, followed by Sylvie's wounded-animal howl, punctuated by Mr. Machismo's retreating footsteps.

~⌇

Marcos Stephanos
1:30 p.m., Friday, 23 October

"To quote your very British mother, Katherine, bloody hell!" Marcos stopped pacing and dropped into the chair opposite Katherine's desk. He slapped his hands on his thighs and, shaking his head, focused on the opposite wall. He took a deep, steadying breath and turned his gaze back to Katherine. "What was Tony thinking? Thank the gods this fiasco didn't happen on a busy day within earshot of our clientele."

"I know. It could have been much worse," Katherine said, drumming a pen against her cheek. "I had just come in, and I could hear the hullaballoo all the way from the front office. I caught Tony as he was bolting down the hall like the devil was after him. It took me fifteen minutes to calm Sylvie, and, by the time I got everyone's side of the story, I was so infuriated I sent the lot of them home. I was ready to call you when you walked in the door. Between dealing with Jill and this, my stress level is over the top."

"Jill? What's Jill done now?" Marcos asked.

"I really think this marriage thing has derailed her, and I suspect she might be dipping her hand in the till," Katherine said. She rubbed her lower lip and looked sideways at Marcos.

"Dipping into the till? What the hell are you talking about, Katherine?" Marcos opened his hands in a give-me-a-break gesture.

"We'll discuss Jill later," Katherine said, with a dismissive wave of her hand. "For now we have to decide what disciplinary action to take with Tony and Paige. Aside from telling Paige to stay home until I called her, I haven't decided exactly how to handle this dress situation." Katherine folded her arms. "Tony is at fault, of course, but he's a major moneymaker for the studio, as is Sylvie. It's a no-contest if someone has to go. You need to understand that." Katherine leaned forward, resting her folded forearms on her desk. Marcos met her gaze. "We don't have a huge investment in Paige as yet, and, if the girl is going to be trouble, maybe we should cut our losses now. I need your unbiased input on this one, Marcos."

Marcos rubbed his forehead. His thoughts were pinging like an out-of-control pinball machine. First, Katherine tried to take out a loan behind his back, then insinuates Jill might be tucking cash payments into her pocket, and next talks about letting Paige go. What the hell was happening? Marcos cleared his throat, started to speak, and stopped. Katherine raised an eyebrow. Her scrutiny made him acutely aware of his body language. He shifted in his seat, blinked to control an eye twitch, and forced his shoulders down from his ears. Clearing his throat again, he leaned forward, his arms on Katherine's polished walnut desktop. His stomach clenched. He badly needed a reboot to this day.

"Okay, here's what I think, at least for the moment," Marcos said. "Let's bring Tony and Sylvie back in on Monday. They can't lose practice time before the competition. We'll call Paige on Monday and tell her to come in on Tuesday for a meeting with all parties. This gives us time to get our ducks in a row. Are we agreed on the time frame?"

Katherine nodded at Marcos to continue. She was fiddling with her pen, flipping it back and forth between her index and middle finger.

"Okay." Marcos took a deep breath. "Sylvie can go back to her normal teaching schedule right away. But Tony...you know Tony is going to be remorseful for about two seconds before he bounces back to being Tony the Superstar. The only way to get through to Tony is to hit him over the head, and that means in the wallet. So, for the next week, he can come in to the studio for run-throughs with Sylvie, but that's it. Joey, Jackson, and I can cover his students. Tony will lose the income from those lessons. He still has to work the Halloween party on Friday, though, and lead a workshop." Marcos leaned back and folded his arms.

"So, what about Paige?" Katherine said. She moved toward the edge of her chair and stared, unblinking, at Marcos. He felt like he was under the vigilant eye of a bird of prey.

"Paige is another story," Marcos said. "The girl is surprisingly naïve for her age and new to this business. I see her as being as much the victim here as Sylvie, but I'll think of something appropriate. Paige has to understand the seriousness of what she's done and also the sheer stupidity of her actions. I'm not in favor of letting her go, Katherine. She has too much potential," Marcos said, striving to sound firm and unemotional. "Right now Sylvie is our top priority. We have to do whatever it takes for her dress to be repaired as good as new. Agreed?"

"Agreed. But…" Katherine dropped her pen. It rolled across the desktop and fell to the floor. Katherine widened her eyes as she slid her hand across the desk, stopping short of Marcos's hand. "This debacle has coincided with a tiny, little, cash-flow issue. Nothing to worry about—"

"Please tell me you're not suggesting we can't cover the cost of mending Sylvie's dress? Exactly what do you mean by a tiny cash-flow issue?" Marcos knew from sad experience that the more innocent Katherine's expression and the wider her smile, the deeper the doo-doo she was about to pile on. And he hadn't forgotten about his discussions with the bank manager.

"Marcos," Katherine said. She dragged the syllables of his name out to a lilt, sounding more like *Marr-coossss*. She lowered her chin and looked at him through thick false eyelashes with what he could only construe as an intimate, teasing expression—one he hadn't seen in a very long time. In spite of himself, he felt his breath quicken. His involuntary salute to her powerful femininity began to muddle his thinking.

"Please don't blow this cash-flow issue out of proportion. It's truly minor and nothing for you to be concerned about." Katherine spoke with a smile in her voice and a toss of her shiny brunette hair, which she wore loose today. The ripple of gentle waves softened her face, dropping years off her personal calendar. "It's that, well, I was in such a hurry to clear my desk, I paid several bills at once. I don't know what I was thinking."

Marcos smiled. When Katherine put her mind to it, she could make herself sound like a maiden in distress in a 1930s film. He sighed. He thought he was long past the sucker stage.

"It's all a matter of timing, Marcos. I'm waiting on a couple of large payments from students to plump the account. It's a temporary issue, believe me. Temporary. Do you think you could be our white knight one more time and cover this little expense until we're clear?" Katherine stood and, leaning on one hand, tugged playfully on Marcos's sleeve to emphasis her words. "You really will save the day."

Marcos shook his head and gave in to the smile he'd been struggling to hold in check. The woman knew how to work him. Always had. His defenses crumbled.

"Oh, and I called and rescheduled Paige's wedding couple, Nikki and Brandon. They'll come on Monday to work with you. Brandon sounded very pleased at the chance to work with the Dance Master," Katherine said, radiating flattery.

"Okay, okay, you win. Tell me how much to write the check for to cover Sylvie's dress, and I'll give the wedding kids their lesson on Monday." Marcos said. He swallowed and pulled at the tip of his nose. He'd always given in to Katherine's pleas, and she knew it. Why should this time be any different? He pushed his chair back to stand and, with a heavy sigh, turned to leave.

"I'm going to walk the half-block to Starbucks, Katherine," he said, on his way out of her office. "I need the air to clear my head as much as I need one of their double-espresso Americanos."

ELEVEN

BUSINESS IS BUSINESS

Katherine Carrington
10:00 a. m., Monday, 26 October

Katherine pushed the heavy glass door partway open with her backside. Her purse was tucked under one arm, and a Macy's shopping bag dangled heavily from one wrist. Between her hands she balanced a huge tray covered in plastic wrap.

"Can someone get this bloody door for me before I drop everything?"

Jill jumped around the reception counter. "I've got it," she said, stretching her arms around the tray before it tumbled out of Katherine's grasp.

"Take the tray into the breakroom, Jill." Katherine adjusted the angle of the shopping bag and, with one hand against the doorframe, regained both her balance and her composure. "Make sure the pastries stay tightly covered to keep them fresh. Actually, it probably doesn't matter. The vultures around here will consume anything," Katherine said, turning her attention to the contents of her shopping bag.

"Yes, ma'am," Jill replied. The heavily laden tray wobbled in her arms.

"Hey, Jill, wait a second," Marcos called out from the hallway. "What's that you have?"

"Marcos, you are the worst vulture of all," Katherine chided. "You can smell sugar a mile away. I stopped at Mother's assisted living home. Evidently they hosted some sort of breakfast open house, and there were scads of Danish and doughnuts left over. I helped myself to a tray. As my mother was fond of saying, 'Waste not, want not.'"

"Since we're running short-staffed today, the extra carbs will keep us going," Marcos said.

Katherine shook her head as she watched Marcos follow Jill, knowing he'd return with his plate piled high. She unlocked her office and dropped her purse and shopping bag beside the desk. Maybe she'd actually indulge in a pastry or two this morning. Visiting with her mother left her craving comfort food. Katherine booted up the computer and folded her arms. Her mother knew how to keep the crap coming. This morning she'd started in on how Katherine never should have left Paul. Dementia had erased the ugly truth. Even after all these years, Katherine felt her face burn when she thought about how Paul-the-philanderer left her for a cliché: a young, busty cocktail waitress. The public humiliation still stung.

The computer chirped to life. Her desktop icons popped up. They were strategically placed to show off the wallpaper: a collage of foster-cat photos. Her thoughts drifted back to Paul. In retrospect, maybe learning about his affair was the best thing that could have happened. It gave her a legitimate out from a marriage that was slowly strangling her.

Paul was a complete control freak who'd kept her on a choke chain. How could someone so passionately private feel justified in reading his wife's personal emails and then berate her for emailing her best friend to vent? And he monitored every penny she spent, even checked the mileage on her car to calculate gas expenses, and then he'd question her about where she went. Paul worked on the assumption that women were weak and, for most men, a wedding ring was a challenge. The relationship scales always tipped heavily in Paul's favor. In the end, she probably came out on top. Katherine felt vindicated when his cocktail waitress floozy left him after five years for someone with more money, and two years later Paul died of undetected prostate cancer. Served him right. She'd never even shed one tear.

Katherine kicked off her shoes. There'd been a few men after Paul, but nothing long term, and certainly no one in a long time. She sighed and stopped herself short from chewing on a loose cuticle. She had to admit she missed the fun of an occasional hot romp between the sheets. At this point in her life she didn't need complications, but some no-strings-attached, uncomplicated sex wouldn't be unwelcome.

"Hey there," Marcos said, popping his head around the door. He slid a plate laden with sugary confections onto Katherine's desk. "Might as well plan tomorrow's meeting over pastries. But before we get started, I'm going to need coffee."

"You know, pastries sound good to me today," Katherine said. "Would you mind grabbing my cup and bringing me a coffee as well?" Heavy-duty sugary carbs weren't a bad second to sex. She'd take what self-indulgence she could get.

Katherine's fingers played over the tray of goodies before settling on a powdered chocolate-filled doughnut. Her mind was still a not-so-merry-go-round of memories, and she couldn't seem to jump off the carousel. After she married Paul, she soon learned that a sadistic streak lurked under his veneer of charm. From the beginning of their marriage he misused the privilege of intimacy. In public, he trotted out all his spouse's little private quirks—all the flaws, fears, and embarrassing moments that are privy only to one's partner. For Paul, Katherine's foibles were fodder to fuel his impromptu comedy routines for friends and colleagues. When her mortification showed, Paul jeered that she was overly sensitive and took things too seriously. He enjoyed saying cruel things to her under the guise of teasing. If she didn't take the abuse with a smile, he accused her of not having a sense of humor. Katherine took a huge bite out of her doughnut.

"Katherine, you have powdered sugar on your chin," Marcos teased. He set two brimming coffee mugs on her desk. "It's a good look on you, but...." He hand her a Kleenex.

Katherine swiped at her chin and glanced sideways at Marcos. "Gone?"

"Yup. Good job. Pass me one of those cream cheese Danish things, please," Marcos said. He put his feet on her desk.

"Really, Marcos," Katherine said. Marcos winked. The man was incorrigible.

"I promise to wipe off any dirty smudges," he replied. "So, I checked today's schedule to make sure Paige's students, Nikki and Brandon, are on for this afternoon." Marcos took a good bite or two of his pastry before continuing. "I've watched Paige with these two, and they sure don't seem to be a match made in heaven."

"I'm not sure there is such a thing," Katherine said. "I've known you long enough to remember your glory days. You used to brag about bailing out of more than one woman's bedroom window in the wee hours of the morning. Didn't sound like any of those married ladies found their match made in heaven, either, unless they foolishly believed it might be you."

"Now that really would have been foolish," Marcos said through a mouthful of Danish.

"On a more serious note," Katherine said, "do you think the ruckus with the dress is going to sidetrack Sylvie's focus in the competition? She's hell-bent on placing in the top three."

"Maybe you could talk with her this week," Marcos said. "You have the best rapport with Sylvie. Remind her you don't have to like your partner to make magic happen on the floor. If she cold-shoulders Tony and there's no chemistry, it will show in their dancing."

"Honestly, Marcos, I'm more concerned about them being able to work together on a daily basis. Sylvie is a big asset to the studio, and I don't want to lose her."

"Neither do I." Marcos slipped his feet off the desk and sat upright in his chair.

"By the way, I called Paige about being here by noon tomorrow. All three of them have now been notified of the meeting," Katherine said. She kept her eyes on Marcos. "I'm going to take the lead tomorrow, Marcos, and we have to show a united front. Understood?"

"I'm with you, Katherine," Marcos said.

His tone was upbeat enough, but the look on his face gave Katherine the impression that the buttery pastry he'd just consumed had turned to a lump of raw dough in his stomach.

~

Marcos Stephanos
1:00 p.m., Monday, 26 October

Marcos sat at the café table closest to the ballroom's entrance, finishing his coffee. Even after a brisk walk to Starbucks and back, he was crashing from a sugar overload. He crimped the rim of his cardboard cup with a fingernail. Chatting with Katherine this morning had been like spending time with the old Katherine, back when she was fun. He should have directly addressed the issue of how to deal with Paige, but at the time he didn't want to ruin the moment. Sometimes avoidance was the best path. But what if Katherine took a hard line at tomorrow's meeting? He sloshed the last dregs of coffee back and forth in the mutilated cup. He was more than a little surprised at how disturbed he was when Katherine suggested letting Paige go.

Marcos ran a hand through his thick, silver-tinged hair. What was wrong with him? Right now, when he should be concerned about Sylvie's agitation over the ruined dress, he was more concerned about Paige sitting at home fretting about losing her job. On Friday he'd come close to hitting her name on his contacts list and calling. He usually shied away from needy women, but this girl definitely brought out his protective side and an unfamiliar possessiveness. He could sense a deep longing in Paige, but for what he wasn't sure. She was still mourning the loss of her mother, but could she be recovering from a broken relationship as well? Marcos became conscious of one leg furiously jiggling. He placed a hand on his thigh to physically quell the movement.

He had to admit he found Paige damn attractive, and, unless he was misreading the signs, she seemed to be equally attracted to him. There was the age difference to consider, but the difference could actually be a plus. Paige's naïvety and lack of life experience provided moldable, raw material. The more time he spent with her, the more he knew that what he needed was exactly that: more. He needed time to figure out where this was going, whatever *this* might be. Or, did he want it to go anywhere? The simplest way to deal with this whole line of thought was to think about something else.

Marcos deposited what was left of his coffee cup in the trash. He had to get his mind back on track. He had to make sure Sylvie didn't run to Katherine before the meeting, adding fuel to the "Fire Paige" hot spot. Tomorrow he'd seek her out and make sure to validate her feelings, and let her know she was their top priority. He had to get that situation under control pronto. But, before he could ponder any longer, Brandon and Nikki appeared at the entrance to the ballroom, their dance shoes already on.

"So, I hear we're your next victims today," Brandon said with his wide, trusting grin. He landed a pulled punch on Marcos's shoulder.

Marcos rolled his shoulder back as if injured. "Don't want to mess with a cowboy with roping muscles, so I'd better do a good job." With a wave of his hand, he invited the couple to sit. "Paige is working with you on a foxtrot, correct?"

"Yeah, a foxtrot," Brandon said. Nikki rummaged in her purse, pulled out a compact, and reapplied her lipstick.

"So, how about if you show me what you've learned. Dance to the count first, and then you can try it to the music you've chosen. Paige told me you plan to dance to one of Nikki's father's old favorites, Frank Sinatra's 'Summer Wind.'"

Brandon stood and extended a hand to Nikki, which she rejected. She tucked her long blond hair behind her ears and gracefully rose from her chair.

Marcos folded his arms and arranged his features in a thoughtful pose as they began to work through their patterns. Brandon counted out loud. Foxtrot would not have been Marcos's first choice, especially Silver-level foxtrot. It was jazzy, but flowing movements and off-the-beat counts took a high degree of skill to do well. Paige had mentioned Nikki thought Bronze foxtrot was too boring. Within minutes it was clear these two were lacking the partnership skills required to pull off this dance. They needed something easier, more upbeat, and maybe even something they could do without having to be in each other's arms. Nikki came close to knocking both of them over trying to back-lead Brandon through a pivot. Instead of reaching out to steady her partner, Nikki continued to force the movement.

"Let's stop for a minute," Marcos said. "I don't see smiles. Are you guys having fun?"

Nikki folded her arms. She assumed a one-hip-out, defiant stance and gave her fiancé what Marcos could only interpret as a classic ice-princess, freeze-you-to-death glare. Brandon looked hangdog and sad.

"Okay, then. Nikki, if you can be flexible with your music choice, I'll show you a dance you can have some fun with. Remember, you are learning a routine for your wedding reception, not a memorial service. You want to look joyful," Marcos said. He forced a smile he didn't feel. "Let me show you a nightclub two-step. It can be danced to songs like 'Because of You' or 'Lady in Red' or 'Glory of Love.' You can use a very relaxed hold and create lots of graceful, shaping actions. Okay?"

"Sounds good to me," Brandon said.

"Maybe you can actually learn to lead this one," Nikki jabbed.

"Both of you watch while I demonstrate the basic footwork," Marcos said. He tried not to grit his teeth at Nikki's caustic comment.

"The leader's left foot slides to the side, weight is transferred, the right foot slides behind the left foot, takes weight in a sort of rock step, and the left foot then slides in front, across the body, and takes weight. The count is *slow, quick-quick*. It's rinse-and-repeat in the opposite direction."

Marcos took Nikki by the hand and faced her. "Keep the movement soft and glide by bending your knees. Slide your foot along the floor. I'll lead you through it. Brandon, you watch what we do and tell us what you think." Marcos expertly led Nikki through the basics, trying all the while to encourage her to follow. He now understood her fiancé's frustration. The woman wanted to be in charge.

"Nikki, a follower has to give over control, trust the leader, be sensitive to his cues, and follow his center. You have to turn off your thinking and stop second-guessing. Your only job is to follow." They danced two more basics.

"Now we're going to add more movement, turning clockwise. This keeps the dance from becoming boring while the couple remains in one place. I'll lead Nikki through an underarm turn, like so." Marcos stopped and bowed to Nikki. "Well, Brandon, what do you think?"

"I like the look of this dance," Brandon said. "I think we could master this and look really good on the dance floor together."

"I think so, too," Marcos replied. He gave Brandon an encouraging pat on the back. What Marcos didn't say was he doubted Nikki could surrender control long enough to follow Brandon through even a two-minute wedding dance. Many years as a dance instructor showed Marcos that partnership dancing boiled down personality characteristics to a strong concentration and narrowed one's field of vision. Negative traits, which otherwise might be glossed over, became glaringly obvious.

Brandon excused himself to visit the men's room, and Nikki immediately turned to Marcos. Her eyes were narrowed and bright with blame.

"You, I can dance with," she said, "but I'm not sure Brandon is ever going to make a good dance partner. I'm beginning to wonder if he is going to turn out to be as awkward in bed as he is on the dance floor. The man has no finesse at all. I can't figure out what he wants me to do, and you can't expect me to follow him blindly."

Nikki's little-girl whine grated on Marcos's nerves, but he froze his features into a placating smile and continued to listen and nod. No way was he getting in the middle of this one. He was a dance instructor, not a marriage counselor. He walked Nikki back to their table as she continued to vent.

"Brandon and I are *off*, and not only on the dance floor." Nikki folded her arms across her chest and made a sour-lemon face. "Our whole relationship is fight and make up. He never listens to me. Taking dance lessons might not have been such a great idea for us."

Brandon bounced back into the room before Marcos had to fill air space with a trite, noncommittal reply. This couple reminded Marcos of why he stayed out of the marriage game.

~

Katherine Carrington
5:30 p.m., Monday, 26 October

Barbara and Ed were having a tête-à-tête at a side table. "So what do you two have your heads together over?" Katherine plastered a charming smile on her face. She was shrewd enough to tread lightly with her core clients, especially in light of Edward not warming to her idea of them spending time together outside of the studio. He'd come around eventually, but until then she needed to keep him happy and spending.

"Well, we met this evening to practice our Smooth routine but got sidetracked. I was telling Edward how we should collaborate on an article or a class aimed at high school juniors," Barbara said. "We could call it Life Lessons 101."

"Sounds like a great title," Katherine responded, one arm wrapped across her torso. Her fingernails bit into her upper arm. "What sort of life lessons would you cover?"

"Well," Barbara responded, her eyes bright with enthusiasm, "maybe a sort of practical survival guide to handling money."

"The secret to accumulating wealth is spending less than you earn," Edward interjected. Katherine smiled and nodded, but in reality she couldn't have cared less.

"I'd also cover the basics of filling out a loan or job application," Barbara said, leaning forward in her enthusiasm, "making a good impression during an interview, and…"

Katherine fixed a smile on her face and waited for Barbara's mouth to stop moving.

"Well, okay, then," Katherine said. She hoped her eyes weren't visibly glazed over. She wished to God she'd kept on walking. "I'll leave you two to your mission to save our youth from the school of hard knocks while I get some real work done." Katherine softened her words with a charming smile directed at Edward. Surely he could see how sappy Barbara was?

Katherine strode across the dance floor and stepped onto the raised platform where the sound system was housed. She'd write notes on music selections for the Halloween party while making mental notes about the students on the floor.

Barbara was the one Katherine hadn't quite figured out as yet. The woman was loyal to the studio and gave freely of her time but seemed rather ordinary. Maybe Marcos could fill her in on Barbara's financial circumstances. They seemed quite chummy. Katherine sighed. She glanced at Edward and shook her head. The Edward she knew could never be seriously interested in an average, dime-a-dozen, middle-aged widow. Barbara surely wasn't a threat.

Linda Wilson, on her way out of the ballroom, waved to Katherine. Linda loved to make people laugh and had no problem doing it at her own expense. Katherine didn't trust the joking-around types; you never knew who they really were. Was Linda an unselfconscious extrovert or insecure—one of those people who got in the first jab before someone else could?

She scanned the busy dance floor. Katherine had pegged one of

Marcos's students as a flashy gold-digger, but, in fact, she was a soft-spoken Lebanese mother of five who just loved bling. Her much-older husband, a foreign-car dealership owner, had a generous nature and never batted an eye over the amount of money his wife spent at the studio. Katherine hoped the woman would continue dancing long after her ancient husband left her a widow.

Mei Le was finishing a lesson with Jackson. All Katherine knew about Mei Le was that she was a pharmacist, and pharmacists made good money. She'd signed a lesson contract just a few weeks ago. Katherine would talk to Jackson about Mei Le entering the next showcase.

She rested an elbow on the platform's railing. And there was that odd student of Tony's waiting to dance with Jackson, who was filling in for Tony for the week. Tall and gangly, she had pronounced knock-knees and looked very awkward dancing. But the woman moved with abandon and complete confidence and loved performing. She acted like she was Broadway's greatest loss. What the hell, everyone wasn't cut out to be a ballroom dancer, but as long as they were willing to part with their money, what did Katherine care?

Katherine spotted Lorna and lowered her head, careful not to catch the woman's eye. If you gave her the slightest glance, she would be all over you in a heartbeat, with a ridiculous girlish burble that spilled out like an overshaken bottle of soda. Lorna was the neediest, most annoying person Katherine had ever come across and so unattractive. But her rolls of tummy fat and missing teeth didn't stop her from wearing outrageous, skimpy costumes and entering every event. Katherine hid her face behind a fan of papers. What was the woman's story, anyway? She seemed a little dim-witted. Katherine knew she was single, always paid with a credit card, and didn't seem to have a job, so maybe she must have family money behind her?

Katherine put down her fan of papers and sucked in her lower lip. To hell with it—as long as a student was willing to spend, who was she to question whether they were a trust-fund baby or deeply in debt? Not her problem. Business is business, and business is about making money.

TWELVE

Vertigo

Paige Russell
11:15 a.m., Tuesday, 27 October

It was a bad omen. Overnight the wind had siphoned enough desert dirt to spew a dung-colored layer of smut across the skyline, obliterating the desert's blue sky. Paige pulled her wide scarf across her face and ran from the apartment's staircase to her car. The dust in the air made her eyes water, threatening to ruin her mascara. She slid into the driver's seat and turned the key. Nothing. Not even a belligerent whine. The battery was deader than disco.

"Great start to my day," Paige muttered. She pulled the useless keys out of the Corolla's ignition, slammed the door, and raced up the stairs to call the studio.

"Good morning. Desert DanceSport. How can I help you have a great day?" Jill chirped.

"Hey, Jill. It's Paige. And I'm not having such a great day, but maybe you can help. I have to be in by noon for a meeting, but my car battery died. I need to hitch a ride."

"Bummer," Jill sympathized. "Let me check the books. Marcos is already here, but Joey works from noon to nine today. He lives out on the east side. Maybe you can catch him before he leaves the house. Wait a sec. Here's his number—555-2697. If you don't reach him, call me right back, and we'll figure something else out, okay?"

"Thanks, Jill," Paige said. "See ya, I hope."

Paige jumped from foot to foot waiting for Joey to answer the phone. She was lucky. He was ready to head out the door and could be outside her apartment complex in less than ten minutes. Paige mumbled a quick prayer of thanks to whoever might be out there listening.

Back outside, she huddled close to a thick oleander bush—a welcome windbreak. Why was the wind always worse in midtown? The building-lined streets were concrete canyons, funneling air currents that swooped in from the foothills. Paige zipped her jacket as dirt and debris whirled around her. A beat-up pizza box skidded its way across the road, coming to rest at the base of the oleander. She pulled her scarf over her nose.

Paige shoved one hand into the pocket of her bomber jacket, mindlessly shredding the Kleenex she found there. Her stomach growled. She'd barely touched any food since Friday, and this morning's coffee threatened to rise into her throat. She bit her lip. Not one person had called over the weekend, not even Brianna, who was supposed to be her friend. Katherine was all business and ice when she called her about the meeting. And Marcos—every time she thought about how disappointed Marcos must be with her, she felt ill. Even he didn't call to check on her, which was a surprise after he'd been so sweet to her last week. She still felt the warmth of his hand when he guided her away from Tony's harassing comments. Marcos's grip felt so protective. She'd felt cared for, a feeling she hadn't had since her mom died.

Before Paige could make herself any sicker with worry, Joey arrived. He adjusted his titanium stud earring in the rearview mirror, flashed a classic Joey-style flirtatious smile, and started a steady stream of studio gossip. Paige slumped in her seat, too numb with fatigue and worry to even try to respond, until something Joey said ripped through her brain fog.

"What? Sorry, didn't catch that. What did you say about Katherine and Tony?" Paige turned to face Joey's chiseled Roman profile.

"Oh… yeah…that. Yesterday I overheard Tony in Katherine's office. Tony wasn't even trying to keep his voice down," Joey said, turning to share a smirk. "I heard him say something about Sylvie being nothing more than a damn drama queen. And then Katherine came back at him and told him to 'shut the hell up,' and said, 'you're lucky you're not being fired.' I beat a retreat before the office door opened. I don't think either one of them knew I overheard. Better to play dumb and stay out of it."

With that, Joey popped in a salsa CD and seat-danced the rest of the way across town. Worked for Paige. She needed time to process. But Joey drove like he danced—fast and hard—and he spun them into the studio parking lot ten minutes earlier than she expected.

"Mucho thanks for the ride, Joey," Paige said, as she jumped out of his comfy Nissan. "I'm going to have a quick smoke, so I'll see you later, okay?"

"No worries. Catch ya later."

"Hey," Paige yelled after him. "If you see Marcos or Katherine, tell them I'm out here and I'll be inside in few minutes."

"Done."

Paige watched Joey swish away. He was the gayest-acting, sexiest straight boy she'd ever known. If she hadn't actually met his wife, Roxanne, she'd have assumed Roxanne was fiction. Paige lit a Virginia Slims and leaned against Joey's car. It was still windy, but not as bad as it was fifteen miles southeast, in midtown. She breathed in the relaxing mix of chemicals and closed her eyes. Lately she was lighting up unconsciously. With twenty cigarettes to a pack and the number of times she made stops at the convenience store, Paige couldn't fool herself about how much she was smoking or how much she was spending. Numbers don't lie, and she could do the math. She took another drag. Between whatever fallout was about to rain on her from her lack of judgment with Tony and her uncertainty over where she stood with Marcos, she was in way over her head. She lifted her cigarette, momentarily fascinated with the way the smoke curled and played in the breeze. Yes, she had to quit this smoking habit sometime, but right now she needed every stress-reducing tool in her limited arsenal.

Paige tapped the ash off her cigarette and watched it trickle to the ground. Movement caught her eye. Ants. Hundreds of tiny, reddish, pencil-point ants were trekking across the broken asphalt on a direct two-lane path, some heading southeast and others marching northwest. At the crossroads, ants stopped to touch antennae, as if to confirm some tribal connection or to make sure they were on the right route. Paige watched, and the process of greeting never varied. *Am I on the right path? Are you friend or foe?* A quick ant-style handshake, and they were on their way again, their place in the order of things confirmed. Paige sighed. If only her place in the world were as clear-cut as that of the ants.

With one last lung-expanding drag, Paige mashed the stub of the cigarette between her finger and thumb and dropped the butt into an outside pocket of her purse. She may have joined the ranks of the smokers, but she'd be damned if she'd join the ranks of the litterbugs.

～

Barbara Bradshaw
11:45 a.m., Tuesday, 27 October

"Hi, ladies. Can I sit with you a minute while I change out of my dance shoes?"

Barbara turned to see a stunning blonde in her early forties standing close to the table she shared with Linda. Barbara smiled and nodded, but her face felt wooden with the effort. She hated herself for being so shallow. This woman was model-gorgeous. Her wide-open, lifted eyes and Barbie-doll contours were a breathing testament to her husband's artistry as a cosmetic surgeon. Barbara bit her lip and reminded herself that envy was one of the seven deadly sins.

She motioned for the blonde to sit, which she did with maddening grace. Barbara sighed. She felt every minute of her age next to this lithe beauty.

"Was that Jackson you were dancing with? Don't you usually take lessons with Tony?" Barbara forced a polite smile.

"I do," the stunner replied, revealing perfectly aligned teeth. "Katherine called me yesterday and offered an exchange lesson with Jackson for today."

"Now that I think about it, I haven't seen Tony since I arrived." Linda jumped into the conversation as she scanned the ballroom.

"Katherine told me Tony isn't teaching this week," the blonde said. She glanced from Barbara to Linda as she spoke, bestowing them with an overwhitened smile. "Katherine didn't say why Tony wasn't available but offered me two exchange lessons with Jackson for every one of my lesson hours with Tony. We dance again on Thursday. I have to run, ladies. See you on the dance floor." Blondie fluttered her fingertips as she left.

"When I got here early to practice before my noon lesson with Joey, the only person around was Jill," Linda said. "Where the hell is everyone today, anyway?"

"Darned if I know." Barbara shrugged. "I had my usual eleven o'clock lesson with Marcos, but he asked if I could shift our noon lesson to one. Of course I told him it was fine. He said something about a mandatory staff meeting at noon."

"Oh, well. If anything's going on, we'll find out sooner than later," Linda said with a shrug. "So what now? You have an hour to kill before your next lesson with Marcos, right?" She was unselfconsciously pulling off her leggings as she pulled on a skirt.

"I do. I'm trying to decide if I want to be lazy and chill or make the effort to practice some of the footwork Marcos is trying to drum into my muscle memory," Barbara said.

"It wouldn't hurt me to practice a bit more," Linda replied. "Joey's working with me on spotting my châiné turns so I can spin more quickly, and I have a lot of mass to spin." Linda placed her hands on her midriff, leaned back, and let out a full-bodied hoot.

"Châinés are tough for me as well," Barbara said, with a grimace. "Marcos tells me to start the turn on my standing foot, turn my opposite shoulder into the direction of the turn, and then pull my thighs together as I bring my feet together and change weight. Yikes."

"Right," Linda said, "and while you're at it, whip your head around to spot the turn." Linda paused to look at Barbara over her glasses. "Joey thinks I'll get better with time, but the reality is I'm getting older faster than I'm getting better. Time isn't working in my favor."

"I've been thinking along those lines lately, too," Barbara said, reaching for her coffee as she spoke. "Actually, I've been sorting out what I really want to get out of ballroom dancing at this point. Have you noticed the big push for competitions and events?"

"I have," Linda said. "But then I do most of them, anyway. However, Joey's encouraging me to increase the number of heats I usually do."

"I'm trying not to get pulled into the competitive vortex. I love the camaraderie of events but hate being watched and judged." Barbara folded her arms. "I've been reminding myself that I started dancing to stay active, have fun, and find a community where I could make some new friends. It was never about winning a comp. The competitive mindset turns it all into a stress. I had enough stress when I was working."

"And when you start comparing yourself to everyone else, it's way too easy to get discouraged and lose perspective," Linda said. "At our age, it really should be about having fun, not trying to prove anything to anyone. I value the critiques I get from the adjudicators, but the only person I'm out to beat is myself. Granted, Joey may not share that perspective." Linda raised her eyebrows and stuck out her tongue.

"I guess I should chat with Marcos so he understands my expectations and can modify his own accordingly," Barbara said.

"Hold that thought for a sec," Linda said, turning her attention to a youngish Asian woman who was hobbling into the ballroom with her dance shoes unbuckled. She sat at the next table with a sigh and a muttered, "Stupid shoes."

"Do you need some help with those buckles?" Linda asked.

"Yes. Thank you," the woman said, nodding to both Linda and Barbara. "I'm Mei Le." She raised the offending shoes. "New. Hate slip-lock buckle. Too hard." Mei Le offered a weak smile, but to Barbara's ear's the irritation in her voice overshadowed the friendly overture.

"Here, let me show you." Linda scooted her chair closer to Mei Le. "We help each other around here." Linda bent to position Mei Le's foot in the shoe and proceeded to give her a shoe-fastening lesson. "Hold the strap firmly against your ankle and adjust the buckle on the strap to fit tightly. Now pull the strap with the fastened buckle past the slit in the metal guide on your shoe, and drop it into the slot. To take the shoe off, slide the strap out of the slot. You never have to actually buckle or unbuckle again, unless you need to adjust the tightness. Okay?"

Mei Le nodded.

"Haven't I seen you on the floor with Jackson? You're new, right?" Barbara asked.

"Yes. New. Just started," Mei Le responded. She smiled at both women, but the smile was short-lived, fading into pressed lips and a frown. "Maybe taking ballroom lessons not good idea," Mei Le said, with the trace of a chopped Chinese accent. "Besides Jackson, have no one to dance with. No boyfriend, no husband, so can't go dancing. Jackson would not go." Mei Le's skirt had hiked up during the shoe-buckling process, so she tugged it down to cover her knees. "A lot of expense and effort for a lot of nothing."

"I'm not sure what you mean," Linda responded.

Barbara met Linda's glance with a shrug. "Me, either," Barbara said, genuinely confused. "Why did you decide to take lessons in the first place?"

Mei Le leaned forward and looked from Linda to Barbara. "I work hard. Need to relax, and so I thought, *Dancing*. Dance studio be good place to meet someone who also likes to dance. But where are single men? In four weeks I don't see single men. Men are too young or too married, and instructor not allowed to go out dancing with student. So, I only dance at lessons or practice parties."

"Well, yes, I hear what you are saying," Barbara said. "But neither of us have husbands or boyfriends, either."

"It like this," Mei Le said. "When you learn new language, you learn because you want to visit another country, or you need language for job, or…you know…you have reason to use new language, right?"

"Right. So why don't you enter a studio event with Jackson?" Barbara said. "We, Linda and I, both learn routines with our instructors so we can dance in the showcases or competitions. That's when you really get to dance. The performance events are your opportunity to get out on the floor and use what you are learning in your lessons."

Mei Le gave a grunt of—what? Disgust, agreement? Barbara set her mouth in a tentative smile.

Mei Le folded her arms across her chest. "I spend fortune for lessons, and then, to use what I learn, Jackson want me to spend another fortune to enter event with him?" Mei Le said. "Jackson talk to me about next showcase and dinner. So for $200 registration, I get $30 dinner, and I spend $1,300 to dance thirty-four two-minute heats, and then I get plastic medal for participation? I don't think so. Sound like big rip-off to me." Mei Le gave another grunt and shrug, stood, and, without another word, strode across the ballroom.

Barbara looked at Linda, completely taken aback. "When one looks at it from the perspective Mei Le presented, there really isn't much one can say, is there?"

~⁀

Paige Russell
12:05 p.m., Tuesday, 27 October

Katherine's office door was open, and everyone else was already seated. Tony was on Marcos's right, and Sylvie was beside Tony. Her chair was angled to one side, perpendicular to everyone else. Katherine sat behind her desk, tapping a pencil on the desktop. She asked Paige to shut the door. Paige complied and slipped into the chair to Marcos's left.

Katherine took a sip of water and started straight in. She wasted no time on preliminaries. She let everyone know they weren't to speak out of turn and made it clear she wasn't going to let the meeting degenerate into a shouting match.

"What you did, Paige, was inexcusable." Katherine's voice was direct and firm. "You haven't been in this business long enough to understand the unspoken rules, and you have yet to spend your own money on a competition gown or Latin costume. I will assume your breach of etiquette, in respect to trying on Sylvie's new Latin dress, was based on ignorance rather than malice or jealousy. We considered letting you go, but instead you are on probation for the next six weeks. You have to prove yourself all over again."

Paige kept her hands folded in her lap. She forced herself to meet Katherine's glacial blue eyes, which were riveted on her. Paige lowered her head again and bit her upper lip.

"Paige," Katherine said. She didn't resume speaking until Paige met her gaze. Katherine's arms were folded on her desk, and she was leaning forward. "Do you have any idea what these costumes cost or what the process is to get one custom made?"

"No. I…I guess I really don't," Paige said. She hated that her voice shook. She clasped her hands tighter. "I know they are expensive, but—"

"Let me bring you up to speed, then," Katherine said, cutting her off. Her voice would have frozen water in a hot spring. "This costume was an out-of-pocket expense for Sylvie. It cost over $3,000, and at that price it was an amazing deal. It was a special show offer from Romey Designs. They had a vendor's booth at the Crystal Ball in Chicago, where Sylvie and Tony competed a few months ago. Sylvie was measured at the competition, and she and Deana Romey worked together on the design. Sylvie chose the fabric and the crystals, which are all Swarovski. Even you should know Swarovski's crystals are the best and most expensive." Katherine paused.

Paige nodded.

"Each crystal is sewn or glued on by hand. The body of the costume is made from a special stretch fabric to allow for ease of movement. After Sylvie competes in this dress two or three times, she'll offer it for resale and order something new. Do you understand how important these dresses are to a competitive dancer and that they're a major investment?"

"Yes, ma'am," Paige replied, ducking her head to hide the tears she was blinking back. She looked up in time to catch Katherine turning an equally stony gaze on Tony.

"For you, Tony, there's no excuse. When you encouraged Paige to try on Sylvie's costume—and I still have no idea what possessed you, but I have a suspicion and it isn't very pretty—you showed complete and utter disregard for your dance partner. Trust is an integral part of a dance partnership. This was the ultimate form of disrespect. You are suspended from teaching lessons for the rest of the week. I've contacted your students. They know their lessons will be taught by someone else. I didn't share with them why. The only time I want to see you in the studio is to prepare for the competition with Sylvie. You owe her that. And you're still expected to conduct a workshop at the Halloween party. Am I clear?" Katherine leaned back, arms folded, shaking her head.

"Yes." Tony was more subdued than Paige, and probably anyone else, had ever seen him.

With lowered eyes, Paige stole a glance Tony's way. If she read him right, he was fed up with all of them right now, and the fact that he was the picture of humble remorse was more a testament to his acting skills than genuine penitent feelings. She bit her lip, stifling a smile. If he thought he could get away with it, he'd probably reach across the desk right now and strangle Katherine on the spot.

Katherine turned to Sylvie next, who was sitting ramrod straight in her chair, one perfectly manicured hand clasped around a knee, the other tightly grasping the armrest. Sylvie held her head high. Her makeup was flawless, her blond curls perfection. It was clear she wanted everyone to understand she was the star of this show.

"Sylvie, I am terribly sorry this happened. I understand Paige gave you a formal apology and you accepted." Sylvie nodded, but barely looked Paige's way. "I don't expect you two to be the best of friends, but I do expect you to rise above this and cultivate a cooperative and cordial working relationship." Katherine paused. "And I hope you understand that laying hands on another instructor will never be tolerated again."

Sylvie nodded again.

Katherine continued, "Your dress is in the capable hands of Olivia Cordova, one of the Romey team of seamstresses. I spoke with her this morning. She said the dress will be returned to you in perfect condition by this weekend. The invoice for the repairs will be handled by us, so please don't worry about this costing you anything."

"Actually, I'm covering the cost of repairing the dress," Marcos said. He looked quickly at Katherine and then cleared his throat and rubbed a finger across his upper lip.

"Thank you, Marcos," Sylvie said, turning a curious-looking gaze his way.

Paige was surprised to see Katherine flush a pale shade of crimson. She didn't care who paid as long as the cost wasn't coming out of her own paycheck, which she thankfully still seemed to have. And, at least for now, Sylvie was making a show of taking the high road.

"So, I have to ask, Katherine," Sylvie said, tilting her head. "Why is Marcos covering what should be a studio expense? I don't understand."

"The studio is experiencing, well…um…a very temporary issue with cash flow—nothing to worry about—and Marcos offered to step in to get us over this tight spot." Katherine's voice faltered. "We all owe Marcos our thanks for being so generous."

"I want it to be clear," Marcos said, "that I stand behind Katherine one hundred percent in how she's handling this matter. You, actually we, the studio, are fortunate none of our students witnessed your little brouhaha. The lack of professionalism displayed by all of you is unacceptable. We won't tolerate anything even close to this happening again."

In the mirror, Paige saw Marcos turn to Tony. Marcos was massaging his knuckles, and his features were rigid. "Tony, I don't want to see you any closer to Paige than necessary, with the exception of using her to demonstrate a dance pattern to a student."

Marcos turned his attention to Paige. She relaxed when she saw his expression soften.

"Paige, you're not completely off the hook. You've been given the benefit of the doubt. I believe you were led astray by a senior staff member who should have known better. As your unofficial mentor, you and I will discuss this in more detail in private. Understood?"

His voice sounded softer than his demeanor, and Paige smiled gratefully. He nodded and smiled back at her. She wasn't sure anyone else noticed.

"Fine, then," Katherine said as she stood. "Tony, unless you have practice time booked with Sylvie, you're free to leave. The rest of you, back to work. We have the Halloween party and dance workshop on Friday, and I need everyone at the top of their game. We are done here."

THIRTEEN

CENTER STAGE

Marcos Stephanos
12:15 p.m., Wednesday, 28 October

With a sweep of his hand, Marcos invited Paige into the soft leather passenger seat of his Miata. She snuggled in and ran her fingers along the dashboard.

"Great car." Her tone was appreciative but her voice barely audible.

Marcos cursed under his breath when forced to squeeze between his sleek sports car and an oversized SUV to get to the driver's side door.

"I…well…I just want to say…." Paige stammered.

Marcos's attention was focused on backing out of the parking space. The tail end of the Chevrolet Tahoe blocked his line of sight. "Okay. We're out. I'd like to know what idiot parked that SUV monstrosity." Marcos glanced at Paige. Her upper lip was caught between her teeth, and she looked like she was fighting tears. "Paige, are you okay?" Marcos touched her clasped hands. They were icy cold and stiff. "What is it? Do you think I'm taking you out to fire you?"

Paige nodded and raised her eyes to his, treating Marcos to the full volume of her tearful, expressive, gray-green eyes.

"Paige, I swear to you, we're just going out for a nice lunch. I thought you needed a break from the studio." The girl was guileless, her feelings transparent as her face softened into a smile and her body visibly relaxed.

"Thanks. Appreciate it. Everyone is giving me looks, and Sylvie won't speak to me. No one gets how crappy I feel and, worse, stupid for trusting Tony. I've barely eaten for three days. All weekend I expected Katherine to call and fire me."

"I wouldn't have let that happen. I'm guessing you forgot yourself in the excitement of seeing the new costumes," Marcos said, merging into traffic. "Everyone makes mistakes. The important thing about mistakes is learning from them."

"Well, I've learned big time from this." Paige paused and swiftly changed conversational gears. "So how long have you had this car?"

"Since 2009. It's an MX-5 Miata, a hardtop Roadster Coupe." Marcos winked at Paige. "What I wanted was one of the limited-edition, twentieth anniversary, MX-5 models, but only two thousand were made for release in Europe. If I ever get to live in Europe...."

"Europe? Do want to live in Europe one day?" Paige's demeanor lightened as she broke out of her self-imposed cocoon of contrition. The familiar inquisitive Paige emerged.

"I've thought about it," Marcos said, downshifting as he approached a traffic jam. "Maybe in the UK or Germany or possibly even Romania. I'd like to study the teaching and coaching techniques taught in the Eastern Bloc. Dancers there are seriously competing at eight-years old."

"Is that why the European-trained dancers usually beat everyone over here?"

"Of course," Marcos replied, turning to bestow his lovely companion with a smile he hoped conveyed sophistication. "They have every advantage. Those people eat, breathe, and sleep competitive ballroom with no concept of free time. They're tireless professionals, and it shows on the floor."

Marcos engaged Paige in companionable chatter while driving past the nondescript, every-town landscape of fast food restaurants, bland strip malls, banks, and car lots. The scenery reshaped into attractive neighborhoods closer to the University of Arizona. This location had 1930s-style homes—porches, lawns, and gardens graced the area, which included a walkable shopping district of small boutiques, cafés, and bookstores. Marcos turned into a small lot and helped Paige out of the low-slung car. Today he was putting his best foot forward. He held open the café door, waving Paige in. A young woman with red-tipped, white-blond hair and heavily made-up eyes greeted them.

"Hello, and welcome to Wylie's Coyote Cafe." The hostess smiled, flashing a silver tongue piercing. Marcos noted how she spoke with the questioning lilt at the end of each sentence so many young people her age affected.

"Can we take the curved corner booth, please?" Marcos asked. Marcos waved to the owner, an old friend.

"Of course." The girl's stiletto heels tapped their way across the hardwood floor. "Your server will be along in a moment. Enjoy."

Paige turned to Marcos, eyes wide, one hand over her mouth.

"I feel like a soccer mom who stumbled into a rave." She giggled. "Here I am, in my black dance skirt, leggings, and no-nonsense ponytail, and here's the hostess, all edgy with her piercings, tattoos, and fishnet stockings. Makes me feel old."

Before Marcos could comment on how the lovely, fresh-faced Paige looked nothing like a soccer mom, their waiter materialized from the dust motes dancing in stripes of shuttered sunlight. He was very clean-cut collegiate, except for the purple-and-black tattoo visible through his open collar.

Marcos checked the wine list. He wanted this to be a celebratory lunch, but he couldn't have this young employee arriving back at the studio snockered. He scanned the selections, hesitated, and then said,

"Bring us a bottle of the Klinker Brick Old Ghost Zinfandel. We'd like two glasses, but also bring a large diet Coke for the lady, please." Paige nodded. "We'll start with your wonderful artichoke and spinach dip. We need comfort food. It's been a trying few days." He directed his last remark to Paige, who smiled a huge Cheshire Cat smile.

Marcos studied the menu, giving Paige time to settle in and relax. In minutes the waiter was back at their table. He uncorked the wine and poured a taster for Marcos. At his nod, the waiter filled both glasses, with affectations designed to infuse Wylie's artsy ambiance with an air of sophistication.

"Paige," Marcos said, "for the record, Katherine thinks I'm chastising you in private and giving you a tutorial on ballroom studio ethics."

Paige nodded, wide-eyed.

"So consider yourself duly spoken to, and let's put the dress disaster to bed."

Paige reached for her wine glass and gulped down half its contents.

"Wait!" Marcos laughed. "The occasion calls for a toast, not a guzzle." He raised his glass. Paige followed his example. "To new beginnings and lessons learned." They clinked rims. Marcos savored the rich and fruity zinfandel, but Paige drained her glass and poured herself a second before Marcos could stop her. He subtly shifted the bottle out of her reach just as their appetizer arrived at the table.

"So, after you take a good drink of your Coke," Marcos softened his stage directions with a smile, "tell me how your apartment is working out for you?" Marcos winked, nodding toward Paige's soft drink, as he spread spinach-artichoke dip on a water cracker.

"It's great," Paige responded, ignoring her Coke and talking through a mouthful of pita bread and dip. "I'm on the second floor. I have a little balcony with a decent view. It's mostly furnished with things I brought to Tucson from Flagstaff, but I did buy one thing here I really love." Paige looked at Marcos, cocking her head to one side.

"So what fabulous item did you buy?" he asked, recognizing a cue when he heard one.

"Two things, really: a vintage telephone table and an old-fashioned rotary-dial telephone I found in an antique shop. The phone actually works, so I have a landline," Paige said, doing a little seated happy dance, somehow avoiding a lapful of wine. "It is so shabby-chic."

Marcos raised his eyebrows at the notion that a rotary phone could be considered an antique. It drove Paige's young age home. "Sounds like a gem of a find. So, how about your social life? Dating much?" He kept the question casual.

"No. I haven't dated anyone in a long time. Been too busy at the studio." Paige, absorbed in overloading a pita point with the thick dip, didn't even glance his way.

"Did you leave anyone special behind in Flagstaff?" Marcos swirled the wine in his glass, enjoying the play of light on the pinkish-burgundy liquid. Paige sat back in the booth and wiped her fingertips on a napkin, her expression wine-softened. If her stomach really was empty from not eating, he should curtail her intake of alcohol. If nothing else, they'd take a head-clearing walk before returning to work.

"I haven't even shared this with Brianna, and she's pretty good at prying things out of me." Paige pursed her lips as if contemplating how much she should say. "I was dating someone at NAU. We'd been a thing for over a year when my mother got sick. I knew Kevin was self-absorbed—he was a drama major, for God's sake—but I didn't fully appreciate how much until my mother died."

Paige topped off her wine. Marcos moved the zinfandel to the safety of his side of the table. This last top-off had to be it for her.

"After my mother died, Kevin was a complete jerk. Since I knew she was terminal, he thought I should have been emotionally prepared. And I had him to make it all better. He said *I* was self-absorbed by not putting him first."

"I'm sorry, Paige. I'm sure that was painful. It's tough when someone doesn't have your back." Marcos laid his hand over Paige's.

He was ashamed of how pleased he felt to know she wasn't romantically involved with anyone.

"Well, that's what you get for dating an acting student. Feelings are something to try on like a new outfit. 'Live and learn' might become my life's motto," Paige said. She gave a short, self-deprecating laugh.

Marcos motioned to their waiter. He felt Paige slip her hand out from under his. "Bring us two turkey-with-green-chili sandwiches, please, grilled on jalapeno cornbread. Since we are splurging on calories today, we'll split a plate of the thick-cut, sweet potato fries."

Marcos shifted the conversation to something he hoped was less distressing than death and old boyfriends. "And family? Any relatives in Tucson?"

Paige made a bit of a face, then wine-washed the spinach off her teeth before replying. "Um, well, I guess sort of, but…no, not exactly. I don't have much family. My grandma lives in a memory-care home in Florida, and my mother's sister also lives in Florida in a resort-style retirement community. Aunt Teresa is seventy-one, nine years older than my mother."

"Your aunt is seventy-one?" Marcos couldn't keep the shock out of his voice. "How old was your mother when she had you?"

"Old." Paige grinned. "My mother was forty when I born."

Marcos digested the *old*. And what did that make him? A relic?

"Anyway," Paige continued, "my mother and aunt were never very close, so we didn't visit back and forth. I don't know her all that well. But I couldn't have made it through the funeral without her help."

Marcos couldn't take his eyes off Paige. Her lovely, smooth skin was flushed with a disarming peachy-rose glow. He mentally admonished himself. His feelings were edging toward the inappropriate. She was both young and an employee. Paige's voice came back into focus.

"Aunt Teresa helped plan Mom's funeral and guided me through the worst of the business end of death. Dying is complicated. She helped me file insurance claims, pay the bills, and list the house with a good realtor. Between the equity in the house and the life insurance from Mom's job, I ended up with enough to live on for a while and still help pay for college." Paige paused. "Whoa," she said, making a spinning motion with her hand. "I sort of forgot what a lightweight I am with wine."

"You might want to slow down a bit, then," Marcos said. It was good to see her unwind, but her getting schnockered was definitely not a good idea. Where was their food? Marcos made sure the wine bottle remained out of Paige's reach. He nudged the untouched glass of Coke closer to her.

"You have plans to finish your degree, then? Why did you leave school in the first place?"

On that note, lunch arrived. The heady scent of grilled fresh green chilies prompted envious looks from the diners at the next table. Paige took a huge bite and busied herself with the sweet potato fries. Marcos, about to dig in, was interrupted by the waiter, who presented a second bottle of wine.

"Compliments of the owner, Mr. Stephanos. I mentioned you were celebrating." The waiter pointed toward the bar.

His old friend waved from across the room. Marcos returned the wave. He felt unappreciative, but additional wine might not be the best idea. He took a bite of his sandwich and glanced at Paige. He was enjoying this private time with her more than he probably should. There was something about this young woman; he couldn't put his finger on it. Reaching for the newly opened bottle, he topped off his glass. He had to be clear to drive safely back to the studio, but it was only wine, and he was famous for holding his liquor. Paige lifted her glass for more. He shook his head, but she countered by raising her glass higher. He knew he should cut her off, but…maybe just a touch more. He'd order coffee after their meal.

"So, leaving NAU, this is how it came down," Paige said. "My mother died at the end of the spring semester of my junior year."

Marcos raised his eyebrows. Paige was twenty-four, old enough to have graduated from college before her mother became ill.

"Yeah," Paige added with a shrug. "I worked between high school and college. In the fall, after Mom's death, I went back to school and moved into a dorm. I tried but couldn't focus, couldn't wrap my head around school anymore. There's more to it, but basically I bailed at the start of this year, found a studio apartment, and got a part-time job at Fred Astaire. The job was low stress. It gave me the time I needed to sort through the last of my mom's things. I also had a lot of emotional crap to work through."

Paige's hand wobbled as she raised her glass to her lips. A splash of wine blotched the tablecloth.

"I was a guilty mess. I loved my mom to pieces, but I wasn't always the nicest kid to be around. As a teenager I was sort of a bitch, and I didn't spend enough time with her after I started college. And when she was in hospice, I didn't visit as much as I should have. I made excuses to not stay. I couldn't accept she was dying. I still feel like shit over it." Paige went quiet and focused on her lunch.

Marcos didn't ask any more questions but gave her time to get some food into her system. They were in no hurry.

"And then, after she died," Paige started talking right where she left off, "the reality of being an orphan sank in."

"An orphan?" Marcos pulled his head back, eyebrows raised. What the hell? Orphan? Paige was not a child.

"My mother was a single mother," Paige said, wiping a stray string of green chili off her chin. "She also became a mother pretty late. It was always me and her."

"And your father?" Marcos asked.

"Not sure. My mother refused to tell me anything about my dad. Once when I had to make a family tree in school, in third grade, I got mad and tore it up because I couldn't fill in one whole side. The teacher called my mother, but even then she just looked sad and wouldn't tell me anything. When I was about fourteen, I really got in her face about who my dad was. She actually cried and asked why she wasn't enough." Paige stopped to consume another sweet potato fry. "Anyway, she finally told me that at around forty she realized she wanted a child more than anything but didn't want a man underfoot all the time trying to control her life. She'd been divorced once. Another story. So, she got pregnant by some guy, and here I am. But what if my father doesn't even know he has a daughter? If it were you, wouldn't you want to know?"

Marcos had no idea what to say. Paige stared, unblinking, like he was bacteria under a microscope. She lifted the wineglass to her lips and sipped, and then sipped some more. When had she refilled her glass? Marcos ran his finger around the collar of his shirt.

Suddenly Paige blinked rapidly and continued with her story. "After Mom died, I started working on finding my dad. I was sort of obsessed, really. My aunt had no information. I don't think my mother confided much in her sister. But then, when I was going through the last of her boxes of stuff…well…I…." Paige stopped in mid-sentence.

"Paige, honey, if this is too difficult to talk about, leave it for another time." His curiosity was piqued, but he wanted to avoid the whole subject of deadbeat dads or whatever else the disturbing tale might be. Dredging this stuff up obviously hurt.

Tears slipped down Paige's cheeks. She pushed her plate away and scooted along the curve of the booth, snuggling against his side. Marcos gently massaged her upper arm. She relaxed into the curve of the booth. He laid his arm strategically behind her. She lifted her ponytail and draped it over his forearm. Her hair was soft and smelled of honey or apples—something natural and sweet.

"It's nice to be close, to feel cared for," Paige mumbled. She buried her nose in his upper chest. "You make me feel like I belong to someone again—protected and safe."

Marcos felt a pang of guilt. He shouldn't have let her drink so much, and her emotional state was exacerbating her condition. Marcos's chest heaved with a deep sigh. Paige was snuggling like a child, but damned if she didn't feel and smell all woman. Attraction was rapidly displacing good sense, and it was becoming evident that, age difference or not, this young woman was just as attracted to him. Marcos tightened his hold, pulling her closer. He tried to keep himself in check but was failing miserably. Having her so close, so needy, was triggering feelings he realized he'd been trying to quash for weeks.

"Paige, it hurts to see you feeling so sad and lost."

Paige sighed and shifted position; he could feel her breasts pushing against his side. Holy Mother of God, things were moving in a direction he hadn't planned, at least not this soon, but the moment felt right. He stroked Paige's hair as he spoke to her, very softly and very gently.

"You need to know you don't have to be alone in life. I can be there to take care of you. I could be so good for you. We need time, but I feel strangely connected to you and deeply attracted, and I can tell you feel the same way."

Paige had gone very still. Marcos took this as a positive sign.

"Listen to me, Paige. I know I should wait, test the waters first, but…." Marcos felt his confidence growing, and he spoke with more authority. "I have feelings for you, my dear. I think we've stumbled into something neither of us expected or planned. We need time to explore what this is, to bridge the age gap and find common ground, but I have a feeling our differences will serve to fill in each other's gaps. And I'm well-situated financially, Paige. I can give you everything you'll ever need or want. Think about it. We could dance together, travel the country, maybe go to Europe if you like. We could—"

Paige stirred in his arms and turned to look at him, her eyes as wide and questioning as a baby owl's. He couldn't stand it another minute. Everything felt right. He tilted her head back, pulled her closer, and kissed her deeply and expertly on the mouth.

With a stifled shriek Paige shoved Marcos hard. In seconds, his backside traveled the few inches to the edge of the booth. With an undignified and loud "Oomph," Marcos found himself in an inelegant sprawl on the cold tile floor.

"What the hell?"

"Marcos! Oh no, Marcos. Oh my God. You don't understand. You can't…we can't….you…." Paige grabbed her purse and leapt over

165

Marcos's prone body, catching his stylish dance pants with her heel, ripping the fabric.

"You what? I don't understand?" Marcos wailed after her. "That I'm too much older than you?"

But the café door had already shut behind her, and she was running toward the open doors of the stopped streetcar.

Marcos tried to push himself up but his hand slipped on the tile. He thudded back down. He was left with the tab, a bruised backside, a damaged ego, and the notoriety that can only be acquired via quick-witted bystanders with camera phones and connections to social media.

~

Paige Russell
3:00 p.m., Wednesday, 28 October

Paige stayed on the streetcar until the motion made her nauseous. She was foggy, couldn't think, didn't want to think. She hit the stop-request button at the Fourth Avenue shopping district, disembarked, and looked up and down the street. She'd taken flight without a flight plan. One thing was clear; she couldn't go back to the studio today. Maybe she wouldn't be missed. Whatever. She'd take her chances on this one.

Paige walked, one hand held over her abdomen like an expectant mother protecting her womb. As the blocks of cracked concrete sidewalks passed under her feet, her head began to clear. Coffee. She needed coffee and someone to talk to. At a small bakery and coffee shop, Paige ordered a double Americano and called the only person she could confide in: someone detached and intelligent, who might not think she was the biggest idiot on the planet. She called Kristi. Next she called Uber.

~

"I'm really glad you were able to make time for me, Kristi." Paige positioned her half-finished Americano out of the way of a careless move. She didn't need spilled coffee on top of nearly upchucking her half-digested lunch on the trolley. "Your receptionist sure gave me a look when I walked in. I must have sounded like a nutcase on the phone."

"What she thinks doesn't matter. You said you needed to talk, and you're my last client of the day, so we can take all the time you need." Kristi, cuticle remover poised in mid-push, lightly jiggled Paige's hand. "Relax your hand. You're super tight, hon." Kristi's cat-like brown eyes were full of warmth, and there was genuine compassion in her voice.

Paige inhaled from her abdomen and exhaled through her mouth, trying to remember the exact technique demonstrated by the yoga instructor on TV. She willed her right hand to soften and looked at Kristi from under lowered lashes.

"I really do need to talk, and you're the one person I trust, so here goes," Paige said. She licked her lips and sat straighter in the chair.

Kristi gave Paige a soft, closed-lipped smile. She opened the bottle of nail color Paige chose—an intense reddish-bronze shade called Boris & Natasha.

"Marcos took me out of the studio today, like out in his car. I thought I was getting fired, but it turned out he had my back." Paige met Kristi's eyes long enough for Paige to see the unspoken question.

Kristi dipped the tiny brush into the richly colored nail polish, and stroked it onto Paige's newly shaped nails.

"It started out great. He took me to a café close to the university and ordered a great lunch and also a bottle of wine, which I guess I guzzled back."

"Paige, you're tightening up again. I need you to relax your fingers."

"Sorry," Paige mumbled through an embarrassed half smile. She took a deep breath and then continued in machine-gun bursts of words. "...and then, when I leaned back to stop the world spinning, I snuggled next to Marcos. He got all comforting and fatherly, or so I thought, and—"

"Or so you thought?" Kristi held the nail brush in mid-swipe.

"Oh my God, Kristi, Marcos came on to me. He started saying all this stuff about how great we would be for each other, and how I wouldn't ever be alone again. And then he leaned over and kissed me. He really laid one on me, Kristi. It was like all the alcohol suddenly evaporated through my skin. I gut-reacted. I was in such a panic to get out of the booth, I knocked Marcos right onto the floor." Paige shook her head, still feeling bewildered.

"Jesus, Paige. I get that the man took you by surprise when he kissed you, but what am I missing here?" Kristi asked. She capped the polish and sat back in her chair. "You're obviously shaken, but why such a reaction? I know Marcos is quite a bit older than you, but I thought you were into this guy, right? You've said how much you want to get to know him better. Even Brianna thinks you have a little crush on this Marcos. So—"

"Oh God, no," Paige said. She waved her fingers in front of her, partly to de-stress and partly to dry the polish. "Yes...yes, I really do want to get to know Marcos better, but everything is such a mess now, I don't know how I'll be able to. I'll try to explain, but you have to understand you can't breathe a word of what I tell you to anyone, okay?"

"Of course, hon. I won't say anything. I'm a great secret-keeper," Kristi said. "I'd hold your hands right now, but I'm not about to ruin the great job I did on your nail polish."

Paige croaked out a laugh.

"Hold on, I'm getting us some water." Kristi walked off and came back with two water bottles. She handed one to Paige.

"Thank you. You'd better settle in. I have to back way up." Paige pulled her legs into a cross-legged sitting position in her chair. She gulped the water, compressed her lips, and took a deep breath. "When I cleaned out the last of my mother's things, I found a worn-out blue folder stuck in a box. I'd bugged my mother for information about my birth father for years, and here she had this folder stashed away the whole time. The only real fights we ever had were over me asking about my father. She always said she didn't know who he was, but...."

Kristi tipped her head to one side and raised an eyebrow

"Okay, I'm getting off track. At first I couldn't make sense out of the papers I found. One was a scrawled note, marked with an age, a date, a faded-out name that looked like Martin Stevens, and some basic info. I thought my mother must have tracked down my birth father—the guy she'd had a one-nighter with. But the age she wrote on the paper was twenty-seven. This was after I was born so my mother would have been around forty-two. But I took what I had and started a Google search anyway."

"Geez, Paige, if your mother had a fling with this guy and you were the result, he would have been only twenty-four or twenty-five at the time. Not totally unheard of, but—"

"If you do the math, this guy would be about forty-nine-years old now. Remember that number." Paige reached for her water, took a sip, and rubbed the tip of her nose.

"A few nights ago I dumped everything out of this damn folder again. I pulled a page out of its plastic sleeve, but this time I noticed how thick the page felt. What I thought was a double-sided blood test printout was two pages stuck together, like someone had jam on their fingers. The edge of the pages started to tear when I peeled them apart. Oh, and important, the folder also contained a referral to a counselor for my mom."

"Paige, you are beginning to sound like you might need a counselor yourself."

Paige placed on hand on Kristi's arm. "Listen to this. Stuck between those blood test pages was information from a clinic in Phoenix about screening for genetic disorders. There were notes in the margins in my mother's handwriting about which sperm banks clinics allowed single women to be inseminated. Sperm banks!"

"Intriguing, but what does this have to do with Marcos?"

"Do you remember how I told you about the first time I saw

Marcos at the dance Expo in Flagstaff, and I applied for the job at the studio soon after? I know it's crazy to upend your life on a gut feeling, but the first time I laid eyes on Marcos my heart thunked and something just clicked. It was a gut reaction. I'm still connecting all the dots, but I think I've figured it all out."

Paige paused and captured Kristi's eyes with her own, and held on for a few seconds.

"Kristi, I'm all but positive that my mother went to a sperm bank to get impregnated. My father wasn't a random one-night stand after all, but he wasn't some guy who was in love with my mother, either. My mother was less than nothing to the man who fathered me." Paige stopped for breath. "My father was a sperm donor. The donor's eye color, his dark hair, his profession, the age is even right. The donor would be around forty-nine now, and Marcos is exactly forty-nine. Do you see what I'm getting at? I think I know who my mother's sperm donor was."

FOURTEEN

Dancing for Your Dinner

Paige Russell
11:15 a.m., Thursday, 29 October

Paige retrieved her sweater and shoe bag from her locker and crept into the ballroom. She felt like all eyes were on her, her every move being judged. She sucked in her lower lip when she spotted Sylvie, who ignored her. Sylvie and a heavyset older student faced the mirrored back wall. The sound system was turned to normal hearing range, so Sylvie's voice was audible as she demonstrated the correct technique for swivels. Her right foot was pointed to one side.

"Now, bring your left toe to the heel of your right foot by closing your thighs. Good. Watch how I swivel on the standing foot and send the toe of my free foot in the opposite direction."

With a twist of her hips, Sylvie performed the movement and then repeated the swiveling action on the new, standing foot. Sylvie's swivel snaked sensuously while her student moved like a hippo in drag. It was difficult to watch. Paige wished she could tell this struggling new student that the learning curve for dance was a steep one, and the top of the curve keeps stretching out of reach, even for the best of the pros. It's the nature of dance.

Paige sighed and slumped against the wall. Making friends in the ballroom world was not looking good right now. Sylvie was no surprise. She was back to being bitchy Sylvie, but then she'd been groomed by bitchy Katherine. Carrie brushed against Paige as she ushered a student into the ballroom without even a quick "hi" or an "excuse me." Even Brianna was standoffish lately. Paige felt ready to choose the sincerity of solitude over the fickle nature of friendship. She hated to think ballroom pros were inherently spiteful, but there was something about all those sequins and crystals that didn't bring out the best in people. Life becomes fake—all about putting superficial stuff first and winning competitions and trophies, at any cost.

Marcos and Barbara Bradshaw were in the center of the ballroom, dancing through Barbara's new foxtrot routine. Paige tried not to look their way, but she couldn't stop herself. Marcos met her gaze head-on with a look somewhere between wary and scornful. His eyes held none of their usual welcoming warmth. Paige raised a hand, but dropped it at half-mast. The man must think she hates him, but then she could hardly blame him after her knee-jerk reaction.

Paige bit her lip and fingered the folded paper stuffed deep in the pocket of her cardigan. She'd copied down some info, hoping to make a few calls to confirm at least some of what she'd learned. Before she had any kind of a serious talk with Marcos, she'd better know what she was talking about. Maybe she'd approach him after the Halloween party. She folded her arms and rocked on her heels. She couldn't leave things the way they were, with no explanation for her behavior, and now she'd lost the luxury of time.

"Hey there. Are you perfecting your dance skills by osmosis?" Brianna shouted in Paige's ear. Someone had raised the volume again.

Paige turned around and smiled. Brianna was finally friendly again. "Yup. That's my new approach. Don't think I'll be asking Sylvie for a tutorial on Latin technique any time soon."

Brianna placed her hand on Paige's back. "Don't worry too much. It will all blow over. Trust me. Stuff happens. After the comp, Sylvie will be in a better head space. Even Marcos is grumpy today. He's been a real grinch."

"I guess I hadn't noticed," Paige said, unable to meet Brianna's eyes. "I sure hope you are right about Sylvie coming around, though—"

"Hey, Paige. Hi." Brandon, the male half of her wedding couple, came bounding into the ballroom. "Sorry to interrupt." He performed a little bow to acknowledge Brianna. Paige had to stifle a giggle. What a sweet guy he was.

"No problem," Brianna said. "I'll leave you two to talk. I have a student coming in any minute, and I'm still in my street shoes."

"So where's Nikki? Isn't she with you?" Paige could hazard a guess why Nikki wasn't with him, but she didn't want to jump to any conclusions and make an ass out of herself.

"Um. Right. Nikki's not with me. She…um…she called off the wedding." Brandon waved his hand in a *no* when Paige started to make a sympathetic sound. "Believe me, it's all for the best—water under the bridge—and I'm moving downstream with the current." Brandon made a wavy motion with his hand.

Paige caught Marcos looking their way. Brandon high-fived at Marcos, and Marcos raised a high-five in return.

"You know, you and Marcos over there probably saved me from making the biggest mistake of my life."

"How so, Brandon?" Paige asked.

"It was learning what a dance partnership should be that woke me up. Nikki and I weren't partners, either on or off the dance floor."

"I'm sorry to hear that, Brandon." Paige gave a little shrug of sympathy.

"It's all good." Brandon had the wide-open grin of a man completely at peace with himself and the world. "But, the good news is, I decided to continue taking dance lessons. Any chance you could fit me into your schedule?"

"I'm sure I can. I would love to work with you." Paige smiled.

She really needed to increase her base of regular students, so this was great news.

"Okay, then," Brandon said. "I'll go get Jill to put me on the books for a weekly standing with you. I'm on a lunch break. Can I postpone signing any contracts until my first lesson?"

"I don't think it will be a problem," Paige said. "I'll walk you to reception. You might have a couple of paid lessons still on the books anyway. Let's go check."

Paige tossed her sweater and dance-shoe bag in the general direction of the couch, took Brandon's arm, and escorted him to the lobby.

~

Barbara Bradshaw
6:30 p.m., Thursday, 29 October

The familiar muted bang of the heavy front door, followed by the metallic thud of keys hitting the entryway table, stirred Barbara out of the comfort of her chair.

"Michael, is that you?" she called, already on her feet. He'd texted as soon as his plane landed, but that was a good hour and half ago.

"Yeah, Mom, it's me."

Barbara collided with her son in the tiled entryway. She grabbed his arm to steady herself and stretched onto her toes to give Michael a hug. He hugged her back with one arm and waved a large brown paper bag under her nose. The tantalizing scent of Chinese food emanated from the bag.

"Sorry to be so late," Michael said. "I'll get my suitcase out of the car later. I'm starving."

"Oh, do I smell General Tso's? Your lateness is completely forgiven," Barbara said. She relieved her son of the bag and headed into the kitchen, where the warm browns and golds of the granite countertops played nicely against the dark woodgrain of the kitchen cabinets. Copper pans hung overhead, catching and reflecting light.

Barbara arranged the takeout containers and serving spoons on the kitchen island.

"Before you walked in the door, I was having a cup of tea and wondering whether I should make us something for dinner or call for delivery." She smiled at her son. "I'm quite pleased you're here, late or not."

"Me, too," Michael said. He slipped his leather jacket over the wrought-iron back of one of the barstools by the island. "Marcos texted me right after I texted you. I made a quick stop at the studio. He wanted us to speak privately before he introduces me around at the Halloween party tomorrow. I hoped bringing home some of our favorite Chinese might redeem me for being so late."

"You know food is always the way to win my heart or my forgiveness," Barbara said, as she pulled plates out of the cupboard and retrieved a bottle of wine from the under-counter wine cooler. "How about opening this white zinfandel?" she asked.

"You know," Michael said, "I wasn't going to call you. I toyed with booking a hotel room for tonight to surprise you at the studio party tomorrow." He reached for the corkscrew and expertly opened the wine. "But I've been your son long enough to know you might be more annoyed than surprised if we didn't have some catch-up time first."

"Smart boy. You know me well," Barbara said. She passed Michael an everyday Mikasa dinner plate. "Help yourself. I'm going to pour more hot water into my cup. I think I can squeeze another cup of tea out of this teabag. I'll have some wine later."

"You have your tea, Mom. I'm having wine. It's been a long day."

Barbara gave Michael time to enjoy the first couple of sips while she busied herself filling plates for both of them. She pulled out the barstool beside her son.

"Did Marcos tell you which workshop dances you'll be teaching for the Halloween workshops?" Barbara asked.

"He did. Marcos wants me to teach one ballroom basics class for sure and then observe whatever else is going on. I'm to make myself as useful as possible during the day and dance with as many students as I can at the evening party. But I do have something else to tell you."

Barbara met Michael's eyes. She held her fork midway from plate to mouth. She hoped her smile would eclipse the motherly concern welling in her throat. Unknowns always worried her, and she didn't want it to show on her face.

"So, what I haven't told you as yet is this. Marcos offered me the opportunity to come on board at Desert DanceSport as an instructor and maybe even as house choreographer."

"Whaaat?" Barbara's fork clattered to the edge of her plate, spilling bits of vegetable-fried rice onto the counter and Saltillo-tiled floor. Her eyes locked onto Michael's.

"We touched on the subject over the phone a week or so ago. My participation tomorrow is an interview of sorts. Marcos knows I haven't done much ballroom since college, but if everything comes together, I might hang up my stage shoes and move back to Tucson."

Barbara's grin was as wide and joyful as a happy child finding a new bike under the Christmas tree.

Michael put down his fork and leaned one arm on the counter. "I'm not sure Marcos has cleared everything with Katherine. I know Marcos has her ear, but it seems that Katherine is the one who makes the final decisions. Marcos said he could work around Katherine, but I'd prefer to be hired with her blessing rather than causing a conflict right off the bat."

"I think that's a wise move."

"So, can I pick your brain a bit about the studio?" Michael said. He reached for an egg roll and dipped one end into the plum sauce, cupping his hand under the eggroll to prevent sauce from dribbling onto the countertop.

"Sure, fire away," Barbara said. "I'll answer what I can." She wondered how Michael was going to be able to form understandable words around the hunk of egg roll he'd bitten off.

Michael chewed and swallowed before continuing. "What do you know about Katherine and how she runs the studio?"

"Katherine is a tough nut to crack." Barbara dipped her teabag in the cup, squeezed it against the spoon, and said last rites over it. "Katherine's never come across as warm. Her demeanor makes it clear she's the boss and she runs the show. She listens to Marcos, though, and maybe sometimes to Sylvie. I've sensed that there might be some romantic history between Marcos and Katherine, but I'm not privy to any details."

"I'll tuck that tidbit away." Michael raised his eyebrows.

Barbara caught the twinkle in Michael's eyes and smiled. "I would describe Katherine as all business, all the time. She's sort of calculating. One of those people who smiles at you like she knows it's expected but doesn't understand why. It feels a little sociopathic." Barbara paused and picked stray rice kernels off the countertop. She turned to look at Michael. "My advice is not to approach Katherine on an emotional level or talk about advancing your career. Everything has to be about what you can do for her and for the studio. But be wary. Lately she's unpredictable, gushing with enthusiasm one minute and snapping at everyone the next."

Michael frowned, and Barbara saw a familiar protective look cross his face. She raised her hand in the international *stop*.

"No, Michael, not at me," Barbara was quick to add. "But I've heard her get pretty testy with Jill and also with some of the instructors. I don't know what's going on with her, so I can't give you much insight. But, in terms of the studio, I probably know more about the inner workings than I should. Marcos talks to me a lot, and, because I help out here and there, I overhear things."

Michael tilted his head. "You help out?"

Barbara shrugged apologetically. "Just little things. I take care of the lobby plants, and I've helped answer phones when Jill is away from her desk."

"Mom!" Michael pushed himself out of his chair. "Mom," he said again. He began to pace. "Let me get this straight. You pay for lessons, you pay registration fees for dance events and outside coaching—from which your instructor benefits as much as you do—and then you volunteer your time to help them run *their* business? You do know that *you* are the client, right?" He emphasized his words with a sideways cut of one hand into the palm of the other.

Barbara shrugged and suppressed an amused smile. The way Michael talked with his hands when he was wound up, you'd think his heritage was Italian rather than English-Scottish.

"A ballroom studio is not a nonprofit, Mom, and the people there aren't your family. You tend to get the two confused. You thought everyone at Dad's office was part of one big family, and where are all of them now?"

"That was different, Michael. I admit I expected them to stay in touch, but…okay, maybe you have a point about my helping at the studio—"

"Mom, I can tell when you're humoring me and when you're honestly agreeing with me."

"Right, but more to the point, dear, what else was it you wanted to ask me about Katherine?" Barbara smiled sweetly and quietly sipped her stone-cold tea.

Michael settled back into his chair and poured himself another glass of wine. "You neatly maneuvered me back onto my own track after a derailment into your business."

Barbara raised both her teacup and an eyebrow.

"Okay, then. I'll stay on my track with a few questions and issues," Michael replied with a smile. "It helps to be armed with as much information as possible when evaluating a new work situation."

Barbara folded her arms and sat back for the ride. Michael began to pace again—a very typical *I'm sorting this through* habit of his father's. He rattled off a list of questions about attrition rates, the number of students, advertising… Italian he might not be, but his expansive hand gestures and excitability were a stereotypical gay giveaway, which she found endearing.

"Whoa there, my Type-A-personality son," Barbara chimed in. "Way too many questions for a quick evening chat, and you need more depth than I can give you. How about if we revisit this after you've talked to Marcos again? I'll try to fill in anything he can't or won't divulge. I might have to do some discreet digging, but I have my ways."

"You're right, I know," Michael said. He rubbed his hand over his bearded jawline. "I'm jumping the gun. We don't even know if I'm a good fit as yet. After tomorrow when I talk with Marcos again, I'll have a better idea of where I need to fill in the blanks. So, how about if we revisit this over breakfast on the weekend?"

"Makes perfect sense to me," Barbara said, through a mouthful of General Tso's chicken. "I think I need that glass of wine now."

∼

Katherine Carrington
8:30 p.m., Thursday, 29 October

"I don't know what was said during your Come-to-Jesus talk with Paige yesterday, but the damn girl never even came back to work in the afternoon and didn't even bother to call. Now you're telling me I shouldn't take her to task over it?" Katherine was beside herself with annoyance. Marcos was fidgeting like a schoolboy called to the principal's office. What the hell was up with him?

"Katherine, I'm asking you to let it go for now. Please. We've had enough disruption around here lately. Let's deal with it after the Halloween party, okay?" Marcos raked one hand through his perfectly combed hair.

"Fine. You win. I don't have time for this right now anyway. I've asked everyone who's still here to pop in to review expectations for tomorrow," Katherine said. She barely got the words out before there was a soft rap on the office door. Brianna came in first, then Paige, Joey, and Jackson. Katherine gave Sylvie a pass because she was teaching a late lesson; Tony she'd talk to in the morning. Carrie was a part-timer and wasn't working this evening. There weren't enough chairs for everyone, so Paige and Jackson hugged the wall. Katherine decided to stand behind her desk rather than have to look up at anyone.

"I'm going to keep this brief and to the point," she said. "Please remember to thank Jackson, oh, and Jill as well, for agreeing to stay late tonight to begin decorating for the party. Even though we're opening late tomorrow, I expect all of you here as early as possible, no later than nine, to put the finishing touches on decorations before students and guests arrive. First and foremost, our annual Halloween party and workshop is something our students look forward to, and we want it to be a fun event for them. However, don't forget the party is also a major promotional opportunity for the studio." Katherine unfolded her arms and leaned on her desk, making eye contact with each captive employee.

Jackson shifted his weight from one foot to the other, eyes fixed on his shoes. Katherine cleared her throat. Once he looked at her, she moved on.

"As you know, we'll have three workshop classes going on during the day rather than regular lessons. If you're not teaching a workshop, be available to even out the numbers, partner participants, or demonstrate the lady's or man's footwork. Remember, workshop classes generate interest in taking private lessons."

"Just a reminder that Michael Bradshaw, Barbara Bradshaw's son, will be spending the day with us." Marcos looked around as he spoke, making sure he connected with everyone in the small room. "Help Michael get oriented in any way you can, and check out his workshop, please. I might want input from you later on his teaching style and also whether he might be a fit with our group." Marcos gestured to Katherine, turning the floor back to her.

"The party will include the usual silly games. Encourage participation. Games build camaraderie. Please introduce people to each other. This is studio family-building time. We'll be selling raffle tickets. Jill can handle most of that for you, and she'll also give out the color-coded wrist bracelets. If someone comes into a workshop without a bracelet, make sure they pay before they participate. The evening will include a costume contest and prizes for the best potluck entrée and dessert." Katherine ticked items off her hand as she spoke. She passed a short stack of papers to Brianna, who happened to be closest to her. "Brianna, please pass these around."

Katherine kept a printout for herself and remained standing behind her desk. "I'm going to read this aloud to make sure you've at least heard it once. I want you to use these statements as talking points with your students tomorrow." She held her paper in front of her with both hands, moving it from left to right and back again until everyone was following it with their eyes. She turned her page around, and began to read.

"Why dance competitions help students take their dancing to the next level…." Katherine's voice was strong and clear as she covered setting goals, improving stamina and muscle tone, having fun, and igniting a passion for dancing. "Does anyone have any questions? Comments?" She asked glanced from face to face. "All right, then, class dismissed." She waved all of them, including Marcos, out of her office.

After the last straggler left the building, Katherine made her rounds, making sure the breakroom coffee pot was unplugged and the lights and fans were off in the main ballroom. Sure enough, one bank of lights was still on, and a cardigan and dance bag were in a jumble half behind and half next to the couch. Paige's name was on the dance shoe bag.

"Stupid, careless girl," Katherine muttered. As she picked up the sweater a flutter of miscellaneous objects slid out of a pocket and landed on the floor. "Bloody hell." Sighing, Katherine bent to retrieve the mess: a tin of breath mints, a small package of Kleenex, a lip gloss, a pencil, and a tightly folded piece of computer paper. She stuffed everything, except the folded paper, back into the sweater's deep pocket. Katherine smoothed the page out on a nearby table.

"What the hell is this?" *Before Confronting Marcos, get facts straight, find out if M was in Phoenix in 1990? what about difference in name, why? what about DNA testing?...* Katherine plopped into a café chair. She creased the page back into its folds and stared off into nothingness. Could this possibly mean what it looks like? DNA testing? But why? Is Paige searching for her birth father? Does the girl actually think that person might be Marcos? How did she connect the names? Or could it be old man Martin she's after? Katherine sat bolt upright. How would he react if he thought he had a daughter or a granddaughter? Maybe he'd want to ensure her future by buying her a piece of the studio? Maybe Marcos would have to step off his pedestal? This was gold. Paige could turn out to be gold. Marcos, a dad? Katherine threw back her head. Her laugh reverberated around the room.

FIFTEEN

Unmasked

Paige Russell
10:30 a.m., Friday, 30 October

"Geez, be careful, girl." Jill was standing on an upholstered chair, stretched on her tippy-toes, trying to pin a string of Halloween decorations high on the wall. "It's not worth a trip to the ER to get all this stuff up." Paige moved closer, ready to steady Jill if needed.

"There. I did it," Jill said. She jumped from the chair, her rainbow headband bobbing crazily on its springs. The wide skirt of her over-the-rainbow costume floated around her. "This was worth coming in early to finish. We did great."

Black cats with arched backs swung from the ceiling; sequined cobwebs twinkled under the overhead lights; bales of hay held piles of pumpkins, baskets of apples, and bowls of wrapped caramel. Witches flew across the walls

"I agree. Totally great." Paige twirled, taking in the transformed lobby. Her side-slit, paisley bell-bottoms whipped around her calves, keeping time with the leather fringe of her vest.

"Hey, did you catch Joey's superhero outfit?" Paige asked. She giggled from behind her hand and arched her eyebrows. "He actually looks pretty darn good in those blue tights."

"I missed him. He must have come in when I was in the hallway on the ladder. But—"

"Excuse me, girls." Like an unwelcome apparition, Katherine appeared out of nowhere. Her black leotard sported a fluffy tail, and a cat-eared headband topped her upswept hairdo. Under the leotard she wore only fishnet stockings. "Paige, may I have a word with you?"

"Yes, ma'am," Paige said. She turned back to Jill with a *What did I do now?* look before following Katherine. Hands clasped, she stood in front of her boss.

"It occurred to me, Paige, that I've been so focused on business, I've been remiss in asking how you're doing, especially in light of a major move and the loss of your mother. I apologize." Katherine placed one hand on Paige's arm.

Paige bit her lip to keep from flinching. The concern in Katherine's eyes looked genuine enough, but...? "I'm okay," Paige replied. "I keep myself occupied with work. Thank you for asking, though."

"What about family, Paige? Do you have siblings? I'm assuming your dad is still alive?"

Paige hesitated. One of Katherine's rules was for everyone to leave their personal lives at the front door. Where was this coming from? "Um...well...My mom was a single mom, and I'm an only child. My grandmother is in a nursing home in Florida. My only aunt lives close to my grandmother." Paige twisted a strand of hair around her finger and shrugged. "I never knew my dad really, so—"

"Oh dear. I didn't mean to open a wound." Katherine moved a little closer. "If you ever want to talk, sweetie, you know I'm here. But, for now," Katherine waved her hand in the direction of the lobby, "you should get back to what you were doing, and I have to get myself into the rest of this costume."

"Okay, thanks, Katherine," Paige said. *Sweetie?* What just happened? She hoped her confusion wasn't written all over her face. She'd never been a good poker player.

"What was that all about?" Jill whispered as Paige slipped behind the counter. "And did you get a load of the V-neck of her leotard? It's cut damn near to her navel."

"Yup. Not too shabby for a fiftysomething," Paige said, avoiding both Jill's eyes and her question. She turned away and heaped cookies from a bakery box onto trays.

"Cars are starting to pull up outside already. Get ready for cray-cray day," Jill said.

Paige ticked her list off her fingers. "Let's see. You're in charge of the color-coded wristbands. I've set up the refreshment tables. I'll add these pumpkin cookies and carrot cake muffins Katherine got from the bakery. You have the big coffee pot all ready, right?"

"Yup. I'll keep coffee going all day," Jill said.

"Are you working overtime? Will you be here through the evening?" Paige asked.

"I'm staying. Katherine wants someone at the front desk all day to take last-minute payments and in the early evening for people who are coming only for the potluck and party. I need the extra hours anyway."

The front door opened and one Goofy, a pirate, two flappers, and a Disney princess streamed into the lobby. Everyone carried a tray or covered container. Yummy mixed aromas escaped into the air.

"Jill, I'd better get these on the table and make sure we have space for more." Paige hurried toward the refreshment tables outside the main ballroom. Someone in a brightly colored Hawaiian-style muumuu was putting out Halloween-themed plates and napkins. The shape was all wrong for another instructor, but who else would step in...? Oh, of course, Linda Wilson. Her voice was a dead giveaway. She was joking and chatting with everyone within earshot.

"Let me help you." Paige rearranged plates and platters and added Katherine's offerings. The variety of treats was overwhelming. Good thing she'd put out the second table.

"I brought the pumpkin bread," Linda Wilson said. "I was supposed to bring a pecan pie." Linda made sure she had Paige's attention and then scanned the crowd.

Paige knew better than to turn back to what she was doing. High-paying students like Linda held an unspoken status and didn't take well to being ignored. A story was pending.

"I had the pie in the oven. It smelled fabulous," Linda said. Her gaze grazed each face as she expertly stopped everyone in their tracks. "Homemade crust and the pecans arranged in a beautiful spiral. I put the pie on the rack to cool and opened the microwave to heat water for tea. And there it was." Linda paused and splayed her hands out in front of her. "The melted butter that was supposed to go into the pie was still sitting in the microwave."

Linda's words were met with sympathetic murmurs. Paige was impressed. Linda Wilson could work a crowd. No wonder she was a top real estate agent.

Linda's eyes rose heavenward, as if questioning the pie-making gods. "So, the whole pie hit the trash can. But I'd made pumpkin bread as well. It's my own special recipe." Linda pointed at a plate of golden sliced bread. Onlookers quickly moved forward to sample Linda's special bread and exclaim over its moist texture.

Paige stepped out of the way as a woman in a bathrobe, covered with stuffed toy cats, maneuvered a tray of nicely arranged, quartered sandwiches onto the table. As if she were hosting the event, Linda greeted her with a big smile and changed the topic of conversation to the costume contest and prizes that would be awarded for the best dishes after the potluck dinner. This party was clearly a big deal to everyone. Who knew?

"Paige, excuse me, I need to get through." She felt a light touch on her back. Marcos! He was dressed as a circus ringmaster. The man's sense of humor was classic.

"Everyone." Marcos clapped to get the crowd's attention. "In ten minutes, at 12:30, our first workshop starts. Michael Bradshaw is your guest instructor. If you are signed up, please begin making your way into the rehearsal hall." Marcos turned toward Paige. "Brianna is assigned to Michael's workshop to demonstrate the ladies' footwork.

I'd like you to stand by to observe, but be prepared to step in and partner someone if needed."

"Of course," Paige replied, matching Marcos's polite, professional demeanor. Her insides cringed. She hated feeling this awkward but had no idea how to ease the tension. Potential scenarios bounced around her brain as she walked into Michael's workshop. Michael acknowledged her with a nod and a big smile.

The ratio of leaders to followers looked pretty even. Good. She might not have to stay long. Brianna, in a short, flirty ice-skater costume, stood next to Michael at the front of the room. She wore leggings under the short skirt. Smart girl. The ceiling fans in this smaller ballroom had swished more than one skirt higher than the wearer expected. On a young, tightly muscled girl it could be a cute moment, but on the older women not so much. Paige shuddered. No one wants to see saggy, aging butt, male or female.

Michael glanced around the room full of chin-wagging students, clapped loudly, and asked everyone to focus their attention where it should be focused, on him. He said it with forked fingers pointing from the crowd to his eyes. His smile was all charm. Paige was impressed. In moments, the chatty group was under control and eating out of his hands. Michael began his spiel, pacing and punctuating his words with broad hand gestures. His energy was contagious.

"We have both Bronze- and Silver-level dancers in this workshop, but it never hurts for even the most advanced dancers to go over ballroom basics." Pointing to a flyer, Michael continued. "We'll cover Dance Frame, Head Position and Connection, Line of Dance, Alignments to Line of Dance, Contra Body Movement, and Swing and Sway. I want to touch on the differences between the dances: the rise and fall and sweeping flow of the waltz, the jazzy slow-slow quick-quick of foxtrot, and the staccato movements of the tango. We have a lot to cover in one hour." Michael clasped his hands together and glanced around the room. From what Paige could see, everyone was fully engaged.

"One thing I want to emphasize today," Michael continued, "especially for you ladies, is a mistake most beginners make, which is focusing on learning patterns. Ladies, if you try to anticipate which pattern your partner might lead next, you are likely to be wrong and you won't be focusing where you should be focusing, on your connection. Connection is everything. You have to turn off your thinking. You are not in control on the dance floor." Michael tilted his head and, with a saucy smile, wagged his finger at the ladies.

"Connection tells you where to go," he continued. "Your only job as a follower is to understand some basic rules of movement, and then go in the direction your partner sends you. Now, for the gentlemen, it's up to you to hold a strong frame, have a good connection with your partner, and focus on the rhythm. You should be feeling the rhythm of the music throughout your body before you take that first step. Begin with simple movements so you can establish the conversation of connection between you and your partner." Michael stopped and made eye contact around the room, leaving time for any questioning hands to go up.

"Okay, then." Michael rubbed his palms together. "We are going to start with a Bronze-level foxtrot. The first two beats are slows, two walking steps: *slow, slow.* Then step to the side for a lilting *quick-quick.*" Michael demonstrated as he spoke. "The movement is jazzy, and you roll through your feet."

Paige was dying for a cigarette. She couldn't stop fidgeting. She lasted about twenty minutes and then signaled to the entrance with a head nod. Michael shot her a thumbs-up. Eyes down, she slipped quietly out of the room, turned the corner, and walked smack into Marcos, who was observing Michael's class.

"Whoops. Slow down, young lady." Marcos caught Paige by both arms and held her at a safe distance, preventing full-on frontal contact. He looked her up and down. "You make a groovy hippie. That's quite the fringed vest you have there."

Paige sidestepped his grasp and straightened her flowered

headband. "It was stashed in the back of my mother's closet. I never thought this was her style, but I guess we never know anyone, really." Geez, even to her own ears she sounded sarcastic. Paige took a breath and tried again. "Sorry I almost ran you over. I need a quick smoke before Tony's workshop."

Marcos nodded, stepped aside, and tipped his top hat, allowing her to move quickly past him. She trotted to the back door, her heart thumping in her chest.

Paige walked several feet away from the back entrance. She'd been reminded more than once about the city ordinance requiring smokers to be twenty feet from the entrance to a building. She lit up, took a long, satisfying drag, and felt her body soften and relax. She leaned against the eucalyptus tree and closed her eyes.

"There she is, the fake little bitch."

Paige's eyes flew open. Sylvie's expression registered outrage. Seemed that her Tinkerbell costume didn't include fairy dust. Paige eyed the large bag of ice Sylvie carried, hoping the plan wasn't to whack her with it.

"W-what? What's wr-wrong with you?" Paige stuttered. "What did I do now?"

"Brandon. Wedding-couple Brandon. Like you don't know. Before I made an ice run, I overheard him talking to Katherine. I guess he thinks you're the cutest, sweetest little thing ever, and he's 'so happy to be taking lessons from you.' He thinks you walk on water. Yeah, sure you do, but it's frozen and thin." Sylvie's voice was low and ugly. "So, going after Tony wasn't enough? Now you've broken an engagement. Are you proud of yourself?"

"No. No, Sylvie. You're wrong. It wasn't like that. I—"

"Don't bullshit me, little Miss Innocent. Everyone thinks you're so naïve, but I see through your smoke screen. You're a conniving little bitch who'll do anything to climb to the top. You secretly want to push me out and train to partner Tony, don't you?"

What was Sylvie saying? This was so unfair. Paige felt tears welling.

She ducked her head and dropped her cigarette into the gravel. She turned to walk away, but Sylvie's hand closed around her wrist. Sylvie pulled Paige nose to nose.

"You stay the hell away from Tony until after this comp in LA. Do you hear me? I need all of his fire so he can explode on the dance floor. After we win, he's all yours. Maybe you two deserve each other you...you fat-assed *puta*!"

Paige wrenched her wrist free. It was reddened and sore. Sylvie flipped her blond curls and stalked into the studio, one arm bracing the big bag of ice against her side. Paige blinked hard and fast. She would not cry. She dropped her face into her hands. Sylvie had everything all wrong. She had no right to accuse her of such awful things. The back door slammed and footsteps approached. Paige braced herself. Oh no, please not Sylvie again. She felt a familiar hand on her shoulder.

"Paige, what's wrong?" Marcos asked. "What can I do to help?"

His gaze took in her reddened wrist. She covered it with her other hand and turned to face him, blinking back tears. She so wanted to feel Marcos's arm around her and confide in him like she used to, but she couldn't. She was too afraid of sending the wrong message. Paige shook her head. "It's nothing. Nothing I want to talk about anyway," Paige said. With downcast eyes she sidestepped around him and ran to the back door, ponytail and leather fringe flying behind her.

～

Marcos Stephanos
1:30 p.m., Friday, 30 October

Marcos felt both oddly defensive and like a fool standing alone in the parking lot. His mood was slipping into exasperation. Dead cigarette butts littered the gravel. "It's starting to look like one big ashtray out here," he muttered, making a mental note to clean the area later. He scanned the back entrance to the studio and rubbed his jawline, lips pursed. Why hadn't he noticed before how tawdry and rundown everything looked? There were weeds against the back wall, greasy-looking fingerprints all over the door, and a crack in an office window. Not good. He had to talk to Katherine about getting some basic maintenance work done. A tacky-looking facility was not conducive to attracting an upscale clientele.

Marcos rubbed his jawline, his thoughts back on Paige. Today wasn't the day to try to smooth things over with her, but this tension between them couldn't continue. What on earth was going through her mind? Was she repelled by the age difference between them? Or was it that he was basically her boss? Marcos held his breath. What if Paige now felt unsafe at work? Could that be it? Christ, the last damn thing he needed was a sexual harassment suit. Was it possible he completely misread her signals?

He took off his top hat, placed it on the bench under the eucalyptus tree, and finger-combed the hat-hair look he knew he must be sporting. Marcos reached for the buttons on the costume's red jacket but then stopped. If he took the heavy jacket off, he wasn't going to want to put it back on. At least Katherine agreed to lower the air-conditioning for today. God only knows what they made these costumes out of, but they damn well held in body heat.

The urge to smoke had passed, so now there was nothing left to do but put the absurd top hat back on, affix a smile to his face, and get back inside in time for Tony's American Rhythm class. What had possessed Katherine to put Paige on the schedule for Tony's class? Had she spaced out on everything that happened recently, or was she setting Paige up for a fall?

Marcos stepped in the back door and immediately pivoted sideways to avoid a collision with someone's plate of sandwiches and cookies. The hallway was awash with a wave of costumed humanity. Closer to the reception area, students were gleefully breaking balloons for the prizes hidden inside, and there was a short line to claim raffle ticket wins. Katherine had outdone herself this year. There were the usual prizes of free coaching, but somehow the Queen of Coercion had maneuvered clients into donating services ranging from massages and makeovers to a tamale-making class and even a cosmetic surgery consultation.

"This is the best Halloween party ever, Marcos." A woman—he couldn't remember her name—was pulling on the sleeve of his jacket. "The studio looks great. Super decorations. I might have to hire you guys the next time I need an event planner." The woman's light laugh rippled out, and the arm grab changed to a light punch. Marcos tipped his hat and moved on, schmoozing his way through the throng. He hoped his overworked crew could keep it together through the potluck and dance party. The kids had the weekend to blow off steam in their own way, on their own turf. As long as they came in fresh on Monday, Marcos was good.

"Hey, Marcos, over here." Michael was standing by one of the treat tables, waving him over with a very large, half-eaten carrot cake muffin.

"Good workshop, Michael," Marcos said. He eyed the muffin and glanced at the table to see how many were left. His stomach suddenly reminded him he hadn't eaten. "I observed most of your class and have only positive things to say."

"Appreciate that. You have a great group of students here. Everyone was receptive, and I was impressed by how many keep notebooks." Michael licked frosting off his fingers.

"What's next for you this afternoon?"

"I'm on game duty," Michael said. He crumpled the cupcake paper and tossed it into the trash can. "I get to supervise everyone whacking the wicked witch piñata before the potluck starts. I'm hoping to watch part of Sylvie's three-thirty workshop. By the way." Michael edged a bit closer to Marcos and lowered his voice. "What's Joey's story? The girls say he's married, but my gaydar kicked in big time, and I'm never wrong." Michael wiggled his raised eyebrows.

Marcos blinked, twice. What? He pulled his head back. "You're on your own with that one, buddy." He laughed and shook Michael's shoulder. "I'm not sure any turn of events around here can surprise me anymore. All I know from Linda is that Joey and the wife pretty much lead separate lives. And, in the nick of time, here comes our lovely leader." Even under the painted-on cat whiskers and heavy makeup, Katherine's face was flushed, and her gaze looked glazed. He hooded his eyes with one hand. Maybe it was just the lighting.

"Haven't seen you all day," Marcos said.

"And there's a good reason, my friend." Katherine smiled. "I've been busy writing contracts for both existing students and their guests. Two more couples have entered heats for the ball in December. Everyone seems to having a great time. The party is a huge success."

Marcos smiled and nodded, leaning in a bit closer. Yup. Katherine's cheeks were flushed, and the flush extended into her very visible cleavage. Was it caused by an adrenaline rush from a good sales day or was there a faint smell of alcohol clinging to Katherine? *Please, God, don't let this day go south.*

"And here comes my favorite student on the arm of your favorite student." Marcos beamed. "Look at you two. Sonny and Cher?"

Barbara tossed her long black wig and kicked up a leg to show off her colorful bell-bottoms and white boots. Edward sported a faux-fur vest, wide leather belt, and khaki-colored bell-bottoms. He'd planted a longish toupee on his head to complete the look.

Barbara opened her arms to give Marcos a hug. "We came for Tony's class and the potluck and dancing. We'd never make it through a full day of workshops and have energy left for the party." Barbara smiled sweetly at Katherine. "Great crowd. Looks like you've pulled off another great Halloween, Katherine."

Marcos was appalled. Katherine barely nodded at Barbara, but instead turned to Ed.

"Save me a dance or two this evening, Edward," Katherine said. "Maybe you'll win the big drawing of a night on the town with your instructor."

Marcos had never seen anyone bat their eyelashes before, but there it was. Katherine could drive a wind turbine with those thick fringes glued to her eyelids. "I'll walk you two over to Tony's workshop." Marcos said. He gave Katherine a *What the hell?* look and got a raised chin in return. Six more hours until 8:00 p.m. Time couldn't pass fast enough.

SIXTEEN

KISMET

Marcos Stephanos
1:50 p.m., Friday, 30 October

Marcos stopped in his tracks. His top hat tilted forward hitting the bridge of his nose; he pushed it up with the back of his hand. Coming at him was a bedsheet-white face with grotesquely rimmed eyes and exaggerated skeletal teeth. The hooded figure was draped in an obsidian-black cloak. It held a scythe in one hand. A shiver ran across the back of Marcos's neck. A familiar giggle floated out of the depths of the hood, breaking Marcos's visceral reaction. He felt more than a bit foolish as the hood slipped down to reveal a tousle of blond curls.

"Amy Fromme," Marcos said with his hand over his heart. The juxtaposition of this black-hooded nightmare with gentle Amy, waving a cookie from a slit in the cloak, induced a bellow of self-conscious laughter from Marcos. "Whatever inspired this angel-of-death look, and what happened to your usual wild-haired gypsy costume? This getup is haunted-house scary."

"Funny you should say that," Amy replied. "Eric and I volunteer in the Angels for Children's walk-through haunted house. I scared myself the first time I put this costume on and looked in the mirror. Wait until you see Eric, all draped in white and chains. Great Halloween party, by the way." Amy bit a hunk out of the oversized cookie, spilling crumbs down her cloak.

"Thanks. So, we've missed you at group class."

"Sorry," Amy said. "We've been going to Carrie's group lessons at our community club house. It's sorta fun to enjoy a cocktail or two during a dance lesson. Loosens us all up."

"Carrie's classes at the club?" Marcos deliberately inserted an upbeat lilt to his voice.

"Exactly. You know that nice couple from Canada, Lisa and George Benton? They snowbird in our neighborhood, and they sponsor a happy hour twice a month. They hired Carrie to teach some ballroom lessons. You knew about this, though, right?" Amy said.

Marcos tilted his head, hoping it was an ambiguous response.

"Carrie's such a sweetie. We really enjoy her." Amy dropped the last half of the cookie into a side pocket. "Marcos, I'd love to chat more, but I want to hit the ladies' room before Tony's class. By the way, Lisa and George were in the reception area a few minutes ago, checking out the cupcake table. Doctors never follow their own orders about diet, do they?"

"Doesn't seem like it." Marcos smiled, tipping his hat. "Great to see you, Amy." He glanced at his watch, sighed, and grimaced. Tony's class was starting soon, but he needed to catch the Bentons first. He'd find Carrie later.

Marcos slipped into Tony's class and tucked himself into an inconspicuous corner. His goal was to observe without looking like a school hall monitor, ready to write someone up. He placed his top hat next to him, unbuttoned the confining jacket, and folded his hands behind his head. The Bentons had been naïvely open with him when he asked about their happy-hour lessons, completely unaware that, by teaching at their club, Carrie had put herself into a precarious position with the studio. He'd deal with Carrie later but not until rational thinking overcame his initial anger.

A cursory head count revealed twenty-two participants in Tony's class, with ages ranging from energetic twentysomethings to the older, Barbara-and-Edward crowd. Marcos knew for a fact that the tall, willowy redhead was at least seventy-one. Every student in the room was intermediate to advanced and serious about increasing their skill level. Marcos made a mental note to talk to Katherine about adding an advanced Rhythm class into the weekly schedule. And speak of the devil, there she was. Katherine sidled through the entrance and leaned against the back wall, a tumbler of orange juice dangling in her hand.

Marcos's attention shifted to Paige as she strolled across the room to join Tony at the front of the class. A tasseled silk scarf wove through the low belt loops of her paisley bell-bottoms, accentuating her flat stomach. Marcos rubbed his forehead, sucking in his upper lip. Paige was avoiding him, and if she didn't break the freeze-out soon, he was going to have to. Tony stood with his back to the mirrored wall. Paige joined him. She slipped off her fringed vest, revealing a clingy camisole. Marcos swallowed hard. Not knowing what was going through Paige's mind was driving him crazy. Their situation wasn't unique. Most couples meet at work. But with strict rules against fraternizing with students, dance teachers dating each other was the norm, not the exception. And he was her superior, if not her boss. Was Paige afraid of losing her job if they got involved and it didn't work out? In today's feminist world, was he a reckless fool to come on to a subordinate? Marcos felt his temples tighten with the threat of a headache.

Tony clapped. Marcos turned his focus back to the teaching couple. Paige was smiling, but there was an aura of tension around the edges. He mentally crossed his fingers that Tony wouldn't be a douche and Paige could hold it together, especially after what he'd witnessed outside.

"Okay, mis amigos, down to business. The patterns we're working on today are Alternating Underarm Turns, Open Swivel Walks, Left-Side Catch, Cradle and Roll Out, Quick Underarm Turn Roll Out, and Circle Wrap. For many of you, these patterns aren't new, but our focus will be on proper technique and arm styling. Paige and I will demonstrate as we go. At the end of the class, we'll run through the entire sequence so you can video. Gracias."

Marcos leaned back, drawing one ankle onto the opposite thigh. He wrapped his hands around the folded knee and tried to focus on Tony's teaching.

"Before we dive in," Tony continued, "let's review basics. The Rhythm dances, especially rumba and cha-cha, involve continuous movement rather than moving only on the beat or the count." Tony demonstrated a basic rumba box as he spoke. He traced his toes along the floor, moving with enviable Cuban motion as he straightened and bent his knees. "I want you to think about the *ands*: one *and* two or slow *and* quick *and* quick. One movement flows smoothly into the next. You want a relaxed, artistic flow." Tony pulled Paige in front of him.

Marcos gritted his teeth.

"Watch Paige as I lead her through a basic rumba box." Tony stepped forward. "Notice how she keeps her weight on the inside edge of her feet, with her toes turned out. As one knee bends, the other leg straightens, which causes her hips to roll around and back, in a figure eight. She never lifts her feet from the floor, but slides them like she is trying to keep a dollar bill under the toe of her shoes."

The low waist of Paige's hippie bell-bottoms rolled seductively around her hips. The tassels on the scarf flicked back and forth like a cat's tongue.

Tony wiggled one eyebrow and shot a wicked look at the group. "Ladies, pay attention to how Paige uses her ASSets with atTITude: ab tucked in, ta-tas pushed forward, and butt pushed out." The room resounded with giggles. Tony smirked in Marcos's direction. Paige, head held high, didn't react.

Marcos's fists closed, and a jaw muscle began to twitch. To his left, he caught a movement. Katherine slipped along the back wall, moving toward him. He breathed himself into a demeanor of nonchalance.

"Now find a partner and get into dance hold, elbows down. You should feel a strong connection through your hands as you crunch and stretch your rib cage," Tony said. "And remember the character of the dance. While cha-cha is flirtatious, rumba is more sensual; the relationship has moved past flirting and on to…well, use your imagination." Tony winked at the crowd and got a laugh in return. This time Paige turned crimson.

"*Slow and, quick and quick; slow and, quick and quick.* Draw out those slows." Tony moved with Paige as one. The room moved with them.

Marcos felt Katherine invade his personal space, looming over him, too close to his chair. She leaned in, pointed her glass at Paige, and whispered, "She's so very young and flexible, isn't she? Everything we aren't anymore. Doesn't it make you feel old to realize your little protégé is easily young enough to be your daughter?"

Marcos felt himself stiffen. The hair on the back of his neck rose. What had Katherine heard? Surely Paige hadn't talked to her? Could she know anything about the lunch incident? Was that comment a *dirty old man* dig?

"Katherine, you're being absurd," Marcos whispered behind his hand. "Since when do we talk about feeling old? What brought this on?"

"Oh, I don't know." Katherine released a stagey sigh. "Maybe nostalgia for my misspent youth," she said, leaning even closer. Her glass tilted, spilling a few drops of liquid on the edge of the dance floor. "I'm beginning to regret not having kids or grandkids to enjoy as I age."

Marcos turned, but Katherine kept her eyes locked on the couple at the front of the room.

"I'm surprised your father hasn't given you more grief about not producing a grandchild." Katherine leaned close enough to whisper in Marcos's ear. "The crazy way you drive that sports car, have you ever thought about writing a will and inserting an 'in the case of progeny' clause? Who knows, Marcos, maybe you have offspring out there somewhere. Heirs to your father's fortune."

Marcos jerked his head to one side. He rubbed his temples. Katherine was on a wildly provocative tangent, and he was in no mood to rise to the bait right now.

"Paige doesn't have a boyfriend, does she? Maybe she doesn't like the young ones. I wonder if she might be looking for a sugar daddy or maybe just a daddy. Who knows?" Katherine tapped the tips of her nails on her tumbler as she spoke.

"Katherine, you're babbling utter nonsense. What the hell is in that glass, anyway?" Marcos stood and reached for the tumbler, but Katherine jerked it out of his way, spilling a few orange drops on her cleavage.

"None of your concern, Mr. Stephanos. I am mourning the loss of my sister on this almost-anniversary of her death." Katherine made a toasting motion. Marcos narrowed his eyes as she shielded the tumbler with one hand. "Whatever it takes to get me through the day." She tossed her cat-eared head.

"Let's step out to the hall," Marcos said. He retrieved his hat and took Katherine by the elbow. He could see more than one set of eyes following them in the mirror. Tony was grinning, probably quite happy to have Marcos out of his way.

"Katherine, what the hell? Is that damn orange juice spiked?" Marcos leaned forward and sniffed the glass. He recoiled and resisted the temptation to wrestle the tumbler away from her. "This is inexcusable, no matter the reason. And what's all that nonsense you were nattering about Paige and your sudden interest in my father's need for a grandchild? What bottle did that complete crap escape from?" As annoyed as Marcos was, he had to compress his lips to avoid smiling. How did you lecture a cat face painted with exaggerated whiskers?

"Marcos," Katherine breathed. She blinked at him, all wide-eyed innocence. "I was teasing, just playing. You take everything much too seriously. We'll talk later when you're in a better mood." Katherine turned tail and strutted off.

Marcos lifted his top hat and scratched his head. Damn that woman. She poked with her passive-aggressive taunts and then, when he got pissed, said "only kidding." He leaned against the wall, not knowing whether to curse or laugh.

Tony's class was winding down. Marcos heard him encouraging students to video him and Paige running through the entire sequence of steps. He pulled away from the wall and turned toward the ballroom, stopped, turned around again, and headed for the main treat table. He needed a heavily iced chocolate cupcake. Better sugar than sugar daddy, at least for the moment.

～

Katherine Carrington
2:45 p.m., Friday, 30 October

"Jill." Katherine poked her head around the corner to the reception area. Jill was putting out wristbands for the end-of-day stragglers.

"Yes, ma'am?" Jill said. Her rainbow headband bobbled.

"I need to speak with as many instructors as are available. Tell them to come to my office as soon as Tony's workshop ends. Oh, and find Marcos and let him know we're meeting before the third class starts. Leave the front desk unattended while you round everyone up."

Not waiting for an answer, Katherine ducked back around the corner and darted through the crowd to the shelter of her office. She closed the door, leaned against the cool wood, and lowered her chin to her chest. Her social smile dissolved into abject misery. Leave it to her bloody mother to call during her favorite party day and accuse her, once again, of being responsible for Kimberly's death. Jesus. She had just been a child wanting to go out for Halloween with her big sister. Joan had lost a daughter, but why couldn't she understand Katherine had lost a sister as well? With a sigh that caught in her throat like a sob, Katherine emotionally regrouped. She pulled the bottle of vodka out of its hiding place in her desk and poured herself a quick shot. The warm liquid mended her frazzled edges. She deposited the bottle of Ketel One back in the file drawer.

Katherine straightened her torso, sucked in her abs, and turned to examine her reflection in the mirror. The black cat costume definitely showed off her curves and taut muscles. What the hell could Edward see in Plain Jane Barbara when he had Katherine right in front of him? Couldn't be Barbara's looks. Maybe the woman was a first-class cook? Katherine laughed a bitter-sounding laugh and blew herself a kiss. She was better than this. If Edward couldn't be more discriminatory in his taste for women, it was his loss, not hers. What was it that awful Felicia at New Haven called her the other day? A narcissist! Did the woman think that was an insult? Katherine tilted her head and ran one finger along a painted-on cat whisker. Smiling, she confirmed to her reflection, "I don't underestimate myself, and I don't believe in false modesty. If that's narcissism, then so be it."

At the sound of approaching footsteps, Katherine shoved the empty shot glass into the still-open file drawer. She was standing behind her desk by the time her minions knocked.

"Door's open."

Marcos filed in first, followed by Sylvie, Joey, Brianna, Paige, and then Tony. Tony found a seat, while everyone else remained standing.

"Since we have a longer break between the second and third workshops, Marcos and I thought this would be the best time to speak with all of you." Katherine didn't miss Sylvie's quizzical head tilt or Joey's closed-off folded arms. "No worries," Katherine said, with a dismissive wave of her hand. "We only want to get your impressions of Michael Bradshaw." Katherine glanced around the room. "Everyone, please speak freely. There are no wrong answers." Marcos was campaigning hard to bring Michael on board. She still wasn't convinced Michael was a fit or whether he could compete for clients and floor time. And, until he was up to speed, covering the extra paycheck could be a bitch.

"I was impressed." Sylvie spoke first. "Not only was his technique flawless, but he was able to translate his movements into words the students could understand." Sylvie stopped to sip from her water bottle. "Michael was clear, didn't throw too much at them at once, and walked around to give one-on-one help. He put together a short bit of choreography, which made everyone feel like they came out of class with more than they expected. I liked his style."

"He's okay," Tony said. "Good moves, quiet demeanor, the students seemed to like him."

Katherine stood with her right arm folded across her midriff and traced a line across her lips with her left index finger. Typical Tony. Praise for other male dancers didn't fall off his lips. He was the top dog, one leg raised, ready to piss on everything to mark his territory.

"From what I've seen and heard, I think he's great," Joey finally piped up.

"I thought he was good, too. Seems like a nice enough guy." Paige shrugged.

"I overheard a few students say they loved his class. Seems pretty cool," Brianna said.

"Thank you, Brianna. Actually, Brianna, you can go," Katherine said. "You're needed more to keep things moving out there."

Marcos opened the door for Brianna and closed it behind her. Arms folded, he stood with his back against the door. As he started to speak, all heads turned in his direction.

"As you all know, we are considering bringing Michael on board. With his ballroom and stage experience, he would make the perfect replacement for Jeremy. Michael will need some coaching in our dance syllabus to teach ballroom full time, but he's a quick study. I'd like to groom him to represent Desert DanceSport on the competitive circuit as well. There are several students he could partner, and I'm sure he'll attract new ones."

At that, Katherine unfolded her arms and nodded. A little more competition for Tony. This could be a good thing. Tony might get his act together if he felt threatened.

"When will you make a decision?" Sylvie asked.

"Soon. Katherine and I have to talk. It's as much Michael's decision as ours. He has to decide if we're the right fit for him as well," Marcos said, moving away from the door.

"I guess we'll leave things there for now," Katherine said. "Make sure our guests are all getting enough attention, and try to pry those wallets open, please. So, everyone out. Oh, Sylvie, I'm going to observe at least part of your workshop. I'm hoping it will inspire more students to develop an interest in paso doble."

Marcos once again held the door open but didn't leave with everyone else. Katherine took a seat, waiting for the other shoe to drop.

"Katherine, we have a problem. Or I should say we *had* a problem. I couldn't find you, so I took action." Marcos folded himself into a chair. "I let Carrie go."

"What? Why?" Katherine walked around her desk and perched on the edge facing Marcos, her cat tail swinging off to one side. At least Marcos hadn't stayed to lecture her.

"Carrie was giving dance lessons to guests of the Bentons at the happy hours they sponsor at their club and also at private parties at their home. Even Eric and Amy Fromme have taken a few lessons there instead of here. Carrie knew the rules. Staff instructors aren't allowed to teach on the side. And worse, she's taken gifts and money as gratuities. The Bentons had no idea anything she was doing for them was in conflict with her employee contract."

"I'm so very disappointed in her." Katherine compressed her lips and shook her head. "She knew better than to undercut the studio. What did she have to say for herself?"

Marcos ran his fingers through his hair. Damp from wearing the hat all day, it stuck out at wild angles. "That's the thing. Had she been apologetic or offered an acceptable line of reasoning, I might have given her a reprimand rather than firing her. She was quite the opposite, very belligerent. She felt justified in taking what she sees as rightfully hers."

"Exactly what did she say?" Katherine asked, arms folded tightly across her chest.

"Carrie went on a tirade about being 'tired of living on the edge of wealth, having her face shoved in everything she'll never have.' It had finally sunk in that teaching ballroom won't get her the lifestyle her clients enjoy. She hates wearing fake diamonds while four-carat diamonds are flashed in her face. Sadly, what she said has a ring of truth to it, but what do these kids expect? Too many come here straight from high school, never continue their education, and don't have a long-range flight plan."

"Agreed," Katherine said. "And these clients she is so jealous of—doctors, financial advisors, engineers—all worked hard to get where they are today. Carrie's thinking is off."

"Who knows what she was thinking?" Marcos shrugged. "I was too upset with her attitude of entitlement to delve very deep. Anyway, I wanted you to hear the news firsthand. I couldn't let this go." Marcos put the top hat back on and touched it in an ironic salute. "Back to playing circus ringleader."

The door had barely closed before Katherine rounded her desk and retrieved the bottle and shot glass out of the drawer. "Between my bloody mother having a wave of lucidity on the eve of Halloween, Edward arriving with sappy Barbara on his arm, and Carrie trying to sabotage us, I bloody well deserve a drink." She swigged back the shot and poured another shot into her coffee cup. She'd top it off with coffee before going into Sylvie and Joey's workshop. Katherine opened the door to a hallway buzzing with happy voices, punctuated with laughter.

∿

Katherine stood at the entrance to watch Sylvie's workshop unfold. There were fifteen people in the room. Jackson would partner the extra lady, making it sixteen. Sylvie led a warm-up sequence, looking every inch the gorgeous Latin dancer. She'd changed out of her Tinkerbell costume and into her Latin practice skirt, black with the fire-engine-red ruffled top. She wore her competition dance shoes with the two-and-a-half-inch heels and her shiny blond curls bounced around a wide red headband.

"Okay, is everyone nicely warmed up?" Sylvie called out. Her face was flushed; the color in her cheeks enhanced her blue eyes.

"First let me give you a little background on paso doble so you can get into character. The music is taken directly from what's played for the matadors at bullfights. The paso doble is similar to samba in the sense that it's a progressive International Latin Dance. A few of you have done at least some samba, right?"

Hands raised, and heads nodded.

"Okay, good. So, forward steps are taken with a heel lead, your frame will be wider and held up more than in the other Latin or Rhythm dances, and there is significantly less hip movement. Because of its inherently choreographed tradition, ballroom paso is danced competitively, not on the social dance floor." Sylvie paced back and forth in front of the group, making eye contact as she spoke.

Katherine loved Sylvie's direct teaching style. She was warm and engaging but still all business.

"Now here's what I want you to think as we work through the basic steps. Men, you are the bullfighters; ladies, you are the cape, or the matador's shadow, or sometimes even the bull. This dance is sharp, staccato, intense, and a bit angry." Sylvie stamped her feet and flipped an imaginary cape. "So, men, form a line on this side of the room, and ladies on the other. Joey and I will dance some basics first. Then Joey will demonstrate the man's part of the pattern. I want you to change partners around the room as we dance. We have one extra lady. Jackson is here to even us out. Once we get the basics down, we'll try it to music. Okay?"

Sylvie looked once around the room for questioning faces, then looked at Joey as if to say, *Are you going to just stand there?* Katherine glanced at Joey with narrowed eyes. He pushed away from the wall he was holding up and walked over to help Sylvie teach her favorite dance.

~

Katherine glanced at the wall clock; it was past 9:00 p.m. Her office door was ajar and she could hear the buzz of conversation dwindling as the studio emptied out: "Best party ever, had a great time, plan to take your class, Sylvie, bye, thank you, great costume, so happy every bit of my green chili casserole was eaten...." Katherine inserted her red thumb drive into a USB port and tried to focus on the screen. She felt off-kilter and exhausted. She glanced again at the bottle of vodka lying in the file drawer, surprised that it was more than half empty.

"Mind if I come in?" Marcos called out.

Simultaneously, Katherine switched tabs on her machine and slammed the file drawer shut. "Fine, come on in—I'm almost done here," Katherine said. She didn't have the energy to try to infuse her voice with enthusiasm.

Marcos slouched into the chair opposite her desk.

"Sounds like the place is finally emptying out," Katherine said.

"Yup. People were having such a good time, it was hard to bring the day to a close. Jill is still here doing some cleaning to avoid coming in tomorrow. Everyone else has gone home."

Katherine patted a stack of papers on her desk. "We have several new lesson contracts signed and a few more sign-ups for the Midwinter Ball."

"Did you enjoy the day? This is your event, the one you wait for all year," Marcos said.

"I did. With the exception of a jarring call from dear old mum, everything was grand," Katherine said. She felt herself tilting a bit in her chair. She leaned forward on one arm and made an effort to sit up straight. Marcos raised an eyebrow.

"Katherine, I understand how upsetting your mother can be, but you can't drink in the studio. How much have you had today?"

"Damn it, Marcos. A sip, a splash in my coffee." She pulled away from her desk and stood, leaning forward on her outstretched palms, and glared across the wood expanse.

"Look," Marcos said. Katherine watched him finger-comb his hair, a telltale sign of stress and frustration. "About a week ago, I found a boozy-smelling glass in the main ballroom. Actually, Paige found it, and I immediately took it away from her. This has to stop, Katherine. Your drinking in the studio is obviously not just a stress reaction to today's phone call. It's more than that, and I won't have it."

"*You* won't have it!" Katherine took a deep breath, fighting to keep herself from shouting. She leaned back too quickly, rocked with dizziness, and only through great effort and strong abs maintained her standing position. "How dare you. I will not discuss this with you tonight, Marcos. You're out of line." Katherine peeled off her cat ears, turned to the small closet, and pulled out her street clothes. "I think it's time for you to head home."

"This isn't the end of this discussion, Katherine. We'll talk when you're more able to focus." With that, Marcos turned around and walked out, leaving the door partly open behind him. Katherine heard him wish Jill a good night as he left the building.

"Damn fool of a man. Who the hell is he to judge me?" Katherine pulled off her costume, tossed it on the floor of the closet, and slipped into sports pants and a light pullover sweater. She opened her large handbag and placed it on the floor under her desk. "Goddamn Marcos. Was he calling me an alcoholic? Screw him." Hearing the sound of her own voice somehow vindicated her feelings. She hated being misjudged. "Whoops. Can't leave Mr. Red lying around for nosy Marcos to find. I'm going to take this little doodad home and create some accounting magic over the weekend." Katherine pulled the red thumb drive from the USB port without even ejecting the device properly and dropped it in the direction of her open purse. She snatched at the straps of her purse, as she pulled her office door all the way open, and stepped into the dimly lit hall. She reached behind her to turn out her office light.

"And how long have you been standing there?" Katherine snarled. She'd almost turned around right into Jill, who was standing stock still outside her office. "Not even going to answer me..." Katherine mumbled, as Jill, silent, backed away. "No matter, too dumb to understand anything I said anyway. Stupid girl."

SEVENTEEN

A ROLL OF THE DICE

Katherine Carrington
10:00 a.m., Sunday, 1 November

A deep rumbling close to her ear stirred Katherine from sleep. An icy nose explored her cheek. "Chi?" Katherine mumbled. She gently removed a probing paw from her ear. A sandpaper tongue caressed her forehead and then her eyelids.

"Okay, Chi, that's enough. For heaven's sake, it's Sunday, my sleep-in day."

Chi maneuvered onto Katherine's pillow. Utter, inner-cave darkness descended as the full weight of Chi's black fluffy body plopped across Katherine's face. Fur played around her lips and itchiness crept into her eyes. Her allergist would not approve, although she did remember him saying it was patients like her who bought him his Jaguar.

Suffocation not being an option, Katherine slipped out from under Chi's rumbling body; her pillow could suffice as a human substitute. Undaunted, the cat adjusted his position and began a contented washing ritual, stretching his toes wide to clean between them. Katherine swung her legs over the side of the platform bed. She massaged her temples; her head was throbbing, and her mouth tasted like how cigars smell.

"Oh, now I remember." An image clicked into focus: an empty vodka bottle sailing into the bougainvillea bushes off the patio. She'd toasted her sister's memory and...well, it didn't matter at this point.

Katherine switched on the bedside lamp, thankful she'd chosen diffused lighting. The frosted globe of the metal lamp softly illuminated the alcove that held her queen-size bed. A lowered ceiling hid curved curtain rods. She pulled open the silver-gray drapery with one hand. A three-quarter wall separated the sleeping platform from a small sitting area. The side facing the sitting area was designed as a built-in bookcase, holding books, ceramic and metal sculptures, and framed photographs of Katherine in flattering dance poses. Her decorating scheme was white and gray with a pop of burnt orange found in a sculpture or picture frame. Katherine glanced around the newly remodeled bedroom suite, feeling very pleased with herself in spite of the headache. Remodeling her townhouse with a home equity loan on her mother's house was a smart move. She patted herself on the back for her financial creativity.

She slipped on a red-and-gold Chinese robe and stepped out onto the large balcony. The view was why she bought this unit. The Santa Catalina Mountains sprawled to the north, and the Rincon Mountains sat on the horizon to the east. The outdoor décor she'd chosen was minimal: a few pots of cacti and succulents and enough seating for herself and one guest. Katherine shivered and pulled the light robe tighter. The chill morning air was clearing her brain fog.

Katherine slid the sliders closed and stared at the cat, happily napping on her satin pillow. "Wait a minute," she said. "How did you get in here in the first place? Did I forget to close the cat-room door last night?" She crossed the room and swooped the cat into her arms. "Guess where you're headed little guy." Chi flicked his tail but didn't protest.

The bedroom's double doors opened to a loft that overlooked the main living area. A narrow staircase hugged one wall; the opposite wall displayed a collection of art. Light flooded the lower floor from tall undraped windows. Her streamlined furniture continued the mainly white theme. Two contoured chairs in robin's egg blue and a white sofa faced a widescreen TV. White, blue, and gray throw pillows added an air of ease with Katherine's favorite pop of orange adding an attitude of surprise. The gray-and-blue Navajo rug, visible under the chrome glass-topped coffee table, softened the expanse of slate flooring.

Katherine carried Chi through the living room to the second bedroom at the back of the townhouse. The door was ajar. She held the cat in front of her face. "I wasn't paying attention last night, Chi, was I?" Katherine pushed the door open all the way. Lady Cat was curled on a blanket, and New Cat breakfasted from a dish of dry cat food. New Cat, still settling in, eyed Katherine warily and then glanced at the open door with interest.

"Not a chance." Katherine closed the door behind her. "And you, my dear," she said, as she deposited Chi onto a high cat tree, "are an absolutely spoiled little bugger." Katherine moved about the room, talking to the cats, picking up cat toys, and checking food dishes. Light played on Chi's yellow eyes, creating an optical illusion of perspective and depth. A feline Mona Lisa, his eyes followed Katherine, but his head never moved.

"Okay, cats, you're on your own for a while. I need coffee and Tylenol. The best thing about you guys is not having to take you for walks with a poop bag dangling from one hand." She shook her head at the sound of her own voice. She was talking to herself more and more these days. As much as she loved the quiet of her townhouse, sometimes it echoed with an emptiness that even her foster cats and redecorating couldn't fill.

In the granite-countered kitchen, Katherine popped a Hawaiian Kona coffee pod into her Keurig, put her Crazy Cat Mom coffee mug on the platform, and clicked the remote for the wall-mounted TV. She poured a small glass of water and pulled a large bottle of extra-strength Tylenol out of a cupboard, along with a bottle of Bailey's Irish Crème.

"What the hell. It's Sunday, and, after death-day anniversary yesterday, I'm entitled." The coffee maker gurgled its last drop into her cup. Katherine added a generous splash of Bailey's, took a satisfying swig, and chased her morning beverage with a swallow of water and three Tylenol. She hit the play-messages button on the landline telephone base. Her fingernails tapped discordantly on the speckled silver-and-black granite, and a clatter of news show hosts prattled on in the background.

The first message was from Sylvie. She said that since Katherine wouldn't be in on Monday, she wanted her to know the Latin costume arrived Saturday, and it was perfect. She was all packed, and she and Tony were leaving for LA from the studio Monday morning. The second message was from Marcos—something about Michael and signing him on. Katherine compressed her lips and hit delete. She pushed her mass of bed-tangled hair off her face.

Suddenly irritated with the background noise, Katherine clicked off the TV and tossed the remote onto the granite counter. "Whatever happened to real journalism? People shouting over each other and jabbering about celebrities doesn't qualify as news in my book. It's all egos and sensationalism." She ran a hand across her eyes. "Damn headache. Shower. That's it. I'll try a hot shower."

Within minutes Katherine was soaping and stressing. A lowball offer had come in on her mother's house, but it wouldn't leave her enough money to cover all bases. She might be able to get her mother enrolled in Arizona's Medicaid. Then she could begin the paperwork jungle to get her into the state's long-term care program. Katherine bit the inside of the lip. That could take forever, and in the meantime New Haven's monthly bill had to be paid. And where had she put the Medicaid paperwork anyway? Damn. Why couldn't she think straight lately? She turned her back to the stream of water and let the heat work out the knots in her neck. Leaning forward, she placed her palms against the marble wall so the hot torrent could cascade down her back. She straightened to rinse shampoo out of her hair and followed with a soothing, lavender-scented conditioner. She needed to calm her mind. Her thoughts were swirling around faster than the water racing down the drain.

Hair wrapped in a soft towel and body wrapped in her robe, she trotted, barefoot, back downstairs. Where was her purse? She needed her Mr. Red flash drive so she could quickly review the accounting spreadsheets before indulging in some TV movie time. Her purse should be… Where was it? Not in the kitchen, not on the couch, not on the table by the front door. Her heart raced. It had to be here somewhere. Panic began to rise. She spun around, and there it was. A leather strap peeked out from beneath the shawl she'd tossed on the dining table last night. So stupid to freak out. What was wrong with her? Her head told her she was too young to worry about inheriting her mother's dementia, but her gut leaked a little acid anyway. She stuffed the thought back into its compartment and shut the lid.

Katherine poured another coffee, added some more Bailey's, and settled into her blue upholstered home-office chair. Her computer sat on an alcove desk by the kitchen window. She sipped the coffee blend and ruminated while the laptop booted. Who would have expected her mother to live this long? The woman was pushing ninety. As harsh as it sounded, not having to pay New Haven every month would definitely ease things. In the interim, a bit of accounting magic could save her tight white ass. It was no big deal. She'd put everything straight once a good offer on the house came in.

The computer chirped to life but Katherine stared out the window, lost in thought. What about the juicy little tidbit she'd found on the scrap of paper in Paige's pocket? That info might be worth something if she played her cards right. She hadn't seen Marcos's father for years, but she knew he liked her. Maybe she could test the waters with a simple, catch-up lunch date?

Katherine reached into her purse for the bright-red thumb drive. She rummaged around but couldn't feel it. Must have fallen into a side pocket. Nope. She upended the purse on the table. She stood, and her robe fell open. A panicky tightness grew in her gut. "No, no, no! It has to be here." She raked her fingers through the pile of belongings strewn on the table. She knew she'd dropped it into her purse before she left on Friday. Could she have been stupid enough to leave it on her desk? Could it have fallen on the floor? Damn it to hell. She pulled her robe closed with a hard tug. No! Not to panic. It was Sunday. The studio no longer had a weekend cleaning service, and, even though she wasn't going in until Tuesday, no one had any reason to be in her office.

"Breathe. It will be okay. You have things under control. It can't be lost." Katherine sat down hard in the chair. The sound of her own voice calmed her. She took another deep breath and willed herself to relax. "I'll call Sylvie back to wish her good luck in the comp, and then I'll ask her to check my office for a red flash drive before she leaves on Monday. Marcos can let her in. She can tuck it into a drawer for me. Sylvie is the one person I can trust to do what I say." Katherine took another deep breath, formed her lips into a smile, and reached for the phone.

～

Paige Russell
Noon, Sunday, 1 November

Next to Kristi's black silk pajama bottoms, black tank, and trendy striped robe, Paige felt caught in a college-dorm time warp. She was decked out in her well-worn Beastie Boys T-shirt and shapeless gray PJ bottoms. Paige tucked an untidy fall of hair behind her ears before filling two mugs from the coffee carafe.

"Who invites themselves over for a morning pajama party?" Paige said, yawning.

"It's technically not morning; it's past noon." Kristi got comfortable on the couch and helped herself to two napkins and a blueberry Danish. "We're in PJs, and I brought Danish, so a pajama party it is. We got lucky with the pastries, by the way. Mrs. Martinez from apartment 242 brought them over. Her husband went overboard at the bakery again, and she's trying to watch her waistline. Her loss, our gain. Probably literally."

Paige chortled and flopped onto the couch beside Kristi, tucking her feet under her. "I don't know about you, but I didn't turn off the lights last night until past two. You actually woke me when you called this morning at eleven-thirty."

"As long as we're not adopting a new lifestyle, one big night out won't ruin us. It was a blast, though, wasn't it?" Kristi said through a mouthful of buttery pastry. "I haven't been downtown clubbing on Halloween night since…well…I don't even remember when. I'm not really a clubber, but I had a great time. Downtown was like one big party."

"Yeah, and once you ditched your fancy Halloween mask and started flashing those big cat eyes of yours, our table filled up with drinks faster than we could drink them. I don't know how you've stayed single," Paige said, smiling at her friend.

"By choice, that's how. Once I finish my degree, then maybe I'll cast my net, but for now I need to stay focused." Kristi rested slippered feet on the upholstered crate-table. She folded one arm across her middle to support the hand balancing the heavy ceramic mug.

"So, no bridal wish book for you, then? No dream wedding?" Paige teased. She pulled her hair off her neck. It was making her sweat.

"I'd love a life partner one day, but marriage, I don't know. I'm for sure not the big-wedding type. I don't get making such a big deal out of one day. Reality is that a week after the wedding, you're washing the guy's underwear and socks, not drinking champagne. Me, I want to focus on the commitment, the long-term relationship, rather than playing queen for a day."

"I need you; you ground me in reality," Paige said. "By the way, what time was it when we left the club last night? Before midnight?"

"A bit later," Kristi replied. "Your last two tequila shots took you right past sexy-funny and on to maudlin-teary. When you started talking to the guys at our table about searching for your dad, it was, shall we say, a call-an-Uber moment."

"I think I remember talking about the dad thing." Paige put her mug down and rubbed her forehead. "That wasn't good, was it?"

"It sure sobered everyone up fast," Kristi said, raising her mug in a toast.

"Sorry," Paige said, with a crooked half grin. "I think it's my twenty-fifth birthday looming. I'd clung to some idiotic idea that Mom was waiting until I hit the magically mature age of twenty-five to come clean about my dad. At first the magic number was twenty-one, but when that birthday came and went, I pushed the date out. Of course, my mother's death slammed that door in my face."

"Are you angry with your mother, Paige?" Kristi tilted her head and leaned forward. "I know you miss her terribly, but it sounds like there's an undercurrent of anger there as well."

"Maybe." Paige paused for a few beats. "I'm going to get more coffee, okay? I'll bring the carafe back with me."

"Okay," Kristi said.

"So, since I've told you all kinds of personal stuff already," Paige said, pouring Kristi more coffee. Kristi was licking pastry bits off her fingers and didn't react. "I guess I can tell you the whole truth about what happened after my mother died, when I went back to NAU that fall." Paige kept her eyes focused on her coffee cup. "I need to say one thing first. Grief can change you. It affects the way you see yourself and the world in ways you could never have imagined." Paige raised her eyes to Kristi's, compressing her lips to stop them from trembling.

Kristi dropped her pastry onto her plate and gave Paige her full attention.

"I struggled all the way through the fall semester. I was actually close to flunking out. I don't even know why I bothered to register again in the spring," Paige said. She took a sip of coffee, cradled the mug between her hands, and switched to a cross-legged position. "I pushed people away, Kristi. I turned down invitations to go out and invites to people's homes for dinner. I was grieving, but it was more than that. I felt like I belonged nowhere, to no one, and being around happy families or couples hurt more than being alone."

Paige stopped talking and twisted her hair away from her face, catching it in the elastic band she'd slid onto her wrist earlier.

"My boyfriend and I broke up. I skipped classes to hang out downtown. You know Flagstaff. It's a college town, so it's packed with pubs, cafés, art galleries, lots of places where you can hide and waste time. And, as you've found out, I'm a lightweight with booze. It didn't take more than a couple of drinks to numb me into making some bad choices."

Paige reached for a pastry and ate the cream cheese out of the center before continuing. "I was lonely and lost and I…well… I ran though several short-term relationships with guys—guys around my own age and much older guys as well. I didn't care. I needed to feel wanted, if only for one night or for a few days."

Kristi cleared her throat and took a big sip of coffee.

"Yes, I know." Paige made a face. "You don't have to say it. Just because I don't hit the bars and clubs now, everyone thinks I'm some kind of angel. Well, I'm an angel with one hell of a tarnished halo."

"Yup, your pedestal will never look shiny again," Kristi said with a smile. "Hey. I'm certainly no one to judge you or anyone else. On a more serious note, Paige, you were only, what, twenty-two when you lost your mother. That's enough to throw anyone, even someone much older than you, into a tailspin. And you didn't have siblings or a dad to share your grief. And it's not like she was in her nineties with Alzheimer's and was miserable, and you knew death would be a blessing. It wasn't like that. Your mom was still young, and then boom, her illness hit and progressed fast. You didn't have time to wrap your head around it."

"Thank you. I knew if anyone would understand it might be you." Paige stretched out her foot and touched Kristi's perfectly pedicured big toe. "It was a terrible time. My whole identity was being my mother's daughter, even if I was a brat sometimes. Suddenly the house we'd lived in was on the market, and I had no home to go home to.

My aunt was back and forth from Florida and really had no idea what was actually going on in my life. I'd lost the only person who loved me unconditionally. Even boyfriends don't love you unconditionally."

"That's for sure the truth," Kristi said, raising her eyebrows.

"I think this is what started me obsessing over finding out if I had a dad out there somewhere—a dad who would want to know me. I hadn't found Mom's blue folder yet. Anyway, sometimes I was so ashamed of myself, I wouldn't leave the dorm room for days—wouldn't shower, binge-watched TV, ate crap. When I tried to act normal, it took too much energy, so I pulled away from everyone. My friends gave up on me, and who could blame them?"

"Well, this friend isn't giving up on you," Kristi said. She jumped up and gave Paige a quick hug.

"Now that you've committed yourself," Paige said with a tilt of her head, "how about if I push the envelope and ask you to come out on the balcony with me, so I can fortify myself with a smoke to continue my story?"

Kristi laughed and shook her head. "You really are a piece of work, but I'm liking that more and more about you. Okay, then, let me get a coffee refill, and I'll join you outside."

Paige grabbed some throws from the back of the couch and her pack of Virginia Slims. She was already exhaling a whitish-blue trail of smoke by the time Kristi stepped outside. She handed Kristi one of the soft Mexican blankets and wrapped herself in the other one, and they each settled into a chair.

"So, here we go," Paige said. "Finally, one day I decided even I couldn't stand myself. That was also the day Aunt Teresa called to say the house had sold, and she was on her way in from Florida to help me set up bank accounts and everything. The timing was perfect. I bailed on the semester but took withdrawals wherever I could instead of failing classes. I moved into a small studio apartment and went into my nun phase, which I guess I'm still sorta in. No guys. Hardly any drinking. That's when I started the overwhelming process of sorting through my mother's boxes."

"So," Kristi said, leaning forward, elbows on knees. "What's your plan with Marcos?"

Paige folded her arms and leaned back, closing her eyes. "I don't know. Everything is so fucked right now."

"Yeah…so?" Kristi countered.

"After my mother died, I would be in tears thinking about stuff like having a wedding without her there. And then I'd obsess about not having a father to walk me down the aisle or parents to be grandparents to my children. That drove the search to find the other half of my history. You know the rest about finding the folder and everything." Paige glanced over at Kristi. "But I didn't really answer your question about Marcos, did I?"

Kristi shrugged and shook her head.

"When I applied for the job at the studio, I didn't have a clear plan. After seeing Marcos at the dance expo, all I knew was I needed to see him again, literally look at him up close. I had to know what kind of a man he was. And now, because of the café mess, I'm not sure what to do." Paige looked at Kristi and bit her upper lip. "Input, please."

"I think you've been through enough loss already, and I'd hate to see you open yourself to more hurt. I understand how badly you want a real father in your life, but biology alone doesn't make someone a dad. And it's not like he would have an emotional tie to your mom. If you hit him with this, be clear in your own mind about your expectations. It's very likely he'll ask what you want from him. And he might be angry. You have to have an answer for him, Paige. Remember what Brianna told us about his marriage to the woman with the young child?"

Paige nodded. Tears tugged at the backs of her eyes at the memory of that conversation.

"What do you think will happen when you confront him? The man that came on to you has to switch gears suddenly and see you as a daughter. And what if he doesn't believe you?"

"I don't know." Paige could barely hear her own voice. "What a mess."

"I'm not saying don't talk to him. He's completely in the dark and you have to clear the air. But be prepared to quit your job if things don't go well. What if he's absolutely mortified by what happened between the two of you, and he can't face seeing you at work every day? What if he's furious and feels stalked? On the other hand"—Kristi reached out and grabbed Paige by one wrist—"and I just thought of this: What if Marcos realizes his attraction to you was for a whole different reason—the pull of blood? Some gut recognition that he misinterpreted as attraction because that's how his male mind works? What if he has a major "aha" moment? You know, after my full-circle ramble, now I'm thinking that the only answer is for you to take your chances, roll the dice, and see what numbers come up."

EIGHTEEN

PERCEPTION IS EVERYTHING

Barbara Bradshaw
10:15 a.m., Monday, 2 November

"Good morning." Barbara held a large Baker's Bagels bag. The heavy front door swished closed behind her. "I come bearing gifts."

"Oh, yum. Bagels. Thank you, Barbara." Paige ran around the reception desk and reached for the bag. "I'll put them out. I think we have a nice tray in the drawer under the mosaic table."

"Perfect," Barbara replied. She pulled off her gloves and shrugged out of her light suede jacket. "You'll find napkins, knives, and tubs of cream cheese in the bag."

Barbara glanced around. The bagels certainly wouldn't be wasted this morning. Joey loitered at the counter, and Brianna was already heading toward Paige. Even Sylvie and Tony, with their luggage in tow, were hanging out. Katherine was the only one absent...oh right—Marcos mentioned she would be out the Monday after the Halloween party. Marcos was in the front office and seemed to be having an animated exchange with Jill. She tilted her head. Now that Barbara was officially helping on a regular basis, Jill usually came in late on the days she knew Barbara would be there. Whatever. She'd find out what was going on soon enough.

The office door burst open, and Jill bounced out, looking flushed and happy. Marcos followed Jill and raised his eyebrows at the crowded lobby. Maybe it wasn't a coincidence so many employees were loitering in the reception area. Marcos cleared his throat and stood with legs apart, making it obvious he wanted to make an announcement.

Jill's voice was the first to fill the room. She jumped up and down like a kid and giggled. "I'm so happy that everyone is here because I have some really exciting news."

Looks were exchanged. Tony folded his arms. Barbara poured herself a cup of coffee.

"I just gave Marcos a week's notice. Steve and I are moving to San Antonio." Jill clapped her hands and released a high-pitched squeal.

Barbara came close to sloshing hot coffee all over herself.

Jill paused for effect. The girl was an attention whore.

Barbara cleared her throat. "San Antonio? So, what happened to Steve's Border Patrol training? Is that off the table now?"

Jill played with the buttons on her sequined cardigan and then looked around and smiled, making sure to engage each person in the room. "It's such a romantic story. Last week Steve sat me down with his iPod with a playlist he made just for me. 'San Antonio Rose' by Patsy Cline and 'San Antonio Stroll' by Tanya Tucker were two of them, and the last one was 'Forever and Ever, Amen' by Randy Travis." Jill clasped one hand to her heart. "It has that chorus about 'loving you forever and forever, amen.'"

The room was quiet. It felt like everyone was waiting for the other shoe to drop. Barbara assumed Jill would take the silence as respectful awe of her husband's romantic nature.

"So," Jill continued, "then Steve broke the news that he's not going into the Border Patrol after all. He applied for a job in the Caterpillar manufacturing plant in San Antonio, and he got it. They offer medical insurance and everything, and I'll be covered." Jill clasped both hands over her abdomen. "And this is the best part — Steve's aunt and uncle have a huge house in San Antonio, and we can stay with them as long as we want." Jill stopped for breath.

Barbara glanced at Marcos, who hadn't said a word. His arms were folded, his expression neutral. Barbara was about to say something about Jill's new situation but stopped as Jill slipped off her cardigan. Something bright caught her eye.

"Um, Jill, what's that on your forearm?" Barbara asked.

"Oh." Jill's face flushed again, and she was beaming. She stretched out her arm. "It's my new tattoo—two entwined San Antonio roses. The color is yellow for the song 'Yellow Rose of Texas.' We got matching tattoos to mark our new start in Texas."

Even Tony moved in closer to get a better look. Brianna murmured her approval. Paige actually drew back a bit.

"Oh, I see," was all Barbara could manage. She felt the color drain from her face. She bit her upper lip. Stupid. She should have learned her lesson the first time. What about all the talks she'd had with Jill about choices and responsibility. Seemed her advice had floated off like milkweed fluff. Barbara sipped her coffee. And her son had just lectured her about being naïve and wasting her resources on those who never changed their ways. Maybe she just wouldn't tell him about this one.

"And there's more!" Jill exclaimed, a few decibels higher than necessary for human ears.

"More?" everyone said in unison.

"I'm signing up for beauty school in San Antonio. Steve's Aunt Charlene is going to pay for me to go. Can you believe it? I am so excited. I'll get as many of the required 1,500 hours in as I can before the baby is born, and I'll finish the rest afterwards." Jill stretched out her arms, ready to embrace the world.

"So, when did you say you were leaving?" Brianna asked.

"Actually," Jill looked at Marcos and then glanced at Barbara, "I did tell Marcos I would work another week, but since Barbara is volunteering at the front desk, and Paige and Brianna can fill in, I would love the extra time to pack and shop for a few new outfits to take and all that stuff." She looked at Barbara with puppy-dog eyes.

"New outfits," Barbara repeated, more to herself than anyone else. What the hell?

"Well," Tony said, looking at his watch and pushing/pulling Sylvie to the door. "This has all been very interesting, and we wish you well, Jill, but Sylvie and I have a flight to catch. Our Uber ride is here."

"Wait. I almost forgot," Sylvie said, stopping halfway out the door. Her suitcase banged against the metal threshold. "Has anyone found a red thumb drive, maybe on the floor?"

Heads shook and "no"s were murmured. Jill went quiet and averted her eyes.

Sylvie flicked her wrist and said, "No big deal. But if you come across one, it's Katherine's." And then she was out the door and gone.

"Paige," Jill piped up in a questioning voice, "can you handle the front desk for a minute while I talk to Barbara alone?"

"Sure, but I have Brandon coming in at eleven o'clock, so make it quick. Okay?"

Barbara raised her eyebrows. Jill motioned Barbara to follow her down the hall. Surely she wasn't going to ask for more money? This time the answer would be no. Jill pushed open the door to the ladies' room and checked under the stalls to make sure the room was unoccupied.

"I have something to give you, but I need to explain first." Jill leaned against the bathroom's long counter. "Something sort of weird happened Friday night after the party. I was here cleaning and tidying. Everyone was gone except for Katherine. I was right outside her office, but Katherine didn't know I was there, at least not at first. She was talking to herself, sort of loud, saying crap about Marcos being nasty to her, calling her an alcoholic, then she started mumbling about Marcos being nosy, studio accounts, working on her magic numbers, and something about a red thumb drive. She almost fell against her desk when she stood to leave. I think…I think maybe she'd been drinking. And then before I could move out of the way, Katherine saw me and she…"

"So, go on," Barbara said.

"She said some really mean things to me." Jill's voice choked. "She said it didn't matter if I was standing there because I was too stupid to understand anything anyway, and she picked up her purse and left. She didn't even lock her private office door. She actually left it partly open. I went in because I thought I saw something fall onto the floor and bounce." Jill unrolled her fist and exposed the red thumb drive. "I found this on the carpet under her desk."

"Is that what Sylvie asked about?" What on earth? Why hadn't the darn girl spoken up?

"Maybe," Jill said. "I was going to put it on Katherine's desk, but she's been so awful to me, I stuck it in my pocket instead. I know that was wrong, but I can't undo it. I looked at it at home, thinking it was maybe pictures of the party, but it's all numbers and some passworded files. I brought it back, and I'm giving it to you."

"Why me?" Barbara asked. "I'm not sure either of us should have this if it's Katherine's."

"Well, I trust you, and you know things; you can figure things out. Maybe you can take a look and decide what to do. Please take it." Jill extended her hand. "I'm leaving today. Except for Katherine, I love this studio and all the people here, especially you." Jill bit her lip and color rose in her face.

"Jill, I'm really uncomfortable with this," Barbara said, but she let Jill place the thumb drive in her hand.

"If there's nothing weird on here, you can give it right back to Katherine, but at least look first," Jill said.

Barbara nodded and slipped the small device into the pocket of her light cardigan.

"Okay," Jill said, obviously relieved. "Let's go back out front. I'll give you some last-minute tips on the front desk until it's time for your lesson with Marcos. I feel sort of bad about leaving so soon, but I don't think it will be hard to find someone to take my place."

~

Marcos Stephanos
2:30 p.m., Monday, 2 November

"Your waltz was excellent today, Barbara. You were lighter than you've ever been. Did you notice how much floor space we covered?"

"I did," Barbara said, smiling. She slipped on her everyday flats and zipped her dance shoes into the black shoe bag. "I think I'm finally getting the hang of the diagonal hip swing."

"And thank you for working with Jill this morning," Marcos said. He wasn't sure Jill's leaving was actually a bad thing, but he decided to keep that thought private.

"Not a problem. I enjoy handling the desk. I can fill in until you get a replacement for Jill. Oh, and on that note, I have a suggestion."

"Listening," Marcos said. He was curious but also cautious.

"There is a young woman I know—a lovely, intelligent girl—who also happens to be my nail technician. She's open to something part-time and is available to work the evening shift in reception, even on a temporary basis. She'd also be happy to exchange some of her hours for dance lessons. I thought Michael might take her on to get floor exposure."

"How about experience?" Marcos bit his lower lip. A nail technician?

"She's wonderful with people and extremely bright. She's taking classes online to finish a bachelor's degree. I feel confident enough in her abilities to recommend her."

"I'm sure Katherine would be fine with that. I'll run it by her and let you know," Marcos said, placing one hand affectionately over Barbara's. "And what about the hours you've been putting in? I can't let you continue to help us out with this for nothing. Maybe I can offer you a few free lesson hours in exchange for your time?"

Barbara shook her head and waved him off as she gathered her belongings.

"Let me walk you out," Marcos said, offering a supporting hand as Barbara stood. "Any chance you have time to sit and chat for a few minutes? There is something else I'd like to talk to you about...something I need your help with, actually."

"Funny you should say that. I was going to ask you the same thing," Barbara replied

She was smiling, but Marcos was concerned. Barbara seemed uneasy. Maybe today had been too much for her? Was asking her to spend time at the front desk an imposition?

Marcos held the back door open and followed Barbara to the bench. Enough sun broke though the patchy shade of the eucalyptus to offer a welcome spot of warmth.

"So," Marcos said, rubbing his palms on his trousers. "I have a situation with a student, and I think you might be the perfect person to help me sort things out."

"All ears," Barbara said.

"Do you know Mei Le, by chance? She's relatively new to the studio, dances with Jackson?"

"Actually, I met her only last week. Why? What's up?"

"She took me aside to talk about canceling her contract." Marcos leaned forward, forearms on thighs, hands clasped. He paused before continuing. "I don't usually discuss one student's issues with another, but I consider you a friend and a mainstay of the studio."

"Thank you, Marcos. That makes me happy to hear." Barbara visibly relaxed. "You can talk to me and know it will go no farther. You know how I feel. This studio is my second home."

Marcos unclasped his hands and rubbed them together. "Here's the dilemma. I don't expect every student who signs an initial contract to become a fixture at the studio, but, in this case, I feel like we've failed Mei Le in some way. By the same token, she hasn't given us a fair chance. I'm still unclear about her expectations, but I was hoping we could encourage her to stay long enough to experience the camaraderie and to begin to feel part of the group."

"Group! That's it, Marcos. I'll talk to her about joining some of the group classes. I can even offer to go with her. Her contract entitles her to one free class a week, and I know she hasn't taken any. You're interacting all the time and switching partners, so you soon get to know everyone. That's how I first made friends here. It doesn't happen only taking private lessons."

"And that's exactly why I like running things past you, my friend," Marcos said, hoping his smile conveyed the warmth he felt. Barbara was as much his friend as his student. "If this works out, I could offer Mei Le a few free heats in the next showcase. If we can get her into the fun of participating, maybe we can change her perception."

"So here's an idea," Barbara said. "Maybe, for future reference, you could start a mentoring program here. You know, buddy up a newcomer with an old-timer like me for the first few weeks. It was Linda Wilson who took me under her wing and helped me get oriented. This place is as much community center as dance studio, Marcos. Actually, I have more ideas for another time, but if we have a plan to help Mei Le settle in, can I run something else by you?"

"Of course. But why the serious face? Should I be concerned?" Marcos said. Barbara had straightened her back and was rummaging in her purse, hopefully not for Kleenex. Was she going to cry? Marcos pulled back. He was beginning to feel uncomfortable. Female emotions spilling all over the place didn't always bring out the best in him.

Barbara held up a red thumb drive by the tip, like it was infected with Ebola.

"I don't know exactly what this is or how important the information on it might be. I'm pretty sure this is the red thumb drive Sylvie mentioned Katherine lost. But before you give it back to her, you might want to give the contents a look." Barbara held out the drive.

"Okay," Marcos said. He thought Barbara was being overdramatic, but that wasn't really her style. He took the USB drive, staring at the small device like staring alone could reveal its contents. He dropped it into his pocket. "There is obviously more to this story. How did you come to have it?"

"I'll condense," Barbara said. "Jill gave this to me after her announcement this morning."

Marcos drew his head back and tilted his chin. He was trying to refrain from comment.

"So," Barbara continued, "Jill was here late after the party...."

Marcos sucked on his upper lip as Barbara revealed Jill's story.

"Yes, you don't have to say it. Jill had no business going into Katherine's office, let alone taking this thing home, but she did. So, you might as well take a look before you hand it back to Katherine. My guess is we'll both be laughing about getting sucked into Jill's dramatics."

Marcos smiled, but he felt a wave of apprehension building in his gut. "I hope it's nothing critical. And I have mixed feelings about looking at the contents when this could be personal, but better safe than sorry."

"Right," Barbara said.

She shifted as if to stand up, so Marcos stood up first and extended his hand.

"I'll come by in the morning to handle the front desk. And if you don't think Katherine will mind me stepping in, I'll start the process of finding a receptionist. No point in letting all my years in human resources go to waste."

"Don't know what we'd do without you, Barbara. If you can find us someone with half your enthusiasm and people skills, I, for one, will be over the moon." Marcos opened his arms to give his favorite student a hug. Too bad she was retired. He'd hire Barbara full-time in a minute.

Slouched in his office chair, Marcos rubbed his forehead. A glance at his beloved Baume & Mercier told him it was not quite 7:00 p.m., but the heaviness of fatigue seeping through his body made it feel more like midnight. What a day. After the banker called, his day had gone from aggravating to enraging, with a touch of exasperation thrown in to test his fortitude. It was just as well Katherine was out of the office. Had she been in, he might have throttled her.

Marcos chewed on the inside of his lower lip. Truth be told, he was as mad at himself as he was at Katherine. He'd let her have free rein with the studio's financial health when he knew the woman could bolt out of control like a runaway horse. Was he too trusting? A sucker? Or maybe too lax? He pushed the word *lazy* out of his mind. He was questioning himself a little too much for his taste. Marcos pulled out the notes he'd taken during his call with Donovan at the bank. What the hell? The studio was in still in arrears on the mortgage, and, as if that wasn't bad enough, balances were dangerously low on a couple of their accounts. Marcos's jaw tightened to a crown-cracking tension. How could that be? Frank Donovan had been more than understanding, which was probably only because Marcos's hefty personal account was at the same bank. He gave Marcos a few days to sort things out, but right now he was more than done for the day.

He pulled his car keys and driving gloves out of the top desk drawer and hit the phone intercom. "Brianna, I'm heading out early this evening. If anyone is looking for me, let them know that whatever they need will have to wait until tomorrow, okay?"

"You bet. See you tomorrow. Have a nice night, Marcos."

Marcos released the button without replying. Right now he needed to go home, hit the Jacuzzi, pour a scotch, and try to regain his equilibrium before dealing with Katherine and her potential histrionics.

NINETEEN

You Can't Tap Dance to Taps

Marcos Stephanos
11:15 a.m., Tuesday, 3 November

Marcos, mesmerized by a video of the Krasnoyarsk National Dance Company of Siberia, barely heard the front door whoosh open. He glanced up from the computer screen just long enough to toss a quick "G'morning" Barbara's way.

No response and no footsteps. Marcos waited a few beats, frowned, and turned away from the screen again. Barbara had paused mid-step. She tilted her head toward the front office behind Marcos.

"What the hell?" Marcos muttered, following her eyes.

There was Katherine, one hand holding the phone and the other gesturing wildly—a pantomime of infuriation. Marcos quietly walked around the reception desk and gave the office door a gentle push. Katherine's voice rose high enough to hear a crisply enunciated "fucking idiot." Marcos remained standing at the office entrance.

"No, it's *you* that doesn't understand." Katherine's voice hit F sharp.

She was standing behind her chair, her back to Marcos. Her

face, reflected in the wall mirror, was knotted in fury. Deep creases bracketed her mouth. There wasn't enough makeup in the world to hide the signs of advancing age.

"No, it's *you* who is being unreasonable. What? Fine, then. And, by the way, screw you!" Katherine slammed the receiver onto the console. "Fucking hell."

Marcos cleared his throat. As quickly as butter left out in the Tucson sun, Katherine's demeanor melted into charm. She turned, smoothing her hair with the palm of her hand.

"We have a minor situation, nothing I can't fix, Marcos." Katherine's tone conveyed indifference, and her shrug sealed the deal. She settled into her chair and crossed her legs, the picture of nonchalance.

"It didn't sound like a situation that was being resolved amicably. What's going on?"

"That was some low-paid, social-services lawyer on the phone. The call was about that student, Lorna—you know who I mean. She's the irritating heavyset girl with missing teeth, who's always fawning all over everyone." Katherine's nostrils flared. She pursed her lips like she was trying to remove a bad taste. "The stupid woman has incurred thousands of dollars in debt on multiple credit cards, spending herself into bankruptcy, and was evicted. Evidently she's on assistance, so how did she even qualify for a credit card in the first place? Her lawyer was assigned through Legal Aide, and some church has stepped in to help her. The bottom line is that Lorna is filing Chapter 7, and, if we get paid at all, it will be pennies on the dollar."

"And exactly how much is owed on Lorna's contract?" Marcos asked. He stood, arms folded, legs spread apart.

"About $8,500. How was I to know she couldn't pay for what she purchased? Her financial circumstances were none of my business. Her car has been repossessed, and the attorney said she might be admitted to a group home. Not quite all there, I gather. I always thought there was something off about her." Katherine looked over at Marcos, radiating outrage.

Marcos remained standing. His lips were set in a firm line, and he felt, for the first time, somewhat immune to Katherine's dramatics.

"It's been a terrible morning, awful." Katherine's voice took on the whine of a petulant child. "First I find out Jill quit and we have to hire a new receptionist, and then there was a stupid clerical error at my bank. They've messed up my account again." Katherine's words spilled over each other. She gripped the edge of the desk. "I'll have to open a new account somewhere else. And anyway, the girl from the bank was really very rude to me on the phone. I won't take that from anyone."

"Katherine." Marcos pulled out a chair and sat down. "The situation with Lorna aside, we have to talk. I took a call from Frank Donovan yesterday. It seems he's tried to reach you repeatedly, but you were always unavailable. He said you've not returned his calls."

Katherine's face was the picture of solicitous concern. "Really? And what did our Mr. Donovan have to say? I'm not aware of any major problems."

Marcos rocked his chair forward and folded his hands on Katherine's desk. He kept his gaze direct. "It seems we're in arrears on the mortgage, Katherine. In my estimation, that can be defined as a major problem." Marcos felt deadened, incapable of even raising his voice.

"As I've told you before, we're experiencing a very minor cash-flow problem. I'm working on the accounts and will have it resolved shortly." Katherine raised her chin.

"Do I have to remind you I'm a forty-eight percent owner in this business, and my name is on the mortgage as well as yours? When I bought in, you wanted me to remain a silent partner. I agreed. And for years I've functioned more as the studio's dance master than as one of the owners. I've been happy to be the go-to guy who oversees the day-to-day flow of the studio. But now I think I've stayed in the back seat for far too long, and things have to change."

"I see," Katherine said. Her demeanor was studied, her face expressionless.

"And then yesterday, when Jill was working with Barbara, she mentioned there's a problem with our account at the office supply store. Barbara was told not to place an order without checking first with you."

"Jill. That damn little troublemaker. As I told you before, I suspected her of stealing. I had to take the petty cash box away from her. I was ready to confront her with my suspicions and fire her, but she quit before I could."

"I think we have greater issues than some unfounded suspicions about Jill, so don't try to derail this discussion."

"What a lot of fuss about nothing," Katherine fumed. She waved a dismissive hand at Marcos. She pushed her chair back and stood behind the desk. "Honestly, Marcos, you don't know anything about the bookkeeping for the studio. You can't walk into my office, after years of amusing yourself teaching lessons, and think you can begin to understand our complicated accounting system." Katherine folded her arms and looked directly at Marcos. "Yes, I'm late on some of the accounts payable. Expenses have been higher than normal. You contributed by bringing Michael in. We've had to pay him as an outside coach. I've done some creative juggling to make ends meet. That's all there is to it. End of story."

"Katherine, quite frankly I am too exasperated right now to continue this conversation and remain civil."

Katherine darted around the desk and placed her hand on Marcos's arm. She opened her eyes wide and curled the corners of her lips. "You don't have a thing to worry about, Marcos. Truly. I'll call Mr. Donovan and have everything straightened out in no time." Her voice had slowed to a comforting purr. "Why don't you relax and leave the bookkeeping worries to me, as you always have? Why change a good thing?"

Marcos glanced at the perfectly manicured hand resting on his forearm. He brushed free of her fingers and strode out the door.

Paige Russell
8:30 p.m., Tuesday, 3 November

Paige poked her head out the back door. The skies were dark. It seemed like just a few minutes ago when she'd caught the last of the sunset finger-painting reds and orange-pinks across the canvas of a dark blue sky. But now there was nothing left but a thin layer of grayish-purple clouds, trying to obscure the first twinkling of stars. Paige wished she could wrap herself in those clouds and disappear for a while, but…it was time to suck it up and deal.

She closed the door, her thoughts flipping like flapjacks. The studio emptied out early this evening, so now was as good a time as any to talk to Marcos. She paused, her hand still on the back doorknob, and nibbled at a cuticle. She couldn't keep sidestepping Marcos, and in light of the cafe incident, she had no choice now but to show Marcos the cards she was holding. Paige took a deep breath. She straightened her spine, threw her dance bag over her shoulder, and went in search of the grand master himself.

Katherine had gone home long ago, but there was light under her office door. Paige moved closer. Someone was tapping on the keyboard. Katherine kept all the personnel files, financials, and tax files in her private office, and no one was allowed in there, except maybe for Marcos. But why would he be in Katherine's office with the door shut?

Paige hesitated and leaned an ear against the door. "Marcos, is that you in there? It's Paige. Can I come in?"

"Wait just a minute, please."

A file drawer slammed, papers shuffled, and then there was the harsh click of a binder snapping shut. Finally the door opened.

~

Marcos Stephanos
8:45 p.m., Tuesday, 3 November

"Paige? I'm surprised you're still here. I thought everyone had left for the day. Come in, please." Marcos smiled what he hoped was a warm, nonthreatening smile. He perched on the edge of the desk in a casual pose.

Paige barely moved from the open door. The look on her face suggested hesitation, as though she might have changed her mind.

"I'm actually pleased you stopped by. I hoped to find time for us to chat and clear the air," Marcos said. He stepped cautiously, waiting for the ice to crack. "I think we have some minor issues to resolve."

Paige smiled but kept silent. She fidgeted with the handle of her dance bag.

"Paige?" Marcos waited until Paige met his eyes. "I hope you know I'd never intentionally hurt or upset you." He reached for her hand. With a flick of her wrist, Paige blocked contact. Marcos frowned. He was not in a patient frame of mind. He folded his arms.

"Marcos, please don't say any more." Paige took a deep breath. "There is something very serious I have to talk to you about."

Christ. Marcos tried not to flinch. Here he was hoping Paige wanted to talk things out, but maybe she was going to announce she'd filed a sexual harassment suit.

"Can I sit down, and can I close the door?" Paige asked.

"Of course." Marcos walked around the desk and took a seat. All things considered, he was surprised Paige wanted to be behind closed doors with him.

Paige dropped the dance bag at her feet and took the chair across the desk. "Marcos, I need to talk to you, but I'm not sure where to begin, so please forgive me if I repeat myself."

Marcos nodded. His chest felt constricted.

"I need to start at the beginning. I've been a mess since my mother died. Her death knocked my feet out from under me," Paige said. "After the initial shock, I was overcome by a feeling of being rootless—I don't know how else to explain it—and it got worse after the house I grew up in sold. I felt lost and abandoned." Using the armrests for leverage, Paige moved further back in her seat.

Marcos reached into Katherine's small fridge and then slid a bottle of water toward Paige. She uncapped it and took a long drink. He wished he could pour himself something stronger.

"My mom raised me alone, and that was her choice, but I always felt cheated not having a dad. I asked and asked who my dad was. When I was old enough to be told, she said the reason she had no information on my father was because I was the result of a one-night stand at some medical conference. She said she's never regretted it and wanted me from the minute she found out she was pregnant. That story never rang true to me, and I always believed there was something she wasn't telling me. I don't look like my mother, so for a while I thought I must be adopted, and she didn't want me to know."

Marcos shifted in his seat. He was as sympathetic as the next guy, but what Paige needed was a therapist, and that wasn't going to be him. Maybe she had some kind of a daddy complex? Whatever the issue was, he was pretty darn sure he didn't want to get sucked into the quicksand. What was it about women's thinking that was always so damn convoluted and complicated?

"Anyway, I wouldn't let it go, and I pushed, and my mom got angry." Paige dropped her eyes and took a breath. "She finally pulled out my birth certificate showing her name, Patricia Kathleen Russell, as my mother, and the name of the father marked as unknown. She was hurt, not just angry, because to her it was like I was saying she wasn't enough. So I dropped the whole subject, but I never stopped thinking that if my father knew I existed, wouldn't he want to get to know me? I'd look at strangers' faces wondering, and I'd sort through my mother's old pictures for men who might look kinda like me. No matter how good my life was or how hard she tried, there was always a hollow spot in my gut that needed to be filled."

Now tears were shimmering in Paige's eyes. Why did the girl keep going on about not having a dad? He felt a niggling little fear that he'd misread her and she might be unbalanced, and here he was alone with her behind closed doors.

"When my mother died, I thought I'd never learn the truth about who my dad might be."

Marcos was too tired for this self-pitying ramble. Did the girl have a point, a conclusion? And what in the hell did any of this have to do with him or her bizarre behavior in the cafe?

Paige stopped talking and licked her lips. She twisted and untwisted her hands, and then dropped them in her lap. Marcos stayed silent, and waited for her to continue.

"And on the practical side, I'm missing chunks of family medical history and info on my ethnic background."

"You have my full sympathy, Paige. I can't imagine how you felt and obviously still feel. My mother is gone as well, but my father is still alive, and I have a large group of cousins. But what does this all have to do with me? I am at a loss here."

"I'm getting there, I promise. After I moved into the studio apartment in Flagstaff, I started sorting through the last of Mom's boxes of stuff. It was a last-ditch attempt to find something that would give me a clue about my father: a letter, a card, anything. I thought that if I could find my dad, maybe he would be surprised and happy to discover he had a daughter. Maybe he had a family, and I could be part of it and belong somewhere again."

"And so, did you find anything to help you track him down?" Marcos said, glancing at his watch. This was becoming tiresome. He was sorry he'd ever opened the door to Paige, both literally and figuratively.

Paige unzipped her dance bag and pulled out a worn-looking, blue manila folder. "This folder provided the first bit of real information, including a name. It was enough for me to go a little crazy for a few weeks in Phoenix checking around. Doors were literally slammed in my face; people hung up on me, and I was accused more than once of being a scammer. So, I gave up, but then two things happened. The second thing was finding some pages I'd missed that were stuck together..." Paige pushed the folder across the table.

Marcos lightly drummed the desktop and shrugged but didn't reach for the folder. This damn girl was sounding crazier and crazier.

"But the first thing was seeing you at the Expo in Flagstaff last summer." Paige pushed the folder closer.

Everything in him stilled. If he had hackles, they would be raised. What the hell did she say about seeing him at the Expo? The girl really was a stalker.

"Marcos, here's the thing. I applied for the job here after seeing you last summer in Flagstaff. In fact, we bumped into each other when you and your partner were winding through the spectators trying to get onto the floor. It was a heart-stopping moment for me."

Marcos laid his hand flat on the desk. "What on earth are you talking about, Paige?" Oh my God. He looked at the closed door. Maybe he should herd her out of here while he still could. This chat was going south fast.

"Marcos, look at me. This is important. This is life-changing. I'm ninety-nine percent sure you're my biological father." She gently pushed the folder closer so the edge of the cardboard was touching Marcos's hand.

"Paige, that's impossible." Marcos fought the urge to demand she take her ridiculous folder and leave immediately. He felt a little dam of acid break in his stomach. He needed to put an end to this nonsense and right away.

"Yeah...well, wait till you hear this. I found a formal-looking typed page with a creased headshot of a dark-haired man, not very clear. The description was: tall, green-gray eyes, college educated, enjoys watching car racing. His ethnic background was pretty much white-bread American. I think the papers in this folder will convince you I'm not nuts."

Her voice trembled and her eyes shone with—what? Unshed tears? A maniacal gleam? Adrenaline kicked in, and with it a full-fledged fight-or-flight response rose into Marcos's chest. What kind of malicious nonsense was she going on about?

"From the very first time I saw you at the Expo, my gut told me I was right. And then the info I found recently confirmed it. There's a minor question about your name, but...."

Marcos's breathing became shallow. Was Paige dangerous? Was she packing a gun in that dance bag? He examined her face. There were no tears running; in fact, she looked very controlled.

"Paige, I'm sorry to stop you, but this is ludicrous. Grief has affected your ability to think straight." Marcos pushed himself away from the desk and strode across the room. He threw his arms in the air, palms toward the ceiling, and turned to Paige.

"I cannot be your father, Paige. Listen to me! I can't be anyone's father. First of all, the timing is all wrong. You were born in, what, 1991? I was about twenty-five then, and how old would your mother have been?" Marcos stopped pacing and stood in front of Paige. "Look at me, Paige, and listen closely. I will never have any children. I contracted the mumps the year I turned twenty-four. I was deathly ill. When a grown man contracts mumps, it often results in sterility. Do you understand what I am saying? I can't father a child, Paige. I had the mumps a full year before you were even born." He stared directly into her eyes. It took everything he had not to grab her and shake her. He was beginning to wonder what he'd ever seen in this sad, deluded young woman.

Paige sat motionless. Her eyes widened, and she bit her top lip. "I didn't know about the mumps," she said, very softly. "But..." She shook her head as if to wake herself up. "But what about before you had the mumps?" Paige looked at him, as calm as the strange stillness before a catastrophic storm. "Did you ever donate sperm for money, Marcos?

Maybe when you were younger? Maybe at twenty-two or twenty-three? I'm not making a judgment. I'm asking a question." She pulled a plastic page protector out of the folder. She held it out, defiant.

The world slowed on its axis. Marcos felt the invisible draw of gravity in every fiber of his being. He stopped moving and locked eyes with Paige for what seemed like thirty seconds. Marcos walked back behind the desk like he was being led to the gallows. He sank into Katherine's large leather chair and looked up, his eyes dry from not blinking. He reached for the folder and opened it, feeling as though its contents held the date of his death.

Paige sipped her water. She remained quiet, and for that he was grateful.

Marcos pulled out the pages. There were faded and creased forms from a sperm bank in Phoenix called Desert CryoFertiBank. Stapled to the inside cover was the donor information sheet with a profile of the donor and a physical description. There was another page of penciled notes, including the name Martin Stevens. Marcos's gut melted like chocolate on a hot day. He couldn't meet Paige's eyes. How could this be happening? When had he lost control of his life?

"One of the things that set me apart from my mother was my unique gray-green eyes," Paige said. "You have the same eye color."

Marcos stared at Paige, noticing for the first time how much her eyes resembled his mother's and his own. Why had he never noticed this before?

"Isn't this you, Marcos?" Paige was now leaning across the desk, balanced on her elbows. She pointed to the donor description. "This gray-green eye color, which we both share, is evidently very rare. I Googled it. Here you can see that the donor's health was excellent. His age is listed as twenty-two. The donor's family background states that his mother was a dancer but later in life became a CPA. His father was an attorney. The donor was a college graduate with a high IQ. Do you have a college degree, Marcos?"

He nodded and somehow managed to croak, "A bachelor's."

"And if you read further, his profession at the time of donation was professional dancer. I don't know how my mother tracked down your name, but on the bottom of the data sheet, as you can see, there is a handwritten notation: *'Martin Stevens, ballroom dancer, Fred Astaire studios in Phoenix, quite good-looking. Seems nice.'* She must have dropped by the studio in Phoenix to check you out after I was born. I think she planned to tell me one day, maybe once I graduated from college. I have to—I need to—believe that. Anyway, my mother was very persistent, and working at finding you wouldn't have been out of character for her. The only discrepancies are that the donor was a nonsmoker, and of course your name isn't Martin Stevens."

Marco sank into the chair. The papers hung from one hand; the other covered his eyes. He started smoking when he was struck by nerves at his first major dance competition and began using a stage name when he was twenty-seven. The sperm donation was done on a dare with a friend. He was twenty-two—a newly hatched dancer and broke. Everything he'd ever heard about karma and life choices catching up with you hit him with the force of a tsunami.

"The clinic. I'd forgotten. Three of us went. The sperm donation was a one-time thing, but we also donated blood for money on a regular basis back then. We were all broke, struggling, dance instructors. I was… But it doesn't matter now, does it?" He finally raised his head and met Paige's eyes. "How did you make the connection from Martin Stevens to Marcos Stephanos?"

"YouTube, Marcos." Paige actually giggled.

Marcos couldn't even manage a smile. He wasn't sure he'd ever smile again.

"Until I found the information about the sperm bank, I was running on gut instinct. The name was major and almost stopped me cold. But then I Googled old YouTube videos, and I found some of a Marcos Stephanos at various competitions, dancing with a Danielle Davino and sometimes with a Katherine Carrington. When I Googled the name Davino, I found even older videos, where she was dancing with a Martin Stevens. Except for longer hair and a tighter waistline, Martin Stevens and Marcos Stephanos sure looked like the same person to me."

"Danielle was my first professional partner. In 1994, at my father's request, I took a stage name—Marcos Stephanos." It took every bit of energy Marcos could muster to verbalize. He was weary to the bone. "It was a deal I made with my father. He'd cut me off financially when I became a dance instructor instead of going to law school. After my bout of mumps, he reconsidered. Long story. So, you've been stalking me?" Marcos managed a weak smile.

"I didn't mean any harm, Marcos. I'm not a stalker in the true sense of the word. Everything I did was necessary research so I could connect the dots. I had to know who my father was and what kind of person he might be. I hit YouTube to try and confirm that I was on the right track. I never expected I'd have the chance to get to know you as well as I have, and I wasn't even sure I would tell you who I was. But then things got complicated."

Marcos had never needed a cigarette so badly and a scotch—a double.

"And I have to tell you something else, too," Paige said. "I've developed very strong feelings about sperm donation—about the children who will one day want to know where they came from, and the casual behavior of the men who aren't really fathers and probably don't want to be. I thought very hard about this, especially after last week." Paige stopped.

Marcos could see that the strain of confronting him was finally hitting her. Her voice had lost its confident edge, and her eyes had dulled with emotional fatigue.

"A person can't do something like donate sperm without understanding that another human being could be the result."

Marcos didn't know what to do. He sure as hell wasn't going to reach out and hug her. That kind of physical contact would put him right over the edge. His flirtatious behavior and everything about last week made him feel ill. Now he understood her flight from the restaurant, and shame warmed his face. This was all too much to absorb.

"Frankly, I can barely form a coherent thought right now." Marcos spread his hands flat on the desk's surface. "I feel very old and deeply tired. And Paige, I hate to say this, but I have to. No matter how much empirical data you have gathered, before we take this any further, actually before we even discuss it again, we need to submit DNA for testing. We have to set emotions aside for the moment and leave any speculation-based paperwork alone and get the facts."

Paige pulled the folder and the plastic sleeve back across the table. She straightened her back and, with a slight frown creasing her forehead, looked directly at Marcos. "Okay. I can deal with that. I understand. I even thought of that myself, so it's not an unreasonable request."

Marcos leaned forward, one elbow on the table. He worked fingertips along his forehead, but the tension wouldn't release. "I feel like I've been tap-dancing through life, and someone has suddenly changed the music from light jazz to Rachmaninoff. I need time to adjust to the beat." His voice came out dry and tired.

"I need you to know I didn't come to Tucson expecting anything from you. That's not what this is about." Paige zipped the folder back into her dance bag and stood. "I'm suddenly wiped out and need to sleep." Paige turned to Marcos before opening the door. "And for the record, aside from a DNA confirmation, as a provider of genes you are not a disappointment. Quite the opposite." She stepped out and closed the door behind her.

Marcos leaned both elbows on the desk. He buried his face in his hands and tried to breathe the knot out of his gut. One day he was drinking scotch in his Jacuzzi, relatively unencumbered, and the next day he has an adult daughter. Maybe. The jury was still out. He was too goddamn old for this. This was not how his life was supposed to go.

"Screw the 'no smoking in the building' rule." He pulled his packet of Gauloises out of his pocket and flipped open his lighter.

TWENTY

Reality Check

Barbara Bradshaw
8:30 a.m., Thursday, 5 November

Barbara's need for coffee overpowered her enjoyment of lazing under the warmth of the duvet. She pulled on a light robe and headed for the kitchen. The house was quiet but not a lonely quiet. There was great comfort in knowing her son was under her roof again, if only for a short time.

Coffee mug in hand, Barbara padded across the Saltillo-tiled living room and opened the shuttered French doors to the Arizona room. The wicker furniture, decked out with inviting, plush, red-and-white striped cushions, offered the perfect spot to watch hummingbirds flit from flower to flower. Big tubs of succulents, flowering annuals, and red hibiscus filled the corners and hung in ceiling baskets. She glanced around with a satisfied smile. In the hot months, this room was her indoor, air-conditioned patio, and in the winter it held a tropical vacation vibe.

Barbara wandered to the windows and drank in the garden. It was too chilly to take her coffee outside, but even from the windows, the ambiance of the garden satisfied her nature-loving soul. The chrysan-themums were in full bloom, and the bottlebrush bristled with red spikes. Gardening, she realized with a pleasant little stomach flutter, was one more interest she shared with Ed Dombrosky. She settled onto a chaise lounge. It was going to be a glorious day.

"So here you are," Michael said. "Great coffee, Mom. Thanks."

"You're welcome." She waited. Michael was hovering. "So, what's up? I have this feeling of waiting for the other shoe to drop. Am I wrong?"

Michael sat down, facing her. "You know me too well. Can I run some thoughts by you?"

"Of course." Barbara leaned back, stretched out her legs, and crossed her ankles.

"So." Michael took a deep breath before continuing. "I'm interested in Marcos's offer at Desert DanceSport, but there's something I have to discuss with him before we go any further." Michael pulled his chair closer.

Barbara placed her cup on a small tiled table. She flipped the handle on the chaise to a sitting position.

"I've given a lot of thought to the direction I want to take with my career." Michael paused. One foot tapped the floor. "I'm tired of the instability and the travel involved with the Broadway roadshows, but I definitely want to stay in the dance world. Teaching ballroom and participating in competitions is a great compromise to stage perfor-mance, and I think I'd be happy at Desert DanceSport, but...."

"But what?" Barbara asked, with the unselfconscious nosiness only a mother can have. She was fully aware she had this maternal character trait in spades.

"I want to be upfront with Marcos about my long-term ambi-tions. He may not want me on board when he finds out I want to pick his brain to learn as much as I can about the day-to-day running of a commercial dance studio." Michael leaned forward. "Mom, my long-term goal is to invest in a business while I'm still young, with many years ahead of me to grow the business. I like the idea of being my own boss and having creative freedom. I could use the money I inherited from both Nana and Dad to get started."

Barbara couldn't keep the surprise off her face. By the look on Michael's face, there was no doubt that subtlety wasn't her strong suit.

Michael laughed. "Yes, Mom, I still have it, every penny. I put most of it into staggered CDs. I knew my inheritance was my one shot to either buy a house or invest in a business. I'm young, but I'm not stupid, and I am my father's son."

"I'm impressed," Barbara said.

"Your little boy is all grown up. I might be a dancer, but flaky I am not."

"I'll say it again, I'm impressed." Barbara couldn't help herself. Her eyebrows rose as she nodded and smiled. "So, my grown-up son, do you have specific ideas in mind?"

"Well…yes," Michael said, reaching for his coffee cup. "My dream is to open my own dance studio."

Barbara gave him her full attention.

"Not just a ballroom studio geared for adults. I want to teach kids as well. I picture a studio offering some interpretive dance, jazz, maybe even theater arts classes. I've thought it through. The kids' classes would be in the late afternoon and early evening, and I'd run classes on Saturdays as well. The adults' classes would be held mainly during the day or later in the evening, which works for most adults anyway, and it might be possible to run some classes concurrently. I'd like the chance to show parents that dance teaches their children the same discipline as martial arts."

"Michael, that sounds wonderful." Barbara was genuinely intrigued and was already wondering where she might fit in as part of this scenario.

"What I need is time working in a ballroom studio to see if what I picture in my head is actually feasible." Michael rubbed his hands together.

"Okay, and…" Barbara said. Her son had stilled and was staring at her, a question in his eyes.

"When the time comes, do you think you might be interested in helping me get this 747 off the ground? Maybe you could handle human resources and interacting with the parents. Of course this wouldn't stop you from keeping up with your own dancing as well."

"Yes, and yes again." Barbara jumped up and planted a sloppy, coffee-flavored kiss on Michael's forehead. She plopped back onto the chaise. She didn't want to dampen Michael's enthusiasm, but she had something she needed to say.

"Michael, you have to understand one thing. I won't be any part of undercutting Desert DanceSport, which would hurt too many people, including Marcos. Let's wait and see where all of this goes. It sounds to me like the studio you picture wouldn't be in direct competition with a strictly ballroom studio anyway."

"Absolutely. We can shelve this for now. It was important to get your take on this idea. At least you don't think I'm nuts to dive into something like this when I'm only thirty-two."

"Nonsense. I think you're at the perfect age to begin thinking long-term. And your business model sounds good." Barbara reached out for her son's hand. "You're being smart. It's hard to make a decent living as a ballroom dance instructor. You're thinking ahead, and I'm one hundred percent behind you." Barbara paused. "On the practical side, I know you have seed money, but you'll also need a business loan. To approach a lender, you'll need a business plan. I can help you put one together. We can take our time and expand it as your ideas develop."

"Sounds perfect, Mom, thank you. One more thing. While I'm working things through, I might have to bunk here with you a bit longer. Would that be an issue?"

Barbara stifled herself. He didn't need to know that she was overjoyed at the prospect of her son living with her a while longer. "Of course, Michael, this will always be your home."

"All righty, then. Now I've really got to get going. I'm late. See you at the studio," Michael said, and before Barbara could answer, he was across the room and gone.

"I guess it's time for me to get moving as well," Barbara announced to the empty room. She hoped there might be a few responses to the ad for a part-time front desk person. Kristi was starting soon to cover the evenings. Katherine, Barbara mused, was being surprisingly blasé about the whole thing and was giving Barbara free rein. She never would understand that woman. From one minute to the next, Katherine ran hot and cold and every temperature in between.

~

Marcos Stephanos
9:30 a.m., Thursday, 5 November

Marcos leaned against the counter in the breakroom and savored both the quiet and a strong coffee. He was exhausted. Three long nights of trying to make sense of the files he'd copied from Katherine's USB drive had worn him out. She'd passworded one set of spreadsheets, but *DanceBitch* was a phrase he'd heard her use more than once—pretty easy guess. Marcos was trying to withhold judgment until he could get a professional opinion, but last night the light flared on. There were *two* sets of accounting books for the studio. No wonder she'd been crazy wild looking for her "lost" thumb drive. Barbara told him Katherine looked like she was going to cry when she learned Barbara had found the USB drive on the floor, behind one of the large potted plants.

Michael poked his head in the door and gave a cheery wave. "Save me some coffee, be there in a sec."

Marcos raised his cup in acknowledgment, not sure he was ready to handle that much cheerfulness. Before he could steel himself to deal with happy, Tony Moreno pushed the door open. Two garment bags were draped over one arm, and he dragged a large suitcase behind him. Sylvie followed on his heels, wheeling one suitcase beside her. Marcos had never seen her so disheveled.

"Why are you two back so soon?" Marcos asked. "Didn't you plan to be gone through Saturday?"

Sylvie and Tory grimaced in unison, but Tony spoke first. "I have a story to tell, but let's wait for the group. I can't go through it more than once."

"I'm only here for the coffee, and then I'm going straight home for the rest of the day," Sylvie added. "We took the red-eye in from LA. Tony and I shared a cab because we left our cars here." She fell into the nearest chair, looking as exhausted as Marcos felt.

Marcos moved out of the way so Tony could reach for the coffee carafe. The front door opened and then swung shut with a thud. Voices echoed around the lobby. The familiar click of Katherine's heels tatted across the tile.

"Good morning," she murmured.

Marcos tipped an imaginary hat. Katherine seemed subdued. Better subdued than the bipolar emotional mess she'd been on Tuesday, frantic about the damn thumb drive. Within minutes of each other, Michael, Paige, and Joey were maneuvering for space in the small breakroom, moaning about needing coffee. Did no one have a coffeepot at home? Paige filled a mug and leaned against the wall, holding the hot ceramic cup like she was warming her hands. A gored skirt flared above her leggings and her thick hair was pulled into a high ponytail. Marcos sighed, the reality of fifty slapping him in the face hard. Sylvie edged Paige out of the way to pull a yogurt container out of the fridge, and, completely out of character, Katherine started a second pot of coffee brewing. By the time Brianna stumbled in, curious eyes roved from Sylvie's face to Tony's and back to Sylvie's.

"So, I heard through the grapevine that something happened at the comp, but my source wasn't clear about what. Couldn't find results posted for Rising Star, either, so...did you two place? And why are you back so early?" Katherine said. She turned toward Tony with an expectant look on her face.

Tony topped off his coffee, glanced at the wall clock, and said, "Long story. I'll cover as much as I can before students begin arriving."

He took a quick sip and put the mug on the counter. "To start, the flight out of Tucson was seriously delayed. And then, because there were no gates available at LAX, we spent an extra hour on board waiting for a gate. Sylvie was ready to open the emergency exit and hike her high heels across the tarmac."

"He's not exaggerating," Sylvie said. "I took my makeup case with me in the cab and did my face on the way to the hotel, and by the time we got there we were ten minutes late for registration. Forget checking into our rooms. We barely had time to get into our costumes, and I had to step onto the floor with my hair just quickly pulled up."

"Which did nothing to help Her Majesty's composure." Tony gestured to Sylvie, who showed him her middle finger.

"Nice behavior, kids," Marcos said.

Undaunted, Tony continued the story. "Nevertheless, we made it through Monday afternoon's preliminaries. Anong Buarin and Larry deVine positioned themselves next to us to show off in front of the judges. In general, the competition was killer. But we were on and hot and made the cut for the finals."

Sylvie muttered something under her breath that Marcos couldn't hear.

"The Latin heats were scheduled for late in the day on Tuesday," Tony continued. "When we walked into the practice room that morning, we heard shouting coming from behind the partition dividing the ballroom into two practice areas. Then, one side pushed open, and out comes Anong, her face all screwed up and red. Right after her was that Deena Watson from Chicago, yelling something like, 'You and your has-been partner are low-life cheaters. You outright stole our new choreography, and you know it.' Anong kept walking but turned around long enough to yell back, 'Prove it. Larry and I don't need any of your losing routines.' Then, before she walked out the door she turned to the room and announced, 'That lying whore Deena is a crazy bitch.'"

There was a major intake of breath all around the breakroom. Words like those weren't tossed around at competitions and, if overheard by a judge, could get you disqualified. Marcos shook his head but motioned for Tony to continue.

"Deena stopped in her tracks, looking like she was going to burst into tears, and then she sort of quietly turned around and went back to the other practice room. Everyone on our floor got back to business. None of us could afford to get pulled into their drama." Tony paused to take a deep breath.

Marcos took a seat; Sylvie got a glass of water; Paige took the chair next to Marcos.

"Late Tuesday afternoon we danced in the first round of finals for Rising Star. There were twelve couples on the floor. We started into our fast and furious jive. Anong and Larry were on the edge of the floor, next to us. Deena and Bob danced in so close it was like they were trying to force us to move closer to Anong and Larry, crowding them off the floor. So there were Sylvie and I, hemmed in by these two loco couples, focused on getting in each other's way." Tony cleared his throat and ran a hand through his hair. He shook his head and then continued. "I still don't know exactly what happened, but as we tried to maneuver out of their orbit, Deena spun into Anong, throwing her off balance. Bob tried to stop Deena's fall, but Anong and Deena's legs were entwined, and all three of them hit the floor."

"And Tony and I kept on dancing," Sylvie piped up. "As we dodged around them, Deena reached up and ripped off part of Anong's costume."

"I can't believe what I'm hearing," Marcos muttered. Katherine stood stock still.

"Tell the rest, Tony," Sylvie said.

"When Deena tossed the ripped piece of fabric, it slapped me in the face, and the sequins caught in my hair. I couldn't see and almost knocked Sylvie down trying to pull it off. The spectators were roaring—some in horror, but some *pendejos* were laughing their stupid asses off. The judges were all standing. Anong's torn costume exposed...well let's just say she was exposed. Check YouTube sometime today. No way there aren't videos out there already."

"Whaaaaaat!" Marcos exploded. All around the room hands covered mouths. Paige was laughing. Katherine's eyes were Cheshire Cat wide.

"So both couples were disqualified from the event. Deena and Bob face disciplinary action, but Deena's accusation against Anong and Larry about the stolen choreography will be investigated. Everyone tried to regroup and continue the heats, but Sylvie's shoulder twisted when I stopped her from falling, and we finished a poor fourth. The whole event was all *mucho chingada*—fucked, big time.

Katherine spoke first. "I'm at a loss for words. I'm sorry for you two. Coming back winners would have raised your teaching rates. It's too damn bad."

Marcos telegraphed a look to Tony. Leave it to Katherine to put dollars before empathy.

"I am still trying to deal with everything," Sylvie said, scraping yogurt off the bottom of the container. "Tony and I had a long discussion on the plane home. I know I should be speaking privately to Katherine first, but I'm just going to say it."

Marcos glanced at Katherine, but she'd already turned her full attention to Sylvie. Katherine folded her arms across her chest.

Sylvie's eyes were locked on Katherine's. "Tony and I have decided to go our separate ways as competitive partners. I still want to pursue the Open Latin championship and eventually make it to Nationals, so I'll be canvassing for another partner." She gave Katherine an apologetic-looking shrug. "I'm truly sorry, Katherine, but I have to put my competitive career first. I'm twenty-nine. If I don't make it over the next two years, it won't happen for me. This is my last shot. I might have to relocate if I can't find a partner willing to move to Tucson."

Marcos could read Katherine's expression at the word relocate. The studio simply couldn't afford to lose two of their top teachers. The coffee began to burn an ulcer-sized hole in his stomach. His fingers twitched with the need to pull out a cigarette. Marcos folded his arms, his jaw clenched.

"Tony?" Katherine looked at Tony with a question in her voice that showed on her face.

"I'm not going anywhere," Tony said. "Desert DanceSport is my home. This is where I belong. I'm happy to take students to compete in Pro-Am events, but I am done with the professional circuit. This year was going to be it for me, anyway, which probably isn't a big surprise to Sylvie. I've been there, done that, and don't want to do it again."

"Well," Marcos said, clapping to get everyone back on track, "I think we need to get on with our day. We have enough to grease the gossip mill for the next few days." He turned to the weary duo. "You two just go on home and get some rest. You look exhausted. I, for one," he added with wicked smile, "will be checking YouTube."

Everyone filed out but Michael. "Any chance we could chat for a few minutes?" he asked.

"It's going to have to be another time," Marcos said. "I will make time for you, I promise." He patted Michael on the arm. The young man put his cup in the sink and followed everyone else out the door.

Marcos sat back down. One elbow was on the table; his chin rested against a closed fist. He'd agonized for the last two nights, but he had no choice. He had to suck it up and eat crow. Lots of crows. Major advice was needed and, if his suspicions turned out to be true, legal guidance. He made his way to the back door and waited until he was safely out of earshot to pull out his cell phone.

Marcos opened his contacts list, took a deep breath, and let it out with an exhale a yoga instructor would be proud of. He couldn't even remember the last time he'd called this number. He waited through three rings.

"Good morning. Stevens, Russo, and Ryan." The receptionist's voice was the perfect balance of upbeat and soothing. "How can I direct your call?"

"Mr. Martin Stevens, please. Tell him his son is on the line."

~

Paige Russell
3:30 p.m., Thursday, 5 November

"Barbara?" Paige said. "I thought your lesson with Marcos was an hour ago. You're still here in the ballroom? Aren't you sick of us yet?"

"You'd think I would be, wouldn't you?" Barbara looked away from her cell phone with an expansive, open smile. "Marcos and I haven't had our lesson yet. He had to run out, and I decided to hang out and wait rather than cancel the lesson. I just got a text from him. He's on his way back to the studio."

"I didn't know he'd even left. Doesn't matter, I guess. Mind if I join you?" Paige rested her hand on the back of a chair. "I have Brandon coming in soon for his four o'clock."

"Sit," Barbara said, extending a hand. "I'm enjoying watching everyone on the floor. Linda and Joey were done a bit ago, and now my son is over there talking Joey's ear off. Those two have been giggling and laughing for the past ten minutes. I'm such a nosy mom. I'd love to know what has them so animated."

"Joey loves an audience. My guess is he's enjoying telling old stories to a new victim."

"I was eavesdropping as Jackson worked with that older couple over there." Barbara dropped her voice to a whisper. "He was trying to help the gentleman with his Viennese Waltz. Jackson kept repeating the mantra: 'Contra Body Movement: CBM creates swing, and swing creates sway.' I'm still not sure the old guy got it. He looked confused."

"It's harder for the men," Paige said. "If they don't get enough CBM, their partner doesn't get the right cue. No one said this stuff was easy, and if they did, they were plain out-and-out lying. It takes years to work up the learning curve, and then you find out you've learned something incorrectly, and you have to start back at square one."

"At least it's not only me who feels that way." Barbara laughed and gave Paige a friendly pat on the hand. "And you still want to do this for a living, huh?"

"I guess I'm still thinking it over," Paige replied, keeping it light; but, in truth, she wasn't sure what she wanted to do anymore.

"Did Kristi tell you I got the okay from Katherine, and Kristi will be working evenings at the front desk starting next week?" Barbara said.

"No, I didn't know. We've both been so busy. I'm going to totally enjoy having her here. I think she'll get along with everyone and do a great job."

"I do, too. Looks like Michael will be giving her some lessons. Oh, here comes Edward," Barbara said, waving him over. She turned to Paige as Ed took a seat. "Ed and I have started taking some joint lessons with Marcos."

Paige leaned toward Edward for a hug. Political correctness did not apply to hugging in a dance studio. Everyone hugged, and she loved how Ed hugged her back with enthusiasm.

"Yup," Edward said. He pulled his dance shoes out of his black drawstring bag. "The few joint lessons we've had with Marcos were eye-openers. Dancing with another amateur is a whole different ball game than dancing with a pro. I didn't realize I've been learning patterns but not how to lead. Now I'm reviving old brain cells and rethinking everything."

"Really?" Paige said. This was an important point of view from a male student. She could put this to use with her own students.

"Absolutely. Katherine is such a pro, she can make up for what I lack—she can back-lead me, so to speak—which makes me think I'm much better than I really am. This amateur-with-amateur stuff is challenging, but I feel like I'm learning to dance for real. And, this lovely lady here is the picture of patience."

Edward smiled at Barbara, and his whole expression softened. Paige blushed in empathy as color rose in Barbara's cheeks. Perfect timing for her to slip away. Brandon was on the other side of the ballroom changing his shoes. Paige excused herself but had barely pushed in her chair when Marcos came charging in the door. He waved to Barbara, mouthed "one minute," and signaled to Paige. He took her arm, walked a few feet away from everyone, and leaned in.

"I took our DNA swabs to the same lab where I got the kit. My connection there—a previous student—promised results in two to three days. I'm still trying to absorb this sperm-donor-daddy thing. It's going to take some time to work my head around it. We'll talk in more depth once the results are in, okay? Can you live with that?" Marcos placed one hand on Paige's shoulder.

"Of course," Paige replied. She curled her lips in a friendly smile, willing Marcos to lose the concern in his eyes. He released her and walked over to Barbara and Ed.

Paige stood still and placed a hand over her middle. She felt different. Something deep inside had shifted. It was like a physical ping or a click. Her insides had expanded to fill in the hollowed-out space that had always been part of her. She felt suddenly self-conscious standing there, rooted to the spot. Brandon was focused on tying his shoes. Barbara and Ed were busy talking to Marcos. Nothing had shifted for anyone but her.

She made herself move and walked to the water fountain to buy a couple more minutes. Paige gulped back mouthfuls of water and then wiped her mouth on her arm. She truly felt okay. If the DNA results were positive, she'd have what she wanted—the knowledge of who her dad was. And anyway, a sperm-donor father was really not as bad as a tacky one-night stand. Paige compressed her lips and nodded. It was time to release the fantasy of the dad who would drop to his knees in a wash of paternal love when he first saw the child he never knew he had. That was a child's dream, and she felt more adult by the hour. Marcos might not have the daddy gene, but with time he could become a great mentor and friend. Finding the missing puzzle piece was enough, and her mission, as such, was accomplished.

TWENTY-ONE

DANCING IN THE RAIN

Marcos Stephanos
11:00 a.m., Friday, 6 November

Marcos nosed the Miata into his favorite parking spot in front of the studio. The lyrics to Madonna's "Papa Don't Preach" sang out from his cell before he could turn off the ignition. Swearing, he stripped off one lambskin driving glove and fumbled the phone out of his coat pocket.

"Can you hold for one second? I'm just getting out of the car." Marcos pulled off his other glove and tossed them both onto the passenger seat. He pulled his lanky frame out of the low car and leaned against the driver's side door, legs crossed at the ankles, one arm tucked across his torso. "Sorry, Dad. Thanks for waiting. So, what are your thoughts?" Marcos lowered his eyes, shaking his head as he absorbed what he was hearing.

"Do you honestly believe the situation is this serious? I'm not sure I'm ready to go there." Marcos walked slowly across the parking lot, turned, and paced back to his starting point. He leaned his backside against the car and began to rock back and forth.

"Yeah, I know you're an attorney, and you know what you're talking about, and your people are experts." Marcos had to smile in spite of his distress. Talking to his dad made him feel fifteen again. "I guess I was thinking in terms of irresponsible managing of the accounts, or some indiscreet borrowing, or, at worst, minor juggling of the books."

Marcos sighed and ran a hand across his forehead. He pulled his key fob out of his pocket and clicked the car door locked. "So based on what your accountant suspects, you're saying we need to have an auditor come in?" Marcos shook his head. This was not turning out to be a cheery morning.

"Okay. Let me know as soon as you have the right person lined up. I'll deal with everything on this end. And Dad, I can't thank you enough for being there for me... Yes, brunch on Sunday sounds excellent... Ventana at nine-thirty?... Good. I'll see you then."

Marcos stared into space, the phone still in his hand. He felt like dry quicksand was shifting under his feet, threatening to bury him in a deep hole, and he wasn't sure he had the internal fortitude to clamber out of it. He sighed; his teeth clenched on his upper lip. If only he could turn back time and have a do-over, wiser and smarter. The one good thing to come out of this ugly situation was a genuine reconciliation with his father. He'd eaten several crows in the process—feet, beaks, and all. He managed a tight smile. There was nothing to do now but wait for his dad to call back. He pocketed his phone and walked to the front door.

"Good morning, ladies." Marcos mustered a cheerful tone. And who was that attractive young woman behind the desk with Barbara? The new part-time receptionist? He felt a genuine smile relaxing his facial muscles. Maybe his day was about to improve? The girl really was stunning: chin-length, blond-streaked, dark hair and the loveliest cat-like, almond-shaped eyes he'd ever seen.

"Marcos, let me introduce Kristi. We discussed her coming in to cover the desk in the evenings," Barbara said. "Kristi, meet Marcos Stephanos, studio manager and dance master."

"Very pleased to meet you, Marcos," Kristi said, extending her hand.

Marcos pulled at his collar. Did this young woman always greet new people with such an intense stare? It was like she was attempting telepathy.

"Pleased to meet you as well," Marcos said, reaching for and shaking her hand. This girl made him feel self-conscious, and that made him uncomfortable.

"Kristi found herself with free time this morning, so she popped by to get the lay of the land, so to speak," Barbara said. "I've given her the million-dollar tour, and we've gone over some front desk basics: the phone, a list of staff members, client names she should know, and the appointment book. She'll be starting on Monday evening. Oh, and Paige invited Kristi to tonight's practice party to get a feel for our studio dance community."

"Paige? They've met already?" Marcos asked

"Paige and I are neighbors. Actually, we're more than neighbors; we've become pretty close friends." Kristi tilted her head, her gaze direct and steady.

Marcos felt scrutinized. His cheeks flared into warmth. Friends? How close? Surely Paige wouldn't have discussed deeply personal matters with someone she couldn't have known for more than a few months? But you never knew with women and their insatiable need to share.

"I'm sure you'll do well here, Kristi. Pleased to have you on board," Marcos said. He strove for a businesslike but warm demeanor. He refused to let his foolish insecurities make him sound rattled. He turned to Barbara. "And where is Paige this morning?"

"She's on the floor with Tony. He's coaching her before her noon client arrives."

Marcos gritted his teeth but managed a perfunctory, closed-lipped smile. He could only hope Tony was coaching Paige in dance technique and nothing else.

"Well, I need to get going," Kristi said. She hugged Barbara. "Thank you for all your help. Tell Michael I'm looking forward to my first lesson." She turned to Marcos as she reached the front door. "It was good to meet you, Marcos. Paige has told me so much about you." With a waggle of her fingers she was out the door.

Marcos responded with the slightest of nods.

"Barbara, where's Katherine this morning?" Marcos asked.

Barbara pointed discreetly toward the window of the front office.

"Really?" The office lights were out. Through the partially opened blinds, Katherine was barely visible in the dim glow of the computer screen. He decided to leave well enough alone for the moment.

"Are you heading home now, Barbara, or do you have time for a coffee and a quick chat?" Marcos asked.

"I'd love some coffee," Barbara said. "I was too busy with Kristi to even pour a cup, let alone drink it. Brianna will be off the floor any minute. She said she'd handle the desk for a while. I'll be back in later today."

"Don't know what we'd do without you, my friend," Marcos said. "As soon as I get a coffee, I'm taking myself out back for a smoke. Join me when Brianna relieves you."

It was a gorgeous day. Whipped-cream clouds billowed over the craggy outcrops of Pusch Ridge, softening its jagged silhouette and breaking the endless monotony of Tucson's blue skies. The air held a tingle of crispness with an overtone of languid late-morning warmth. For Marcos, it was the kind of day that forced him to peel off his fall jacket and raise his face to the sun. A woodpecker rat-tatted away above his head, and mourning doves lamented plaintively across the rooftops. Marcos crossed his legs and leaned back on the bench, amusing himself with daydreams about beaches in the south of France. He imagined things were as they used to be when Katherine was someone he trusted implicitly and life was carefree and uncomplicated. The saying "Ignorance is bliss" held new significance.

"Okay, move over. I want to share some of that sunshine," Barbara said, settling in close to Marcos. She placed her coffee cup on the bench beside her. "So, what's up?"

"Well, to start with, life has become complicated and messy, and most of it I can't share with you, at least not yet." Marcos turned sideways on the bench, allowing eye contact. "So if I seem impatient or out of sorts, just know my bad moods have nothing to do with you, ever."

Okay," Barbara replied. "Now you have both my attention and my curiosity." She took a long sip of coffee and then cradled the cup.

Marcos rubbed his hands along his thighs and turned to look at Barbara. "As much as I've shared with you, there are some important bits of information I've kept to myself." Marcos raised both eyebrows and ducked his chin. "The fact is, years ago when Katherine was trying to buy this building, I stepped in with the additional funding to secure the loan. I invested on the condition that I'd be a full business partner. I own forty-eight percent of Desert DanceSport."

"Wait," Barbara blurted. "You're a forty-eight-percent owner? But then who's the Mr. Stevens whose name is on the mortgage with Katherine's?" Barbara's hand flew to her face. "Oh, I'm such an idiot sometimes. I didn't mean to blurt that out. Michael did a little digging for history on the building, and he told me what he learned. Sorry, I—"

"No worries. Don't be embarrassed. I'm surprised more people haven't figured it out. With Google at our fingertips, it's close to impossible to keep anything a secret anymore. Let me explain."

Barbara bit her lip. Marcos gave Barbara a quick wink to put her at ease. She looked absolutely mortified at her indiscretion.

"Marcos Stephanos is not my real name. It's a stage name I took a few years after I started dancing professionally. My legal name is Martin Edward Stevens; my father is Jacob Martin Stevens."

"What?" Barbara's lips compressed as she swallowed. "Your father is the big-time attorney J. Martin Stevens? Even I've heard of him."

"Yup, in the flesh. My grandfather founded the firm, which my father expanded to Stevens, Russo, and Ryan. After I graduated from Arizona State, I was supposed to attend an out-of-state law school. The expectation was for me to join my father's firm and follow in his footsteps, the same way he followed in his father's footsteps."

"Geez. I didn't even know you'd gone to college. Sounds like you had a lot to live up to."

"To put it mildly. My career path was a given all my life. But one day I wandered into a ballroom studio in Phoenix. Dancing was like a drug. I couldn't get enough. When I told my father I was going to train as a ballroom instructor, he went through the roof, as did my grandfather, who was still alive at the time. Our family name was prominent in the community, and the law firm had an excellent reputation. A ballroom-dancing son was an embarrassment. When I refused to cave, my father cut me off. I damn near starved over the next few years."

Barbara was wide-eyed.

"Yeah, I know," he said. "This is the stuff soap operas are made of." Marcos attempted what he hoped was a self-deprecating grin. "My father is not a cold man, Barbara. He lived life under his own father's thumb and expected me to do the same. Even now he doesn't always adjust well to plans being changed unless he's the one changing them. Anyway, I got very ill when I was in my midtwenties and almost died. After that, before my mother passed away, my father contacted me. I was about twenty-seven. He let me know he'd never written me out of the will and was prepared to extend an olive branch. He couldn't bear to see his son struggling financially anymore. I'm sure my mother was behind this 'change of heart.' He not only gave me the money he'd set aside for law school, but he set me up with a trust fund. There was one condition attached. I was to assume a stage name. He still didn't want the family name associated with anything as tacky as dancing. He made it clear he wasn't proud of what I was doing. In his eyes, women paying you to dance with them is not any different from being a gigolo."

"Yikes," Barbara said, covering her mouth.

"Yeah. That was pretty strong. I never changed my name legally, only professionally. My dad has never seen me dance, and, until recently, we've not exactly been lunch buddies." Marcos raised his hand when Barbara motioned as though to speak. "In my father's defense, I have to say, as disappointed as he was with me, the trust fund was generous. I'm able to live as comfortably as I would have as a highly paid attorney, which is more than I can say for most ballroom dance instructors, even studio owners."

"Whew," Barbara said. "I feel as though I just got off a carnival ride. That's quite a story. So, you're not Greek, then? I figured Stephanos was Greek…and all that dark hair."

Marcos threw his head back and roared. Barbara looked astonished. "Oh my God, Barbara, nothing so exotic. Martin is Scottish in origin. I'm pretty much ordinary white bread."

"Sort of like my gene pool—a cross of English and Danish," Barbara replied.

"On to more serious matters," Marcos said. "Since you've been pulled into the white lie of what happened to Katherine's lost USB drive, I can fill you in on a bit more." Marcos compressed his lips and took a minute to sort out what he wanted to say. "I've always kept a low profile and let Katherine handle the financials. It was our unspoken deal: I'd manage the creative end, and she'd manage the business end." Marcos drained his cup and set it on the gravel. "This informal arrangement has more or less worked for us. I recently became aware of some cash-flow issues and learned that some of the instructors' paychecks have bounced. Turns out that's the real reason we lost Jeremy earlier this year. And you know Katherine's been off. You've even commented yourself on how erratic her behavior can be. Anyway, the turning point was after you passed me Katherine's red thumb drive, and I examined the contents."

"I hope I did the right thing." Barbara looked worried.

"You did, trust me. I can't go into detail except to say the drive contained some very confusing spreadsheets. They've been reviewed by my dad's accountant." Marcos paused and rubbed his temples. "The accountant strongly suggested that we bring in an auditor." Marcos placed one hand over Barbara's. "Please remember, what I've just told you is one-hundred-percent classified information. This is not something I want you to share, not even with Michael, okay?"

"I understand, of course. I have a very selfish question to ask right now." Barbara paused, put down her now-empty cup, and folded her hands in her lap. "Except for the fact that I have a lot of money on the books here, I shouldn't be asking, but...where does this leave the studio?"

Marcos opened his mouth to answer but closed it as Linda Wilson's Mercedes pulled into the parking lot with Joey Bustamente behind the wheel. "What the hell?" Marcos said. "Why is Joey driving Linda's car?"

"Um, well, they go out for a brunchy thing once every couple of weeks before Linda's lesson. I assumed you knew."

Joey jumped out of the shiny new Mercedes, walked nonchalantly around to the passenger side, and opened the door for Linda. With a quick wave they headed to the back door.

"No, I didn't know. Instructors aren't allowed to socialize with students. Although," Marcos raised his eyebrows and smiled, "I guess it could be said we are doing exactly that."

"Yes we are." Barbara looked at him with a mischievous smile. "Remember, Linda isn't a kid, and Joey isn't dating her. Joey's a senior instructor; he's paid his dues and can make good judgment calls. It's the newer instructors who need stronger guidelines. Most of them are still too young to have much common sense."

Marcos sighed. "All I see is trouble with having one set of rules for one and a different set for the other. But you have a point. Seniority and seasoning should factor in."

"Anyway, back to your story, or should I say confession." Barbara's smile was tentative. "And back to my question, which I probably shouldn't even ask. Are things so bad the studio might close? I don't know what I'd do without this place." Barbara massaged her upper arms. "The people here, the other students and the staff, are my extended family. As the kids say, they're my tribe."

"If I have to pull every penny out of my trust fund, the doors to this studio will never close." Marcos shook his head. "Right now it's hard to think past feeling gut-punched. Katherine and I go way back, and I can't believe she'd betray our friendship. I'm reserving judgement on Katherine until I see what happens with the audit."

"I appreciate your trusting me enough to confide in me, Marcos. I'm sorry you're dealing with all of this, and I promise not to say a word."

"Thank you for that. We'll sort it all out, I'm sure. I'm trying not to overreact. On another subject, I'm pleased you and Edward are taking some joint lessons with me. Not only do I enjoy both of you, but if the worst happens with Katherine, Edward won't be left in the lurch. He's a major player here, and we value him both as a client and as a friend."

"He'd be pleased to hear you say that. So…I know you have a lot on your plate, but could you make some time to meet with Michael? Maybe sooner than later? He has some ideas he wants to run past you, and now might actually be a good time to hear what he has to say."

"I'll make the time," Marcos said. "I promise."

~

Paige Russell
5:00 p.m., Friday, 6 November

Paige sat down at one of the ballroom's café tables. She felt around in her dance bag for a golf ball, placed it on the floor, and ran the ball under her arch. It hurt, but in a good way. Bless Brianna for teaching her this trick to stretch out the bottom of her foot. The last thing she needed was the dancers' nemesis, plantar fasciitis.

"See you next Friday, Paige," Brandon called out.

"Bye, Brandon." Paige gave him a quick wave. "Good lesson."

Without Nikki dragging him down, Brandon was learning quickly. Today he led a fast swing without any yanking like he was whipping his lariat to rope a calf. Paige relaxed back in her chair but continued to run her foot over the golf ball.

"Good girl," Brianna said, pointing at Paige's foot as she ran past.

Paige signaled a thumbs-up and glanced at the wall clock. Yup. Brianna was a few minutes late for her five o'clock client. Having Kristi here was going to help so much. Expecting the instructors to juggle the front desk, phones, and lesson times was asking too much.

Two tables away, within earshot, Marcos was winding things up with a woman Paige hadn't seen before. He leaned forward, one foot on a chair, while his student scrolled through her cell phone. From what Paige saw of their lesson, this woman had either previous dance experience or loads of natural talent. She'd had caught on to Marcos's instruction for tango very quickly. Since he usually passed beginning students to a less-senior instructor, he must have this one pegged as a potential participant in competitions.

"So, two hours a week for now, then," Marcos said. "Wednesdays at two and Fridays at three, correct?"

"Works for me," the woman said. She sounded very New York. "I enjoyed my lesson. Looking forward to next Wednesday."

Marcos gave the woman a hug and walked her to the ballroom entrance, then headed over to Paige.

"What's up with the golf ball? Arch issues?" Marcos asked.

"I'm doing damage control. I might put arch-support inserts in my practice shoes. Or maybe I need a new pair of shoes. Who knew they would wear out so quickly?" Paige replied.

"Consider keeping a couple of extra pairs with varying heel heights in your locker. Rotating heel height throughout the day can help stretch those tendons and prevent overuse."

"Good idea," Paige replied.

"How tight is your schedule at the moment?" Marcos asked.

"I have an hour-plus break. Was going to grab a bite. I'm staying this evening to work the practice party."

"Is your foot good enough for you to walk to the deli with me? We can chat and pick up some food at the same time."

Paige slipped on her street shoes and stood. "Yeah, I'm good. I can leave my shoes here for now." She held the suede-soled, black leather dance shoes by their shoelaces and plopped them beside a couch. "I'm happy to get out in the fresh air. I'm loving these cooler temps. Much more like what I was used to in Flagstaff."

Marcos held the back door open and guided her across the parking lot to the side street that led to the deli. She couldn't understand why some women found these gentlemanly gestures condescending or offensive. She loved them.

"You haven't experienced a real Tucson summer yet, have you?"

Paige turned to Marcos to answer his question. "Not the intense heat everyone talks about. I got here in August, in monsoon season. Wasn't thrilled with either the hammering rain or the lightning bolts. I much prefer the peaceful precipitation of Flagstaff's snowfalls."

"Hmmm. Peaceful precipitation. You really surprise me sometimes," Marcos said.

Paige basked in his smile. A large rock, freed from the riprap on the slope, lay on the ground in front of her. Paige maneuvered around it. There were no sidewalks along this side street. It bordered a stretch of rocky, open desert.

"How was your coaching with Tony this morning?"

"It was okay," Paige replied. "Tony is Tony." She shrugged. "We worked on my Cuban motion, so of course he had to place his hands on my hips to physically show me the correct movement. He can't stop himself from taking advantage of a situation. I don't take it seriously anymore. I've decided he's harmless." Paige shrugged again, pursing her lips.

"Uh-huh."

"It was all cool. Really." Paige nudged Marcos with an elbow. She hoped his concern came from a fatherly place and nothing else. "Tony is a pain, but he's a great dancer, and I can learn a lot of Rhythm and Latin techniques from him. I'm getting used to his macho-ness, and I think I'm getting better at handling his ego. It's all okay. I mean it."

"All right, then. Moving on to a more important subject. Our DNA test results are back." Marcos glanced sideways at Paige.

Paige stopped walking. Her heart skipped a beat. She wasn't sure how ready she was to hear the results.

Marcos continued walking. "Come on, keep up."

Paige was still rooted.

Marcos turned back. "Okay, then, let's stop for a minute before I'm the one to trip over a rock." Marcos pulled out his phone and swiped through his messages. "I don't have the written report as yet, but my friend at the lab called and then texted the results early this morning. Here...I'll give you the gist of what he sent me. Evidently, our cheek swabs collect something called buccal cells." Marcos looked away from the phone, obviously enjoying the science behind the testing. "I've also learned that a DNA test profile is actually a set of DNA markers, up to fifteen, used to determine paternity and identity. Pretty interesting stuff. Dan, my lab connection, told me the tests compare the DNA sequence of the child to that of the alleged father, and the alleged father can be excluded as the biological father with as little as one mismatch between DNA profiles."

Paige shook her head. What the hell did that mean? She didn't like his use of the word "alleged." Paige kicked at the dirt easement. She was only interested in the answer. Screw the technical stuff.

"No?" Marcos looked at Paige with a slight frown. "Well, I won't bore you with all the details, then, but I've Googled for more information on this process, and I have to say the nerd in me finds it fascinating."

Paige could barely breathe. Marcos nudged her forward again, and, as they started moving, she gulped in air. You can't hold your breath while walking. Paige, looking at her feet, bumped right into Marcos when he suddenly stopped. They were standing outside the deli. It was the first storefront in a short strip mall at the edge of a new housing development. Paige walked over to a small picnic table by the front door and sat down.

"Marcos, could you find the text message again and scroll to the results, please." She wasn't so sure she was hungry anymore.

"I'll read you the part of the actual report he texted." Marcos scrolled through his texts again. "Here it is: 'Martin Stevens is not excluded as the biological father of Paige Russell. Not excluded means the paternity report results show 99.9999 percent confidence that the male tested here is the biological father. It means there is a paternity relationship.' Then Dan typed in 'Congratulations, dad.'"

Paige dropped her face into her hands. She didn't want to cry and fought to hold back the tears. She looked up at Marcos. "It's true, then. It's really true. You're my biological father."

Marcos gently placed both hands on Paige's shoulders. "I was prepared to deal, whether positive or negative. But, even now, faced with the undeniable reality of the DNA tests, I can't wrap my head around discovering I have an adult daughter." He rubbed one hand along his jawline. "I'm not sure what you might be expecting, Paige. If you're hoping I can morph into a daddy type, I don't know whether I can make the jump. Quite honestly, fatherhood was never really in my life plan. So now I have a lot of mental adjustments to make. It's going to take some time to absorb and process this."

Paige studied the face of this man she now knew was her blood. "I understand, Marcos; I really do. Just knowing who my father is means everything to me. For now, honestly, that's enough."

Marcos held Paige at arm's length, looking down into her eyes. "Paige, you have to understand, I'm not sure I have what it takes to be a dad—anyone's dad. I know I want the chance to get to know you on a deeper level. We have to start over. I can fill you in on family history and help you add the missing pieces to your family puzzle. We'll sort this out in time. But right now I'm starving, so let's go inside, order sandwiches, and have our first father-daughter lunch together."

Paige pulled away and nodded. Marcos, always the gentleman, once again held the door open for her. She could barely focus on the words on the chalkboard menu. Now she knew, without a doubt, where her unusually colored eyes and her dancer's walk came from. All the gears meshed, and her engine was running smoothly. The thought struck her that she would always be anchored firmly to her mom—the woman who wanted to be a mother more than anything else in the world. Looking at things from what she hoped was a more mature perspective, she knew in her heart she'd always been loved and wanted. And, as an extra bonus, Marcos hadn't freaked out at the news about the DNA results. He actually was interested in exploring what having a daughter might be all about. Appetite restored, Paige placed her order.

TWENTY-TWO

PAYING THE PIPER

Katherine Carrington
10:45 a.m., Monday, 9 November

Katherine pursed her lips. Eyes narrowed, she stared at the monitor—her focus absolute. A light sweat broke out on her brow. Two Excel windows were open. One spreadsheet showed the payables and receivables, as money came in and out of the accounts. The other showed a different version of reality with several entries brightly highlighted and color codes at the top of each page. The colorful screen tracked the increasingly complicated litany of borrowing from Peter to pay Paul. Too many entries were "loans" to her that she somehow needed to pay back. A triple rap on her office door broke her concentration.

"Katherine?"

The last person she wanted to talk to right now was Marcos. She was annoyed to the bone with his condescending attitude and was in no mood today to deal with him. She closed Excel, took a deep breath, and pressed her tongue against her teeth. She would get rid of him as quickly as possible.

"May I have a word, Katherine?" Marcos said, as he pushed the door ajar.

"Of course, Marcos." Katherine kept her voice controlled, well-modulated, honeyed. "Come in. You know I always have time for you." She stood but stayed behind her desk. Hopefully, standing would negate any thought of an invitation to sit down.

Marcos strode into the office with an unfamiliar air of authority, shutting the door behind him. Really? Without even asking? A writing pad was tucked under one arm, and he carried his laptop, which he slid onto her desk. Katherine stood stock still and waited for Marcos to come to the point of his visit. Instead he barged behind her desk. She folded her arms and stepped out of the way. He wasn't giving her much choice. He pulled opened the file cabinet against the wall and removed several file folders. What the hell?

Marcos stabbed the intercom button on Katherine's phone, connecting him to the front desk. "Brianna, Katherine and I need privacy, so please refrain from sending anyone back here. Don't put any calls through, either, until I tell you otherwise, understood?"

"Sure, Marcos. Whatever you say," Brianna replied through the speaker.

"Sit down, Katherine," Marcos said. He slid into Katherine's empty chair, pushing things aside on the desk to pull his laptop in front of him. He motioned her toward the visitors' chairs on the other side of her desk.

So much for her plan to stay standing and get rid of him quickly. This arrogance was a new and disagreeable side to the Marcos she knew. Katherine felt her upper chest tighten. Something in her gut told her this time she wasn't in the driver's seat. She slipped into the extra chair and sat poised on the edge.

Marcos flipped a page on his writing pad and opened his laptop, angling it so she could see the spreadsheets he'd opened.

"Katherine, I spent several hours last week and over this past weekend trying to reconcile our accounting spreadsheets with our bank balances. I've had more than one long talk with Frank Donovan at Capital Savings and Loan. Everything is a confusing mess. What I've found, among other things, is that hard copies of the paid-in-full contracts don't equal the deposits for said contracts. The same goes for special events. We also have entries for items purchased for the office that are nowhere to be found. Some of your travel expenses to events are higher than the actual receipts. Too many things don't add up. I found discrepancies going back into last year."

Katherine's indignation at Marcos's brash intrusion began to wilt under the intensity of his level, unemotional gaze. There were shadows under his eyes, and his voice reflected the coldness in his expression. She felt uneasy about the direction this conversation was taking. Katherine lowered her eyes and willed herself to slow her breathing. With a little shake, she straightened her back. An adversarial approach was always her best line of defense.

"Exactly what do you mean, Marcos?" Katherine drew herself up and raised her chin. "Are you telling me you actually had the audacity to enter my private office and dig around in my files? How dare you question my management of the studio's accounts?"

Marcos held up his hand to signal her to stop. "Katherine, no histrionics, please. I'm too tired."

"Marcos." Katherine licked her lips and softened her voice. She couldn't let him sense the wave of panic threatening to consume her. She looked down and gathered her thoughts. Katherine raised her eyes to Marcos and tilted her head to one side, hoping the expression she wore was contrite enough to pacify him.

"All right, I…I admit I've borrowed a bit here and there and paid myself a few salary advances and bonuses. It's really a negligible amount, Marcos, and nothing to make a huge fuss over." Katherine raised her head higher, her confidence building. Who was Marcos to question her like this, anyway? "This is my company, Marcos, so in reality I'm only borrowing from myself. It's been a difficult year, and my personal expenses temporarily flew out of control." Katherine flashed a smile geared to either win her adversaries over or unsettle them enough to force them to back off. She blinked. Marcos wasn't responding. She folded her arms.

"Katherine, we go back a long way," Marcos said. He leaned forward, palms up. "I've been with you since before Desert Dance-Sport. I saw you through your divorce. We've danced together, cried together, and worked hard to build this studio together, but I can't let our history get in the way of keeping this business healthy. Too many people rely on us. And Katherine, do I have to remind you, I'm as vested in this studio as you are."

"Now wait a minute—"

"No, Katherine, you wait a minute. The simple fact is that I've been lax about staying in the financial loop. To be honest with both of us, I've been lazy. And it has to come to a halt." Marcos shook his head. "I'm probably as much at fault here as you might be. I failed to recognize the signs of stress. It was easier for me to shut my eyes and go home every night and have a scotch than to dig deep enough to find out what the hell was going on with you." Marcos ran a hand through his hair and stopped to take a deep breath.

Katherine smiled a tiny, tight smile. He didn't meet her eyes. Was he softening? Had he realized he'd gone too far? She jumped in. "Marcos," Katherine cooed, stretching over the desk toward his hand. "I'm sorry you're upset, but nothing is as bad as you think it is. Let me—"

"No, Katherine." Marcos was on his feet.

Katherine pulled back. She flashed from conciliatory to cold.

"Katherine, an outside auditor is coming in to review our books: everything from receivables and payables to profit and loss statements, to taxes both owed and paid. Actually, he should be here any minute. I expect he might be back in again tomorrow." Marcos walked over to the file cabinet and pulled the keys off their hook. "Until he's finished, I'm asserting my authority as your business partner. I'm taking the keys to the file cabinet, and, once we walk out of this office, it will remain locked until the auditor arrives. It might actually be best if you went home for the rest of day. You look like you need the downtime, anyway."

Katherine stood up, speechless with anger. She held her breath for a few beats before gathering together her personal things. Marcos held open the door. With an old-world, courtly gesture, he ushered her out into the hall. She was too stunned to protest.

A smallish, tight-faced man with bushy eyebrows and thick black-framed glasses was standing in the hallway a few feet away. Katherine tilted her head and offered an inquisitive smile. He didn't return it. She had a hunch this weaselly looking little man wasn't prone to smiling. He must be the auditor.

Marcos strode ahead of Katherine and held out his hand in greeting. "I take it you're Mr. Miller of Cranston and Miller?"

"Yes, I am." The odd-looking man in the impeccable suit shook Marcos's hand.

"And I assume you are Marcos Stephanos, or is it more correct to say Martin Stevens?"

Katherine didn't move. This nasty little man knew Marcos's real name. Her gut tightened.

"Katherine, I am going to show Mr. Miller to your office. If you decide to go home, I'll call you when he has reviewed our ledgers and has a recommendation."

Katherine bit her tongue to keep herself from saying something she might regret or, worse, could be used against her. She wrapped herself in as much dignity as she could muster and walked rapidly away from both Marcos and this unlikable Mr. Miller. Hot tears built behind her eyes. She made an abrupt left turn into the ladies' room and slammed open the door.

"Sweet Jesus." Barbara's voice barely registered in Katherine's mind.

She felt Barbara grab her under an arm. Barbara steadied herself on the bathroom counter, keeping them both upright.

"Katherine, are you all right?" Barbara asked, her voice a mixture of shock and concern.

Katherine pulled away from the annoying woman and breezed past her. "I just need everyone to leave me alone right now," she muttered. Every-damn-one was invading her personal space today. "That nasty little man needs to mind his own business. That's all. What I do with my own money is my business. He's trying to cause trouble." Katherine pushed into the last stall and clicked the door shut behind her.

"I…um…is there…? Can I…?" Barbara's voice penetrated the stall door.

Katherine willed her away.

"Okay, then, I guess I'll leave you alone if you're sure you're all right."

A moment of silence followed before Katherine heard the welcome sound of retreating footsteps followed by the bathroom door swinging shut.

~

Marcos Stephanos
1:30 p.m., Monday, 9 November

"And she was mumbling more to herself than really talking to me," Barbara said. "It was something about that 'nasty little man causing trouble' and not 'butting into her personal business.' I've never seen her like that. Do you know what she was talking about?"

Marcos took Barbara by the arm and walked her out of earshot. "Look, I'm going to need you to do some damage control for me until I have a handle on what's going on and figure out what to tell everyone. Katherine was referring to the auditor my father sent over, Mr. Kyle Miller. Dad's firm has worked with Miller's company for years. They're very well respected. Anyway, Miller's in Katherine's private office, and he might be here through tomorrow. To say Katherine is upset right now is the least of it. I had a sort of confrontation with her earlier and suggested she go home."

"Oh. Well, that explains a lot. So, what do you need me to do?"

"Help me keep a lid on things. For all intents and purposes, our Mr. Miller is a tax accountant who's helping us with a new program to simplify our taxes. People are going to see him as he goes in and out, and they'll have questions. He's very discreet, but he'll need coffee breaks, and I expect he'll leave for lunch. I'll come up with an explanation for Katherine's absence. If we can prevent the rumor mill from grinding, we can stave off drama."

"I'll do whatever I can. I'm on the desk for this morning," Barbara said.

Marcos could feel her looking at him. She had a questioning "Can I say something?" look on her face. "Okay, what?" He couldn't suppress a smile.

"Well, here's what I'm thinking. Maybe I should postpone looking for a full-time receptionist until you have a better handle on studio finances. I can continue coming in for a while; you have Kristi in the evening now, and the instructors have been good about sharing front desk duties. What do you think?"

"I hate to say yes, Barbara, because I don't want you to think we're taking advantage of your kind and generous nature. But…yes, I think you're right. Could you give me maybe a few weeks to sort things out? Does that sound doable?"

"Of course. Oh…" Barbara visibly brightened at the sight of her son. Michael had a Starbucks tray in his hand with three coffees.

"Hi, everyone. Coffees all around. A latte for my mom and, Marcos, a double Americano."

"Thank you, you are right on time," Marcos said. "Barbara, Michael and I will be in the front office for a bit. Feel free to interrupt if you need me for anything."

Barbara gave Marcos a thumbs-up as she reached for the ringing phone.

Marcos waved Michael into the office and motioned for him to sit. He suddenly felt his age. Barbara had told him how Michael worked out every morning, and it was obvious he was a working professional dancer who took care of his instrument. His muscles were visible under his Henley T-shirt. Marcos was tempted to rest his feet on the desk but thought better of it. He leaned forward, forearms on the desktop.

"The Americano was thoughtful, Michael. I appreciate it. Your mother suggested it might be a good idea for us to talk as soon as possible."

"Yes," Michael said. "Thank you for making the time." Michael leaned back a bit, both hands on the edge of the desk. "Marcos, I have to be honest with you. I've been here long enough to hear a few worrisome rumblings. Rumors about paychecks being delayed or even bouncing, repairs to the building being postponed, and a few more things that allude to cash-flow problems. Before I call my current employers to tell them I'm officially moving on, I want to be sure I am moving into a stable situation. I hope my frankness doesn't offend."

"I actually appreciate your directness," Marcos said. He sat back and crossed his legs. After all the subterfuge lately, he was ready to deal with someone straightforward.

"I'm not sure if I should even say this, but Katherine seems a bit, well, volatile," Michael said. "That isn't a comforting quality to see in a business owner."

"I can't deny that, either. The studio is experiencing a cash-flow issue, and, yes, Katherine has not been herself."

"Okay. I hope we can talk more about both issues. But what I have to talk to you about is probably more important than my reservations about the stability of the studio. I can't hire on here without being honest about my long-term plans."

"Go on," Marcos said. He uncrossed his legs and folded his arms.

"I'm in my thirties now, and starting to think ahead in regards to my career. I want to stay in the dance world, but I'm interested in doing more than eking out a living as a dance instructor." Michael rubbed the back of his neck and lowered his eyes, as if gathering his thoughts.

"Take your time," Marcos said. He reached for his Americano and took a deep sip.

"I want to learn the studio business from the ground up, Marcos, because my hopes are to one day open my own studio." Michael tapped the heels of his hands together and then entwined his fingers. "Not a studio that would be direct competition with Desert DanceSport but one with a broader focus than only ballroom dance. I am overflowing with ideas right now. And I'm not just a young kid blowing smoke, in case you are wondering. I actually have some cash to invest from a family inheritance. But I need more seasoning in the business, and I could get that here. But would you and Katherine still want to hire me knowing my plans?"

Marcos laughed. He slapped the desk. He couldn't help himself. This young man was bright, motivated, and honest to a fault. It was a refreshing combination.

"Let me interrupt your thought flow right there." Marcos placed both hands on the polished surface of the desk. "To address your initial concern, I have to first ask you to take a leap of faith. I definitely want you on board with this studio. Michael, I'm a forty-eight-percent owner in both the business and the building and, as such, can make this decision independent of Katherine." The look in Michael's eyes was worth all the previous angst of the day.

"What?" Michael smiled, but the smile reflected confusion. "Now I feel a bit like an idiot. Does my mother know this already?"

"Yes." Marcos folded his arms on the desktop. "We can go into all the details one evening over a couple of scotches, but for now that's all you need to know. I want you to sign an employee contract and get you on the payroll right away. Things might go south soon, and we might have to institute a temporary freeze on hiring or on making major changes. I want you locked in before that." Marcos held his hand up in response to Michael's alarmed expression.

"No worries. I promise. That's all I can say for now. This studio is my future, and I'll put everything I have into it to ensure its stability. And, for the record, I'm not averse to taking on someone who's brimming with ideas and enthusiasm. I actually might need your energy and creative drive to help push things forward. So, why don't we take a minute, and you can outline your ideas for me, and I'll fill you in on what you need to know afterward."

Michael nodded and started talking. "I envision a studio that offers not only ballroom dance lessons but country western as well, and jazz and theater arts classes for kids. There would be two tracks for purchasing lessons—one for those adults who only want to learn to dance socially, but social dancers could cross the track anytime into the competitive side of both ballroom and country western…"

Michael outlined ideas in the air with palpable enthusiasm. Marcos relaxed, caught in the wash of words. He leaned back in Katherine's cushy desk chair and put his feet on her desk. For the first time in days, he felt energized and hopeful.

TWENTY-THREE

DUPLICITY

Katherine Carrington
10:00 a.m., Tuesday, 10 November

"Damn it, Chi, that hurts." Katherine pried the cat's claws out of her flimsy tunic top. Unperturbed, Chi continued to purr and pummel her thighs. His toes widened with each push, extending his claws. Katherine mentally kicked herself for bringing the cat outside and then kicked herself again for taking off her leggings. She wasn't getting sun so much as she was getting reddish welts on her thighs from Chi's happy feet.

Life was interfering with her plans for a pleasant morning. Her pastry run was damn near spoiled after being stuck behind a customized Monte Carlo through a very long construction zone. A pounding beat from its over-amped stereo vibrated her Camaro. The dumb-shit driver with the soon-to-be-damaged eardrums came close to being a victim of road rage. By the time Katherine reached the bakery and selected her pastries, she needed a strong drink almost more than the sweets. Then she dropped her keys twice trying to unlock the front door of the condo. Dropping things irritated the hell out of her. There was no way she could be faulted for the generous splash of vodka she added to both her coffee and her orange juice.

Katherine reached for her second cinnamon-apple Danish. Chi was being lavish with his love this morning and was now working on her abdomen. She pressed on the pads of one front paw to release claws from her tunic top. She hated to hurt his feelings, but she was going to have to put him inside. The light fabric of her top couldn't endure such enthusiasm. With a sigh, she scooped up the shiny black feline, carried him to the door, and scooted him into the house. She shut the screen on the French doors before he could make a mad dash back outside. She rarely brought him out, but he'd been so lonely since the other two foster cats went to their forever homes; he deserved a treat. Maybe next time she'd open a can of tuna instead of offering her thighs for his emotional gratification.

Katherine glanced at the pink bakery box, feeling only the slightest pang of guilt at the sight of what was left. "Screw it," she said. Her weight was a few pounds lower than normal, and her stress level was several notches higher. She bloody well deserved whatever it took to deal with the absolute crap coming from Marcos. Katherine reached for her large coffee mug and enjoyed a deep swallow of her favorite Kona blend. She stretched out on the chaise lounge. The day was warm for November, and the sun felt as indulgent as the pastries tasted.

She closed her eyes, but revenge scenarios played out beneath her lids. Marcos had to pay for his scathing assassination of her character yesterday. Drawing outrageous conclusions about the state of the studios accounts was way out of line. Marcos could bumble around the accounting software and talk to the bank all he wanted, but he'd only learn so much. There was no way he would come across her private set of spreadsheets, because they only resided on her red thumb drive. Katherine's eyes flew open. She sat up. Barbara... It was that damn Barbara who'd found her red thumb drive and returned it to her. Surely the woman didn't have the audacity to look at the contents of the drive? She wouldn't have understood what she was looking at even if she had. But Marcos would, and those two were thick as thieves. Katherine pressed one fist against her mouth and ran her knuckles along her lips. She swung her legs off the padded lounger, reached for her coffee mug, and headed indoors. Another cup of coffee would help her think—another coffee with a little boost from Grey Goose.

Katherine sat at the kitchen bar with her refilled mug between her hands. Chi rubbed his head around her ankles. Her thoughts whirled and twirled faster than a majorette's baton. Who's to say her money-moving wasn't to ensure nice bonuses for the instructors…hmmm… because she suspected Marcos planned to peel out a nice amount to fill his own pockets? That line of thinking might not be too hard to sell. He needed to pay for all the undeserved distress triggered by this auditor nonsense. Maybe it was Marcos's turn to have his character questioned? That scrawled list she'd found in Paige's sweater pocket sure read like the girl was targeting Marcos. Was she his love child? Could Paige be scheming to extort money from Marcos or his father? That bomb would rock the hell out of Mr. Perfect's world. Maybe she should call Daddy Steven's office and put a bug in his ear. Or, even better, she could work on Paige. It wouldn't take much to paint a picture of Marcos as someone who'd always been sorry he'd never had children. Poor, lonely, aging Marcos. Katherine smiled. Father or not, if she played this right, Marcos could end up looking like a damn fool or, even better, a deadbeat dad.

Katherine glanced at the kitchen clock. Stuck at home today or not, she needed to do something with her hair and change out of this coffee-splattered tunic top. Looking her best helped her think with more clarity.

"Okay, Chi cat, we're heading upstairs."

Katherine stood too quickly and a wave of dizziness caught her off guard. Her hand flew out for balance, knocking the coffee mug off the counter and scaring Chi, who darted between her feet, dropping her to her knees on the hard tile floor.

"Son of a bitch," Katherine howled. One hand slid through a

puddle of coffee. She pushed herself onto one knee just as the phone rang. "Really, are you bloody kidding me?" She used the edge of the counter to pull herself up and limped across the kitchen to the phone.

"You've reached Katherine Carrington," she said.

"Hello, Katherine. This is Felicia from New Haven." Felicia's voice was hesitant, and she paused for a few seconds. "Katherine, I'm sorry to be the bearer of bad news, but I'm glad I didn't have to call you with this at work. Dear, your mother passed a short time ago. There were no warning signs. She must have slipped away sometime after breakfast. I'm sorry there wasn't the opportunity for you to be with her."

"What? Did you just say that my mother passed away?" Katherine dried her coffee-sopped hand on her tunic.

"Yes, dear. I'm terribly sorry. You left mortuary arrangements with us. Would you like us to call the funeral home for you?"

"Yes…thank you. Please do. I'll be down to New Haven as quickly as I can, to handle whatever needs to be done." Katherine pressed the end-call button and stood, staring out the kitchen window, phone in hand.

Marcos Stephanos
2:45 p.m., Tuesday, 10 November

"You've got it, Barbara," Marcos said. "That was beautiful." He stepped back and held his student at arm's length.

"That felt right for the first time," Barbara said. Her eyes outshone the large diamond studs in her ears.

"It's hard to master a Slip Pivot, and you executed it perfectly. You were light as air as we danced. I'm very pleased."

"Then we are definitely adding these new patterns to our routine?" Barbara asked.

"Absolutely, yes. Learning to maneuver around one's partner is tricky, and you are definitely there. And, the Fallaway Reverse to Slip Pivot is a Gold-level figure."

"I'm pretty darn pleased with myself," Barbara said. "I want to add these patterns to my notes. Do you mind if I take the last few minutes of lesson time to jot things down?"

"Of course not. Remember to add the Whisk to a Wing as well. I'm really pleased with the progress you've made in the past few weeks." Marcos held Barbara's elbow as they walked to their table.

"What about Edward Dombrosky, Marcos? If Ed and I are going to dance together in the Midwinter Ball in December, do you think we can get up to speed with this routine?"

"I talked to Ed earlier this morning. Sorry, meant to tell you. He's on board with us scheduling a few extra hours a week as you suggested, and he seemed enthusiastic about you two registering for the ball."

"I'm excited about it as well," Barbara said. She pulled a small notebook out of her dance bag and jotted down notes.

Marcos settled into the nearest café chair. He didn't have another lesson on the books until after four. He watched Barbara write her notes and draw little diagrams. She was so conscientious. This lady knew how to have fun but still took her instruction seriously enough to be a worthy competitor on the floor. She truly didn't realize how good she was. She and Ed just might make a formidable amateur couple in competitions.

"Okay. Done," Barbara said. She closed her notebook and unsnapped her dance shoes. She turned to face Marcos. "It's so quiet in here today. Where is everyone?"

"Bookings are heavy today from three through nine this evening. It's one of those days where everyone seemed to have someplace else they needed to be in the early part of the day." Marcos crossed his legs and cupped one knee with both hands. "Since it's so quiet, I think we have enough privacy to talk for minute or two without having to go outside."

"Certainly. What's up, or should I say what's up now?"

"I learned something interesting when I talked with Ed this morning." Marcos rocked back and forth and then steadied himself.

"I found ledger notations for expenses related to building upkeep, like rewiring the ballroom for speakers. I thought Edward did the rewiring for free, but the accounts payable show a payment of $1,500. I didn't say anything to Ed but felt him out about what he's been charging the studio for future reference. Ed said he's never charged more than a couple of hundred for any work he's done, including the new thermostat he installed by the reception area. He expects reimbursement to cover his costs, but that's it." Marcos raised his eyebrows. "Katherine, it seems, was paying him quite well, at least on paper. And of course there are no receipts to match the amounts that were supposedly paid out."

"What?" Barbara said, leaning forward. "I can't believe it."

"Yeah, I couldn't, either," Marcos said. "Then I looked deeper and found similar notations to small contractors. Some checks were cut, but now I have to wonder how many $2,500 jobs were really $1,000 jobs." Marcos uncrossed his legs and placed his forearms on the table. "How could I have been such a trusting fool all this time? It's not like I wasn't wise to Katherine's games and her ability to manipulate people. I've seen her in action. I just never expected to be on the receiving end. I don't know whether to be angry with Katherine or just sad."

"I'm so sorry, Marcos, on many levels, really."

"There were actually a few more instances I remember now. When we had the men's bathroom retiled, Katherine said she knew a guy. I never saw a hard-copy receipt, but I was told the cost of the job was over three grand. So, now I have to wonder how much went to her guy and how much went into her pocket."

Marcos's head dropped. He fiddled with the cigarette lighter in his pocket. The downside to chatting in the studio was not being able to smoke. Marcos turned back to Barbara.

"My perception of Katherine has done a 180-degree flip. I always believed, deep down, she was a friend—someone I trusted enough to be in business with. Her duplicity has rocked me to the core. Now all I see is a manipulative, overly made-up, aging prima donna with a tarnished tiara that matches her tarnished soul. I'm not even sure how to put my feelings into words."

"Dare I ask where you go from here?"

Marcos shook his head, lips a straight line. "I just don't know. I think Katherine is an unhappy, misguided woman who needs help. But, with all I know now, even if she went into therapy, I don't think I could ever trust her again." Marcos bit his lip and shook his head. "I'm torn between wanting to see her ruined and wanting to get her help."

"That's a call only you can make, Marcos. And you can't force someone to do anything. But, off the subject for a moment, did you have a chance to talk to Michael?"

"Yes. Our discussion was very promising. I believe in Michael's vision, and I have no qualms about him working for the studio. I've asked him to hang in on faith. I don't want to lose him to another ballroom studio because everything is so unsettled here right now. And Michael's future plans are just that, in the future. We'll deal with all that down the road."

"Marcos…Marcos." Brianna, standing at the ballroom entrance, was waving the handset from the base station at the front desk. "Sorry, but Katherine's on the line. She told me to find you and interrupt you no matter what you were doing."

"Okay, then. Bring it here." Marcos raised his hand, and Brianna ran over.

"Hello, Katherine?" Marcos said. He glanced over at Barbara.

Katherine was speaking full voice, her tone very commanding. "Marcos, I want you to know I'll be out of the studio for the next few days. My mother passed away early this morning."

"Oh dear. I'm so very sorry to hear that, Katherine." Marcos tilted his head Barbara's way. "Is there anything we can do?"

"No. I have everything covered. There won't be a funeral. Mother wanted cremation. I'll plan a memorial of some kind for a later date.

First I have to deal with things at the adult care and the usual paper trail relating to a death. You can help by keeping things under control until I come back in. I don't want to walk into a mess."

Marcos bit his lower lip and took a deep breath before answering. "I understand you're stressed right now. Let me know what you need, and I'll make time—"

"I can't chat, Marcos. I can't listen to your imaginary dramas right now when I have a real-life crisis to deal with." Katherine hung up.

Marcos handed the phone back to Brianna. "Katherine lost her mother this morning, Brianna. If anyone asks why she is out of the studio, please let them know what's happened. Oh, and would you or Paige order flowers from all of us?"

"Of course," Brianna said. "And I'll make sure to get a card everyone can sign."

Marcos turned to Barbara, "I feel like a cold-blooded jerk, but at least now I don't have to come up with some bullshit story about why Katherine isn't coming in."

~

Paige Russell
9:30 p.m., Tuesday, 10 November

Standing on the cement balcony in bare feet might not have been such a great idea after all. Even the heavy Mexican blanket she'd wrapped herself in couldn't counter the chills the cold cement conducted up her shivering legs. A loud rap on the apartment door gave her the excuse to wimp out and go inside. Must be Kristi. Paige slipped on fuzzy slippers on her way to the door.

"Hey, kiddo, you look like you're freezing," Kristi said.

"I am. I'll be fine in a minute. I was standing on the balcony in bare feet."

"Okay, then. Hey, I'm surprised you want company this late. You work tomorrow morning, right?" Krista said.

"Yeah, but I really needed to talk. If I went to bed, there's no way I could sleep anyway. You're not too tired to hang for a while, are you?"

"Nope. Actually the change of routine—working at the studio in the evening—is sort of energizing. I'm having fun. I went in early today for my first lesson with Michael. It was great. I wasn't, but the lesson was." Kristi stuck her tongue between her teeth and made a clown face.

"You'll do fine," Paige said. She tossed off the blanket, pulled a beer out of the fridge, and held it out. "Never too cold for a beer, right?"

"You bet."

"Before I called you to come over, I'd been talking to my Aunt Teresa, the one in Florida I've told you about." Paige motioned for Kristi to sit.

"Is there a problem? Is your aunt sick? You don't look too happy." Kristi settled onto the couch and rested her feet on the upholstered top of the crate table. She took a sip of beer.

Paige chewed on her bottom lip. She could feel her face flushing. "No, she's not sick, at least not physically. Honestly, Kristi, I don't know whether to cry, scream, or throw this damn Dos Equis bottle through the window. I want to break something. I'm angry, frustrated, and I'm not having warm and fuzzy feelings about family at the moment. Maybe my whole perception of family is fantasy stuff from watching too many Hallmark movies."

"Damn, honey, now you really have to tell me what happened. But wait, I'm starving. Do you have any of those crackers we started on a couple of nights ago?"

"Yup. I bought another box. Help yourself. Look in the cupboard next to the stove."

"Is there any of that jalapeno cream cheese left in the fridge?" Kristi asked, already halfway across the room.

"I think so," Paige said.

Kristi sat beside Paige, opened the box of crackers, and popped the lid of the cream cheese. She spread a napkin on the crate table and placed everything within reach.

"Here's the thing. I called my aunt to share my news about Marcos. She knew how I've always felt about finding my father, but she never wanted to talk about it or hear much about it. Of course, I never said anything to her about why I really came to Tucson. I didn't need her telling me how crazy she thought I was."

Paige pointed to Kristi's chin. Kristi dabbed at the cream cheese on her face.

"Anyway, we were having this good catch-up, and then I told her I had some really great news." Paige twisted her lips. "I told her about Marcos and how I discovered Mom had gone to a sperm bank and all. I thought she'd be floored and maybe impressed with my detective work."

"And she wasn't? Is that why you are so upset?" Kristi covered her bare legs with one of the Mexican blankets Paige kept on the back of the couch.

Paige rocked back and forth, lips compressed, and turned to face Kristi. "My aunt got really quiet. Then she said, 'Well, I'm sorry you found out. It's all such a sordid business. I never wanted you to know what your mother had done to bring you into this world.'"

"Oh my God?" Kristi put her hand over her mouth. Paige met her eyes.

"Yeah. Not what I expected. Then she went on about how disgusting it all was, the whole dirty business—her words—of men selling their sperm. And about how she'd tried to talk my mother out of even thinking about such nonsense, and how she told my mother she needed to find a nice man, marry him, and have a baby the old-fashioned way. The only positive thing Aunt Teresa said was 'At least Marcos sounds like a decent man and not some low-life, homeless guy selling his sperm to buy drugs.' She said she'd never been happy about her sister's choice, but that didn't mean she wasn't happy about me. I turned out all right, after all." Paige turned to Kristi. "After all? What the hell is that supposed to mean?"

"Paige, for once I have no words." Kristi pressed her lips together and shook her head.

"You and me both. Aunt Teresa made my mother promise to never tell me about the sperm bank. She said she warned my mother it would mark me for life; I would feel like, get this, 'some unwholesome science experiment.'" Paige shook her head and connected with Kristi's sympathetic eyes. "Now I understand why my mother and Aunt Teresa were so estranged. I also get why my mother was afraid of what I would think and why she kept everything such a huge secret. My aunt said my grandmother was 'kept in the dark because it would have killed her.' I guess my grandmother was unhappy enough about her youngest daughter having a baby without benefit of marriage. Aunt Teresa said that if my grandmother had known my mother was pregnant by an anonymous sperm donor, she might have disowned her. A lot of this is guilt stuff coming from the family's strict Roman Catholic background. Now I understand why my mother never was a churchgoer."

"It's sad that religion closes some hearts rather than opens them. I've never understood that," Kristi said. "I can't even imagine how you must feel right now."

"I feel almost sick, Kristi. I've been lied to my whole life." Paige gestured with her half-finished beer bottle, widening her arms. "I'm not so angry with Mom anymore. She was made to feel, well, sinful for doing what she did. No wonder she hid it from me. I never knew my aunt was so judgmental. I don't want to tell Marcos about this. And now I'm wondering how his family, his dad, is going to take the news. Maybe his father will be horrified as well. Maybe instead of having a family to belong to, I'll always be everyone's dirty little secret. I don't know what to think anymore about anything."

"Are you serious about not wanting to share any of this with Marcos?"

"I don't know," Paige said. She put her beer on the side table and folded her arms. "He looks pretty stressed lately. I'm hoping I'm not the reason. I'm questioning whether me staying at the studio is the best idea for either of us. I'm not sure I want to invest two years or more trying to become an advanced ballroom dance instructor. I want to be part of Marcos's world, but I don't know, in the long run, what's best for me."

"Okay, but for starters…about Marcos looking stressed, don't assume everything is about you. Didn't you say he said he has a lot on his plate right now? You're going to make yourself crazy if you're not careful," Kristi said.

"Make myself? I think I'm there." Paige got up and pulled another beer out of the fridge. "Want another?"

Kristi raised her half-full bottle and shook her head.

"I think I could be a really good dance instructor, Kristi. I discovered I'm good at teaching. I'm enjoying being part of the team at the studio. Even though instructors compete with each other for students and at competitions, working there is like belonging to an exclusive club. And then there's the local dance community. Everyone is tied together by this crazy passion for what they do. We get each other."

"So what's the other side of the coin, then? Why do you suddenly have misgivings?"

"Well, on the flipside, there's the jealousies and financial struggles. Most dance instructors teach because they love dance, not because they hope to get rich. Many have other jobs on the side. Money seems to always be an issue. You work for years, ruin your knees or your back, and end up with no real savings or other saleable skills. I hate to say it but Mom had a point about me getting that teaching degree."

"Look, Paige, you're tired. This isn't a good time to make long-range decisions. Keep in mind that life is never black and white but a dozen shades of gray. I know you don't want to hear that right now, so I'm not going lay some big, uplifting pep talk on you."

"Damn!" Paige sat bolt upright. "I thought of something else. If I stay at Desert DanceSport, will Marcos and I have to tell everyone about me being his daughter? How will that go over? I didn't even think about that until right now."

"Well, there's one thing for sure, if you make an announcement

to the staff, Tony will sure as hell back off and stop being obnoxious."
Kristi laughed a low, silky laugh.

Paige laughed with her. "You have a point there. It might be worth
it just to see his face."

TWENTY-FOUR

THE LAST DANCE

Marcos Stephanos
11:00 a.m., Thursday, 12 November

"The best place for us to talk, Dad, is in Katherine's office. Mine's private but not as spacious, and if we need anything from the files, everything is right there." Marcos stifled a grin at the sight of his tall, silver-haired father. Was there ever a day when the man didn't wear a custom-tailored business suit?

With a sweep of his hand, Marcos ushered his dapper dad into Katherine's office. Jacob Martin Stevens nodded a quick thank-you and took a seat. Marcos flipped on the overhead lights and walked around the desk to take Katherine's chair. He pressed his lips together in a useless attempt to stifle a smile as he watched his dad absorb the décor in Katherine's private sanctuary.

"I see your partner has exquisite and, I must say, expensive taste," Martin said. "Her selection of paintings is stunning, especially that one"—he pointed across the room—"the beautiful, coffee-colored woman lost in devouring a mango." Martin paused for a moment and cleared his throat before continuing. "The walnut-framed mirror has to be an antique, and I'm guessing her crystal decanter is either Waterford or Godinger."

"Godinger, I believe, is what she told me." Marcos raised his eyebrows again and made eye contact with his dad. "Let's say Katherine has refined sensibilities, which brings me to my thoughts on the direction we should take in terms of dealing with her."

The older man shifted in his seat and tilted his head. "Go on," he said.

"I'm not, in any way, minimizing what Katherine has done. I'm still dumbfounded." Marcos paused and rubbed his palms together. "But I can't bring myself to think about putting her through a court battle, the end result of which could be…well, I can't even go there." Marcos leaned back in his chair, one arm folded across his midriff, a rounded fist pressed against his lips.

Jacob Martin leaned forward, one arm resting on the desktop. "Do I have to remind you that, based on the spreadsheets on that USB drive, our accountant made it clear that this is not a simple case of skimming a bit off the top for play money? And then Mr. Miller's audit confirmed the gravity of the situation. His findings were worse than any of us expected, and, in my eyes, his report was a game changer. I'm sorry to say it, but the plain fact is Katherine's been playing you for a fool, son."

Marcos's throat tightened. A wave of disbelief mixed with deep disappointment washed through every fiber of his being, turning his blood to lead. He now understood the old expression "having a heavy heart."

"And, on top of all that, you've discovered she falsified amounts paid to contractors. I don't want to see you hurt, personally or financially, by the current state of affairs, but doing nothing is simply not an option. At the very least you must dissolve the business partnership. If you can't come to terms with filing formal charges, we have to come to a consensus on a suitable out-of-court solution."

"I understand what you're saying." Marcos propped both elbows on the desktop, prayer-folded his hands, and gently rapped steepled fingers against his lips before continuing. "Katherine and I go way back, Dad; you know that. We worked together to build this business. I've known Katherine long enough to know that she is, in many ways, a hard woman—determined, strong, lacking in trust, and completely self-involved—but inside she's broken and hurt. She puts up a protective wall few can penetrate. I've always been able to sneak through the cracks, but lately even I can't get a reading on her. She might need professional help."

"Quite honestly, son, what I know of Katherine leads me to believe that, no matter what, she'll land on her feet," Martin countered.

"She does have that knack." Marcos raised his eyebrows and attempted a wry smile. "I'm not defending her behavior, you understand, but I've come to terms with the fact that I've played a part in this disgraceful situation. For too long I've been willing to let Katherine shoulder the day-to-day running of the business, while I enjoyed myself on the dance floor. I've neglected my responsibilities. And worse, I closed my eyes to obvious signs that something wasn't right. I wanted to avoid messiness. You've told me enough times that I tend to choose the easy road."

"That I have."

"Well, those days are over. I think your self-indulgent son has finally developed a long-overdue sense of responsibility."

"I wouldn't be here supporting you, Marcos, if I didn't believe that to be true." Martin shook his head. "It's still difficult to call you Marcos. As far back as your great-grandfather, first-born sons have used the name Martin, whether it was a middle or first name."

Marcos opened his mouth, but his dad's waving hand cut him off.

"And yes, I know, it was me who asked you to take on a stage name. Nevertheless, it's awkward on my tongue. But continue. You have a plan of action in mind?"

"I do. I've given this a lot of thought; I need your input on the legalities." With both hands on the armrests, Marcos pushed back in the chair. "Here's my thinking. Once we stress the seriousness of the situation to Katherine and let her know that what she's done is a prosecutable offense, maybe we can catch her off balance. Then, before she has a chance to regroup, we hit her with a proposal she can't refuse. If we give her too much time, she'll come back at us with some crazy scheme. I also think I can sell Katherine on the benefits of stepping away from the business. That keeps her reputation intact, and the studio wouldn't be spotlighted with bad press, which matters as much to her as to me. Maybe then I can then find a way to pick up the pieces. I need your input on all the financial and legal ramifications, of course."

"What you suggest could be workable, Marcos, but I want to handle the interaction with Katherine. I have no emotional ties. But you're getting ahead of yourself. Even under normal circumstances, buyouts can get messy. You and Katherine have been operating without a written partnership agreement, so I'm not sure how what you propose would play out in legal terms. However, there's an attorney with my firm who's well versed in acquisitions. We'll ask her for a professional opinion. I do believe that co-owning a for-profit business still creates a general partnership, even if you didn't file documents with the Arizona Corporation Commission. Think of your situation as an uncontested divorce. No matter what the law states, if both parties are in agreement, their decisions take precedence."

"Sounds complicated," Marcos said. He fought the urge to slam his fist through the wall. He couldn't remember ever feeling this overwhelmed and out of control.

"Quite frankly, son, running some ominous-sounding legal terminology past Katherine might be all it takes to get her to concede and meet our terms."

All Marcos could muster was a tight-lipped nod.

"Why don't you leave the details to me? I have financial people we can bring in to slant the outcome in your favor. It all has to happen very quickly, though. You might have to come up to speed on some accounting and business partnership terminology, so you understand what's being proposed. The main numbers my people will look at are the studio's fixed and current assets." Martin paused.

Marcos could his see father's mental wheels turning as he wondered how much his dancer son understood of what he was saying. Marcos bit the inside of his lip. Why did so many people equate dancer with dim?

"To be more specific," Martin continued, "your current business assets are cash, accounts receivable, and inventory, of which you have none because you sell a service, not a product. Your fixed assets are more long-term, such as this building. And, before anything, you must schedule a meeting with the mortgage company to deal with payments that are in arrears."

Marcos nodded. He would never admit it, but his eyes were beginning to glaze over. He shook himself back to attention. "I'm ready to do whatever it takes."

"Then my next question is this: When do we, or I if you prefer, sit down with Katherine and lower the boom?" The senior Martin Stevens sat back in his chair, crossed his legs at the ankles, and folded his arms.

"I'm ready any time. The sooner, the better. I'll contact Katherine today. She might be close to tying up loose ends regarding her mother's death. But right now I need to change gears. How about if we duck out for some lunch? My treat while I still have some cash left in my pockets." Marcos's smile was more of a grimace. "And there's actually something else quite important that I need to discuss with you, something completely unrelated to the studio. I warn you, this might very well have to be a two-martini lunch."

～

Katherine Carrington
1:30 p.m., Thursday, 12 November

The island in Katherine's kitchen was completely covered in file folders, binder clips, stapled and loose pages, pens, and an open vodka bottle. Her cell phone was propped in a metal holder within reach, and two coffee cups sat at opposite ends of the counter: one freshly filled placed next to her laptop and another forgotten half-empty cup at the far end. Katherine ran a hand through uncombed hair and tucked it behind her ears. As she dropped her head to focus on paperwork, stray curls drooped into her eyes. With an exasperated expulsion of air, she reached for an elastic band and twisted the straggly strands into a messy ponytail.

"Thank the gods for buyers from Seattle with pockets lined with money. If only it were a seller's market here as well," Katherine muttered. She clicked her pen and began to sign the sales agreement her realtor had dropped off. She pushed one set of papers to the side and scooped up another. This was a much more acceptable offer than the first and couldn't have come in at a better time. "Well, Mom, you kept the house in good shape and chose a nice neighborhood, so it looks like I'll come close to paying off that second mortgage." Katherine raised her coffee mug and toasted her mother's advantageous decisions.

"And now, on to New Haven." Her mug met the table with a jolt. Katherine dabbed at the sloshed liquid with the tip of her robe. She was a few months in arrears at the nursing home, and they required a last-month fee as well. Well, they were going to have to wait until she closed on the house, and they had to like it or lump it. Luckily, the house was ready for immediate occupancy, and the buyers were antsy to move in. Katherine glanced at the wall clock. She still had plenty of time before she had to shower and dress. Her appointment with Westward Title wasn't until four. She rat-tatted her nails on the countertop. Her left index fingernail was broken, and her nail polish was peeling. She folded her fingers: out of sight, out of mind.

Katherine's thoughts flitted from one worry to the next like a crazed cactus wren. She glanced at the clock again. If she left a little early, she could kill two birds with one stone. She'd take one of her mother's outfits to the funeral home, although dressing a body for cremation was incomprehensible to her. She'd already picked a simple casket, no disrespect intended, but her mother was being cremated, for God's sake. It wasn't like there would be a big funeral with the casket on display. A simple memorial service could be done when life calmed down and she could deal. Right now she was inundated with loose ends that needed tying, and more than a little pissed off with Marcos and his newfound authoritarian attitude. She couldn't take on anything else. Katherine dropped the pen to reach for the vodka, but in mid-reach, the phone trilled. Sylvie. Okay, she'd take this one.

Katherine inhaled deeply and put a smile in her voice. "Hello, Sylvie, how are you?"

"I'm good, Katherine, but I called to ask how you're holding up. Marcos told us about your mother. I'm so sorry. It's strange not to have you at the studio."

"Thank you, Sylvie. And also thank you for the card. I'm doing as well as can be expected," Katherine said. She infused her voice with the expected sadness that she couldn't seem to muster. All she felt was numb.

"Will there be a funeral?" Sylvie asked.

"No, no funeral. I might plan a small memorial service at a later date. I should be able to pick up her ashes on Monday."

"Oh, okay. Well, then, if you have a minute, I'd like to tell you what's going on with me."

Katherine reached for her cup and then the vodka. She splashed a decent amount into her cooling coffee. "Go on," she said. Sylvie's attention span for anyone other than herself was limited.

"Well, what I haven't told anyone is that I've had an ad running in some of the dance magazines for a few weeks. I received a response from a Romanian dancer. Actually I got to meet him at the competition in LA. He's been looking for a new professional partner as well."

"And…?" Katherine responded.

"Well, we discovered that we're on the same page as far as wanting to hit the major competitions and win. We found time to dance together in one of the practice areas, and our connection was instant. We felt like we'd been dancing together for years. And, Katherine, he's in pretty good financial shape, which is a huge plus."

"So what does this mean, Sylvie?" Katherine asked, already knowing the answer but wanting to hear it from the horse's mouth. She took a deep sip of her enhanced beverage.

"Well, it means I'll be leaving Desert DanceSport sooner than I expected. End of December, actually. Valer—that's his name—is on an H-1B visa with a studio in Santa Barbara. He's their in-house coach and choreographer. He also competes with a pool of amateurs who enjoy traveling to competitions. Valer can't leave that studio, Katherine. He can't come to Tucson. He's been there three years and is on track for a green card. It just so happens they need an experienced female instructor, and they're happy to take me on. I really have nothing to keep me in Tucson." Sylvie paused; Katherine stayed silent. "Katherine, dancing with Valer, I could have a real shot at a national title. I can't pass on this chance."

"I see." Katherine tapped the countertop, ignoring her ratty-looking nails. This was going to leave Marcos in a bind for sure. This turn of events would make Marcos realize he needed her at the studio now more than ever. Of course, losing Sylvie would mean jumping back into teaching again until Sylvie could be replaced.

"I really, really hate to spring this on you when you're out dealing with your mother's death. But I didn't know when you'd be back, and I wanted to tell you before I told anyone else." Sylvie's words stumbled over each other in a nervous-sounding rush.

"I appreciate that, Sylvie. But I think you need to tell Marcos as soon as you can. Things are up in the air with me right now, and I don't know exactly when I'll be back in. Marcos can decide how to tell the group. I'm assuming you've told Tony, correct?"

"Well...no, actually I haven't. I will, though, soon. I don't think he'll care that much."

"Give him the courtesy anyway, Sylvie, and don't wait too long."

"Hey, by the way, it's been really weird around here since you've been gone. Some strange guy was holed up in your office for a couple of days, and then a very nice-looking older man has been in the studio, hanging out with Marcos. I think Brianna said his last name was Stevens."

"Stevens? I'll have to ask Marcos. Thank you for calling, Sylvie. I do appreciate you talking to me before you told anyone else. I wish you well. Bye." Katherine hung up and slumped in her chair. Trying to focus on Sylvie's words had zapped what little energy she had.

So, Jacob Martin Stevens himself was in the office? What was that all about? Marcos and his father weren't exactly chummy. Katherine couldn't remember Marcos spending more than a handful of hours with his father over the past several years. She couldn't even remember the last time she'd seen the man. She tapped a staccato beat on the kitchen countertop. Funny, now that she thought about it, she'd left a message for Martin Stevens at his office last week, and he had never returned her call. Katherine dumped out the remains of her coffee and poured a shot of vodka into the empty cup. She took a deep sip. What could Marcos be up to? Surely he wasn't thinking he could run the studio without her. There was no way they could get along without her, and besides, she had no plans to sell her part of the business. "Marcos can't push me out and lose Sylvie as well. Stupid man." There was the phone again. She leaned over to check the caller ID: Marcos. Well, speak of the devil.

Katherine stood and leaned against the kitchen bar. Cell in hand, she took a deep breath and steadied her voice. "Hello."

"Katherine. It's Marcos. How are things?"

"Very well, thank you. I've accepted another offer—a much better offer—on my mother's house. I'm finalizing things this afternoon actually, so I don't have much time to talk. Besides asking how I am doing, what do you need?" Katherine picked up a pen and jiggled it idly between her fingers.

"I want to give you a heads-up, Katherine. We have numbers back from the auditor's report. My father has stepped in to help us wade through all the legal issues. I know you're dealing with your mother's death and the sale of the house and all, but it's important we meet as soon as possible."

Katherine tossed the rest of the vodka back. She didn't respond.

Marcos paused for a moment and then continued. "I have to be honest. My father is representing my interests, which means he will also ensure that the best interests of the studio are met. He'd like us, the three of us, to meet and find a way to resolve this situation we find ourselves in. Frankly, Katherine, this is a lot more serious than I think you realize. I'm hoping we can resolve our issues out of court. Are you available to meet at the studio rather than my father's office, say, tomorrow morning around ten?"

Katherine felt bile rise in her throat. Out of court? What was he talking about? When did court come in to this? She took several deep breaths. "I think I can manage that," she said. Her stomach flipped, and her heart began to race. "I do have to go now, Marcos. I have an appointment this afternoon. I'll be there tomorrow, and I'll be on time."

Katherine clicked the phone off, spun around, and threw up in the kitchen sink.

TWENTY-FIVE

DANCING FOR YOUR LIFE

Paige Russell
7:30 a.m., Friday, 13 November

"Hey there. Knock, knock."

"Hi, Kristi." Paige raised a hand in greeting without tearing her eyes away from the page she was scrolling through. She rebalanced the laptop resting on her thighs and dug her toes deeper into the edge of the crate table's upholstery.

"How come your door was unlocked?"

"Huh? Oh. I ran downstairs to get the last couple of days' mail. I guess I forgot to lock it when I came back. Thanks for coming over so early."

"As long as you don't mind that I'm still in my PJs. Is that last night's pizza?"

Paige could feel the words on the screen drilling their way into her brain.

"Paige? Did you hear me?" Kristi said. "The pizza. Is it from last night?"

"Yeah. Cold pizza is great for breakfast. Coffee's hot. There's plenty of pizza, so help yourself." Paige stayed focused on the screen, fingers on her mousepad.

"Ummm…would you mind if I made myself some toast?" Kristi asked.

"Go for it." Paige heard Kristi rummaging around the kitchen, but couldn't tear her eyes away from the website she'd found.

"Paige… Paige…" Kristi tapped Paige on the shoulder. "What on earth are you doing?"

"You're not going to believe what I found." Paige pushed the laptop onto the table and leaned back into the couch cushions. "I've been here most of the night. Found some amazing websites and blogs last night. Dozens of people sharing their experiences about finding birth parents. I can't believe I've never come across any of this stuff before."

"So what got you going on this?" Kristi sat next to Paige and sipped her coffee.

"Ever since Marcos ordered the DNA tests and we got the results, my emotions have been all-over-the-place crazy."

"I thought you were super happy Marcos turned out to be your biological dad."

Paige reached for another slice of pepperoni pizza and munched a hunk back before continuing. "Of course I'm happy, but…there's like something else. I think during the whole dad-search thing I was on a major adrenaline rush. It was all about the research and proving I was right. I thought about it all the time. And then, after I got my answer, the balloon deflated, and I started feeling a weird sadness and low energy. It's like I've lost a booster rocket."

"So, if I'm hearing you correctly," Kristi said, "this would compare to having a semester-long project at school. It takes over your whole life, and then suddenly you're done. You're happy and relieved, but you also have this lost feeling like, now what?"

"Yeah. Sort of a letdown I didn't expect. And then I started thinking about all the years I lost, not having a dad, when all the time he was so close. I keep imagining how different everything could have been. I'm still getting past that one. Anyway, last night I searched for how other people reacted to finding either biological parents or children they gave up for adoption. In the middle of it all, I found a whole online community of people conceived with donor sperm."

"Wow. This is heavy. Who knew? You sure looked mesmerized when I came in."

"Kristi, these blogs are amazing. Some are advice pages, and some are stories from kids searching for their roots. There's one guy with a sperm-donor dad who found out he has three other siblings from three different mothers. Anyway, everyone uses the word 'obsession.' It's not just me. So many posters said the search process made them kind of crazy and took over their lives. And everyone's reaction to sperm donation being their start was different."

Paige fought the urge to open one of the sites and read Kristi some of the stories. She paused to munch on the last of her pizza slice.

"Between the sites where people were adopted and were looking for birth parents and the sites where sperm donors were their dads, everyone had some picture in their heads of what their birth parent would be like. They imagined what would happen when they met. When they finally did meet, sometimes it was as wonderful as they thought it would be, and other times it was a huge wake-up call. No matter what, it was life changing. These stories have for sure changed my thinking. Finding my dad was not the end of the story but the beginning of a new chapter."

"Very profound, hon. You and Marcos must both have a jumble of emotions to sort out."

Kristi's smile was comforting. Paige felt thankful to have someone to share all of this with. No one at the studio knew, not even Brianna.

"And get this. I learned something I'd never heard about before." Paige reached forward and opened the laptop. "See." She pointed to the title of the page she had been examining when Kristi came in. In bold letters, the page was titled: "GSA, Genetic Sexual Attraction."

"What in the hell does that mean?" Kristi leaned forward for a better look. She stared at Paige over the rim of her mug with wide and curious eyes.

"Maybe it explains Marcos's behavior—the weird attraction to me. It happens, Kristi. There are studies." Paige sat back and crossed her legs yoga style. "It's this bizarre thing that happens—usually after learning there's a blood connection. It's like a bonding, a feeling of fitting with someone—belonging, I guess." Paige pointed to the open laptop and traced her finger under the text on the screen. "Here's an article about how the attraction is 'a byproduct of delayed bonding that would normally have taken place in infancy and then throughout a lifetime of being father and daughter.' It goes on to explain feelings get all mixed up, like falling in love. Because adults bond through physical intimacy, these feelings can become way complicated. The article explains that until these new feelings get sorted out, everything can be a big mess. Oh my God. I have learned so much."

"This is really deep stuff, Paige. But I guess it explains a lot." Kristi raised her eyebrows, which made her brown eyes look even bigger.

"I know." Paige sat still. She shook her head. "I have to let this stuff sink in, and then I'll send some of the links to Marcos. But right now I don't want to overwhelm him. Our new status is pretty fragile, and all this stuff's a bit scary." Paige tilted her head. "And, no matter what, I think Marcos has to learn he's much too old to be running after girls as young as me." She grimaced.

"I'm thinking you might want to sidestep that one." Kristi bit her lip, but her smile spilled out around the corners of her mouth. "Marcos might be close to fifty, my friend, but he's one heck of an attractive man, so good luck there. But, changing the subject, at least you can't say life is boring."

"For sure. I'm on a merry-go-round, and it keeps spinning faster and faster. Oh, and there's more I wanted to tell you. Holy crap. How could I forget? Late yesterday afternoon, Marcos called me into Katherine's office and introduced me to his father. His father, Kristi. My grandfather!" Paige bounced up and down in excitement.

"What!" Coffee spit out of Kristi's mouth. She wiped the dribbles off her chin with a pajama sleeve.

"Yeah. Can you believe it? I was stupid tongue-tied. His name is Jacob Martin Stevens, and that's a whole 'nother story, but…he was very kind and shook my hand. He said I have my grandmother's eyes, and he was looking forward to getting to know me better. I've caught glimpses of him in the studio lately but didn't know who he was. He's a very elegant gentleman. A lawyer, I think."

"Sounds to me like you caught the brass ring on that crazy merry-go-round you're on." Kristi compressed her lips and nodded. "I don't want to sound like an old lady here, but you've really changed—matured is a better word—an awful lot in just a few weeks."

"I actually feel older," Paige said. She rocked back and forth and cocked her head. "I've been talking to Barbara a lot. One day we were discussing Jill. I said how Jill's craziness taught me to never become a goofy dreamer who runs on emotion. Barbara said we learn as much from bad examples as from good, and it's the choices we make that shape our lives. And you," Paige grabbed Kristi's arm and shook it, "you've taught me not to think always in black and white, and that's huge. And you know, for so long I thought I had to know who my father was to know who I really am. But now," Paige straightened and raised her chin, "I think we're not so much about where we came from but about where we're going. We make who we are ourselves."

"You, kiddo, are turning into quite the philosopher." Kristi raised her cup in a toast.

"I have so much more I want to talk to you about, but now I have to hustle and get ready for work. We need a wine-and-chat night soon. I have a lot to sort out, but I feel like the whole world is opening up to me."

〜

Marcos Stephanos
9:15 a.m., Friday, 13 November

Yawning, Marcos listened with mounting impatience as the Krups coffee maker growled its way through the bean-grinding cycle. He stared mindlessly out the window until the sound of brewed coffee trickling into the pot roused him to awareness.

As he poured his first cup, his father's Mercedes swooped across the front parking lot. He watched his dad park at the far end. Marcos's lips formed a half smile. Looked like some things never changed, and Mr. Jacob Martin Stevens was as paranoid as ever about someone's car door dinging one of his expensive vehicles. Marcos strode to the studio's entrance to open the door. He motioned for his father to take a seat by the colorful Mexican-tiled coffee table.

"Morning. Thanks for coming ahead of schedule. I wanted some time to talk before meeting with Katherine," Marcos said. "Black, right?" At his father's two-fingered salute, Marcos filled another tall ceramic mug with the rich-smelling brew. He settled into the chair across from his dad, placing both mugs within easy reach.

"I've never taken the time to absorb the lobby décor," Martin Stevens said. "It's well done, very Southwestern but not kitschy cowboy."

"I can't take credit for any of this," Marcos replied. "This is all Katherine." Marcos crossed his legs and leaned forward. "Thanks for agreeing to come to the studio rather than us trekking downtown to your office."

"You're welcome. I think the studio will be less intimidating for Katherine, and we might be able to catch her with her guard down. Good coffee," Martin said, after taking his first sip.

"That it is. Katherine has good taste in everything from art to coffee," Marcos replied. The coffee was strong, and his mind fog was beginning to clear.

"Ideally, we can come to an agreement with her today," Martin Stevens said, crossing his legs. "I plan to emphasis the seriousness of the situation so it's clear to Katherine. As it is, the woman is lucky you don't want to file charges against her, but she doesn't need to know that upfront." Martin took another sip and put his cup down. "I have to insist on one thing. Any subsequent meetings or discussions will be conducted at my office. I want my staff available to prepare any necessary legal papers or to act as notaries."

"Agreed," Marcos said. He stared into his cup, hoping for divine guidance in the coffee dregs. He sighed and put it down. "Oh, by the way, off topic, I got word Sylvie will be leaving Desert DanceSport in December. She'll be a huge loss to the studio, but it looks like we won't be shorthanded for long." Marcos rubbed one hand along his forehead. "Michael knows a ballroom dance instructor in the Phoenix area—a young woman who wants to move back to Tucson. He showed me some of her dance videos. If things go well with restructuring the company, we'll make her an offer as soon as we can."

"Put the brakes on, son. If we can avoid a court case against Katherine and all the negative publicity that would entail, if we can get her to back away from the business, *then* you can start making plans but not until then. Next time around, I encourage you to conduct business on more than a handshake." Martin folded his arms.

"I won't fight you on that one," Marcos said. He leaned forward and rested his hands on his thighs.

"Since we still have about a half hour or so before Katherine arrives and no one else is here as yet, I'd like to change the subject and talk about young Paige for minute," Martin said.

"Okay." Marcos tried to gauge his father's mood from his tone. Marcos casually sipped his coffee but felt his father scrutinize him with the acumen of a hunting hawk. He couldn't stop himself from launching into a stream of nervous chatter. "I totally understand your surprise at learning you have an adult granddaughter. Trust me,

I'm still trying to sort my way through the reality of unintentionally fathering a child. Between that shocker and Katherine's duplicity, I'm on emotional overload. I haven't had a chance to fully absorb everything and react. So, what are your thoughts after sleeping on the news?"

Martin rubbed his jawline. "Well, once my brain started functioning after the initial shock of hearing about Paige, I've been trying to adjust to this unexpected turn of events. Yesterday, when you introduced her to me, I found her to be a nice young woman, very unassuming. She bears a strong resemblance to your mother as a young woman. Paige has her eyes, as do you. But, family resemblances aside, I am pleased that you were levelheaded enough to have DNA tests run. This is not the sort of thing you believe on someone's word."

"And? What else? I know that look," Marcos said.

"I…ah…well." Martin cleared his throat. "I'm assuming this young woman didn't know much about you, besides your profession, when she made the connection between you and the donor clinic. Seems like she did her research to track you down, and I have to wonder exactly how much research she did." Martin paused to sip his coffee. "Do you know if she did any digging into your family background?" Martin tilted his head and leaned closer to Marcos. "What I am getting at is this: Did she know you stand to inherit quite a bit of money? Do you know her well enough to disallow the fact that she might have an ulterior motive for seeking you out as her biological father?"

"My God, Dad. I know you're a lawyer, but—"

"No buts about it." Martin raised his chin. "I live in the real world. Once we've settled this business with Katherine, I hope to invite Paige to lunch for a chat. To be frank with you, if I detect any hint of her being a gold-digger, I won't hesitate to draw up something akin to a prenup or write an addendum to my will."

Marcos gritted his teeth. He was surprised at how defensive and protective he felt about Paige. His fingers tightened around the armrest of the chair until his knuckles hurt. Right now was not the time to start a verbal sparring match with his father. He took a deep breath. His father was an expert at reading body language, and it would be unwise to let his agitation show. Marcos reminded himself to pick both his battles and the timing.

"I understand where you're coming from," he finally said. "I have every reason to believe Paige is looking for closure to a lifetime of questions. She knows nothing about my circumstances, only that I drive a nice car and smoke expensive French cigarettes." At the memory of his ego-driven statements at the café about being financially well off, Marcos blanched. With any luck, Paige didn't remember much of what he said.

"For now I can accept you having no reason to doubt her intentions. I'll still do my own digging." Martin gestured, palms up. "On the other hand, son, if no red flags go up, I'll make every attempt to accept her as family, if that's what you want."

Marcos's adrenaline rush subsided. He patted himself on the back for knowing when to keep his mouth shut. A few years ago, this type of discussion with his father would not have ended well. "I appreciate that. I think you'll be pleasantly surprised when you get to know her."

"Now," Martin said, "what do you know about this young woman's mother? About the other side of her DNA, so to speak."

"Dad, don't tell me you're going to start with the old 'who are her people' line of thought. Her mother was a registered nurse and did a good job of raising a daughter alone. Short of there being a mass murderer in the family Paige hasn't told me about, I don't think there are any skeletons in the closet. And, more importantly, we have to evaluate Paige on her own merits."

"I admit my first impression was a good one, but I believe in erring on the side of caution," Martin Stevens replied. He raised his eyebrows and attempted a conciliatory smile.

"I think that's Katherine's car outside." Marcos flipped his wrist to glance at his watch. "Right on time. It's not quite ten. Time to batten down the hatches."

TWENTY-SIX

EXIT STAGE LEFT

Marcos Stephanos
10:00 a.m., Friday, 13 November

Marcos couldn't remember the last time he'd seen his father in action, and he was curious to see which chess piece the old man would move first. He was to act as second chair, to let his father take the lead.

Martin Stevens walked behind Katherine's desk to sit, so to speak, at the head of the table. With a gracious motion of his hand, he invited Katherine to take the seat across from him to his left. Marcos pulled out the chair next to Katherine. Martin folded his hands on the polished desktop and looked at the folders in front of him. The silence was broken by Katherine; Marcos fought to keep the surprise off his face.

"I hope we can resolve this muddled piece of business without any acrimony," Katherine said, her voice clear and authoritative. "I'm sure the situation with the company's finances isn't nearly as problematic as you all are making it out to be. This is all a tempest in a teapot, and I'd like to get things resolved as quickly as possible, and get back to work."

Katherine pressed her lips together and held her head high. Her demeanor screamed, *Why am I even here?* Her hair was loose and softly curled. She was fully made-up from a set of thick eyelashes to perfectly applied lipstick, and she was dressed in a take-no-prisoners, power-red sweater, gray pencil skirt, and skyscraper red heels. The woman meant business.

Marcos glanced across the desk at his father, who seemed unperturbed. His hands remained on the desktop, his expression unreadable. Martin Stevens looked directly and calmly at Katherine, not saying a word. Marcos looked from one player to the other. Katherine loosened the red-and-silver scarf draped around her neck. Her tremor was barely visible.

Martin cleared this throat and opened one of the folders on the desk in front of him. "As you are aware, Katherine, we had the studio's financials professionally reviewed by an auditor. This file folder contains his report." Martin's voice was low and controlled. "I also have here"—he opened a second folder—"the studio's profit and loss statements for the past two quarters. We compared the P&L to the company's liabilities and to net income, which, as I'm sure you know, is calculated by subtracting total expenses from total revenues." Martin paused to push the folders across the table toward Katherine. "Although you've suffered some setbacks this year with the loss of a major income maker, the studio has done quite well in terms of sales."

"Exactly," Katherine said. "So why all the fuss and feathers?"

Marcos shook his head. Katherine tossed her hair like an ingénue and attempted a disdainful smile. Could she have an ace up her sleeve, or was she a master at bluffing?

Martin leaned forward. He placed his elbows on the polished wood desk, rubbed the tips of his fingers together, and directed an unsmiling gaze at Katherine.

"On the surface, the company's balance sheet looks healthy. This is in direct conflict with the fact that too many of the studio's accounts payables are behind, and you have been unable to make payroll on more than one occasion. The mortgage is also more than three months in arrears. It seems you're low in working capital. Again, unexplainable by what we saw on the balance sheet, until this came to our attention." Martin reached into the vest pocket of his jacket and pushed a silver thumb drive across the desk. "This USB is one of mine. The spreadsheets on this drive are a copies of the files stored on your personal red USB drive, which I understand went missing for a couple of days. I'm sure you must understand we're painfully aware that you were keeping two sets of books."

Katherine ignored Martin's thumb drive. She sucked in her upper lip and plucked at the scarf around her neck. Her eyes remained fixed on some point above Martin's head. Marcos could see her chest rise and fall as she took a few deep breaths. Martin sat back, the picture of patience. Katherine tapped her weapon-like fingernails on the desktop and glared at both Marcos and Martin like an irritated nanny forced to deal with truculent children.

"You have both worked yourselves up over nothing," Katherine said. She flattened her hands on the desk. "I'm particularly disappointed in you, Marcos. Your disloyalty saddens me, and it's a shame you've wasted your father's time in your spurious effort to discredit me. Nosing into my private spreadsheets was like someone walking into the middle of a conversation and taking everything they heard out of context."

Katherine closed her eyes for a few seconds. She shook her head and then glanced from one man to the next.

"So let me put both of you straight. What I have done is nothing more than a bit of creative accounting. Everyone does it from time to time. It's a simple matter of deferring deposits. Contracts paid in cash were entered in the ledger and the contracts filed, as per usual. The only thing missing from the picture was the actual money that exchanged hands. Really, gentlemen." Katherine's voice took on a conciliatory tone. "The simple truth is I was forced to borrow from the studio's accounts to cover some personal expenses that were burying me. In due time, all the monies would have been put back." Katherine opened her hands and shrugged in a *Don't you see?* gesture.

Martin waited a beat. "The fact remains, Katherine, that taking money from the studio's accounts to cover personal expenses is not borrowing; it's theft, plain and simple." His voice was steady and unemotional. "And juggling the books is not an acceptable way to stave off being found out until the situation can be corrected."

Marcos's head spun in the aerodynamic drag as Katherine changed emotional gears.

"Now look here, Martin. You are forgetting this is my company. Mine. One can't steal from oneself. I don't know what you two think you've cooked up, but I'm not going to sit here and listen to any more of this. I might even sue you for defamation of character."

Katherine started to stand, but Martin waved her back down. "I do believe what you've done was not necessarily malicious in intent," Martin said. His voice had softened an imperceptible notch.

"Of course it wasn't." Katherine sank back into the chair and held her hands in front of her, fingers spread. "You must know my intention was to pay everything back." She shifted her gaze to Marcos. "Marcos?"

Marcos felt himself flinch. This was the first time a hint of fear flared in Katherine's eyes. He held himself back.

"Whatever your intention, Katherine, you have committed a serious crime. It's called embezzlement." Martin tapped the auditor's folder.

"That's absurd." Katherine's voice raised an octave, sharp around the edges. "How dare you even use that word to me." Her eyes moved wildly from Martin to Marcos. "One can't embezzle from one's own company."

"My dear," Martin said, as though explaining the obvious to the obtuse, "have you forgotten you don't own this business outright? You and Marcos signed an agreement some years ago, making Marcos a forty-eight percent owner in Desert DanceSport. His name is also on the mortgage."

The intercom on Katherine's desk buzzed. Marcos stood and leaned across the desk to punch the button. "Yes," he said.

"I'm in and at the front desk. Saw your note." Paige's voice broke through the silence in the office. "Wanted to let you know someone is out here in case you need anything."

"Thank you, Paige. All I need is for you to make sure we are not disturbed. And hold all calls, please."

"Gotcha," Paige replied.

Marcos settled back into his seat but not before he saw an odd little smirk playing at the edges of Katherine's lips.

Martin swiveled his chair to directly face Katherine. He sat back and folded his arms. "Let me explain exactly what you're up against. I don't want there to be any misunderstanding. The auditor's report was worse than any of us expected. Not only is the mortgage three months in arrears, but over $24,000 is unaccounted for. This is not borrowing, Katherine, this is embezzlement, and in Arizona, embezzlement at this level becomes a felony." Martin leaned forward, every syllable full-on attorney. "To be clear, the statute states that if the amount embezzled is more than $4,000 but less than $25,000, the theft is considered a Class 3 felony."

Martin paused and looked at Marcos with an expression clearly conveying a warning not to speak or show any weakness in resolve. He continued.

"Katherine, a Class 3 felony is punishable by a maximum of 8.77 years in prison. On top of that, in most embezzlement cases, the defendant may be required to reimburse the victims, in this case Marcos and the business, for the amount embezzled in addition to any criminal fines that may have to be imposed."

Marcos rubbed at his temples. His father's voice faded into background noise as he continued to bring Katherine up to speed. These legalities were a rerun for him, and he sank into a stupor under the barrage of hard-core legal terminology. The sound of his name jolted him back to awareness.

"Marcos cannot recover losses from you, Katherine, because I believe you are completely overextended, even after selling your mother's home."

"That may be, but I can't help but feel all this is some kind of veiled personal attack," Katherine said. Her voice took on a self-righteous tone. "I'm stunned you would even use the word prosecute." Katherine opened her purse and pulled out a small, folded sheet of paper. "I jotted down some notes I copied from a piece of paper Paige dropped on the floor of the ballroom. Looks to me like Marcos might have something to hide from you, Martin. Maybe Marcos has an ulterior motive here and is attempting to deflect attention away from himself by attacking me." Katherine turned to Marcos and pushed the folded paper across the desk. "I don't know what to make of this, Marcos. Maybe you're still in the dark, but it looks to me like you're about to be blackmailed. But then, maybe you know that already. Are you in need of a cash influx, Marcos? Could this be what you're hiding from your father? Why don't we all lay our cards on the table and see who folds first." Katherine pushed the paper to the center of the table.

"What in the hell are you talking about, Katherine?" Marcos reached for the paper, but his father's hand was quicker.

"What's on that damn piece of paper?" Marcos asked. Right now he was done with Katherine playing games after he'd gone to bat for her with his father. He knew his anger showed in his voice, and he didn't care.

"So you're saying, Katherine, that what you have here you copied from a personal note that belonged to Paige. In other words, from something that was private and didn't belong to you," Martin said. He leaned forward and folded his hands on the desktop. "If you think you're playing a winning hand, my dear, it's time for you to fold. And, before my mood changes to less than amenable, you might think twice before trying to bring my granddaughter into the mix."

"Granddaughter," Katherine murmured. "So I was right." She looked wide-eyed from Martin to Marcos and then visibly slumped in her chair.

Marcos shook his head. Any sympathy he might have had evaporated. He knew Katherine didn't have another card to play, and what she'd tried was a cheap bluff.

"I think we are done here," Martin said, standing. He flipped his wrist to look at his gold Rolex. Marcos knew the movement was calculated. Martin turned to Katherine with a disarming smile. "Katherine, I would tell you to get your own lawyer, but you can't afford one and, frankly, you don't have a leg to stand on. So, why don't we call this meeting over, and you and I discuss potential scenarios over a late brunch. I for one could use a martini. Marcos, I'll come back to the office to check in with you later this afternoon."

"What?" Marcos said. "Really?" Was that an appraising eye his father ran over Katherine as she rose from her chair? Katherine cast a practiced, vulnerable look Martin's way. What the hell was this?

Martin held the door open, gently placing a hand on Katherine's back as she exited the office.

Marcos stepped up and held his father back by one arm. Leaning forward, he whispered, "I'm calling a staff meeting tonight, so I need to know what the hell you're up to, old man. And don't deny it, because the look I saw in your eyes is a clear conflict of interest."

"Not at all, son," Martin replied with a wicked smile. "I'm one hundred percent in the driver's seat, but there's no reason not to enjoy the scenery while traveling down the road."

∼

2:00 p.m., Friday, 13 November

"Paige." Marcos placed what he hoped was a fatherly arm around her. "I really appreciate you helping out in reception as much as you have been. With any luck, we'll be able to hire a full-time receptionist soon, at least someone for the peak hours of the day."

"No problem." Paige glanced at Marcos with a soft, closed-lipped smile.

"Good. One thing more, please check the roster to confirm everyone's working through the party. I need to call a quick meeting at the end of the night, and I want everyone here. Oh, and would you send out a group email or text to give everyone enough notice. I don't want someone slipping out the door and later telling me no one told them to stay late."

"Sure. I can do that right away."

Marcos could hear the question in Paige's voice. He was tempted, but it wouldn't be fair to fill her in before everyone else. It was a moot point anyway because his father was back from lunch and on his way in the door, and Katherine wasn't with him.

"Good afternoon," Martin said, giving Paige a friendly nod.

Marcos saw a flush of color rise in her cheeks. She nodded back at his dad and smiled, but bubbly Paige had suddenly become quiet, almost shy.

"Marcos, let's talk for a few minutes. Can we use this space?" Martin gestured toward the front office. "I think I have some interesting news for you."

"Certainly," Martin said. He held the office door open for his dad. "Paige, please hold calls and tell anyone looking for me that I'll be busy for a while."

Paige responded with a thumbs-up.

"Where's Katherine?" Marcos asked, as he shut the office door. He turned on the light and closed the blinds.

"I brought her back here and walked her to her car. She's on her way home but is coming back after the party for the staff meeting." Martin rubbed his palms together. "I think we have a very workable plan, but we need to move on it before Katherine rethinks. I'll keep this short and sweet for right now. Next week we'll hammer out the details and complete all the paperwork."

"So tell me how your private little chat went." Marcos asked. He bit his lip and hoped to God his father hadn't succumbed to Katherine's charm. She was gifted with a cobra's ability to hypnotize its prey into submission.

"It went quite well." Martin crossed his legs and sat back in his chair. "I limited Katherine to one cocktail. I wanted her relaxed but clear-headed. We didn't talk about the studio right off the bat but began the discussion with personal matters like the sale of her mother's house, money owed to the nursing home, and her own finances. It sounds like she can settle things with this New Haven place. But she took out a home equity loan against her mother's house, which ate into profits on the sale. She seems to have considerable credit card debt and has run up some smallish store accounts with outstanding balances. So, the sale of the house won't begin to save her. And because she can no longer move funds around from the studio's accounts, she will most likely have to file bankruptcy."

"Better Katherine than the studio," Marcos said. He felt mean-spirited.

"I'm relieved to finally hear you say that. After I managed to get Katherine to talk about her debt load, I laid the facts in front of her regarding her creative accounting with the studio monies. That's when she began to grasp the gravity of the situation. The woman has managed to dig herself into a deep, dark hole. When the reality of the situation sank in, she damn near reached across the table to slug back my scotch." Martin chuckled, obviously amused.

For the first time Marcos was acutely aware of the fundamental difference between himself and his father. Martin could chuckle at the image of Katherine being faced with ruin, while Marcos felt only dismay, even though he was angry with her. He could see why his father was such a formidable opponent in the courtroom. The man was energized by confrontation and enjoyed the maneuvers of manipulation, while he found it draining. In a magical moment of self-realization, Marcos let go of the guilt he'd carried from not following in his father's footsteps.

Marcos swallowed hard before he spoke. "So, after all that, did you two come to any resolution or strike a bargain?"

"We did. We discussed ending your business partnership. Under ordinary circumstances, if your partnership was to be dissolved, you would buy Katherine out. Katherine is now painfully aware the only buyout on the table is her avoiding prosecution, fines, and a possible jail sentence."

"I wish I felt better about all this. I still can't believe it's happening," Marcos said. He rubbed the back of his neck and slowly shook his head.

"Well, it is, so buck up," Martin said. His voice took on an academic tone. "In a nutshell, this is what is going to happen. First, Katherine will sign a quitclaim on the building." Martin chopped an open palm with side of his other hand to emphasize his words. "This is the legal, quick-and-dirty way to get the mortgage into your name. I'll have the paperwork ready for her to sign this weekend. Early next week, you meet with your lender to bring the mortgage payments up to date. You might have to use your private funds. Are you able to do that?"

"Yes, sir, I am."

"Good. Katherine has agreed to walk away from her stake in the business. By taking her name off the mortgage and putting the building in your name only, she will essentially be giving you any monies that would have gone to her if and when the building sold. In simple terms, she loses the twenty-five grand she put down, and also her share of any equity accrued over the years. Once things have stabilized and if you and Michael decide to sign a business partnership agreement, the mortgage on the studio can be refinanced in both your names. You might be able to lower the payments in the process. Something to think about for future reference."

"I know we have no choice but to remove Katherine, but it's rough. I never thought—"

"This is business, Marcos, pure and simple. It's best to sever this limb with an electric saw instead of an old, rusty handsaw. Keep in mind that, under the circumstances, you're doing Katherine a favor."

"I know, but..." Marcos let the thought die. He didn't want to sound weak.

"Also, I strongly suggest you call a locksmith before the end of the business day and arrange to have the locks changed on Saturday. You can let Katherine in on Sunday to clear out her personal belongings, when the studio is empty."

"As you suggested, I called the staff meeting for later tonight,"

Marcos said. "There have been murmurings about both cash flow and Katherine's absence. Everyone knows something's up. Now, without going into unnecessary detail, I can simply announce Katherine has decided it's time to move on. And Katherine being in attendance should quaff any gossip before it starts."

"She'll be the star of the show," Martin said, followed by a good chuckle.

"Seriously, Dad? Exactly what's funny here?"

"I saved the best part for last. You'll like this, I promise. Over after-lunch coffee, I presented Katherine with a plan to move her life forward. She was actually excited about the idea. And"—a smile crinkled Martin's eyes—"I felt the need to break the cold-blooded attorney stereotype. So, I've taken the liberty to speak with an old friend, and here's what we came up with…"

~

9:15 p.m., Friday, 13 November

Marcos wasn't expecting to see Katherine already in the break-room, but there she was, leaning against the back counter, arms folded. He nodded his hello and stood where he could make eye contact with everyone. As the staffers jostled their way in, there were a few "Hi, Katherine"s, but they were outnumbered by curious looks. Marcos counted heads. He held back a sigh. Even at the end of a long day, the kids had enough energy to playfully tease and elbow-jab each other, while all he felt was a longing for his Jacuzzi and a double cotch. He stepped forward and clapped.

"Thank you, everyone, for staying a bit late. I promise to keep this short, but there are some big changes in the wind I need you to be aware of. Let's start with this quote: 'Life is nothing without a little chaos to make it interesting.'"

The room settled into studied silence.

"I think it's best to turn things over to Katherine." Marcos extended a hand, and she stepped forward.

"I have some exciting news," Katherine said. She glanced around the room, smiling and bestowing her famous winks, which held the promise of a wonderful secret she was about to share. Everyone looked expectantly at their boss. Marcos could see the wheels turning. He would bet his Miata that bonuses were on more than one instructor's mind.

"First, I want you to know I love you all, and Desert DanceSport has always been my heartbeat." Katherine paused for effect, her smile as sincere as that of a priest sweet-talking a choirboy. "However, running this business has become more of a stress than a blessing for me, and it's time for a change. Timing being everything, I've been presented with an offer I simply can't refuse."

Katherine waited for the murmurs to subside.

"I'll be leaving Desert DanceSport to run the dance and entertainment program for a major cruise line. This is the opportunity of a lifetime, and I can hardly wait to get started. In fact, today is my last day at the studio. The cruise-line company needs me in LA within a few short weeks. In the interim, I'll be taking care of personal business so I can be free to leave."

"What about your house, Katherine?" Sylvie piped up. "Are you, like, selling and moving to LA for good?"

"It's been suggested that I set up my condo as an Airbnb, so that's another bit of business I have to get organized. I plan to market it as a vacation spot for people who enjoy hanging out with cats. My foster-care connections will make sure any cats in residence are taken care of. So keep it in mind for friends and relatives visiting Tucson." Katherine tilted her head to the left and raised her shoulders in a coquettish *How's that for brilliant?* gesture, which Marcos would have bought into had he not known the truth. The woman was giving the performance of a lifetime. He hated to admit it, but he was still more than a little in awe of her.

It was Joey who brought up the inevitable question. "So, who'll be running the studio? You're not selling out, are you? What happens to all of us?"

Survival mode superseded congratulatory mode, and the room filled with voices, questioning each other and questioning Katherine. Marcos stepped forward, silencing the group.

"The second part of this informal news release is that I will be buying Katherine out." Marcos glanced toward Katherine and changed his mind about announcing the pending partnership with Michael. That could wait. "I'm asking for your trust as we move forward. I have exciting plans to share with you, but tonight is Katherine's time to say goodbye and share her news. Over the next couple of weeks, I'll meet privately with each of you to discuss your thoughts and career goals." Amid applause that Katherine joined in, albeit weakly, Marcos turned the meeting back to his soon-to-be-ex-business partner.

"Everyone," Katherine said, the ring to her voice commanding attention, "I hope to come in one day next week and say personal goodbyes, but right now I have a few things to take care of in my office. It's late, and I'm sure you all want to get home."

Chairs scraped the floor, water bottles and glasses were put down, smiles and glances were sent Katherine's way, and everyone drifted off. With the exception of Sylvie, no one walked up to their boss to give her a goodbye hug.

"My car's parked out back," Katherine said. "I'd like to walk into the ballroom one last time."

"Of course," Marcos said, following behind her. He stopped at the entrance to the ballroom while Katherine took a few steps out onto the floor. Half the lights were still on. She stood on the floorboards, shoulders back, chest high, tailbone tucked—the consummate dancer. Reflections from the mirror ball caught the reddish-blonde highlights in her dark hair. Under the softness of the subdued light, Katherine could have passed for forty. She turned and glided over to Marcos, her hips fluid and her feet turned out. She reached for the panel of light switches. As one by one the banks of lights in the ballroom dimmed, Katherine's image faded in the mirrors.

She'll do okay, Marcos told himself. My dad is right. In a year she'll be back for a visit, showing off the wealthy widower she captured on a cruise, someone to take her comfortably into her retirement years.

Katherine drifted past Marcos and reached into the purse she left in the hallway. She turned back toward him and handed him her studio door keys. Her eyes glistened with a sheen of tears, but her smile conveyed confidence.

"Well," Katherine said, "to quote Jack London, 'Life is not always a matter of holding good cards, but sometimes, playing a poor hand well.'" She stretched high on her toes, leaned into Marcos, and gently touched his cheek with her lips before turning away. And without even a backward glance, Katherine strode down the hall and exited the studio by the back door.

ACKNOWLEDGMENTS

The first person I have to thank is my husband, David, for his belief in me and his unwavering support. My husband not only doesn't stand in my way, he steps aside and opens doors, encouraging me to run through them.

I also must thank the nonprofit NaNoWriMo, sponsor of a month of nonstop writing craziness known as National Novel Writing Month. The first draft of this novel was the result of my 2011 NaNoWriMo. If not for the encouragement of fellow writer, Kristi Jenkins, I wouldn't have taken my first jump into "NaNo" way back in 2007. That month of writing changed everything.

Mucho thanks and deep appreciation go to the past and present members of my talented writers' group, Vista Writers. Without your critiques, insights, edits, encouragement, and great cookies (Eva), this book would not have taken shape. I couldn't have done it without you.

A special thank you goes to Joshua Cochran, author, poet, and writing instructor at Pima Community College. Participation in Joshua's Special Projects class in 2014 gave me the confidence and the skillset to revise and expand my initial draft. Joshua has continued to be a guiding light and mentor, generously performing a content edit on one of my last revisions.

I owe a debt of gratitude to my outstanding BETA readers, Susan Vanatta and Julia Potter. I appreciate every minute you took from your busy lives to read the entire manuscript of DBTB. Your insights were invaluable. And, Susan, your ballroom dancing was the yardstick I measured myself against. I always fell short.

To my editor, Linda Sawicki, I extend a huge thank you. It was pure serendipity that we crossed paths, and I still can't believe I was lucky enough that you took me on as a client. Your eagle-eye editing and astute suggestions put the finishing touches on my manuscript.

Marketing consultant and fellow writer, Paula Johnson, is responsible for so much of the behind the scenes work. She designed my webpage and held my hand while I learned to create posts. She tutored me on the importance of author mailing lists and developing a social-media presence. Paula also published some of my earliest writing on her e-zine, *Rose City Sisters*. Thank you, Paula, for your encouragement, patience, support, and unflagging sense of humor.

And thank you to the first-rate publishing team at Wheatmark, Inc.: Grael Norton, Lori Conser, and Lorraine Elder. Without you this book would not be a reality. You've made a dream come true.